Gentle Birth Choices

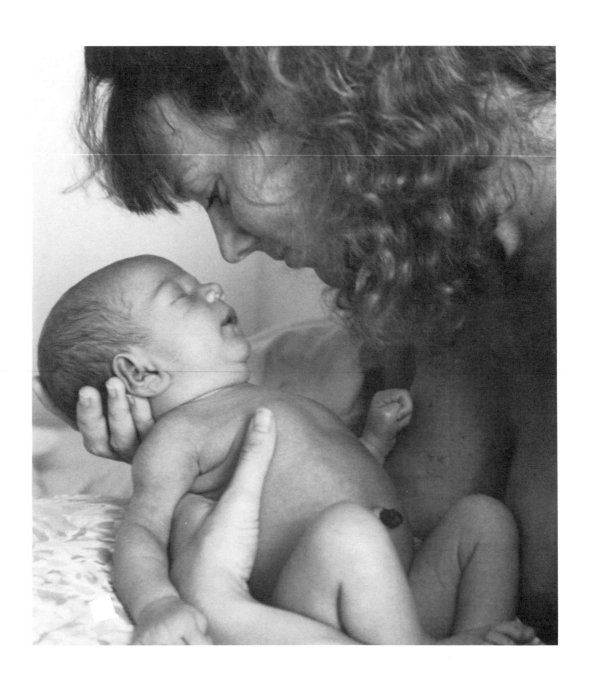

Gentle Birth Choices

A GUIDE TO MAKING INFORMED DECISIONS ABOUT

BIRTHING CENTERS • BIRTH ATTENDANTS
• WATER BIRTH • HOME BIRTH • HOSPITAL BIRTH

BARBARA HARPER, R.N.

Photographs by Suzanne Arms

Foreword by Robbie Davis–Floyd, Ph.D., author of
Birth as an American Rite of Passage

Healing Arts Press
Rochester, Vermont

Healing Arts Press
One Park Street
Rochester, Vermont 05767
www.gotoit.com

*Note to the reader: This book is intended as an informational guide. The remedies, approaches,
and techniques described herein are meant to supplement, and not to be a substitute for, professional medical care or treatment. They should not be used to treat a serious ailment without
prior consultation with a qualified healthcare professional.*

LIBRARY OF CONGRESS CATALOGING-IN-PUBLICATION DATA

Harper, Barbara, 1952-.
    Gentle birth choices : a guide to making informed decisions /
  Barbara Harper.
      p. cm.
    Includes bibliographical references and index.
    ISBN 0-89281-480-2 Book
    ISBN 0-89281-528-0 Box Set
    1. Natural childbirth. 2. Childbirth. I. Title.
    RG661.H37 1994
    618.4'5–dc20   93–20959
                                       CIP

Printed and bound in the United States

10 9 8 7 6 5 4 3

Text design by Randi Jinkins and Virginia L. Scott

Healing Arts Press is a division of Inner Traditions International

Distributed to the book trade in Canada by Publishers Group West (PGW), Toronto,
Ontario
Distributed to the health food trade in Canada by Alive Books, Toronto and
Vancouver
Distributed to the book trade in the United Kingdom by Deep Books, London
Distributed to the book trade in Australia by Millennium Books, Newtown, N.S.W.
Distributed to the book trade in New Zealand by Tandem Press, Auckland
Distributed to the book trade in South Africa by Alternative Books, Ferndale

This book is dedicated to my daughter, Beth Elaine Braunstein, with the hope and prayer that she will be able to approach pregnancy, childbearing, and parenting with a brighter, more positive outlook than I was given when I was her age. Let us initiate our daughters into the beauty and mystery of being women. Let us instill in them the confidence that we were born to have babies with dignity, power, and love.

Contents

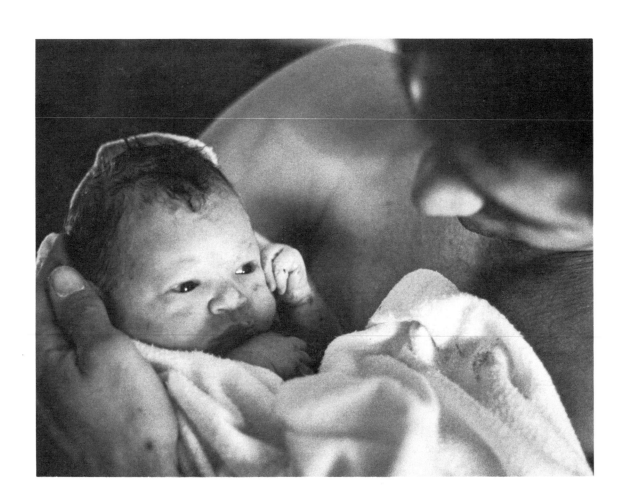

Foreword

This book beautifully conveys the magic, wonder, and excitement of birth as it can be when women approach it as a natural process that they can trust, and when practitioners remember to honor its sacred nature. In this comprehensive look at birth potentials and possibilities, Barbara Harper lays out the spectrum of alternatives available to today's women, informing and empowering them to make true choices. Here she performs an invaluable cultural service, for "freedom of choice" is often not available in a culture that tries hard to channel birthing women into the straight and narrow way of technocratic birth.

We in the United States live in a technocracy—a society organized around an ideology of technological progress. The core values of the technocracy center around science and technology and the institutions that control and disseminate them. In every society, core cultural beliefs and values are most highly visible in the rituals that accompany important life transitions like birth, puberty, marriage, initiation into a religious or occupational group, parenthood, and death. Rituals at the most basic level are enactments of these core cultural values and beliefs. Thus it is not surprising that the core values of our technocratic society would be most visible in the rituals with which we surround the birth process.

Basic to initiation rites across cultures is the removal of the initiate from normal social life. Once so removed, initiates are stripped of their individuality—their heads are often shaved or their hair clipped short, their clothes and adornments are taken away and they are dressed in identical gowns or robes. They are then subjected to hazing processes designed to break down their normal ways of thinking. Once this cognitive breakdown is well under way, the initiate is bombarded with messages about the core values of the culture. These messages are conveyed through powerful symbols. Symbols operate through the right hemisphere of the brain—their messages are emotionally felt, not intellectually analyzed, and their impact is often very powerful. These symbolic messages serve to rebuild the belief system of the initiates in accordance with the dominant beliefs and values of the group or society into which they are being initiated.

It is not difficult to see striking parallels between this cross-cultural initiation process and hospital birth. Birthing women are removed from their social setting and taken into the hospital—a powerful institution organized around our culture's supervaluation of science and technology. Their clothes are taken away, they are dressed in hospital gowns, and their pubic hair is shaved or clipped, symbolically desexualizing the lower half of their body and marking it as institutional property. Labor itself is a natural hazing process—the pain of contractions leaves women disoriented and wide open to internalize the symbolic messages they are sent. The powerful cultural symbols that convey these messages are the intravenous (IV) line, the electronic fetal monitor, the Pitocin drip, and all other myriad technological procedures through which most birthing women in the United States must undergo during their rite of passage into motherhood. What messages do such procedures convey into the bodies and emotions of birthing women?

The IV is the symbolic umbilical cord to the hospital. It makes a birthing woman appear to be dependent on the institution for her life, just as the baby in the womb depends on her for life. This of course is a perfectly accurate mirror of American society—in fact, we *are* dependent on institutions for our lives. The frequent examinations of the cervix to see if it is dilating fast enough (and the Pitocin drip that is administered if dilation is slow) convey strong messages about the importance of time in American society and the importance of on-time production by our body-machines. The electronic fetal monitor is there to warn of possible malfunctions—like the IV, it powerfully symbolizes the woman's dependence on the institution and its technology. Episiotomies express our strong cultural belief in the superiority of the straight line. (The medical myth that "clean, straight cuts heal faster than jagged tears" is one of the many medical myths surrounding birth that Barbara debunks in chapter 3.) The flat-on-the-back (lithotomy) position keeps the woman "down" in relation to the medical staff's "up," expressing our cultural value on hierarchy and reinforcing women's structural subordination at the moment of birth. Forceps and cesarean sections allow the physician to be the birth giver; they clearly express our culture's insistence on the necessity of restructuring natural processes. The all-too-brief brief bonding period allowed in many hospital delivery rooms conveys the message that society gives the baby to the mother and then has the authority to take the baby away. (Most newborns are whisked off to the nursery shortly after birth.)

The separation of self from body and mother from child that begins in the hospital is continued in countless American homes. Babies are constantly put into their separate cultural spaces—carried in plastic rockers or strollers, put down to play in playpens, put to sleep in cribs, and fed with plastic bottles. In no other culture is there so much separation between parents and child. It is no wonder—and no cultural accident—that our babies bond to technology and grow up to be voracious consumers! Their constantly increasing levels of consumption drive our economy, and so the technocracy feeds itself.

In order to appreciate this book most fully, it is important to note what it is not. This is not a book designed to perpetuate the technocracy. This book is not based on principles of separation but of connection. The dissociation of the woman from her own bodily experience and the separation of mother from baby so common in hospital birth are not to be found in these pages. Barbara Harper seeks to heal the wounds generated by our separation-based technocratic way of life. She writes of the possibilities for reconnection through childbirth that are present when the woman takes charge of her birthing experience by finding the setting and the practitioner(s) who will truly nurture her as she labors. Ideally, these should and can be people to whom it does not occur to take the baby away from the mother, who would never dream of asking her to give birth lying flat on her back, who will hold her, dance with her, laugh and cry with her instead of offering her drugs. So pervasive is the technocratic model of birth, so intensive the training of most medical people in that model and those techniques, that it takes a book like this one to let American women know that such options do exist, that such choices can be theirs.

It is true that many women will not want the choices this book offers. The epidural rate stands at 80 percent not because doctors everywhere are forcing epidurals on unwilling victims but because the majority of birthing women ask for—and often insist upon—the mind-body separation the epidural creates. As women in American culture, we are encouraged to regard our bodies with a great deal of ambivalence. We are taught that what is most important about our bodies is their beauty, the degree to which they conform to the aesthetic standards of the day—flat tummies and all. We are not taught that pregnancy is beautiful; not told that it can enhance, not detract from, our attractiveness and sexuality; not encouraged to glory in the astounding changes pregnancy brings. Instead, too many of us see pregnancy as an out-of-control biological process that ruins our figures and takes over our lives. Pregnancy becomes something to overcome, to prove that we can go on with our busy lives in spite of its pull on us to take life at a different pace. Women I have interviewed speak of their distaste at having to "drop down into biology." It is of course understandable that women with this attitude would welcome, even demand, the freedom from biology granted by the epidural, would appreciate the fetal monitor for the sense of reassurance it brings, would even sometimes prefer the orderliness and controllability of cesarean over the uncontrollable and chaotic biological process of birth.

American women are generally supported in this attitude by hospital-based childbirth classes that do not teach them of the wonder and mystery and sweaty, intense power of birth, but rather prepare them for each and every hospital procedure by educating their intellects instead of honoring their bodies. In contrast, Barbara Harper speaks of the connection that is possible when women let go of the fear-based desire to dissociate from their bodies, when they plunge deep into the body, deep into birth, allowing their bodies to be their teachers and their guides. Birth wisdom, as Harper shows, comes most completely not from the outside but from deep within the woman's physiology. Those of us who listen to our bodies as we give birth, who follow the dictates of flesh and muscle, who rock and moan, sway and sing, do not generally find that our bodies will tell us "Lie down, put your feet in stirrups, tighten the monitor belt, and push!" Rather, the voice of the body says, "Walk around, grunt and breathe, breathe deep into the depths of your belly, of your soul. Feel yourself, be yourself, live this moment, this holy time of birth.

Reach down, feel the wet warm head of your child about to be born. Reach up, hold on to the people who will support you. Plunge deep into yourself as you flow with the powerful contractions. Give birth to yourself, to your own embodied power, even as you give birth to your child."

I want to let you know what this insightful book has in store. After explaining in chapter 1 what she means by "gentle birth, " Barbara Harper provides in chapter 2 a succinct and useful history of the medicalization of childbirth in the West—a necessary precursor to understanding what has gone wrong with standard hospital birth practices today. In chapter 3 she takes on the medical myths that support the technocrat's efforts to make it look as if babies are best produced by science and technology, not by women. These myths, these stories made up to justify the technocratization of birth, say that women's bodies are inadequate to produce healthy babies without medical and technological assistance; the hospital is the safest place to have a baby; maternity care can only be properly managed by a physician; once a cesarean, always a cesarean; birth needs to be sterile; drugs for pain relief won't hurt the baby; it's better not to eat or drink during labor; birth is more difficult after age thirty-five; baby boys need to be circumcised; and on and on. Some readers may be shocked, but I urge them to continue through this chapter. Barbara is unafraid to take on our deepest cultural assumptions and show where they do real harm to mothers and babies. We all have much to learn from her insights.

Chapters 4 and 5 narrate the history of childbirth reform in the United States, providing an invaluable guide not only to the past but also to such recent developments as the rise of freestanding birth centers and the midwifery renaissance. Chapter 6 offers exciting descriptions of the emergence of waterbirth as an option for women all over the world, including much practical advice on using water for labor and on the logistics of planning a waterbirth. In chapter 7 we are reminded of the importance of connectedness. The author shows us how ignoring the mind-body connection leads to unnecessary interventions, while awareness of it can facilitate gentle birth. She brings vividly to life the findings from prenatal psychology studies that show babies are conscious beings who share the same bioenergy system with the mother, and that this relationship, when explored consciously by the mother, can yield rich rewards for parents and child. Chapter 8 provides a practical guide to the current range of gentle birth choices and suggests ways to make your choices work for you and your family.

This book is exactly the sort of guide that pregnant women have been needing to help them sort through the myriad choices and options that confront them in the 1990s. Women themselves have been instrumental in creating these options and alternatives, and Barbara Harper is one of those women. Her own quest for alternatives to the technocratic norm lead her to be one of the first women in the country to give birth in the water—an enlightening embodied experience that inspired her to want all women to know the true range of their choices. Through creating the Global Maternal/ Child Health Association and Waterbirth International, she has made the full spectrum of choice available to thousands of women in the United States and abroad. This book, and her remarkable video "Gentle Birth Choices," are her next major milestones on that road.

It is my hope that mothers, fathers, and birth practioners will choose to be guided by the information, the loving and accepting attitude toward women's bodies in all their untrammelled fluidity, and the profound wisdom that Barbara Harper offers them here.

Robbie E. Davis-Floyd, Ph.D.
Research Fellow, Dept. of Anthropology
University of Texas at Austin
Author of *Birth as an American Rite of Passage*
(University of California Press, 1992)

Acknowledgments

I want to thank all the parents who shared with me one of the most intimate experiences of their lives. Without their patience and trust I could not have proceeded. Each birth taught me something about myself and about the way God works within this universe. Each child brought renewed hope for a kinder, gentler way of being with one another in this life.

Each and every person with whom I have ever spoken about birth, and especially water birth, has in some way influenced the writing of this book. I talked about this book for years before it was ready to be written. The consistent encouragement I received all along the way from my family and friends is deeply appreciated. My children—Beth, Sam, and Abraham, born in 1978, 1984, and 1986—were, of course, the reason for writing about this subject. They provide me with a connection to all women who have given birth and with a great hope for the world of the future.

Harry Kislevitz has given me much more than his love and support. He encouraged me to research water birth in the very beginning. He wanted me to have the opportunity to be on the leading edge of something that he knew intuitively would be of great benefit to humankind. He was there to participate fully in the births of Samuel and Abraham, being everything a father could be for his sons. He never questioned my holistic approaches to childbearing. He cut their cords, yet he will always remain truly connected to our children. For this I am forever grateful.

Author Barbara Harper relaxes in the sun between contractions, just a few hours before her son Abraham is born at home in the hot tub.

Dr. Michael Rosenthal has been my inspiration, teacher, and friend. I appreciate his patience with my writing. Dr. Robert Doughton was my cheering section on numerous phone consultations. His reminders to "keep breathing" were invaluable. Certified nurse-midwife Marina Alzugaray passed to me a special awareness about birth and showed me what it is like to dance through the birth process. Binnie Anne Dansby brought birth into my consciousness and taught me to see the power of creation within birth.

Mirtala Cruz has given me sanity at times when there was none, and her water baby, Kelly Vanessa, was a very special gift for all of us. There are numerous people who deserve mention: Penelope Salinger for reading through each rewrite and giving me assignments; Mary Judge for never letting me forget that I had to complete this; Phil and Judy Babcock for encouraging me emotionally and keeping me balanced physically; my Christian midwife sisters, Carol Guachi, Renee Stein, Jan Trintin, and especially Mary Cooper, who have consistently kept me in prayer—thank you and God bless.

My final midwives for this book were Nicole Van DeVeere and Elise Schaljo. Without their constant support and encouragement, I would not have been able to "push" this work out of me and into the world. Not enough can ever be said about how wonderful midwives are!

And finally I must thank my mother, Ruth Eileen Protsman, for giving birth to me, and her mother, Estella Harper Lemonyon, for watching over me to this day.

Introduction

Choice is a political issue. How and where a woman gives birth and who attends her are not simple issues—hospital versus home birth or midwives versus doctors—but matters of control and responsibility. As women echo their dissatisfaction with discrimination, sexual harassment, and violence, their voices have never been stronger. The struggle for reproductive rights has brought the word *pro-choice* into our consciousness. I get frustrated when I contemplate just how much energy is focused on abortion when choice is also a vital issue for women having babies. Women the world over are seeking true choices in childbirth: not which hospital to go to or what the decor of the birthing room will be but the opportunity to manage their labors and births. Women want to be in control of their bodies during birth and in charge of their babies after birth.

Even though I was a thoroughly informed pregnant woman in 1978, who had completed nurse's training in 1974, my involvement in decisions around my maternity care was extremely limited. I had been in active labor with my daughter, Beth, for over twenty-four hours when the nurse came into the labor room and started to prepare for something. I asked her what she was doing, and she said that the doctor had ordered a prep for a cesarean. I refused to cooperate and asked to see the doctor. The doctor had already decided the course of action and was only going to inform me before I signed the consent papers. I was not even consulted or given a choice. I did not consent and demanded proof that my pelvic outlet was smaller than the diameter of my baby's head. The baby was not in distress, and neither was I. I knew that I could deliver normally. The orderlies came and wheeled me down to X-ray, where the radiologist and the obstetrician confirmed through X-ray pelvemetry that the size of my pelvis was indeed quite adequate and that the baby was actually very small.

The doctor said that I could *choose* to go on suffering or I could get it over with and have my baby a lot sooner, implying that a cesarean was preferable to a long and arduous labor. I *chose* the former. I was then given massive doses of Pitocin, an internal fetal monitor was put in place, I was given narcotics intravenously without my consent, and I was given a complete shave. When my baby came flying out of me, the nurse held a hand on her head until a first-year resident could gown and glove to "deliver" the baby. My obstetrician, discouraged by my slow progress, had gone home for dinner and wasn't even in the hospital. He finally arrived at the last moment in order to repair the severe laceration I had incurred. My perineal scar was not as deep as the wound to my psyche.

To add insult to injury, the nursing staff would not let me see my baby for about twelve hours. They said that I needed to rest. I remember pounding on the nursery window as I watched a nurse bottle-feed my baby, which was totally against my specific instructions. I was escorted back to my bed by the nursing supervisor and within a few minutes was offered a sedative (ordered by the doctor). I endured the next two days in a mixture of new-mother anxiety, anger, and frustration.

The whole experience and the memory of the humiliation and disappointment led me to seek alternative approaches five years later, when I became pregnant with my second child. This time I vowed I would be as informed as possible and totally in charge. I talked to mothers with rosy-cheeked babies in the health-food stores and inquired if they had had home births. I finally found out who the midwives of my community were and sought them out. I was also interested in water birth. The whole idea fascinated me, even though the nurse in me wondered about the possible harm for the baby. I went to great lengths to have my questions answered.

My search for information about water birth and how a woman could have a positive birth experience took me to France, to a little farming community outside Paris. When I arrived in Pithiviers at the Hospital Generale, I had expected to see a less institutional-looking building. It was indeed a state-run institution that just happened to have a distinctively different obstetric unit run by midwives and one distinctively different obstetrician, Michel Odent. The minute I stepped onto the maternity floor, I knew something dynamic was going on there. Full-color photographs of women in various stages of labor and giving birth filled the wall on one side of a large meeting room. On the other side a large mural depicted women giving birth in squatting positions. A peek into the patients rooms revealed large double beds with bright spreads, rocking chairs, and cradles for the babies. No nursery? No hospital beds? What was the birthing room like? I interviewed the midwives, and after an hour I was allowed into the birthing room. A couple was in labor, and the midwife had to obtain permission for me to watch their birth.

My heart leapt with joy at the chance to watch this birth, especially since I was seven months pregnant. I watched a young French woman climb out of a large, round tub filled with water adjacent to the birthing room. She squatted and, with her husband's help, released her baby with a few moans and one loud cry. She sat down on the sheet-covered floor and proceeded to rub her baby's back. What an incredible sight! This woman was totally in charge. The midwife had said nothing and done nothing but watch her give birth.

The only other births I had experienced were in the hospital during my nurse's training and, of course, my own birth. The birth in Pithiviers only reinforced the conviction that I would never go to a hospital again to have a baby, especially as long as obstetricians were in control. I could not comprehend the discrepancy between birth in American hospitals and this seemingly simple community hospital in France. What were we doing wrong?

I saw the deep, deep scars that women were left with, not just in the United States but all over the world. Women and their families were living with the humiliation and sense of powerlessness that modern technology had given them. Their births had been taken away. Many women and most young girls think of birth as an illness that is bloody, sickening, and painful. Very few women have ever seen a birth unless they have been a nurse in a maternity unit in a hospital. I began to feel anger and frustration again.

3

My anger intensified when I came home from France and met with my obstetrician in Santa Barbara. When I naively attempted to share the information I had gathered in France, he dismissed me as a radical, a person only concerned with self-gratification, and, what was worse, a potential "child abuser." My doctor vowed to report me to the "authorities" if I attempted a home birth or an underwater delivery of my baby. He went to his bookshelf, pulled out a book, and threw it down on his desk, yelling at me, "I know who you are. You are one of them!" It was *Immaculate Deception* by Suzanne Arms—a book I had not even read yet.

The birth of my son, Samuel, was so powerful that I could barely comprehend its impact. I had constructed a tub large enough to hold approximately seventy-five gallons of water and placed it in my bedroom. The lay midwife I had hired to attend me during my birth was there, though I labored mostly alone, walking, singing, cooking, and talking quietly with my partner. I remember feeling totally alive. I could feel the energy of each contraction with every fiber of my being. I sensed the baby's movements, and I could actually feel my cervix dilating during contractions. I felt the baby's head with my fingertips when it was in my vagina. When I got into the water, it felt like a lightning bolt hit me. The water intensified each contraction yet made the sensation less painful. My body was birthing this baby, and I simply allowed myself to witness it. I experienced the birth that I had wanted and desired for so long. I was empowered.

I began talking about water birth immediately. By the time my second son, Abraham, was born in 1986, I could think of little else other than how to facilitate the documentation of water births. I especially wanted to record how positive and empowered births changed women's lives and their attitudes about themselves. Pregnant women and midwives started writing to me. I held classes in my home, wrote articles, lectured, and traveled all over the world with my children seeking information about water birth and gentle birth.

The idea of water birth began to shock people out of their complacency about birth. If a woman thought she wanted a water birth and had no other orientation to gentle birth, she had to educate herself on the best possible way to obtain the birth she desired. Couples began to work to create options for

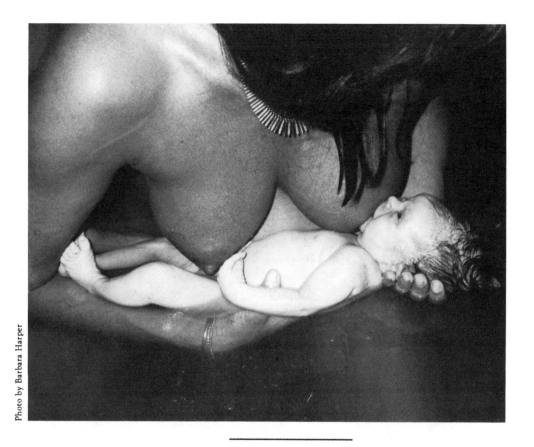

Photo by Barbara Harper

Noel, breast-feeding baby Zen immediately after her water birth, came all the way from Bali to find an experienced water-birth midwife in California.

themselves that previously did not exist. More and more couples sought the services of midwives or doctors who were willing to listen and who agreed that women should be allowed to be in charge of their birth experiences. Sometimes couples would take on the task of educating their practitioners about what they wanted. Couples had to take responsibility for their own health and well-being. They couldn't just hand their lives over to someone else: "Okay, Doctor, whatever you say." Women and men began to "just say no" to controlled and managed childbirth.

Establishing the nonprofit organization Global Maternal/Child Health Association (GMCHA) in 1989 was the realization of a dream for me—a dream in which I helped women empower themselves with information and awareness about their own abilities and all their options. GMCHA provides families with information and resources. We strongly support the belief that women have the ability to have a natural gentle birth experience and that midwives should be the primary care providers for maternity care. Our office now processes hundreds of requests for information and assistance each month. Over one thousand women have sent us birth stories that resoundingly testify to the fact that when labor is left alone and not medically managed, the majority of women will birth instinctively with power and dignity. Birth is the continuation of a normal female physiological cycle.

This book has taken many convolutions and turns, but it has continued to lead me on a path of discovery and awareness. The book itself started out as the story of water birth, but as I researched and listened to all the women who wanted a water birth, I heard a similar story. Over and over the women were saying, "I want to give birth the way *I* want to." I have realized through my work that I have more than a job or a dream—I have a calling. The more I surrender to it, the more I accomplish. It is the same in birth.

The more women I talk to, the more I hear them say, "I wish I had known that I had options when I was having my baby." This feedback has served to reinforce my desire to communicate to those who will listen and to begin creating gentle birth choices for all women, their families, and especially the babies. The very core of our society is deeply affected by the way we give birth. I want women and men to be challenged by what I have written. My strongest desire for this book is that women will come together, use the information to support each other, and help each other cry out, "Take back our births!"

I

Gentle Beginnings

Human birth is the most miraculous, transformational, and mysterious event of our lives. It is also an experience that is shared by every single member of the human race. The birth experience indelibly imprints itself in the lives of both the mother who is giving birth and the baby who is being born. In today's high-tech, industrialized, computer-run world, our cultural perspective of birth depends greatly on who controls the birth experience.

For centuries medicine has been trying to investigate, calculate, and predict within a certain degree of probability the outcomes of birth. In the twentieth century, doctors poise themselves, ready to intervene at any given moment, needing to know what is happening at all times during the birth process. It has never been a priority of obstetrics to consider birth from the mother's perspective or to ask what could be done to make her birth more fulfilling.

A gentle birth begins by focusing on the mother's experience and by bringing together a woman's emotional dimensions and her physical and spiritual needs. A gentle birth respects the mother's pivotal role, acknowledging that she knows how to birth her child in her own time and in her own way, trusting her instincts and intuition. In turn, when a mother gives birth gently, she and everyone present acknowledge that the baby is a conscious participant in his or her own birth. The experience empowers the birthing woman, welcomes the newborn child into a peaceful and loving environ-

A happy mother makes a happy baby.

ment, and bonds the family. The goal of a gentle birth is to reclaim the wonder and joy that are inherent in the beginning of a new life.

Gentle births occur throughout the world: in homes, where births have traditionally been natural and without intervention; in birthing centers, which are becoming more popular as women demand greater freedom in giving birth; and in some hospitals that are responding to the needs and desires of today's families. Women worldwide are seeking more natural, family-centered ways to birth their children and experience this passage into motherhood as life-affirming, without the suffering and trauma that have been traditionally associated with labor and delivery. Women are realizing that their births do not have to incorporate the biblical "curse of Eve," that is, birth as a painful burden that women must endure in order to have children. Instead, more and more women and their families are viewing labor and birth as one of the most extraordinary experiences of their lives, a time when they can witness the strength and sensuality of the female body. Women also know that birthing a baby can be hard work, the type of exertion that will test their endurance both physically and emotionally. Because of this they want optimal education and support.

Today, with the combined advances of medical technology, drugs for pain relief during labor and birth, and an increase in the number of neonatal intensive care units, people might think that women have more birthing options than ever before. They may also believe that birthing is safer than at any other time in history. This is not necessarily true. The United States offers the most advanced technical obstetrical care in the world. Ninety-eight percent of all births in the United States take place in hospitals, attended by physicians. Yet when this country is compared with others worldwide, it ranks only twenty-third in maternal and infant mortality and morbidity rates, with 9.9 deaths of babies for every 1,000 live births.[1] As of 1990 one of the safest countries in the world to have a baby was the Netherlands, with only 7.6 deaths per 1,000 births. In the Netherlands only 40 percent of births take place in hospitals, and over 70 percent of all births are attended by professionally trained midwives, either in homes or birthing centers.

While there are additional factors to consider when comparing these two countries' birth outcomes, such as socialized medicine and accessibility to prenatal care, it cannot be denied that there is a strong case for reconsidering the consequences of the "medicalization" of childbirth. Two basic questions many parents and health care professionals ask as they reassess the medical model for modern birth are (1) What have we sacrificed for technology's promise of safer births? and (2) Can we trust birth to be a normal and safe process that flows naturally, or must we "control" the process with technology? The truth is that birth, like death, is an innate part of life and in most cases does not require the medical intervention and control we have been told is necessary.

Consider Christen's quest for a gentle birth for her son. During the seventh month of Christen's pregnancy, she and her husband realized that the kind of birth they envisioned for their first child was not likely to happen. Christen, who was born with cerebral palsy, had fears and concerns about her ability to have a normal birth because of her physical disability. When she expressed her concerns to her obstetrician during her prenatal visits, they were brushed aside.

The couple felt that their needs were being neglected, so they decided to confront the physician about their desire for a "natural" birth, which might include laboring and birthing the baby in water. Christen's doctor informed her that it would be necessary for her to have continuous electronic fetal monitoring and an intravenous (IV) line in her arm; she would be allowed no food or drink; and during delivery, stirrups would be used, although she could sit almost upright in the new hospital bed designed to help women "push" their babies out. Christen was told she might be able to use the shower during labor but that she would need constant monitoring, especially since her physician had recently prescribed medication for a possible heart condition.

The response from Christen's obstetrician crushed her expectations but strengthened her resolve to have a normal, natural, gentle birth. Home birth was not an option for Christen because of her medical condition. Her next step in the search for a gentle birth was to seek support and information from Global Maternal/Child Health Association (GMCHA). She asked for a referral to a doctor who would listen to how she wanted to birth her baby.

Christen and her husband made an appointment to meet Dr. Michael Rosenthal, medical director of the Family Birthing Center in Upland, California. They felt very comfortable at the birthing center, where they found the atmosphere friendly and helpful. They didn't even mind the three-hour drive to get there. Rosenthal felt confident that Christen could have a normal and healthy birth. No one talked about IVs or fetal monitors. Christen was treated like a healthy pregnant woman without a feared "disability" or "medical condition." Christen's options had expanded, and she felt she was in charge again.

Once Christen was in active labor, she progressed quickly, moving about freely and sipping water or eating as she needed. Rosenthal and one of the center's labor nurses stayed with the couple throughout the labor, offering encouragement and reassurance. Christen walked and sat in a rocking chair, and she found that her most comfortable position for labor was sitting on the toilet. She was surprised that sitting upright and relaxed on the toilet could be so comfortable. Christen handled the intense work well and didn't feel the need to labor in a tub of water. After three hours of labor, Christen realized that the baby was ready to be born. She leaned back with her husband's support, and the baby slid out into Rosenthal's waiting hands. Christen's tears of joy were mixed with sweat from her intense labor as she held her new son close to her body. Her husband and a few family members gathered around to share in the awe of those first moments with their new child.

Christen called GMCHA a few days after her birth to thank the staff for the referral to Dr. Rosenthal and all the support she had received. In relating her birth story, Christen said, "All of my life I was taught that I couldn't trust my body. I couldn't trust it to move how I wanted it to or to be healthy. Yet I instinctively trusted my body and its ability to birth my baby. I just knew I could do it. I felt the energy of the birth moving through me, and I just let it happen. It was so incredible. I'm so happy that we went to the birthing center. Now I know that I can do anything!"

Christen took the experience of her birth and applied it to mothering her baby. She knows she will be able to do whatever it takes to be a mother. Christen was truly empowered by giving birth. Every day thousands of women, like Christen, seek a birth experience that they intuitively know will be best for them and their babies. They know that there is far more to birth than just getting the baby out of their bodies. That is one of the reasons women are asking for gentle births.

The idea of women having choices when birthing their babies has only begun to emerge as a woman's right in the past ten years. Until recently it did not occur to most women to question or challenge a physician's procedures during labor and delivery or a hospital's policy in the maternity ward. To do so implied that you were not a caring mother and that you were willing to risk your baby's safety for your own selfish needs. However, in recent years many parents, childbirth educators, midwives, and physicians have asserted the need to again treat birth as a natural process, saving technological intervention for births that are truly high risk. Many doctors throughout the world feel that if birth is allowed to proceed normally, at least 75 percent of the time it will take place without any complications that require intervention; but in hospitals in the United States, interventions are routinely used in more than 90 percent of all births.[2, 3]

A growing number of medical studies strongly indicate that the excessive use of technology in childbirth has contributed to a rising cesarean rate and other unnecessary complications. Ironically, the countries with the highest number of obstetricians and the lowest number of midwives have the highest cesarean rates. In 1970 the cesarean rate in the United States was 5 percent; in 1990 it was 25 percent.[4] That means one out of four women give birth by undergoing major surgery. A 1987 report citing individual hospital cesarean rates named over one hundred hospitals in the United States that had rates from 35 to 53 percent.[5] The World Health Organization (WHO) has called for a reduction in the cesarean rate because of the increased risk of maternal and neonatal mortalities. They recommend that no hospital should have a cesarean rate over 10 percent each year and maintain that those who do are intervening too often in the birth process.[6]

Dr. Edward Hon, inventor of the electronic fetal monitor (EFM), has said, "When you mess around with a process that works well 98 percent of the time, there is potential for much harm."[7] In response to a survey conducted by the GMCHA, Dr. Josie Muscat, an obstetrician and the director of the St. James Natural Childbirth Center on the island of Malta, stated that he has found that 98 percent of all births at his clinic are natural and without complications when women are not disturbed with medical procedures during labor but instead encouraged with love and support.[8]

The elements that make up a gentle birth are certainly nothing new or revolutionary. Many have been a part of childbirth for thousands of years. However, many of the traditions of gentle birth wisdom have been lost or devalued, particularly during the twentieth century, as medical technology and procedures have transformed birth into a medical event.

Ingredients for a Gentle Birth

Before describing the important elements of gentle birth, I want to point out that these are merely suggestions. Gentle birth is not a method or a set of rules that must be followed. Rather, it is an approach to birth that incorporates a woman's own values and beliefs. Every birth is a powerful experience—sometimes painful, always transformational. Each birth is as unique as the woman giving birth and the baby being born. There is no illustrated owner's manual.

Many women's early social conditioning that makes them believe they are unable to give birth normally must be replaced with a newfound understanding of the philosophy of and the ideas behind gentle birth. When women realize that their bodies know how to give birth and that their babies know how to be born, they gain confidence. Only then is gentle birth a possibility.

A gentle birth takes place when a woman is supported by the people she chooses to be with during this most intimate time. She needs to be loved and nurtured by those around her so she can feel comfortable and secure enough to follow her natural instincts. A birthing woman must be trusted so she in turn can trust herself, her body, her partner, her baby, and this process of giving birth. Her intuition must be respected. During a natural gentle birth, a woman feels and senses the power of the birth and uses this energy to transform every part of her own being. A gentle birth is not rushed. The baby emerges at its own pace and in its own time, received into the hands of those who love and recognize it for the divine gift that it is.

Some of the most important ingredients for a natural gentle birth are described on the following pages. Each woman has individual needs and preferences, so again, use these elements only as guidelines.

PREPARATION

The education that best prepares a woman for a gentle birth is one that empowers her through information and a belief in her ability to give birth naturally. The original childbirth educators were mothers who labored in front of their children and included them in the folk medicine of the day. Pregnant women asked their mothers about a pain or an ache, and the mothers responded by saying, "Oh, I had that with all three of you." For the daughter to experience her mother giving birth is worth a whole course in childbirth education. In sharing her mother's labor and giving birth, she learns about the essence of this miracle firsthand.

Today childbirth educators have taken over the job of mothers whose memories of birth were obliterated with drugs, unconsciousness, and the medical treatments of the day. There are many styles of education and preparation for birth. One of the most important components for all methods of childbirth preparation is a healthy attitude. Women pay attention to their bodies throughout their pregnancy by eating healthful foods, avoiding stress, sticking to a physical exercise program, being cautious about exposing themselves to harmful chemicals or toxins, and maintaining a positive emotional outlook. While preparing for a gentle birth, it's important to keep an open mind as to how the birth will actually proceed. Flexibility is essential, because in some cases medical intervention may be necessary.

I recommend that a woman look into her attitudes, ideas, and beliefs about birth. This may include exploring her feelings about her sexuality, her relationship with the baby's father, and her relationships with her parents. A woman who is comfortable with her sexuality will feel less inhibited sexually during the birth. A woman who has examined her own birth will not be likely to repeat the pattern of that birth in the one she is preparing for. A woman who has a good sense of herself will not be easily swayed away from what she knows to be right for herself. A woman who is at peace with her partner and her family members will find comfort in and draw strength from those bonds and will want to include those people in the birthing experience.

A REASSURING ENVIRONMENT

When a woman is in a comfortable, distraction-free, reassuring environment, she is more likely to shift into a more instinctive level of concentration or consciousness that will enable her to labor spontaneously. Making this shift helps tremendously in reducing the sensation of pain. The levels of certain brain chemicals, called endorphins, increase throughout pregnancy, reaching a peak during labor.[9] Endorphins have a major affect on the perception of pain and feelings of well-being; they are the body's natural painkillers and tranquilizers. As the body responds to the natural oxytocin that causes the

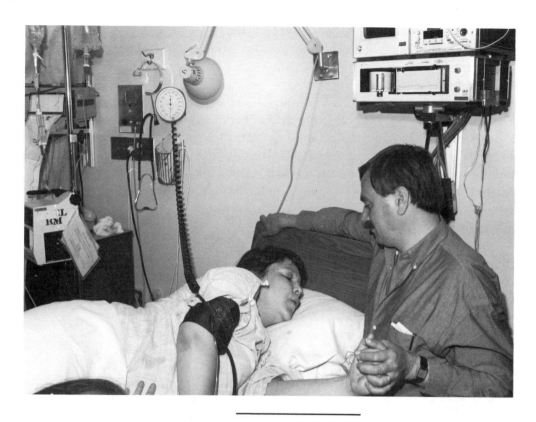

*A woman tries to ignore her surroundings and
concentrate on her contractions.*

uterus to contract, more endorphins are released into the system, reducing
the pain and creating a sense of well-being. Runners describe a similar response in long-distance running, which they refer to as a "runner's high."

The uterus is a large muscle with a difficult job, but endorphins work in
cooperation with the uterus. As the contractions of the uterus become longer
and stronger, more endorphins are released. If a laboring woman is treated
impersonally in a hospital's cold surroundings, bombarded by IV hook-ups,
medical paraphernalia, bright lights, loud noises, and separation from her

loved ones, her response will be one of fear and inhibition. The body responds to fear by tightening, thus blocking the release of endorphins and releasing the chemical adrenalin, which influences the body's "fight or flight" response. Adrenalin can actually slow or stop labor altogether. It sends mixed signals to the laboring body, sometimes causing a racing heart and an intensification of pain. In *Birth Reborn* Dr. Michel Odent writes, "For the body's natural powers to come into play, they must be left alone.... Giving women painkilling drugs and synthetic hormones [artificial oxytocin] during birth, as is common practice in most modern hospitals, destroys the hormonal balance on which spontaneous labor depends. Certainly pain itself can slow labor down, but when drugs are not used, the body can defend itself effectively and naturally against it."[10]

Equally disruptive to a laboring woman is the imposition of time constraints for birthing the baby. When a woman in labor shifts into a deeper level of concentration, she removes herself from concepts of time. Unfortunately, laboring women are often threatened with various kinds of interventions if they are "taking too long": the artificial rupture of the amniotic sac, the administration of synthetic oxytocin (Pitocin), or a cesarean section. Generally the intention is to help quicken the birth process and to ensure the mother's and child's safety, but often the greatest assistance is to simply let the mother continue with her labor, unhurried and undisturbed. Midwives traditionally allow labor to unfold in whatever time is necessary, especially if the mother is active, rested, and eating and drinking, and if the baby shows no signs of stress.

On one occasion a certified nurse-midwife (CNM) in California had been attending a woman during her first labor, at home, for over thirty hours. She suggested to the woman that perhaps a change of scene was in order and drove the couple to the beach for an early-morning walk. The woman's contractions actually slowed down and she was able to sleep for several hours. When she woke up, she ate, showered, and went for one more walk. By that time it had been almost thirty-six hours. Her contractions increased, and after forty hours she birthed her baby in warm water. The mother's level of energy and her confidence and trust that everything was normal never swayed. The midwife had faith in the woman's ability to birth her baby without

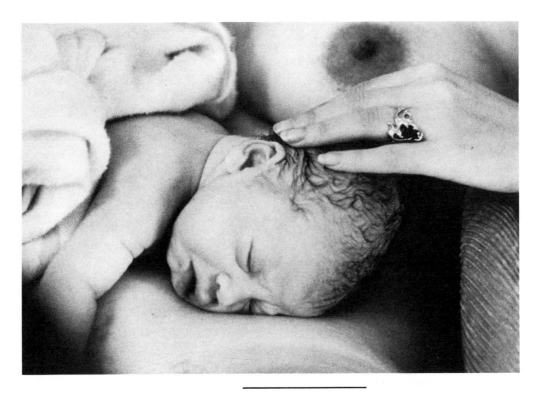

A newborn rests peacefully on her mother's abdomen
after a long and exhaustive labor.

intervention. In hospitals the length of time a woman can labor without having interventions used has decreased over the last two decades. Doctors used to let women labor for up to forty-eight hours and not think it was abnormal. It is now not unusual for interventions to be used to speed the labor after only six or twelve hours.

FREEDOM TO MOVE

If a woman is physically active during labor, her baby is constantly repositioning in the womb, readjusting and descending, preparing for the birth. Requiring a woman to be in bed during any part of her labor and decreasing her ability to move increases the need for interventions.

A growing number of childbirth professionals share the conviction that the worst possible position for giving birth is the traditional "lithotomy," or lying-down position, a posture still insisted upon by most Western doctors. The past president of the International Association of Obstetricians and Gynecologists, Dr. Roberto Caldeyro-Barcia, has stated: "Except for being hanged by the feet, the supine position is the worst conceivable position for labor and delivery."[11] When lying on her back, the woman's enlarged uterus compresses the major blood vessels and diminishes the amount of oxygenated blood available to the placenta, possibly placing the fetus under distress. Additionally, the lithotomy position forces the woman to push against gravity during the delivery. Rarely does a woman choose to lie down during labor or delivery because it is so painful. Most of womankind will give birth in the vertical position if there is no obstetrician or labor nurse around to make them lie down.

The two most widely chosen birthing postures throughout the world are kneeling and squatting. In cultures where women still control childbirth, women naturally squat, kneel, or lean against a support person in a semisitting position. These same women who squat or kneel during the birth are also active and moving throughout their labors.[12] Taking a woman off her back and putting her upright does more than merely change her position. It gives her control of her body. It removes her from being a patient upon whom the birth is performed and empowers her to become a woman giving birth.

It appears that the lithotomy position remains in favor today in Western medical practices only because it is convenient for the attending physician. By sitting on a stool at the end of a bed or table, he or she can easily observe the development of the delivery, intervening as needed—and besides, "that's the way it's always been done." Dr. Michael Rosenthal observes, "At the Family Birthing Center it seems so absolutely natural for women to labor and deliver vertically. It is very hard for me to walk through labor and delivery in the hospital and see a woman lying flat or even semiprone on a bed or table."

After observing laboring women for several years at the Family Birthing

Center in Upland, California, Dr. Rosenthal realized that women instinctively know how to give birth and, when not impeded by medical interventions, do so in their own way. Rosenthal decided to take birth out of the delivery room, with its narrow metal obstetrical table, and create a private, homelike atmosphere for birthing women. A laboring woman at the center is encouraged to remain active and to take any position she wishes, whether standing, sitting, or squatting, on the floor, on the bed, or in the bath—whatever feels right for her. Rosenthal believes that a woman in labor needs a place where she can do exactly as she likes, where she can feel free physically and emotionally. Laboring women are not forced into positions or told to be quiet or to control themselves. They are supported with calm reassurance, understanding, and tenderness. The birth is not hurried. When allowed to take its own course in this way, the birth usually progresses easily and spontaneously for mother and child.

QUIET

An important element for a gentle birth is quiet, not only for the laboring mother but for the baby. It may seem a difficult requirement at first, but in a quiet, hushed atmosphere the mother remains undistracted, able to stay centered within herself. In a calm environment a laboring woman can concentrate during the contractions, and in the time between the contractions, she may rest and sometimes even sleep. A sense of intimacy can be extremely important to the woman, knowing that when she comes out of a contraction, there will be a pair of loving arms to hold her and the privacy to hug, kiss, share a joke, or mend a hurt with her partner. While in labor a woman can shift back and forth from deep concentration during contractions to a lighter, playful state between contractions. Intimacy and the ability to concentrate enhance a woman's endurance and ability to focus on the work of birthing her child. Unnecessary chatter by the doctor, midwife, or others present can be distracting to a woman in labor.

A baby born into a quiet environment is not startled by the intensity of sounds and voices. If you stop and listen for just a moment and pretend you have never heard any sounds before, you get an idea of how terribly frightening the raw, unfiltered sounds of a conventional delivery room might be to the newborn. Imagine hearing for the first time the crackling sounds of a hospital intercom, the exuberant cry of observers, and the clanging of stainless-steel basins and instruments.

Ideally, the baby is best welcomed into a quiet place, a safe place, an environment that is free from bright lights and jarring loud noises. American obstetrician Dr. David Kliot, who has incorporated the elements of gentle birth into the hospital births he attends, observed, "There really was a sensational change in the atmosphere of the delivery room when the lights were turned down. We are all so accustomed to 'lights, camera, action,' to the swinging electrical doors, intercoms going off, basins clanging. It's hard to imagine how much noise there is until it stops. With all the commotion, all the instrumentation, the emotional content of the moment for the woman and her husband could be virtually ignored. As soon as the lights were dimmed, however, all eyes were automatically directed toward the birthing process."[13]

LOW LIGHT

Low light is soothing. We seek it as a refuge from the bright light of the workplace and from the fluorescent lights of institutions. We return to low light to rest, reflect, relax. We meditate or pray in the dim light of holy places. We make love in candlelight, in the moonlight, or in darkness. When ill, we recover our strength in the dim light of our sick room.

During the birth process, low light provides the most comfortable environment for mother and child. Low light creates a relaxing and private atmosphere in which a special, intimate event can occur. A room lit with natural light, candles, or very low wattage electric light provides an ideal ambience for a laboring woman. After the birth, the child's eyes are spared from bright lights. The most amazing thing has been witnessed in darkened birthing rooms: Newborn babies almost immediately open their eyes and gaze at their mothers. Gazing into the eyes of your newly emerged child, who seems peaceful and present, is an unforgettable moment.

Dr. John Grover, one of the first physicians in the United States to undertake a Leboyer-style delivery in a hospital, observed, "I noticed immediately that babies born in this peaceful, twilight atmosphere seemed calmer and more alert than those I had delivered in the past. After awhile the nursery nurses began to comment, 'Ah, you've brought us another gentle birth baby!' without my having to point out the fact. When I asked them how they could tell, the reply was, 'Oh, most babies are either asleep or crying most of the time; yours look about more, they seem to follow us with their eyes.'"[14]

Grover, as well as many other physicians, experience no trouble attending births with reduced lighting. Not only does the human eye adapt to dark, but other senses become keener. Midwives report that perceptions, especially the sense of touch, are actually heightened in low light. A midwife from Ohio related that her attention was much more focused on the mother when the room was dark and quiet. It was actually easier for her to sense changes in breathing, which can be the very first signs of distress or tension. The midwife could then talk to the mother and help her relax.

Births that take place at home by firelight or candlelight may seem to some like a return to the dark ages, but the participants, including the care providers, view these births as sacred events. Dr. Donald Sutherland, an obstetrician in Australia, describes feeling privileged to be able to witness the tenderness of a two-second-old baby gazing into his mother's eyes. Sutherland openly wept when he said, "They [the other physicians] don't know what they are missing."[15]

THE FIRST BREATH

Once the child is born and comes into contact with the air, his breathing begins naturally. There is rarely a need to artificially stimulate a healthy, normal newborn's breathing, especially by hitting or slapping. If stimulation is necessary, a gentle rub on the back or on the feet is usually enough. With the first expansion of the chest, air enters the baby's nose and throat. As the lungs expand to accommodate the air, the fluid that earlier filled the tiny air sacs is absorbed into the blood and lymphatic circulation.

Some practitioners feel that the first breath can be gradual or abruptly painful, depending on when the umbilical cord is cut. When a baby takes his first breath, he crosses a threshold to a new world. Until this moment, the mother is supplying the baby with oxygenated blood through the placenta and umbilical cord. By keeping the newborn attached to the umbilical cord while it is still pulsating, the transition to breathing with the lungs is gradual

Cradled and protected in his father's arms, the baby eases into his new life.

and gentle. The newborn begins to breathe through newly operating lungs while simultaneously receiving oxygen from the placenta via the umbilical cord. The baby can fill his lungs gradually, coming to terms with the new element, oxygen. It usually takes fifteen to twenty minutes before the blood flow through the cord decreases substantially and stops. Physicians are traditionally in a hurry to cut the cord in order to speed the process of the delivery of the placenta. In a gentle birth the cord is often not cut at all until the placenta has been expelled by itself.

During the time between the birth of the baby and the cutting of the cord, the newborn is placed on the mother's abdomen, face down, arms and legs folded under. If the mother is upright, the baby can be held in the mother's arms, where essential body contact between the two is maximized. This period of tranquility marks important transitions for both: The baby moves from *being breathed for* to *breathing alone,* and the mother experiences the infant who was once inside her now as an individual beside her, separate but still deeply dependent.

THE FIRST CARESSES

The newly emerged baby who is immediately placed in his mother's waiting arms receives the immediate benefit of skin-to-skin connection. The baby is slowly massaged, caressed, or held with loving hands. The mother is simply there with her child, communicating with her touch that this child is welcomed, loved, and long-awaited. This simple act has the power to calm and soothe a newborn beyond anything else. In a gentle birth the mother is asked to determine the sex of her baby either by looking or feeling under the warm blankets. Finding this part of the baby's body can be part of a whole-body massage.

Touching and massaging the newborn is beneficial for the mother as well. Dr. John Grover notes, "I have philosophically given a great deal of thought to helping the mother deal with her sense of physical loss as the baby is born. Her reaching down and touching the baby as it is coming out, and actually helping to bring it onto her stomach, seems to matter a great deal in many cases. But probably more important is the subsequent skin-to-skin contact with the wet, squirmy infant. It is surprising that more has not been written about this phenomenon. How could a woman who has carried a fetus inside herself for over nine months not feel a sense of loss when it physically leaves her body?"[16]

Touching and holding the baby in the moments after he has been born is

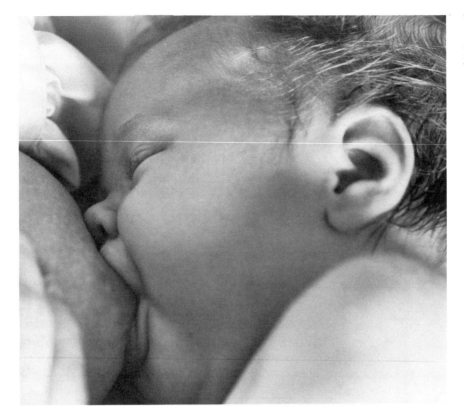

extremely important for fathers, siblings, and other family members as well. Hospitals require family members to wear a gown and mask while in the delivery room. This creates an artificial barrier for skin-to-skin contact with their new babies, as well as with their partners. Fathers often feel overwhelmed by the intensity of the birth experience. Some feel excluded; some remain distant, not wanting to "get in the way." Fathers can be encouraged to remove their shirts so they, too, can pick up their babies and hold them against their skin. For many fathers, the child is not real until they hold the baby in their arms or touch the baby in the moments after birth. It is then, gazing at their new child, that birth becomes real; emotions surface and unbreakable bonds are formed.

THE BABY AT THE BREAST

The ideal time to begin breast-feeding your baby is within the first moments after birth. When the mother is awake and aware and has given birth to an alert baby, it is easy to watch for the early cues that the baby is seeking the breast. The baby's head will turn, his mouth will twitch and form an oval shape, and his tongue will move in and out. This is called rooting. If the baby is in his mother's arms, these signs can't be missed, and the baby is gently guided to the nipple. Researchers have documented that newborns left on the mother's belly will actually crawl to and attach themselves to the breast within the first twenty minutes following birth. If the baby is not put to the breast within the first hour after birth, he may lapse into a drowsy state that can continue for up to twenty-four hours, making nursing more difficult. For early nursing to develop easily, the baby's senses must be stimulated to function fully. In a gentle birth, mother and child are free to communicate with each other without inhibition. The cuddling, talking, stroking, and loving that take place immediately after the birth provide the mother and baby with the opportunity to continue the symbiosis that began nine months before, in the womb.

Babies enjoy nursing immensely. When you see a baby at the breast, it is clear that he is engrossed in a most wonderful, sensuous activity. Breast-feeding contributes to a baby's emotional life. All the smells, touch sensations, sights, and sounds of nursing enrich the experience. While breast-feeding, a mother communicates her feelings and emotions to her infant in many different ways. The way she looks into the baby's eyes, the way she touches and holds him, her movements, her voice, her breath—and even the taste, smell, and feel of the breast from which the warm, nurturing milk flows—all communicate love and acceptance to the baby.

By issuing statements about the benefits of nursing, WHO is working to reverse the trend to bottle-feed, which started in the mid-1950s. Statistics show that infant mortality rose proportionally, especially in developing countries, when bottle-feeding replaced breast-feeding. In a poor country a bottle-fed

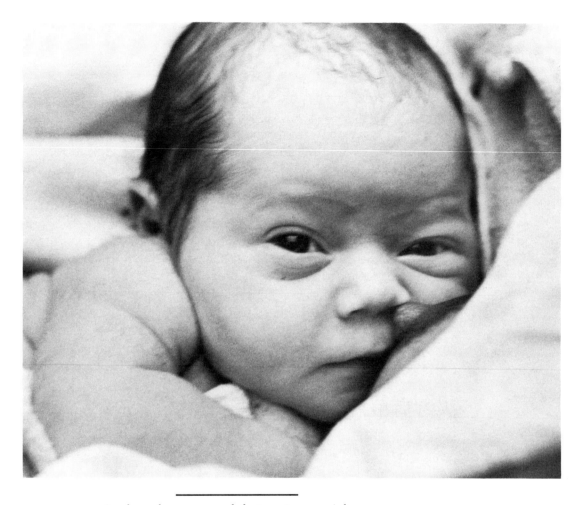

*Awake and aware, snuggled up against mom's breast
just one hour after birth.*

baby is twenty-five times more likely to die than a breast-fed one. In an effort
to reduce infant mortality, one of the goals of WHO is to see infants worldwide breast-fed for the first six months by the year 2000.[17]

The routine hospital practice of separating infants and mothers and giving infants glucose water or formula has actually been shown to cause harm to the infant. The infant may suffer from an irritable bowel, and if the glucose is inhaled into the lungs, the resulting aspiration can be very dangerous.[18] In addition, offering the baby something other than the breast interrupts the natural rhythm that needs to take place for breast-feeding to work. Breast-milk supply is dependent on the amount of stimulation the nipple receives from sucking. The rhythm and flow of breast-feeding is a delicate balance that can be easily disturbed by supplements or glucose bottles.

The first breast milk, colostrum, is a very nutritious, balanced substance meant to sustain new life in a perfect way. Colostrum is higher in protein and lower in fat and carbohydrates than mature milk, so the baby needs very little to get off to a good nutritional start. Colostrum is also high in natural anti-bodies that protect the baby from infection. In addition, colostrum is a laxative, which helps to ensure that the baby's bowel is cleared of meconium, the sticky, tarry first stool. If the first bowel movement is delayed more than twenty-four hours, a baby is more likely to develop jaundice, probably because the meconium is reabsorbed through the intestines.

The process of encouraging the baby to nurse shortly after birth is extremely beneficial for the mother. The baby's sucking at the breast stimulates the immediate release of two hormones in the mother that are important for postnatal recovery and health. The hormones, oxytocin and prolactin, work together to stimulate milk production. Oxytocin also causes the mother's uterus to contract, which is important in preventing hemorrhaging, and stimulates the uterus to return to its normal size. Prolactin helps prepare the breasts for milk production and is secreted as a direct result of the baby's sucking so that milk can flow. Prolactin also inhibits ovulation; breast-feeding has been used worldwide as a natural form of birth control, although it is not considered a reliable contraceptive. Breast-feeding can also increase a mother's sense of well-being and give her an immediate sense of her ability to mother. It is a special and satisfying feeling for nursing mothers to know that they can feed and nurture their babies with their own milk.

BONDING

Perhaps no aspect of conventional birthing has caused as much distress for new mothers, fathers, and babies as hospital policies that require enforced separation at a time when the parents most want and need to be with their babies. There is no good medical reason to separate a healthy newborn baby from his mother. The separation of mother and child immediately after birth harkens back to the days when mothers were routinely drugged for labor and delivery and were virtually unconscious. It was felt that they needed time to "sober up" before they could relate to or care for their babies.

Dr. Robert Bradley, an American obstetrician and author, wrote, "I'm sure the humane society would and should arrest me if I did to animal mothers what we do to human mothers—take their babies away from them at birth and put the babies in a big box with a glass window where the mothers could see their babies but couldn't hold them or touch them."[19]

Sheila Kitzinger, well-respected British childbirth educator and author, noted, "A screaming baby alone in its cot or lined up with rows of other screaming newborns is a neglected baby. He cannot know that help is near, that milk is coming in half an hour, or twenty minutes or even five minutes. He cannot know that loving arms are waiting to hold him. He is to all intents and purposes completely isolated and abandoned."[20]

When Santha was seeking an alternative approach to her previous hospital birth, she recalled her three-year-old son telling her, "I remember [when I was born] they put me in this box and they made me go to sleep and I wanted my mommy." Santha responds, "That was really sad to hear. I remember wanting to be with my son, but he couldn't be with me because he had to go through all these hospital procedures."

In a gentle birth the child is not suddenly taken away from his parents and put into a little bed alone in a nursery far from his mother, who is the only person in the world safe and familiar to him. There is no reason or justification for such a practice. In a gentle birth the mother is awake and aware, highly conscious, energized by having given birth, and extremely eager to spend time with her child—touching, looking, feeding, resting, or sleeping together. The newborn needs and wants the comforting presence of his mother, her warmth, touch, sound, and smells. After a gentle birth most mothers experience an incredible high that helps them overcome their exhaustion. They come alive immediately upon seeing the baby. If a mother

Mother and father share the thrill of holding their just-born baby.

really is too tired or too uncomfortable, she can rest and the father or other family members can hold and love the baby.

One reason given by hospitals for separating a baby from its mother is the mother's need for rest, but the disturbance of the mother's sleep for feedings is actually reduced when the child sleeps with her. Sheila Kitzinger explains in her book *Breastfeeding,* "It is a very different matter for a woman to wake up and roll over, lift her baby from a cot at the bedside and cuddle it up to her breast, perhaps falling asleep while the baby is still suckling and waking to find it still nestled against her body. The disturbance is minimal, and both mother and child get the chance of extended flesh-to-flesh contact and loving closeness."[21]

The hours and days after birth are extremely important ones; they can deeply affect the future relationship between the child and the parents. Time spent together during those first few hours and days after the birth lay the groundwork for a profound relationship with one another. Becoming deeply bonded is vital for the family and can be wonderfully satisfying to all.

And, one might ask, why should it be any other way?

2

The Medicalization of Childbirth

Parents who seek a more gentle, family-centered birth experience ask many questions before deciding how they would like their birth to be. They want to identify the medical procedures and technological advances that make sense and the ones they feel are unnecessary. In order to evaluate the efficacy of modern obstetrical practices, it is important to first understand how some of these technical interventions originated and what attitudes they reflect. How did childbirth evolve from a woman-centered, integral part of home life to a hospital-centered, physician-controlled medical event? How did a natural process come to be seen as a pathological state that required the intervention of doctors, drugs, and medical technology? How and why did the reproductive processes of women become the realm of male physicians?

Our Legacy of Birth

Until the twentieth century, birth, like death, generally took place at home. Some of our grandmothers and most of our great-grandmothers were born at home without interventions, naturally and gently. Giving birth was unique to women, binding them together. This bond crucially influenced how their emotional and physical strengths were defined. Women eagerly supported one another through the birth process, often traveling long distances and staying for days or weeks to aid their birthing relatives or friends. Older daughters

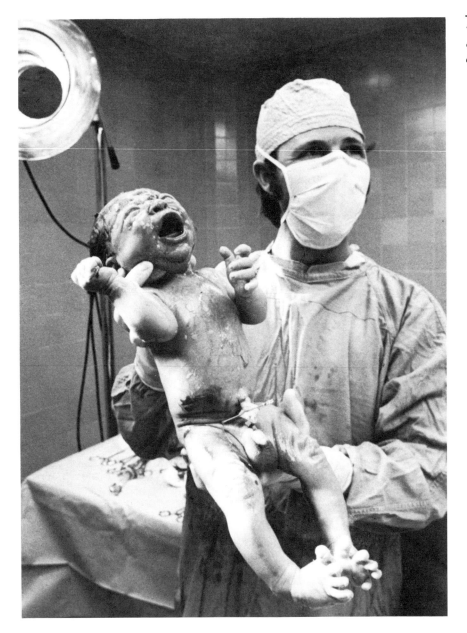

The shock of entering the world in a modern delivery room.

assisted at their mothers' births and mothers, in turn, were commonly called upon to attend their daughters' births. Women who were experienced with the birth process and who had often birthed children themselves came to be known as midwives, respected and sought after for their knowledge and services. It was not uncommon for a woman to be pregnant or nursing for half her lifetime, particularly when the average life expectancy was low.

Women of these times struggled with conditions that complicated pregnancy, birth, and recovery. Diets were less than adequate, sanitation poor, and housing often substandard. The lack of birth control and frequent pregnancies yielded a high infant and maternal mortality rate. Deaths from maternity-related causes at the turn of the century were approximately sixty-five times greater than they are today. The largest single cause of death in 1900 was systemic infection after birth, commonly known as childbed fever or puerperal fever. These infections, especially in women in early charity hospitals, most frequently resulted from physicians' ignorance of the effects of bacteria.[1] The fever was spread from patient to patient by medical personnel, and the use of unclean instruments and linens greatly contributed to the problem. Surgery during pregnancy had an equally high rate of infection and death. As a result, a woman's greatest fear in birth was death; during each pregnancy she coped with the thought that she may only have a few more months to live.

Women eventually traded their comfort and shared experience of childbirth attended by midwives for the promise of safer, faster, and less painful labors and births. This process evolved gradually over centuries, but it can be seen most dramatically beginning in the 1860s with the movement of the physician into the birthplace and the evolution of routine hospitalization for childbirth. The rapid development of the field of obstetrics in the late 1800s and early 1900s, coupled with the growth of related medical technology and hospital procedures, began to make women feel inadequate about their ability to give birth. They no longer trusted their bodies, their instincts, or the wisdom of their grandmothers. Doctors increasingly discredited women birth attendants and eventually controlled the education and licensing of midwives. While 95 percent of American births took place at home in 1900, only 50 percent did so in 1939.[2]

Today 95 percent of American babies are born in hospitals, with a perinatal mortality rate that still remains higher than in twenty-three other countries.[3] Some hospitals conceded to the natural-birth movement by offering more birth options, but most institutions continue to treat birth as a potentially dangerous, life-threatening medical problem rather than a naturally occurring life process. The medicalization of childbirth can be traced to the gradual shift not only from home to hospital but from attending midwife to attending physician.

From Midwife to Physician

Physicians were gradually introduced into the birthplace, due in part to early restrictions against midwives' use of any kind of instruments and to the eventual professionalization of the field of medicine. As early as the thirteenth century, midwives called on male "barber-surgeons" to remove a fetus in a long or difficult labor. These early surgeons were really no more than barbers with sharpened blades and instruments—instruments that women were banned from using by the Catholic Church.[4] In cases where the baby died in the womb, barber-surgeons used an instrument to perforate the infant's skull. The cranial contents were removed and the dead baby was delivered, sometimes after being surgically dismembered. Occasionally this action spared the life of the mother; in other cases it only prolonged her death. Cesarean sections were sanctioned by the Church in order to attempt to save the baby when it appeared that a mother was dying any time during her pregnancy or labor. Instruments were also created to infuse water into the uterus to baptize an unborn baby being buried with a dead mother.

The Church was extremely influential in the lives of all people during this time but especially in the lives of women. Women healers and midwives were often targets for Church-sanctioned public condemnations or witch hunts. The use of metal instruments would have made midwives more powerful than men, and the Church was determined to prevent their use at any cost.

Forceps were invented in 1588 by Peter Chamberlen. Their original purpose was to remove dead babies and speed the process of labor by pulling babies out through the birth canal. The Chamberlen family kept the design, manufacture, and use of forceps a well-guarded secret for almost a century. Doctors themselves, the Chamberlens did not want the tool to be used by other birth attendants, especially midwives. By the seventeenth century, forceps were being used by surgeons to try to save babies from dismemberment and death. Lives were saved, but mothers and infants suffered from a host of forceps-delivery complications, including unspeakable pain, infections, and permanent injury. Physicians classified forceps as "surgical instruments," and the same restrictions on their use by women continued. Perhaps as limiting as actual restrictions, most midwives, who were not usually paid in cash, could not afford to have a set of forceps forged for themselves. Thus, midwives and the families they attended were forced to rely on "specialists" for difficult births.

By the early 1800s urban middle-class women in England and the United States began inviting these "technically" superior men with their surgical instruments to attend their births, along with the traditional midwife. The inclusion of these barber-surgeon midmen (as some women called them) quickly turned childbirth into a successful business, whereas previously it had been women serving other women.

Medical education was standardized in America in the nineteenth century, and men entered medical schools in great numbers. Women, particularly midwives, were excluded from this formal training as a result of the prevailing attitude that women were "inherently incompetent."[5] The Victorian ethics and mores of the day restricted male students to mere book knowledge as far as female anatomy was concerned; thus many physicians graduated without even examining a pregnant woman or seeing an actual birth.

As advances were made in all areas of science and technology, it became easy to convince the public that medicine offered a superior way of both explaining and controlling the human body. In their new role as technically superior advisers, physicians were summoned more frequently to the bedside of upper-class birthing women. In Philadelphia from 1815 to 1825, a span of just ten years, the call for midwives vastly decreased while the number of physicians increased greatly.[6] The only voices to protest this takeover were a few supportive physicians and midwives who believed that men and their technology had no place around birthing women. In the 1820s midwives in England organized, and they charged the new male doctors with "commercialism and dangerous misuse of the forceps." Physicians responded by demeaning midwives as ignorant "old wives" who were unscientific and superstitious.[7] Thus began the battle between physicians and midwives—a struggle that unfortunately continues to this day.

Nineteenth-century doctors felt obliged to offer women the technology of the day. Rather than let nature take its course while attending a birthing woman, they needed to prove themselves as physicians by doing something. They often used bloodletting to relax a woman in labor, sometimes draining her blood to the point where she fainted or lost control. The use of opium or opiate derivatives to minimize the pain of childbirth also gave physicians an advantage over midwives. The playwright Eugene O'Neill often referred to his opium-addicted mother as a tragedy of his own birth; her doctor had given her opium during and after the birth, thus setting the stage for addiction.[8] Doctors commonly used forceps, bloodletting, and opium for perfectly normal labors.

Ether and chloroform were introduced in the birthplace in 1847. In the 1850s Queen Victoria of England went against public opinion and the teachings of most Christian churches by accepting the use of chloroform during the births of her seventh and eighth children, setting the trend for her countrywomen. Medical opinion was initially opposed to the use of ether and chloroform for birth because of the risk of unpredictable complications. However, by the end of 1848, these drugs were used in more than half of all births attended by physicians.[9] It was difficult for doctors to stand by and witness what they saw as immense suffering when one whiff of a chemical could alleviate all memory and pain. Women readily complied with this new practice.

The Promise of Science

Motivated by fear of death and permanent injury, women in the late nineteenth century embraced the promise of improved birth outcomes through the use of "science." Families who could afford specialists with the latest

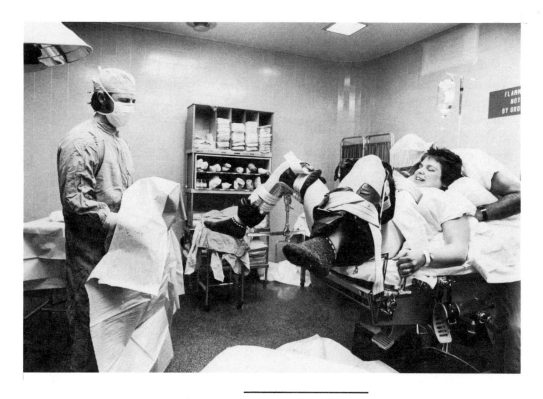

The modern scientific improvement on natural childbirth: Raise a woman, lying on her back, three feet in the air, legs strapped and forced wide apart; numb her body with drugs; and urge her to push the baby out.

technology readily sought them out. Women saw the use of drugs in childbearing as a gift that released them from the pain and suffering biblical tradition had taught them was their lot. Rather than giving up control, they saw themselves as retaining control over a frightening and potentially harmful experience.

Hospital births, which also began in America in the mid-nineteenth century, extended the promise of science to women of low social classes. Unmarried, poor, or immigrant women who had neither the family support nor the financial means to afford a specialist turned to charity hospitals for their time of "confinement." These institutions welcomed even destitute women as birthing patients to supply the new, more clinically oriented medical programs with "teaching material." In these first charity hospitals, birthing women encountered the male physician, usually in training, who could not do much to aid them. In many cases the only reason the physician took charge of charity cases was to gain knowledge and experience. It was unusual for student doctors to actually participate in the birth process due to Victorian codes of modesty.

As medical technology developed during the 1920s and 1930s, there emerged yet another group of women who chose to birth in hospitals. Upper-middle-class and wealthy women hired specialists, soon to be called obstetricians, from urban medical schools. Their ability to pay gave them access to the latest technology in private, newly built maternity hospitals or in private suites in general hospitals. The place of birth moved rapidly from home to hospital, with hospitals becoming the setting for half of all U.S. births by 1938.[10]

American physicians and midwives were increasingly in direct competition for patients. Midwives were shut out of an ever more exclusive medical establishment in the United States. The Flexner Report, a privately funded national survey of American medicine in 1910, criticized the lack of uniform licensing procedures for physicians and the inadequacy of their training. This led to even stricter admission standards, higher tuition, and longer periods of training at U.S. medical schools.[11] There was deliberate discrimination against African Americans, Jews, women, and working-class poor students; the role of the physician was thus reserved for primarily white upper-class men who had the money and the social status to meet medical school requirements.

Meanwhile, the American Medical Association (AMA) launched an "educational" campaign in the 1920s and 1930s to improve the quality of health care as well as the status of doctors. Midwives, still banned from attending medical schools because of their sex, were labeled "uneducated, low-class and non-medical."[12] Physicians throughout the United States actively pursued the elimination of the midwife. Articles against the practice of midwifery were written in professional journals, and lobbyists were hired to urge legislatures to enact strict laws governing the licensing of midwives. The public was warned with exaggerated stories of the dangers of birth outside the control of doctors and hospitals. From 1910 to 1920 the majority of midwives practicing in places like New York City were European immigrants who had been well trained in their native countries. However, the AMA saw them as a threat to the new field of obstetrics and denounced foreign-born midwives as "uneducatable [sic] and a threat to American values."[13]

As a result of this campaign and other factors already mentioned, attendance at childbirth not only shifted from midwives to doctors but from the jurisdiction of women to that of men. The Sheppard-Towner Maternity and Infancy Protection Act of 1921 addressed the problem of rising infant and maternal mortality rates and the lack of proper care for the underprivileged and poor. Fourteen states used federal funding to establish midwifery education programs and care for all pregnant women and children. In 1929 the AMA was effective in lobbying against the use of midwives, and the bill failed to be renewed.[14] By 1930 midwifery was virtually eliminated in the United States, except among the poor of the rural South. In 1935 midwives attended only 11 percent of all American births, but only 5 percent of those births were of white babies.[15]

As the midwife disappeared, the obstetrician/gynecologist, a specialist dealing only with female patients and their reproductive processes, brought forth a new era of childbirth. In 1930 the new American Board of Obstetrics and Gynecology refused to certify any doctor who did not exclusively treat female patients. This eliminated an enormous number of doctors whose practices dealt with gynecological problems and birth as part of the treatment of entire families. The object in establishing this specialty branch of medicine was purely economic. The specialty decreased the competition, thus increasing the chance for a monopoly. With the midwife gone and the family practitioner barred from entrance into this specialty, the field of obstetrics began to expand into the branch of medicine it is today. Ironically, the word *obstetrics* is derived directly from the Latin *obstetrix*, which means midwife.[16]

The idea that childbirth was inherently dangerous and needed constant technical intervention grew with the development of obstetrics and the medical profession. A 1920 article by Dr. Joseph B. DeLee in the new *American Journal of Obstetrics and Gynecology* outlined the horrors of birth for both mother and baby. According to DeLee, labor was a crushing force that threatened the baby and was responsible for "epilepsy, idiocy, imbecility and cerebral palsy" as well as death. For the mother, DeLee compared giving birth to "falling on a pitchfork, driving the handle through her perineum." He believed that "only a small minority of women escape damage during labor." DeLee concluded that labor itself was *abnormal*: "In both cases, the cause of the damage, the fall on the pitchfork and the crushing of the door is pathogenic, that is, disease-producing, and anything pathogenic is pathologic or abnormal."[17] DeLee recommended the routine use of episiotomy and forceps to spare women from these potential afflictions.

The episiotomy is an incision made into the thinned-out perineal tissue in order to enlarge the vaginal opening. Its purpose is to avoid overstretching, undue damage to the pelvic floor, or trauma to the baby's head. DeLee claimed that the stretching and tearing of the perineum resulted in such gynecological conditions as a prolapsed uterus, tears in the vaginal wall, and a sagging perineum. Though first tried in Ireland in 1782 by Dr. Fielding Ould, the episiotomy was not used in the United States until a century later and only became popular with DeLee's endorsement.[18] American physicians, who found tearing of the perineum to be a problem in hospital births, began to insist that the clean, surgical cut of the episiotomy was easier to repair than a natural jagged tear. What they failed to realize is that tearing was largely due to the lithotomy position in which women lay on their backs with their knees elevated, causing undue stress on the perineum. In addition, as soon as the baby's head was visible the doctor would often grab it with forceps and pull, causing the baby's big, blunt shoulders to rip the woman's perineum. Doctors also believed DeLee's claims that the episiotomy would restore "virginal conditions" and make the mother "better than new," implying that women were irreparably damaged in normal childbirth and thus less sexually desirable.

What person could resist such arguments, given the state of knowledge about childbirth and women's health at the time? Even the media sold women on the advantages of medical science and technology in childbirth. As early as 1920 articles in the *Ladies Home Journal* and *Good Housekeeping* urged women to "see an obstetrician early. . . . Choose a doctor you have faith in. . . . You can trust him to guide you through."[19] Women remained haunted by their underlying fear of permanent injury or death. At the same time, midwives were hampered by laws limiting the extent of their involvement or even their right to practice at all. They occasionally had to stand by while birthing mothers hemorrhaged or died of childbed fever, knowing that if they could practice as they wished, they could save them. It was precisely these situations that led women to be swayed by the promise of safer and less painful childbirths. They surrendered some of their most valued traditions in childbirth, traditions that included the support and comfort of their families, a basic trust in their bodies, and the right to be attended in birth by other women. All of these traditions were traded for what they thought would be the protection of life and health during birth.

Pain Relief: The Era of "Twilight Sleep"

The promise of complete pain relief probably brought more women into the hospital than any other reason. "Twilight sleep," introduced in Germany in 1914, appeared to solve many problems connected with birth, from both the doctor's and the patient's points of view. Twilight sleep consisted of a combination of morphine for pain relief in early labor and scopolamine, an amnesiac that often caused hallucinations. Under twilight sleep a woman could still feel and respond to her contractions but supposedly would not remember what happened. The amnesiac component of twilight sleep separated a woman from her body, which could writhe, toss, and even feel pain but all outside her cognizance. The birth itself was not part of the mother's conscious experience because the increased use of scopolamine as labor progressed usually resulted in a heavily sedated mother who was totally unconscious for the delivery. In addition, women had to be carefully guarded from hurting themselves, which sometimes required them to be strapped or tied to the bed for hours as a result of the hallucinogenic side effects of the drug.[20]

Many of the early supporters of pain relief in childbirth were suffragists with strong beliefs in women's rights. Suffragists, many of whom were women physicians, organized the National Twilight Sleep Association in 1915 in the United States. They sponsored rallies in department stores so that ordinary women would be able to hear about the drugs that could ease them through their trial. They published articles and led women's groups, dealing with such topics as pain relief and the "new science" of obstetrics. Through their efforts the public learned of the possibility of a shorter and less painful labor. The suffragist twilight sleep supporters claimed it was the dawning of a new age in childbirth.[21] Little did they know that by insisting on physician-attended births and the use of twilight sleep as a pain killer, they were actually giving up the control over their births that they were fighting so hard to obtain. More and more women began requesting twilight sleep. Physicians readily agreed to the public demands and institutionalized the use of anesthesia in obstetrics. By the 1930s public and medical opinion were in agreement that some form of narcotization should be used for every labor. Scopolamine, one of the main ingredients in twilight sleep, continued to be used until the 1960s when the drugs were gradually replaced by analgesics, such as Demerol, and anesthetics administered through spinals, caudals, and epidurals.

The era of twilight sleep is described in nursing school today as the age of "knock 'em out, drag 'em out obstetrics." A mother of five and grandmother of six who was attending her daughter's home birth in 1990 commented that although she had given birth five times, she had never seen a birth or a newborn baby. "All my labors went really fast," she recalled. "With my first one, I got to the hospital and knew that the baby would be born soon. I could feel it; I wasn't scared. But just as I was about to have what felt like the biggest orgasm of my life, they put a mask over my face and I missed the whole thing. I can't believe that I let them do that to me!" Shortly after her new granddaughter's gentle arrival, this woman, while rocking the baby with tears rolling down her face, exclaimed, "I had no idea birth could be so beautiful!"

Hospital Births for Everyone

The promise of painless childbirth, seen as a right by some women in the early part of the twentieth century, became the standard of obstetric care. The uniform approach to childbirth in the hospital provided an appearance of safety but robbed women of their freedom. Every woman was treated the same way, even though every labor and birth was unique. The standard of care required that women be the passive recipients of all that medical science offered, for her own good and the baby's well-being. Obstetrics placed great emphasis on the ability to predict complications in labor and birth. Every case was seen as a potential disaster, with every physician playing the role of a potential hero. This view of birth stripped women of the chance to experience the emotional and social aspects of childbirth. In other words, women became baby machines, treated like repositories for little uteruses that contained little fetuses, all of which were subject to the control of the physician. During the 1940s, 1950s, and 1960s, the birth process was turned into an assembly line managed by skilled technicians and machines. Time limits were established for the first and second stages of labor, with some hospitals actually instituting the policy that a woman could only be in the delivery room for a specific length of time.[22] With the development of oxytocic drugs to induce or speed up labor, doctors could manage birth even more effectively. Drugs were given to slow a labor until the doctor or the delivery room was ready; then Pitocin could be used to get the labor going again. Cesarean sections replaced the use of high forceps, and fetal monitors helped detect fetal distress that resulted from the use of drugs and anesthesia. One intervention inevitably led directly to the next, until every birth was a medically managed, staged, and produced event.

By 1950, 88 percent of all births in the United States occurred in hospitals; five years later 95 percent of all births took place in the hospital setting. In 1960 it was almost unheard of for a woman to give birth anywhere but in a "modern" obstetrical unit in a hospital.[23] With hospital births for everyone, women had given the responsibility for decisions concerning their births to physicians who promised less pain, fewer deaths, fewer fetal injuries, and no birth defects from difficult and long labors. Women voiced their primary concern like this: "Doctor, give me a healthy baby. I don't care how you do it." They rationalized, "I may lose control over certain aspects of my birth, even my independence, but the promise of a perfect baby is worth the trade-off."

Unraveling Diagnostic Procedures

Women in the 1990s need to inform themselves about the latest technological advances that are applied during pregnancy and childbirth. Well-informed women who know the risks and benefits of tests and procedures can decide which ones make sense to use in their particular situations. Many diagnostic procedures are performed merely to provide documentation in the event that an alleged physician error leads to a malpractice case. Understandably, the doctor or midwife desires as much information as possible about the chemical and physiological aspects of a woman's pregnancy. Unfortunately, when tests are performed without regard for each individual's situation, a subtle message is transmitted to the woman that tells her she cannot possibly be considered normal until her health has been verified by tests. Routine testing assumes that abnormalities will be found and that a physician will be needed to manage them.

Ultrasound is the most commonly used prenatal diagnostic procedure. High-frequency sound waves are beamed into a pregnant woman's uterus in order to take a "picture" of the baby. The information is displayed on a television monitor, usually in full view of the parents. In the case of complications or questions during a pregnancy, ultrasound provides valuable information that can assist a physician in making a diagnosis. Valid uses of ultrasonic diagnosis include judging the age of the fetus when there is a difference between the actual and expected size; determining a fetal presentation and assisting in turning the baby if it is breech; viewing the placenta and fetus when there has been vaginal bleeding; determining a multiple pregnancy; monitoring fetal growth when it is suspected that the fetus has not been growing normally (fetal growth retardation).

If a woman has none of these concerns during pregnancy, ultrasonic diagnosis should not be routinely performed. Although initial studies show no side effects from the use of ultrasound, there have been no conclusive long-term studies on its effects on the fetus; therefore, ultrasound should only be used when there is some medical indication for the procedure and not just to view the baby, determine its sex, or take a picture of it to show at the office.

Alpha-fetoprotein (AFP) is a natural chemical normally produced by all fetuses. AFP crosses the placental barrier and shows up in the mother's blood, which can be easily tested. When an abnormality occurs in the fetus's neural tube, an excess of AFP is released into the amniotic fluid. Neural tube defects result from a lapse in the prenatal development of the brain (anencephaly) and spinal cord (spina bifida). The incidence of these defects in the United States is approximately 1 per 1,000 live births. High AFP levels can also indicate a multiple pregnancy, fetal death, and low birth weight. Low AFP levels can indicate chromosomal abnormalities, in which case an amniocentesis is usually recommended.

The AFP test is performed during the second trimester, between fifteen and twenty weeks of pregnancy (preferably at sixteen to eighteen weeks). The test poses no risk to either mother or baby. The major drawback of AFP testing is its high rate of false highs or lows, as great as 98 percent, which can often lead to more invasive testing or extreme worry for the mother.

Chorionic villi sampling (CVS) is used for very early detection of possible chromosomal (genetic) abnormalities. It can be performed as early as nine to eleven weeks of pregnancy. It requires a small sample of developing placental tissue for analysis, which may be obtained either through the abdominal wall or through the vagina and cervix. Most recent studies indicate a greater risk of miscarriage in women who undergo the CVS procedure than in women who do not, and a much greater risk of damage to the baby than amniocentesis. There have been no conclusive tests proving its safety and accuracy.

Amniocentesis is a fairly invasive procedure that tests for genetic defects in the fetus. Because these defects tend to increase with maternal age, amniocentesis is now practically regarded as a routine procedure for women over thirty-five years of age.

The test involves inserting a hollow needle into the mother's abdomen and removing a sample of the amniotic fluid that surrounds the baby. The amniotic fluid contains cells, excreted by the fetus, that reflect its genetic makeup. These cells are analyzed to detect genetic defects. The most common disorder screened for through amniocentesis is Down's syndrome; other genetic disorders include hemophilia, sickle-cell anemia, and Tay-Sachs disease.

There are accompanying risks to performing amniocentesis. Ultrasound is used along with the procedure to ensure proper placement of the needle, but fetal movement can sometimes result in injury to the baby. The risk of miscarriage is 1 in 200.[24] Fetal death sometimes occurs, and amniocentesis has been associated with orthopedic deformities.[25] And, needless to say, amniocentesis is extremely painful for the mother.

45

The use of amniocentesis has also been associated with early sex determination and the controversial practice of selective abortion if the fetus is not the preferred sex. According to the latest reports, parents still desire male babies twice as often as female babies. In addition, women will sometimes accept diagnosis that indicates severe handicaps and choose to abort what turns out to be a perfectly normal fetus. Even when abortion is chosen for the "not medically perfect" baby, couples may experience an enormous amount of guilt, influencing subsequent pregnancies and births. Consenting to amniocentesis is a decision that takes careful and thoughtful consideration.

The glucose tolerance test (GTT) is used to rule out gestational diabetes, or what is now referred to as gestational glucose intolerance. It is a condition pregnant women sometimes experience. The hormones of pregnancy suppress insulin release, allowing a mother's blood sugar to be higher during pregnancy and thus providing more glucose to nourish her fetus. Occasionally the pancreas, where insulin is made, cannot handle the stress of pregnancy and the insulin/glucose levels become severely unbalanced, causing the blood sugar to remain too high during part of the pregnancy. Prolonged exposure to this high blood sugar level causes the fetus to grow excessively large, resulting in such complications as premature birth or respiratory distress. Gestational glucose intolerance is more common in obese women, older mothers, or those with a family history of diabetes. If detected early enough, a mother's diet may be adjusted to keep her blood sugar from getting too high. Occasionally extra insulin is needed.

The GTT is usually recommended at 24–28 weeks and repeated around 32–34 weeks in women who are considered high-risk. The woman drinks a sweet liquid called glucola, and her blood sugar is checked one hour later. If the one-hour test is positive, a more accurate three-hour test is done. The reliability of a test that has a woman drink a concentrated sugar substance on an empty stomach, however, is questionable. The GTT is done under abnormal conditions and, therefore, often shows unnatural results. An alternative is to measure the blood sugar levels two hours after a heavy meal and to encourage the woman to do normal activities to help her body process the glucose.

The Results of Medical Intervention

What are the results of medical manipulation of a normal physiological process? Have technology and medical intervention lived up to their promises? During this period in which childbirth became a medical event, there *was* a great decrease in the number of infant and maternal deaths. There are many possible explanations relating to the advent of technical intervention that could explain this decrease. New antibiotic drugs spared women from septicemia. Hospital blood banks were established, along with blood typing and transfusion techniques, in the late 1930s.[26] Housing and sanitation conditions improved. Most pregnant women's diets were healthier than their mothers' and grandmothers' had been. Birth control and abortion helped control the timing and number of pregnancies. Yet even though the obstetricians claimed medical superiority, the infection and complication rates were much higher in hospital births than in home births. Women who have needed technology can attribute the safety of their lives and their children's lives to the advancement of medical science and obstetrics. But the labor and birth experiences of the majority of women with normal pregnancies, as well as the birth experiences of their babies, have been affected in many unforeseen and permanent ways.

What price have our children paid for this supposedly advanced technology? Women who sought to liberate themselves from the more uncomfortable and sometimes lethal aspects of childbirth lost much in the process. Women and families must cope with children who have obvious birth-related injuries as a result of the use of forceps or drugs, or through mishandling of the labor. How do families rationalize the child whose abilities to love, trust, and learn may have been impaired by the drugs given to the mother during birth? How has the use of drugs altered women's perceptions of childbirth? What are the personal costs for women who experience intimidation, loss of freedom, humiliation, and even abuse while giving birth?

Interventions in childbirth are usually administered by kind, well-intentioned hospital personnel for what they consider appropriate medical reasons. Unfortunately, those reasons do not alleviate the humiliation a woman feels when she is shaved in order for the perineum to be a "clean" surgical area, or the discomfort she feels when she is given an enema so that she won't "contaminate" the surgical site during birth. It doesn't lessen her embarrassment when she is asked to remove her clothes and put on a hospital gown, or her helplessness when her loved ones are excluded and she labors alone. A woman's trust in her own body and her ability to birth normally is shattered by repeated vaginal examinations in order to assess her "progress" during labor. A mother's self-confidence wavers when her newborn is taken away to the nursery to be cared for by "medically superior" professionals.

The American system of maternity care sends women the message that they are not capable of giving birth without the help of physicians and hospitals. From rules that prohibit eating and drinking during labor, to constant electronic fetal monitoring and subsequent interventions for fear of malpractice suits, the medicalization of childbirth has become the norm. With our concern for comfort and our sincere interest in protecting our children's lives, we have helped create the modern medical myths concerning childbirth. The emotional richness, the transformational power, and the amazing energy of birth have been ignored. The centuries of feminine wisdom about the birth process have been lost in the creation of this new medical mythology. These myths and the technocracy that accompanies them have drastically altered women's self-perception and have given society a distorted view both of womanhood and of the birth process itself.

3
Dispelling the Medical Myths

A wealth of information and research shows that the medicalization of childbirth has been detrimental on many levels to mother, baby, and family. Yet the dichotomy between practice and the ideal remains. The medical management of birth continues; women yield to physician and hospital control; they have made very little progress in achieving the changes that research and instinct tell us are necessary. Is it possible to view birth as a normal physiological process with the birthing woman in control, or is it necessary to approach every birth as a potential emergency "just in case"? How can we overcome the attitude that birth is dangerous and begin to protect the woman's right to birth in privacy and peace?

All over the world, many questions similar to these are being asked by childbirth advocates and parents who are looking for alternatives to today's medical model for birth. There is a growing understanding and appreciation of childbirth as a normal and natural process, one that offers a unique opportunity for emotional, spiritual, and personal growth for the mother, baby, and family. Proponents of gentle birth are reevaluating the standard obstetrical practices of hospital births. Each one of the practices has been studied and researched. The stacks of data accumulate, and when they are all read and evaluated, they all say the same things. These findings, coupled with a greater understanding of birth, indicate that the prevailing practices and beliefs about childbirth are based on false, outmoded, or unverified assumptions.

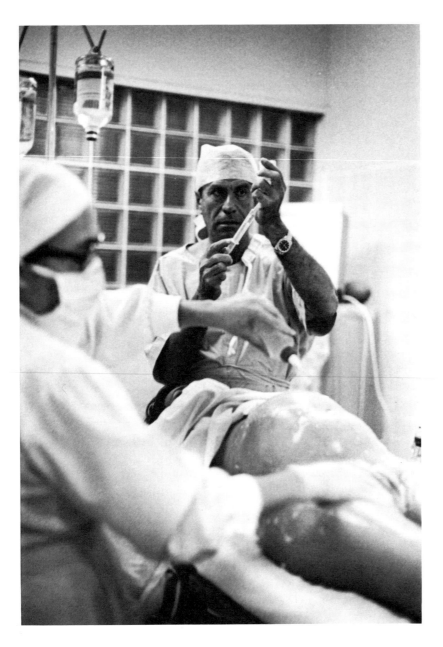

Doctors prepare a woman for surgical birth. Many people believe the medical myth that "once a cesarean, always a cesarean."

The unnecessary procedures and outdated attitudes concerning women and childbirth rob a woman, her baby, and her family of the emotional and spiritual opportunities inherent in life's most creative and powerful experience. The general public's perceptions about childbirth practices are unfortunately based on myths that support the belief that the more physicians can monitor and control the birth process with up-to-the-minute technology, the better the chances for a "successful" birth. Only in recent years has anyone acknowledged women as the center of the birth process and babies as conscious participants.

In the past most women have accepted the myth that their bodies are inadequate to birth their babies without a physician's directions and interventions. Women are encouraged to doubt their bodies' wisdom, their physical strength, and their intuition. In labor and birth a woman waits for the doctor to tell her when to "push" and accepts that an episiotomy may be best or that childbirth is unbearable without pain medication. The language of childbirth reveals whom we see as the person in control of the birth process. It is common to say the doctor or nurse *delivered* the baby, when in reality it was the woman who *birthed* her baby. When women accept their primary role in the birth process and acknowledge the ability of their bodies to birth their babies into the world, they will reject this ideology. Our language will then reflect this fundamental shift in the perception of childbirth. Our children will have a different understanding of birth.

In this chapter we will look at what could be considered the "medical myths" of our time. These myths concerning childbirth include commonly used obstetrical practices that are unnecessary and that actually interfere with the normal physiology of the birth process. You must become an informed consumer and decide for yourself what makes sense in childbirth.

Myth: The Hospital Is the Safest Place to Have a Baby

The modern image of birth perpetuated by the media is that of a woman lying in a bed in a sterile hospital, draped for modesty, hooked up to various monitors and equipment, with a physician or nurse "directing" or "coaching" her through the process as though it were an athletic event. When a woman today asks a physician about the possibility of birthing her baby at home or in a birthing center, it is very likely that she will be discouraged by her doctor, who will state that the hospital is the only place that will guarantee a safe birth. It is important to clarify that safety is measured by death (mortality) or illness (morbidity) during the labor and birth process and shortly thereafter. The United States has consistently high maternal and perinatal mortality and morbidity rates compared to other industrialized countries. In 1990 the United States was ranked twenty-third by the Population Reference Bureau, which publishes the mortality and morbidity statistics.. This means that there are twenty-two other countries where it is safer for women to give birth than in the United States.[1]

The countries with the lowest mortality and morbidity rates are those countries where midwifery is an integral part of obstetric care and where home birth is commonly practiced (see chart on page 53). The Netherlands has had a consistently high ranking among all countries since the 1970s. In 1987 perinatal mortality in the Netherlands was 9.8 deaths per 1,000 live births, whereas in the United States it was 10.8 deaths. This may not seem like a significant difference until the numbers are sorted out a bit more. For midwife-attended births this mortality rate dropped to 2.1 deaths per 1,000 live births.[2] In the Netherlands midwives attend more than 70 percent of all births; 40 percent of all births are home births. While there are additional factors, such as socialized medicine and prenatal care, to consider when comparing birth outcomes between the Netherlands and the United States, there is a strong case for home births attended by midwives. Dr. Michel Odent authored a 1991 report for the World Health Organization (WHO) in which he stated, "The priority must be to challenge the universal propaganda that

---

* There are several different ways to define mortality. Infant mortality includes deaths from birth through the first year of life. Neonatal mortality includes infant deaths from birth to less than twenty-nine days. Perinatal mortality refers to fetal deaths from twenty-eight weeks' gestation up through infant deaths of less than seven days. In the United States perinatal mortality is defined as deaths of the fetus from twenty weeks' gestation up through infant deaths of less than twenty-eight days.

home birth is dangerous. . . . The best means by which to challenge the current beliefs are the statistics from the Netherlands."[3]

One of the largest studies comparing outcomes of hospital births and out-of-hospital births, which includes home and birthing-center births, was conducted by the U.S. Center for Disease Control between 1974 and 1976. North Carolina was the site of the study, which included over 242,000 hospital births and 2,200 out-of-hospital births. In this study it was necessary to differentiate between out-of-hospital births that were planned by women who received prenatal care and births that happened accidentally (for example, while en route to the hospital) or where there was no preparation or qualified person in attendance. The results of this two-year study showed that the infant death rate in hospitals was 12 per 1,000 live births, whereas the death rate for planned, attended home births was 4 per 1,000 live births. The infant death rate in unplanned or unattended home births soared to 120 per 1,000.[4] This study demonstrates that if the birth is planned for and attended by doctors or midwives who are experienced with the birth process, birth is safer at home.

INFANT MORTALITY FOR 1989
(Infant deaths per 1000)

1. Japan	4.9	9. Netherlands	7.6	17. Australia	8.8
2. Sweden	5.7	10. Hong Kong	7.7	18. Spain	8.8
3. Finland	5.8	11. Norway	7.8	19. United Kingdom	9.1
4. Switzerland	6.8	12. Canada	7.9	20. Belgium	9.7
5. Taiwan	6.9	13. West Germany	8.3	21. U.S.A.	9.9
6. Ireland	7.4	14. Austria	8.3	22. New Zealand	10.0
7. Singapore	7.4	15. Denmark	8.4	23. Italy	10.1
8. France	7.6	16. East Germany	8.7	24. Israel	10.7

World Health Organization census statistics.

In 1976 Dr. Lewis Mehl and a group of researchers at Stanford University conducted a comprehensive study that focused on the differences between planned home births and planned hospital births. They studied 2,092 births, half of which were planned home births and half of which were planned hospital births.[5] The women were also matched for age, socioeconomic level, and risk factors. Researchers analyzed each birth for length of labor, complications, and infant health after birth, as well as all procedures that were used during the course of labor and delivery. In the entire study there was only one infant death, and that death occurred in the hospital. The results of this particular study show that the mortality statistics for hospital birth and home birth were identical. Aside from mortality rates between hospital and home births, this study also dramatically revealed that complications and interventions during birth were far greater in births that took place in the hospital than in births that took place at home. Five percent of home-birth mothers received some form of medication, whereas 75 percent of hospitalized mothers received medication. There were three times as many cesarean sections in hospital births as there were in the planned home births with subsequent transfer to hospital. Hospital-born babies suffered more fetal distress, newborn infections, and birth injuries than home-birth babies. The episiotomy rate was ten times higher for mothers in the hospital, and they suffered twice as many severe perineal lacerations. The increased episiotomy rate and severity of perineal lacerations for hospital births was most likely the result of the use of forceps and the lithotomy position for birth. Another interesting aspect of the study was that physicians attended 66 percent of the home births, implying that when childbirth can be removed from a hospital setting where a birthing woman is considered a "patient" and placed in an environment where birth is treated as a natural event, there is less likelihood of intervention.

One of the safest alternatives to hospital birth is to give birth in a freestanding birthing center. The National Birth Center Study, conducted between 1985 and 1987, studied 11,814 women who gave birth in freestanding birthing centers in the United States.[6] The results demonstrated that for basically healthy women with no prenatal complications, birthing centers are a safe and economical alternative for childbirth. Certified nurse-midwife

(CNM) Kitty Ernst, director of the National Association of Childbearing Centers, conducted the study with the Center for Population and Family Health and the School of Public Health at Columbia University. The study was undertaken in reaction to statements from the American College of Obstetrics and Gynecology (ACOG) that discouraged the use of birthing centers because of the lack of data proving their safety. The overall infant mortality rate for the eighty-four birthing centers in the study was 1.3 deaths per 1,000 live births. There were no maternal deaths. The rate of cesarean sections in the backup hospitals was 4.4 percent, compared to a 1990 national average of 25 percent. The birthing centers studied in the National Birth Center Study used few invasive, uncomfortable, or restrictive procedures. Many offered measures to provide comfort and support for the women during labor. The midwives who attended the women during labor and birth had also provided prenatal care to the women throughout their pregnancies. The women who used birthing centers expressed great satisfaction, and the general consensus was that they would use a birthing center again.

Some doctors object to the validity of the National Birth Center Study because the general population giving birth in birthing centers is low risk and cannot be compared to the overall hospital population. Women who use a birthing center are low risk at the time of birth because they had consistent prenatal care, and women who needed the attention of specialists were screened for hospital births. Ernst suggests that this study demonstrates the effectiveness of birthing centers in their continuity of care rather than their questionable safety. Even though the study was reported in the *Lancet* in 1987, it was not until December 1989 that the study was published in the *New England Journal of Medicine.*[7] Ernst believes that there was a delay in publishing the birthing center study in a major medical journal because the findings challenged some core beliefs that physicians and hospitals adhere to in order to justify current obstetrical practices.

Another important report on the safety of birthing center and home births is the Alternative Birthing Methods Study, commissioned by the California legislature during the same period that the National Birth Center Study was being conducted. This mandated study explored consumer needs, availability of alternative birthing services, barriers to obtaining birthing services, insurance options for childbirth alternatives, and the educational preparation of parents. The study concluded that the maternity care system in California has many problems. One of the main problems identified was the poor availability of care, both economically and geographically and in both urban and rural areas. Another major problem was the emphasis placed on medical protocols and procedures for women having normal pregnancies. This included mandatory hospitalization for normal birth.

As a result of this study, the following recommendations were made to the 1986 California legislature:

1. Gather specific data about the practice of CNMs and freestanding birthing centers

2. Introduce new legislation creating a separate category of licensed non-nurse-midwives in order to meet the growing needs of people seeking home births

3. Procure state funding for midwifery education, more autonomy for CNMs, educational materials regarding birthing services for consumers, and affordable insurance for birthing providers.[8]

For childbirth reformers in California the Alternative Birthing Methods Study was considered a landmark study that could transform the current hospital-based system of childbirth. Unfortunately, the politics of the California legislature changed when a more conservative governor was elected, and the suggestions in the study were laid aside.

These and other studies have shown conclusively that childbirth can be safe outside a hospital environment, provided a woman has consistent prenatal care and is supported by a midwife or a physician during labor and birth. In order to prepare for a gentle birth environment outside a hospital, it is important to first reexamine the generally held belief that hospitals are the safest place to birth.

Myth: Maternity Care Should Be Managed Only by a Physician

Because most births in the United States take place in a hospital, it is assumed that physicians provide the only competent maternity care available to women. However, studies have shown that CNMs offer equal if not better maternity care for pregnant women. As of 1990 there were 130 accredited freestanding birthing centers in the United States,[9] and almost all of them employed CNMs and nurses for maternity care. There are approximately four thousand CNMs employed in hospital and birthing-center settings throughout the United States.[10]

Midwifery is practiced throughout the world, though in the United States only 5 percent of all births are attended by midwives. Countries with the highest rate of midwife-attended births (the Netherlands, Scandinavian countries, and Japan) also have the best maternal and perinatal mortality statistics. For every 250 midwives in Japan there is 1 obstetrician.[11] Maternity care in these countries is based on a midwifery model that emphasizes competent prenatal care and education and empowerment for the woman giving birth (see chapter 4). The midwifery model of maternity care assesses all the circumstances—physical, emotional, and spiritual—that may influence the outcome of a pregnancy. Midwives refer clients to physicians only when there is a medical problem.

A common argument against the use of midwives is that they have less formal education than doctors. While it is true that doctors' formal medical education is more extensive in the areas of obstetrics, they are not necessarily more experienced than midwives when dealing with normal labor and birth. Dr. Michael Rosenthal at the Family Birthing Center in Upland, California, admits, "I didn't learn about women in childbirth by going to medical school but rather by watching women giving birth normally." He adds, "Doctors are trained to intervene. Midwives aren't trained to do cesareans—it's not in their realm. Subsequently they utilize other methods to guide a woman through a vaginal birth."

A significant study that strongly indicates midwives' competency for normal maternity care was conducted in Madera County, California, between

1961 and 1966.[12] At the time of this study CNMs could not legally practice in California, so the state legislature temporarily legalized nurse-midwifery for the benefit of the study. The outcome of the study showed that as a result of the care provided by the CNMs there was better attendance at prenatal clinics, and the prematurity rate dropped from 11 to 7 percent. The neonatal mortality rate also fell, from about 24 infant deaths per 1,000 live births to about 10 deaths per 1,000 live births.

Despite these dramatic results, the special California law was later repealed and the use of CNMs was considered illegal until 1975 when a law was passed making nurse-midwifery legal in California. After the study was concluded and the CNMs had discontinued practicing, the prematurity rate increased by almost 50 percent and the neonatal death rate tripled, despite the fact that more doctors moved into the area to provide maternity care.[13]

In addition to the medical competency of midwives, an important aspect to consider is the psychological support that midwives provide. The majority of midwives are women, and many have given birth themselves. Their first-hand knowledge of giving birth and their sharing of that experience, woman to woman, cannot be replaced. Pregnant women are also less likely to be overly dependent on a midwife, who generally assists women in becoming educated about the birth process and encourages them to trust their instincts. In comparison, it is common for pregnant women to see their doctors as authority figures and for doctors to readily assume that role. Even the language that most midwives use differentiates their views of childbirth from those of physicians. Physicians have patients but midwives have clients. A physicians "delivers the baby," which implies control, while a midwife helps the woman "birth her baby."

WHO and the International Confederation of Midwives (ICM) support the use of midwives for pregnancy, birth, newborn care, and the development of the infant, as well as for offering counseling and education to the community. In 1990 ICM, who represents midwives in eighty-two countries, joined WHO to create a position statement on midwifery. This statement declared that when midwifery was utilized for pregnancy and childbirth, outcomes for mothers and babies were more favorable. These two organizations urged all countries to offer midwifery education, insisting that the increased availability of more midwives would improve birth outcomes throughout the world by the year 2000. WHO and ICM believe that when midwives practice, birth is safer for mothers and babies.[14]

The midwifery model of maternity care, as opposed to the medical model of maternity care, offers considerable advantages, particularly when considering a gentle birth. Midwives offer personalized prenatal care, respect for birth as a normal process, and encouragement for making informed choices. Qualified midwives offer competent maternity care for women seeking normal, natural, gentle births.

Myth: The Electronic Fetal Monitor Will Save Babies

The electronic fetal monitor (EFM) is one of the most widely used technological interventions in modern obstetrics. Fetal monitoring allows physicians to listen to and evaluate the baby's heart rate throughout labor and birth. There are two types of EFMs. The external fetal monitor consists of two straps that are placed around the abdomen of the laboring woman; they are equipped with ultrasound devices that record uterine contractions as well as the baby's heart rate while still in the womb. The internal fetal monitor involves inserting an electrode into the skin layer of the baby's scalp while it is still in the womb in order to transmit the baby's heart rate.

The first breakthrough in monitoring a baby's heart rate came in 1917 when a headband was added to the stethoscope. The headband allowed the doctor to listen to the baby's heartbeat while leaving his or her hands free to palpate the uterus and determine the intensity of uterine contractions. Many midwives still use this kind of stethoscope while monitoring women during labor. The ultrasound stethoscope, or fetoscope, developed in the 1960s, refined the art of what is termed "auscultation," or listening to the sound of the baby's heartbeat. The accepted way of evaluating the infant during labor was to auscultate the baby's heart rate periodically. How often and for how long depended entirely on the practitioner and his or her level of experience. Recent studies on the effectiveness of the EFM to diminish the risk of injury

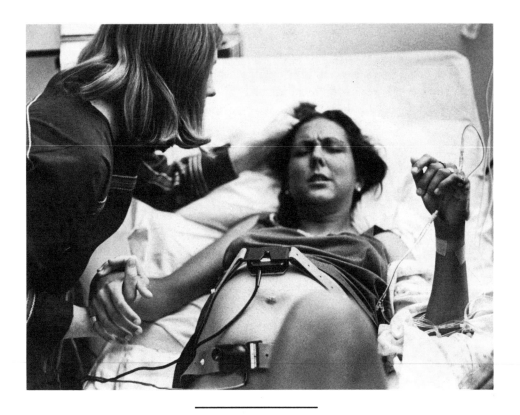

The electronic fetal monitor keeps a woman restrained and flat on her back, the worst possible position for labor and birth.

or death for the baby during childbirth show that the EFM is no more effective than a trained nurse who listens and evaluates the baby's heartbeat with a fetoscope.

Fetal monitoring to determine the well-being of the baby during labor has always been a concern for midwives and physicians. Variations in fetal heart rate and consistent patterns of change are difficult to detect with occasional monitoring. Doctors felt that constant monitoring and evaluation would help detect early signs of fetal distress. This in turn would prevent possible birth-related defects and complications in the baby. The first EFM was available in 1968 and was heralded as the greatest obstetrical advance since forceps. Doctors believed the EFM would eliminate the guesswork in labor. They could constantly observe the fetus with the EFM and more accurately monitor an infant whose mother had been given drugs. Physicians also believed that the EFM would reduce cesarean and infant mortality rates.

The large, cumbersome machine that housed the fetal monitor began showing up at the bedsides of laboring women in hospitals across the United States. As early as 1973, initial studies were released that supported the existence of a correlation between patterns of fetal heart rate and signs of fetal hypoxia, or oxygen deprivation. In the 1970s it was still believed that lack of oxygen during labor could cause epilepsy and cerebral palsy, as well as myriad problems ranging from mild learning disorders to criminal behavior.[15] Physicians believed that the EFM could detect early fetal distress due to oxygen deprivation. Early detection would give them sufficient time to intervene, usually with an emergency cesarean, in order to prevent injury or death.

By 1978 nearly two-thirds of all births were electronically monitored. Nurses were trained to read the tracings of the EFM strip as a guide for intervention. The EFM strips were (and still are) used as legal protection against potential lawsuits. Medical literature was flooded with research on fetal heart-rate patterns, variations, and decelerations that gave credit to the fetal monitor in the detection of potential problems. The physicians' common response to questionable data from a fetal monitor was to perform a cesarean section. With the use of the EFM, cesarean rates throughout the United States gradually climbed. Interestingly enough, there has been no change in the number of cases of cerebral palsy, birth-related injuries, or neonatal mortality.[16]

Could there have been something wrong with the initial reasoning? Did the EFM actually eliminate the guesswork in monitoring the fetus during labor and birth? By the 1980s some obstetricians were questioning the accuracy of the EFM readings. Physicians would perform an emergency cesarean based on an EFM reading that indicated probable fetal distress. When the surgery was completed, they would be surprised to find a perfectly normal, healthy infant. Dr. Michael Rosenthal stated, "It wasn't making sense. I would do a C-section for what appeared reasonable cause and out would come a baby with a high Apgar [a visual rating system for determining a baby's health immediately after birth] and no distress. I began looking for what could be causing the variation on the strip [fetal monitor tracing]." What Rosenthal eventually found was that often all that was needed to improve the apparent status of the baby was to change the mother's position in labor.[17] Many other practitioners and childbirth reformers experienced the same unmistakable correlation between the rising cesarean rate and the widespread use of the EFM. As early as 1980 the National Institutes of Health cautioned against the use of the monitor for low-risk pregnancies, predicting that it would only contribute to more cesareans.[18]

In March 1987 Columbia University hosted a medical conference entitled "Crisis in Obstetrics: The Management of Labor." Dr. Edward H. Hon, inventor of the EFM, asked his colleagues to consider the causes of the rising cesarean rate in the United States. He stated that he never intended the EFM to be used in routine obstetric management. "If you mess around with a process [birth] that works well 98 percent of the time, there is a potential for much harm."[19] Hon stressed that physicians lack patience with the childbirth process and subsequently use the monitor, which can wrongly determine fetal distress. He concluded, "The cesarean section is considered as a rescue mission of the baby by the white knight, but actually you've assaulted the mother."

Dr. Mortimer Rosen, who convened this conference on current controversies in the use of obstetrical technology, stated that the recent dramatic progress of technology has been accompanied by a change in patient expectations.[20] Patients today *expect* a perfect outcome. This shift has caused physicians to be more cautious and to perform cesareans sooner rather than later. Unfortunately, the fear of litigation now plays a central role in physicians' decisions to intervene.

The EFM was thought to be a miracle technology that would wipe out cerebral palsy because it could alert doctors to early fetal distress. In actuality it is known to wrongly identify fetal distress 15 to 80 percent of the time. One 1982 study reported that EFMs had a 74 percent false-positive rate.[21] This means that in this study 74 out of 100 times the monitor tracings indicated distress when there was none. Doctors have also found that sometimes the monitor indicates that there is no distress when in fact there has been severe oxygen deprivation or even infant death. In addition to the inconsistency of the EFM to accurately monitor fetal distress, researchers find that there is no relationship between fetal distress and certain disorders. Dr. Karin Nelson and Dr. Jonas Ellenberg have written several books on cerebral palsy, in particular about its relationship to the events of labor and delivery and the origin of chronic neurologic disorders. They essentially ruled out fetal oxygen deprivation during labor and delivery as a cause of neurologic disorders. Their research also revealed a consistent cerebral palsy rate within the population since 1940. There has been no decrease in the number of children born with cerebral palsy since the introduction and widespread use of electronic fetal monitoring.

Mothers are also concerned about the use of the EFM, especially those who have experienced emergency cesareans because of apparent fetal distress. One mother related, "I thought that everything was fine. I had just started pushing, the doctor had only been in to check me once in over six hours. He came in, looked at the monitor strip, and ordered the nurse to move me to the operating room for an immediate C-section. He didn't even tell us what was wrong. No one did. I'm happy about my baby, but it took me over a year to get past my anger and disappointment about my birth."

During the 1980s women organized groups such as the Cesarean Prevention Movement, now known as the International Cesarean Awareness Network (ICAN) and Cesareans/Support, Education and Concern (C/SEC) to offer education and support to other women who had had cesareans. These consumer groups sponsored educational conferences, gathered statistics, and networked with mothers throughout the United States. Both organizations support couples in finding information to make informed birth choices. They also encourage pregnant women to give birth vaginally after a cesarean.

Dr. Kenneth Leveno stated in 1986 in the *New England Journal of Medicine*, "Not all pregnancies, and particularly not those considered at low risk of perinatal complication, need continuous electronic fetal monitoring during labor."[22] In 1990 an even stronger statement came from Dr. Roger Freeman, who has written textbooks on the interpretation of the fetal monitor. Freeman published an editorial in the *New England Journal of Medicine* entitled

"Intrapartum Fetal Monitoring: A Disappointing Story." He thoroughly reviewed previously published studies comparing the outcomes of labors that were continuously monitored and those that were monitored by nurses listening at regular intervals with fetoscopes. In all cases the outcomes were the same! Freeman's conclusion is that the fetal monitor was adopted for surveillance before any conclusive studies indicated that the monitors produced the results they were designed to achieve. Freeman suggests that before the fetal monitor is discarded a study should be undertaken comparing no monitoring at all during labor with either auscultation or EFMs. Freeman asserts that only then can we determine if monitoring makes a difference.[23] Recent studies indicate that, at best, an EFM can only detect whether an infant is doing fine or whether it is in a "possible" state of distress. A low heart rate may indicate a sleeping baby, while a rapid heart rate may be a response to a stimulus or drug or may just indicate an active baby.

Myth: Once a Cesarean, Always a Cesarean

The cesarean section has been the most commonly performed surgery in the United States since 1983, surpassing both the tonsillectomy and appendectomy. In 1970 only 5 percent of all births in the United States were by cesarean. By 1978 this figure had increased to 15 percent; by 1986, 25 percent of all babies were born by cesarean, which must be considered major abdominal surgery. As of 1990 the national average for cesareans in the United States was still about 25 percent.[24] However, a 1987 survey of individual hospitals revealed cesarean rates at some hospitals were as high as 53 percent.[25]

In 1990 more than 900,000 women in the United States had cesareans for a variety of reasons. Some of the reasons indicated on medical charts included fetal distress as indicated by the EFM; breech presentation of the baby; genital herpes in the mother; cephalo-pelvic disproportion (CPD), a condition in which the mother's pelvis is too small for the baby to pass through; and dystocia, a term used for a labor that has not progressed along "normal" patterns. Within each of these "reasons" for a cesarean is a gray area that is left to the discretion of the attending physician. While no one questions that

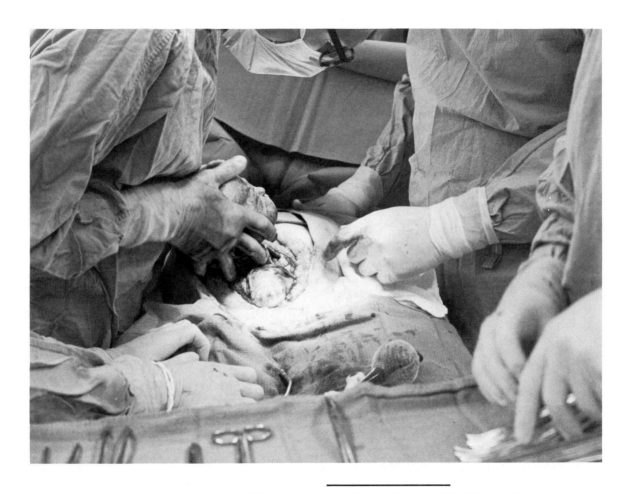

*The baby is removed through surgical incisions in the
abdominal wall and the uterus.*

some cesareans are absolutely necessary, one must ask what has happened
between 1970 and 1990 to increase the average cesarean rate in the United
States from 5 percent to 25 percent.

The reason given by doctors today for approximately 40 percent of all

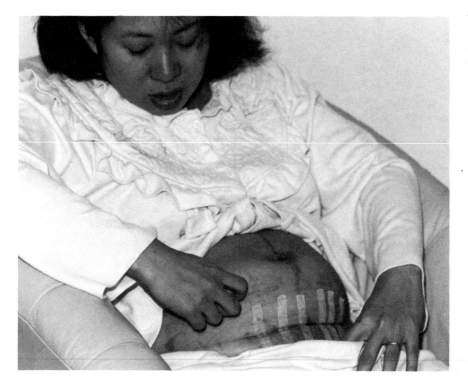

This mother examines her abdominal scar one week after her cesarean.

cesareans is *dystocia*. A woman whose labor has not progressed along "normal" patterns may be advised to undergo a cesarean, although an exact definition of what it means to progress normally varies tremendously with each doctor. When a laboring woman's cervix does not efface and dilate, or when the baby does not descend during a prescribed number of hours, many physicians will diagnose dystocia and consider the diagnosis reasonable grounds for performing a cesarean.[26]

A typical hospital scenario during a slow labor is to administer the drug Pitocin, a synthetic version of oxytocin, which a laboring woman's body produces naturally. Pitocin is given in order to speed up and intensify contractions. Thus, when women are given Pitocin, they are often offered a painkiller as well. While the Pitocin works to quicken the labor, the drugs for pain relief have the opposite effect. In addition, the administration of Pitocin effectively restricts the movements of the laboring woman because she is required to have an intravenous (IV) line and an internal fetal monitor. These restrictions can slow labor even further. If the Pitocin does not work within a certain time limit, a laboring woman will often hear statements like, "We've tried everything; do you want to do this for another twelve hours?" or "You just weren't meant to have this baby vaginally."

In this situation, a physician views a cesarean as an opportunity to save the mother from a "long and difficult" labor. Unfortunately, the mother will never know what the outcome might have been if time had not been the determining factor in calling for a cesarean.

The myth of always having to birth by cesarean after the first cesarean became a rule of thumb for physicians in the early part of the twentieth century, because their diagnosis of CPD, or true dystocia, usually applied to women who had polio, rickets, or a small or deformed pelvis. The reason given by physicians for about 300,000 of the 900,000 cesareans performed in the United States in 1990 was still dystocia.[27] However, Dr. Michael Rosenthal at the Family Birthing Center in Upland, California, has observed, "Oftentimes women will give birth vaginally after they have had cesareans for a diagnosis of cephalo-pelvic disproportion, which means the baby's head is too big for the mother's pelvis. Yet, the babies these women gave birth to at the birthing center were bigger than the ones they were sectioned for!"[28]

From a childbirth reformer's perspective, a term such as "failure to progress" is really failure of the doctor to be patient. It is common knowledge that the longer a woman labors in the hospital, the greater the possibility for medical intervention. In addition, fear of a lawsuit will often motivate a physician to be excessively cautious and perform a cesarean rather than wait. As one doctor so aptly stated, "The only cesarean I have ever been sued for is the one I didn't do."

In the past, women were easily convinced by their physicians to schedule an elective cesarean for their next birth because the experience of a long labor ending in a cesarean the first time was so frustrating and painful. In the early 1980s cesarean consumer groups began to encourage women to attempt a vaginal birth after a cesarean (VBAC). Women organized cesarean support groups to work through their feelings about their previous cesarean births and to express their fear, anger, grief, or disappointment. After women "processed" their feelings, they were then supported in preparing for a vaginal birth and locating a physician who would assist them.

Deborah relates, "I went through five doctors before I finally gave up my search to find a doctor who would *let* me give birth vaginally. For three months I didn't get any prenatal care. I didn't have any insurance anyway, so I called a lay midwife in the next town. She saw me reluctantly, but when I explained the circumstances of my first cesarean, she agreed to come to my home for the birth. You see, I had a cesarean for a foot-first breech baby, and this [second] baby seemed to be head down. The [vaginal] birth went just fine. My daughter watched the whole thing and held the baby with me just minutes after he was born. I'm so glad I stayed home."

In the early 1980s women who pursued a VBAC found the medical community resistant to their efforts. At that time, ACOG had developed strict guidelines for VBACs. These guidelines allowed only for a short "trial labor" and ruled out any woman who had had a previous cesarean due to "failure to progress." Physicians feared that the intensity of strong contractions might stress the uterine incision and lead to sudden uterine rupture. This is a potentially dangerous situation for both mother and baby and can be difficult to detect. ACOG revised its guidelines in 1985, suggesting that physicians could treat VBAC attempts almost like any normal births, with the exception of certain requirements: electronic fetal monitoring, IVs, and the presence of an anesthesiologist in case emergency surgery was required. By 1988 ACOG made the dramatic statement that "routine repeat cesarean sections should be eliminated," setting VBAC as the new standard of practice, potentially eliminating one-third of all cesareans[29]—a standard that many physicians today do not follow. This shift was due in part to consumer pressure, as well as to medical studies disproving the assumption that once a cesarean, always a cesarean.

Dr. Michael Rosenthal and CNM Linda Church attended more than 250 VBACs at the Family Birthing Center between 1985 and 1990, more than 70 of which were water births. One woman who came from Alaska to the California birthing center had a water birth after two previous cesareans.

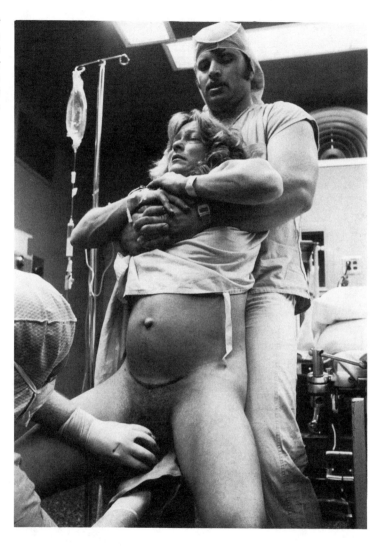

Notice the cesarean scar on this woman's belly as she births her next baby vaginally. Her husband supports her from behind, so she can comfortably semi-squat to push her baby out.

Afterward she wrote, "I knew that I could do it. Once I got into the tub, I knew I couldn't get out." Another woman, Mona, who had had two cesareans, said about the birth of her third child at the Family Birthing Center, "Thank you all for believing I could do it! The other doctors quite literally destroyed my confidence in my ability to birth vaginally."

VBACs have received substantial attention from the medical community. Informative books like *Silent Knife* and *Open Season* by Nancy Wainer Cohen and Lois Estner, and *The Cesarean Myth*, by Mortimer Rosen and Lillian Thomas, have helped draw attention to this issue. Dr. Bruce Flamm has conducted the most comprehensive study to date on VBACs, focusing on ten southern California hospitals. Flamm has correlated the experience of his own obstetrical practice with the study's findings in his book, *Birth after Cesarean: The Medical Facts*. Flamm emphatically states, "Most women who attempt a natural birth after cesarean section will succeed. This has been proven beyond a shadow of a doubt."[30] Dr. Michael Rosenthal has found that 86 percent of the VBAC women who come to his center give birth vaginally.[31]

Myth: Birth Needs to Be Sterile

During the past forty years of childbirth in the United States, there was a time when women were routinely strapped down to obstetric tables with their hands restrained in order to maintain a sterile field for the birth. The enema and shaving of a woman's pubic hair were ordered by doctors to avoid contamination of what physicians considered the "surgical site." In the process of creating a sterile field, the medical model separated the woman from her perineum. Doctors treated a sterile vaginal area on a level devoid of the human element and inherent emotions.

When giving birth, a woman's instinct is often to reach down and feel the baby's head as it emerges. How unfortunate that women are often robbed of this experience in the name of sterility. The truth is that birth cannot possibly be sterile, and there is no indication that nature ever intended it to be. When the baby emerges from the birth canal, he is covered with a film of the mother's vaginal bacteria. The baby is immune to these bacteria because he has shared the same ecosystem with the mother for the last nine months. While in the womb the baby receives the mother's antibodies through the placenta, and after birth he continues to receive these antibodies from the mother's colostrum during the first twenty-four hours of breast-feeding.

There is no need to protect a newborn baby from healthy parents.

What is the purpose of these hospital procedures? Who are we protecting from infection, if not the baby? There are no elaborate sterile procedures in a home or birthing-center birth. Sometimes gloves are not used by midwives because they consider human, skin-to-skin touch an important part of the emotional support they offer to women. However, because of the risk of AIDS and hepatitis, the use of gloves is generally recommended.*

Hospital policy usually requires anyone attending births to wear gowns, masks, and booties, or what are commonly referred to as "scrubs." Perhaps we have lessened our ability to be emotionally connected with the birth by requiring these clothes in the hospital. The drapes remove a woman from her body, her sensuality, and the experience of birth. The masks say, "I am keeping my distance." The emotional experience of a birth can be lost when it becomes a business transaction between the birthing couple and the doctor, garbed according to a dress code of green suits, masks, and gloves.

When women are free to wear whatever they want during labor and birth, and family and friends with them are not restricted with hospital gowns and masks, there seems to be greater verbal interaction and more emotional vulnerability. A woman who can remove her clothes to get into the shower or bath usually finds it easier to drop many of her inhibitions and surrender herself to the physical experience of her birth. She seems to be more willing to make noises, move around, and in general not conform to anyone else's ideas about how her birth should proceed. Fathers often join in more readily, willing to be physically close to their partners and sharing the emotional intensity of labor and birth. One father instinctively took off all his clothes and jumped into the birthing tub at the Family Birthing Center. He wanted to catch the baby as it was born into the water. The midwife had never experienced anything like that before, but she thought to herself that it was their birth—who was she to judge his behavior?

---

* An important point to take into consideration regarding a sterile environment for birth is the risk of exposure to the HIV virus. Virtually all hospitals have instituted "universal precautions" that require midwives and physicians to wear goggles as well as other protective clothing during birth. This procedure is justified, especially when working with people in high-risk groups for HIV and hepatitis. It is done not to keep birth sterile but because the attendants need to protect themselves.

Myth: Drugs for Pain Relief Won't Hurt the Baby

Medical science originally believed that the placenta was a protective barrier between the mother and the baby, a filter that blocked the fetus from harmful substances ingested by the mother. However, in 1961 the shocking effects of thalidomide, a tranquilizer taken by pregnant women in Europe and Australia, proved that the placental barrier theory was completely false. Babies were born without limbs, particularly arms, a condition produced by thalidomide's effect on the developing fetus.[32] Public outcry subsequently demanded more accurate testing of drugs prescribed by doctors for pregnancy and birth. Consumers pushed for advertising, and for the first time pregnant women were routinely warned of potential hazards of over-the-counter and recreational drugs. These warnings now include cigarettes and alcohol, as well as many environmental elements such as microwaves.

Childbirth advocates are now questioning the safety of drugs commonly given to women for pain relief, as well as the anesthetic agents administered during childbirth. Women need to be routinely and thoroughly warned by their health care providers about the possible effects of drugs on their babies and on themselves. Studies need to be done to chart the long-term effects on children whose mothers received drugs during childbirth.

The 1992 *Physicians' Desk Reference* lists all drugs manufactured in the United States and describes the possible side effects. Under each of the anesthetic agents commonly used for epidurals for women in labor, the *Physicians' Desk Reference* plainly states that there are no long-term studies on the effects of these drugs on the fetus. Nor have there been any long-term studies on the impact of these drugs on the child's life.

Dr. Bertil Jacobsen of Sweden's Karolinska Institute is conducting a study on the long-term effects on children of morphine, Demerol, and phenobarbital taken by the mothers during labor. He is examining whether babies whose mothers received barbiturates were born in a mood-altered state. Jacobsen believes that as these children grow and reach puberty their hormones shift, restimulating the imprinting that took place at the time of birth. The subjects of the study, teenage drug users and those with suicidal behavior, are showing a high correlation between their drug abuse and the amount and timing of the drugs given to their mothers during labor.[33]

The developing brain of the baby is susceptible to insult from drugs because it continues to develop for up to two years after birth. In addition, drugs have a far greater impact on the baby than on the mother because of the baby's body size and the limited ability of a newborn's liver to excrete drugs. All drugs used in obstetrics are toxic for babies. Recent studies on babies whose mothers received obstetrical drugs for pain relief demonstrated a variety of adverse effects, including damage to the central nervous system; impaired sensory and motor responses; reduced ability to process and respond to incoming stimuli; interference with feeding, sucking, and rooting responses; lower scores on tests of infant development; and increased irritability. It is important to note that bonding with an infant that is motor or sensory impaired or suffering from drug withdrawal will be affected as well.

There is considerable evidence, both scientific and empirical, that narcotics cross the placenta in sufficient amounts to cause neonatal depression. For instance, studies have revealed that large amounts of Demerol, a drug commonly used for pain relief during labor, can be found in a newborn if the mother received the drug within five hours before giving birth. Demerol can also contribute to a mother's feelings of depression after birth, since narcotics generally cause depression.[34]

Sedatives containing barbiturates that were given to a mother in labor have been shown to adversely affect the infant's sucking reflexes for up to five days after birth. "Floppy baby syndrome" is the common term given to babies who exhibit a condition characterized by poor muscle tone, lethargy, and sucking difficulties. Withdrawal symptoms for a newborn can last up to two weeks and may include irritable crying and body tremors as the baby's body attempts to metabolize and excrete the drugs.[35]

Current studies are examining the possible effects on an infant when a woman receives an epidural or spinal block, a common procedure in hospital births. The epidural consists of an injection of an anesthetic agent, sometimes coupled with a narcotic, into the spinal column to numb the lower half of the body. Some studies suggest that the side effects of an epidural cause the baby to become nervous and jittery, while other studies show that the baby is drowsy after birth. The varied results depend on which drug and how much was used.

There is little research on the effects of drugs on the baby during childbirth and later as the child grows. Basically, the jury is still out. Drugs for pain relief during labor need to be offered cautiously, particularly since the long-term effects are not known at this time. It is a woman's right to choose whether or not she wants drugs for pain relief; however, the general consensus in the United States is that most women *need* drugs to withstand the pain of childbirth. Unfortunately, many women have not been encouraged to experience their labor and birth without drugs but instead have been told that pain medication will make it bearable. It is not uncommon to hear women who may only be a few months pregnant already declaring that they will get an epidural as soon as they arrive at the hospital because they fear the pain of labor will be too great. In turn, out of a misguided sense of kindness, doctors and nurses who genuinely believe that narcotics comfort a woman in labor and ease her pain are likely to encourage that woman to make use of the availability of drugs.

A few simple measures applied during labor—such as walking, changing positions, and staying off her back—can greatly reduce a woman's need for medication. Emotional support and encouragement from loved ones and childbirth attendants can also make a tremendous difference. When a laboring woman has a loving hand to hold, someone to rub her back, or the option of a warm tub of water to labor in, she may never need to consider drugs for pain relief. When a woman feels in charge of her labor and birth and is confident of her ability to birth her baby, drugs will become a little-used option.

Myth: An Episiotomy Heals Better Than a Tear

The episiotomy, or cutting of the perineal tissue, is commonly used in about 90 percent of hospital births in the United States.[36] The episiotomy is performed as the baby's head is crowning just before birth. The rationale used by obstetricians to justify the use of an episiotomy has included sparing the mother from perineal tears, saving the baby's head from damage, hastening the birth, and preventing serious damage to the woman's pelvic muscles.

Many midwives and childbirth reformers realize that an episiotomy is not necessary in most cases. When an episiotomy is performed, it carries the risks of any other surgical procedure: excessive blood loss, hematoma formation (a form of swelling or bruising), infection, or abscessing. Sometimes trauma from an episiotomy of the anal sphincter and rectal mucosa leads to loss of rectal tone and, in severe cases, a fistula, or hole, between the vagina and rectum. An episiotomy can complicate the postpartum recovery. There have been no conclusive studies that prove that an episiotomy would save the muscles from being stretched and losing tone or that it would yield a tighter vagina than one that is stretched naturally. Gentle birth advocates agree that it is important to abandon the routine use of episiotomy and to only use the procedure when a birth becomes difficult due to the baby's size or presentation.

Several important factors can prevent perineal tearing and the need for an episiotomy. One is for the mother to be in an upright position. Another is the ability to change positions while birthing her child. Most practitioners feel it is necessary to get the baby out as quickly as possible after the cervix has completely dilated. They ask women to strain, hold their breath, and bear down. These actions can lead to maternal hypotension (low blood pressure). If the vaginal tissues are distended too rapidly, the possibility of lacerations and the indication for episiotomy increases. The combination of birthing in the lithotomy position and strained pushing will cause the perineum to tear. If a woman is in a vertical squatting position or on her hands and knees when birthing, the pelvic area opens up. She is now working with the force of gravity instead of against it. Under these conditions there usually should be no need for an episiotomy. When a woman is allowed to move and change positions, she is in control of her birth.

A woman who is left alone while birthing will often place a hand on the perineum or on the baby's head as it is crowning. She can work with the contractions and slowly ease the baby out without tearing the perineum. If she has a strong urge to push, she can hold back by changing her breathing pattern to light pants or by vocalizing her energy, which will inhibit her from bearing down. In this way, the baby's head can slowly stretch the perineum.

Many midwives will apply hot compresses and warm oil to the perineal area between contractions to encourage relaxation. Sitting in a tub of warm water will help the perineum stretch, as will assisting the woman to relax her pelvic area. Midwives observe a "resting" phase toward the end of the first stage of labor. They report that some women often do not have the urge to push as soon as dilation is complete and that, in fact, the contractions slow down a bit. One California midwife described her experience: "The mother asked me to check her while she was in the birthing tub. I told her that she was complete and to listen to her body to know when she needed to push. She rested and moved slowly about for almost an hour. At one point she asked me if she should be pushing, and I told her only if she felt a strong urge. She didn't, so she continued to rest. All of a sudden her eyes widened and she said as she reached down, 'The baby's here.' Within four minutes the baby was in her arms. She hadn't pushed once. The baby had descended slowly and then, whoosh, was out in the water." As long as the baby and mother are doing well there is no need to bear down in an effort to "rush" the baby out.

The work of Dr. Michel Odent and others have shown that the second stage of labor is not usually lengthened when it is allowed to proceed in an entirely instinctive manner. In a gentle birth, a woman does not need to be coached to push. Instead she needs to trust her instincts and open up to this wonderful process of letting go of the baby instead of pushing it out.

Myth: It's Better Not to Eat or Drink during Labor

If active labor lasts longer than twelve hours, a woman will probably get tired and hungry. A 1984 survey of U.S. and U.K. hospitals found that not one hospital allowed a woman to eat or drink what she wanted during labor.[37] About 50 percent allowed ice chips for a woman's thirst; some now allow clear liquids, such as water, iced tea, or popsicles. In either case, the calorie requirements and nutritional needs of the laboring woman have been virtually ignored. The rationale behind these restrictions is that if the woman were

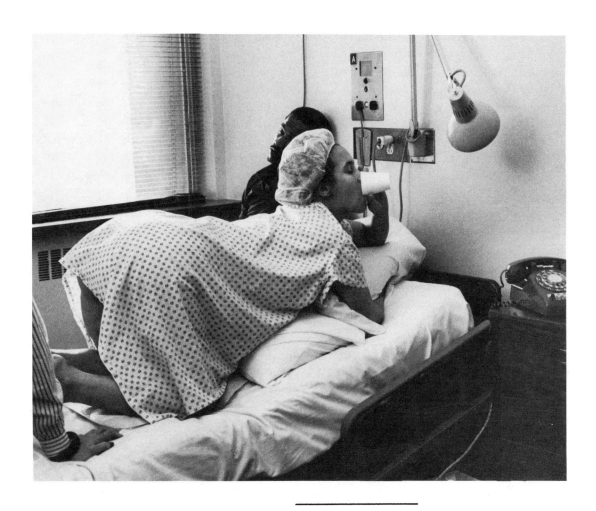

Eating and drinking during labor prevent
dehydration and exhaustion.

given general anesthesia or a high epidural, she would be susceptible to vomiting. The anesthesia would keep her gag reflex from working, thus increasing her risk for aspiration pneumonia.

In reality the practice of withholding food or liquids increases the risk of dehydration and negative nitrogen balance in the laboring woman. There have been no scientific studies of the nutritional needs of laboring women; however, all women who have experienced labor know that it is a major aerobic event, burning up thousands of calories. A great deal of stamina is called for, not only physically but emotionally. What a time to tell a woman she can have "nothing by mouth"! Many women don't feel like eating during labor, but they should always have the option.

In an attempt to compensate for this lack of nutrition, an IV line is usually inserted into the mother's arm for continuous administration of fluid. Although the dextrose or lactated ringers substance in the IV fluid does provide some calories, it is both insufficient and inappropriate to her needs. The presence of the IV complicates the labor in many ways. Any puncture of the skin increases the risk of infection. It also immobilizes a woman in labor, encumbering her freedom to move. She can walk, but someone has to help her manage the IV pole, the tubing, and the bag or bottle. This is the last thing a woman in the midst of a contraction wants to be bothered with. Being hooked up to an IV also carries the psychological implication that birth is a state of illness. Many women just resign themselves to being patients in hospital beds instead of active birthing women. The IV also makes it much easier to accept drugs. If a woman is faced with a painful shot, she may think twice about taking pain medication, but if it can be painlessly injected through the IV that has already been inserted, she finds it more difficult to object. Many women reach a point in their labor when they feel like they cannot take any more and are ready to throw in the towel. It is at these times that family, friends, or the birth assistant can make all the difference with reassuring words or encouragement. Unfortunately, at these times it's also the easiest to accept pain relief via the IV.

Given the option to eat, especially in early active labor, women at home and in birthing centers choose easily digested carbohydrates such as bread, cookies, toast, fruit, rice, or pasta, as well as light proteins such as cheese or yogurt. Some women like to sip milk shakes or protein shakes for strength. Dehydration shows up as dry lips, a racing pulse, and a lack of urination. A woman who needs protein will often become easily discouraged during labor and have a visible lack of energy. Her uterus may even get tired, in what is called uterine inertia. All of these situations can be remedied by asking her to eat and drink. By encouraging a woman to keep drinking fluids during labor and even offering spoonfuls of honey, midwives report that women often regain their strength and are able to accomplish a natural birth. If women in hospitals who were preparing for normal vaginal births ate and drank as they desired, the problem of food in the stomach could be dealt with by inserting a naso-gastric tube and suctioning out the contents of the stomach if an emergency occurred. The prohibition of food and liquids during labor is an example of a cultural practice instituted for good reasons, but those reasons no longer exist with the knowledge we have today.

Myth: Family and Friends Interfere during Birth

Some hospitals today still have policies that restrict the number of people a woman can have supporting her during her birth. A chosen support person must attend childbirth classes and carry a certificate of completion in order to be present for the birth. Nurses have reported that they occasionally falsify these certificates so that fathers can be present for the birth of their child. Partners or support people can be separated from the mother because there are no clean scrub suits in the correct size. Can you imagine the disappointment for both the father and mother if at the last moment he is told he cannot come into the delivery room because he has neither a certificate stating his qualifications nor a scrub suit in his size?

Enforced separation of the birthing woman from her support system strongly contributes to a woman's level of anxiety or fear. Current research on hormones and their effect on the laboring woman points to the fact that fear adversely affects blood flow and uterine contractions. During a normal labor there is an increase in the flow of catecholamines, which activate the fight or flight response in both the mother and the baby. The stress of being alone during labor, separated from loved ones and surrounded by strangers, is enough to trigger an increased level of catecholamine release in the mother. This can produce weaker uterine contractions, prolonged labor, a decrease of blood flow to the uterus and placenta, and an increase in the amount of hormones released. The baby interprets these responses in her mother as stress and her hormone production increases, which in turn can cause distress, heart rate abnormalities, and even colitis and the release of meconium into the amniotic fluid.

Studies have shown that babies born by elective cesarean without active labor have absent or reduced levels of catecholamines, indicating that labor stimulates their release. For the baby the release of the catecholamines is vital because these hormones help regulate breathing efforts after birth. If they are not present, as in a baby who was born by cesarean that was not preceded by normal labor, the infant may experience respiratory distress. Niles Newton, one of the founding members of the International Childbirth Education Association, conducted interesting studies involving mice giving birth in different containers and contrivances. Her findings were significant. Mice whose labors were environmentally disturbed experienced significantly longer labors, as much as 72 percent longer under some conditions, and gave birth to 54 percent more dead pups than did the mice in the control group who birthed in a natural environment. Newton presented her data to colleagues at the 1974 National Congress on the Quality of Life, an American Medical Association (AMA) conference. Newton emphasized that the human mammal (that is, the human mother), which has a more highly developed nervous system than that of the mouse, may be equally sensitive to environmental disturbances in labor.[38]

Marshall Klaus and John Kennell, the pediatricians who wrote about maternal-infant bonding, published a study in the *British Medical Journal* in 1986. The study randomly assigned more than 400 laboring women either to continuous social support, which included back massage and verbal reassurance, or to routine hospital care with minimal support. Among women who received routine hospital care with minimal support, the rate of cesarean birth was more than twice that in the supported group. The women who were assigned labor companions and received massage, emotional encouragement, and support consistently experienced much shorter labors. The difference was approximately seven hours as compared to fifteen hours for those who did not receive help.[39]

A few simple measures can reassure a woman in labor and reduce her stress. Never leaving her alone in labor and providing strong emotional support, as the Klaus study points out, have been proved to decrease labor time and prevent distress in the fetus. Bonding with the newborn is also enhanced when a woman is supported throughout the process.[40] If she is feeling loved and nurtured, she is more available to nurture her baby. It is important for her to choose a person upon whom she can depend for emotional support. Many women want their husbands or partners present and choose an additional person as well to support them through the process of labor. Hospitals need to recognize how the procedures, thoughtless routines, and unnecessary interventions that accompany hospital births increase stress, actually creating the problems that the interventions are trying to avoid.

Myth: The Baby Needs to Be Observed in a Newborn Nursery

A number of hospitals today allow newborns to room-in with their mothers. But the routine procedure is to separate babies from their mothers for some period of time immediately following the birth, reuniting the baby and mother only three or four specified times during the day. The rationale behind forced separation is to prevent newborn infections and to allow the mother to rest. Mothers who receive drugs or anesthesia during birth certainly do need time to "sober up" before they can care for their newborns, and the babies need time to let the effects of the drugs wear off. Most babies experience some form of respiratory depression when narcotic agents are used during labor and birth and do need more careful monitoring. But for the normal, unmedicated birth, separation interferes with some very vital functions.

In 1989 Dr. Marsden Wagner, an American-born pediatrician who is currently a consultant to the Maternal/Child Health division of WHO, lectured a group gathered in Jerusalem for an international symposium on pre- and perinatal psychology. Wagner stated emphatically, "I am convinced the procedure of placing all newborn babies in one room was the biggest mistake of modern medicine." He further refers to the newborn nursery as "a cradle of germs, separating babies from their mothers at the most sensitive point of their relationship."[41] Dr. Wagner also cited several studies that link separation

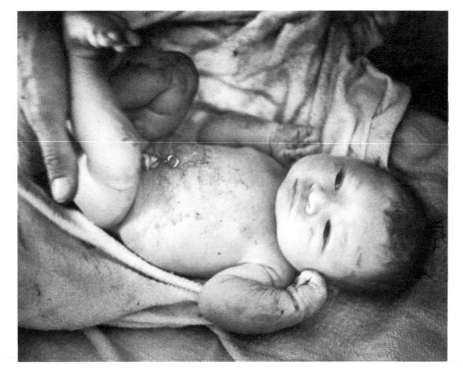

at birth with subsequent child abuse. The importance of the maternal-infant bond in the first few hours after birth has been the subject of many books in the past decade. Most noted in this field is the work of Dr. Marshall Klaus. Bonding is not a science, but there are identifiable characteristics that are associated with this process of emotional attachment.

The first few hours after birth are called the maternal sensitive period.[42] The mother becomes deeply involved, on an emotional level, with her newborn. The first hour after birth is also a time of quiet alertness for the newborn. Later the baby goes into a deep resting stage for several hours, during which it is difficult to rouse him. The mother who holds and communicates with her baby immediately receives a sense of fulfillment and gratification. She lightly touches the baby with her fingertips and then gradually massages the baby's body. Her voice becomes high-pitched and she looks into the baby's face. They greet each other eye to eye. At birth the baby can see perfectly well from distances of about twelve to eighteen inches, just the distance from mother's to baby's face when he is cradled in her arms. This period is not restricted to mothers. Fathers and siblings bond emotionally during this sensitive period as well. Fathers of home-birth babies often talk about watching or assisting with the birth and holding the baby shortly afterward. Most men feel that this experience deepens their relationship with their partner. When siblings are included in the birth or in the first few hours after birth, they exhibit less sibling rivalry. Unfortunately, it is still a rare hospital that welcomes small children to experience the birth of their new baby brother or sister.

The procedures that go on in the nursery can just as easily be done at the bedside, with the whole family participating. Heart rate, lung sounds, muscle tone, reflexes, and skin color can all be assessed while the baby is in his mother's arms. In healthy newborns with good respiratory function, these procedures do not need to be carried out immediately. Everything can be delayed for, at the very least, an hour. This quiet time can give the mother and father a chance to be intimate, initiate breast-feeding, and sense the new responsibilities this new creature brings.

Most parents love participating in the overall examination that takes place shortly after the birth. Siblings like to count fingers and toes. A great deal of teaching and information can be shared about this new person by including the parents in this process. A portable or sling-type scale to weigh the baby can be brought to the bedside. Many new dads like to observe the scale and make the pronouncement of how much their baby weighs. Washing the baby is often not necessary, especially with a water-born infant. The Leboyer bath is still an available option, either in the delivery room or at the bedside. The more responsibility the parents are encouraged to assume, the more confidence they exhibit. The nurse or midwife becomes a supportive assistant to the parents, offering gentle instruction only if it is called for. For the woman who truly needs to rest and have undisturbed sleep, the nursery provides an alternative, but it should remain an option for those who choose it and not something that is forced on all mothers.

Removing the baby to the nursery increases the risk of an infection. Every hospital is terrified of nursery staph infections. Newborns who become infected risk being subjected to everything from aggressive antibiotic treatments to, in some cases, even death. Where do the babies get the infections? Simply from the noses and hands of hospital nursery personnel. When the mother keeps her baby with her, she cuddles him, kisses him, massages him, and covers his whole body with a film of bacteria. This is important because the baby is familiar with her bacteria, which protects him from other foreign germs.

Taking the baby away from his parents also takes away their responsibilities. Caretaking of the baby starts immediately. For the woman who wants to assume this responsibility, taking the baby away from her is an insult to her abilities. She loses confidence and begins to wonder if she really is capable of taking care of a newborn. Perhaps those experienced nurses know something about babies that she doesn't. After all, while this may be her first experience with a newborn baby, they do this all the time. Nothing can shatter a mother's self-confidence more than to have a nurse breeze through bathing and diapering her baby. Even casually doubting her ability to mother impacts on her relationship with her child.

One of the strongest emotions to affect a woman at the time of birth is loss. The physical passage of the baby from intrauterine to extrauterine life means loss on many levels. Many women enjoy being pregnant, feeling their babies inside, and exulting in their increased self-awareness and sensitivity. A lot of attention is focused on the woman when she is pregnant. As soon as the baby is born, everything and everyone is focused around the baby's needs. Many women also feel a sense of loss when the actual birth does not match their expectations, especially if they were planning a gentle birth and ended up needing a cesarean section. The feelings at the time of birth are numerous, and it is sometimes hard for a new mother to sort out just what is going on. She may be in shock over the birth and may display behaviors that resemble anything from denial and disbelief to fear, anxiety, guilt, hostility, crying, and lack of concentration. Physically she may exhibit sighing, weakness, shortness of breath, fatigue, and chest pain. All of these signs and symptoms are directly related to her grief over the loss, either real or imagined. In a hospital birth these manifestations are only complicated by the real loss of her baby to the newborn nursery. The easiest way to ease her emptiness is immediate and continuing contact with her baby. The physical closeness helps mitigate the sense of loss. If she is lovingly supported, she is also generally better able to process her feelings.

A single woman who had had a relatively easy home birth retained the placenta for a time that most doctors would consider abnormal. Instead of panicking, the midwife supported the mother through this period just as she had done during the birth. As they talked, the midwife asked the mother why she was not willing to let go of the pregnancy. The mother cried and admitted that as long as she was pregnant, she felt loved and nurtured. She had a fear that as a single mother she wouldn't get the support she needed to be a good mother. The midwife asked her to hold her baby and to tell him what a good mother she was. As she cradled her newborn in her arms, crying, she felt a huge contraction, stood up to go to the bathroom, and the placenta quite literally fell out. This is an example of the birth attendant helping the mother work through her feelings. Recognizing and dealing with these emotions, having maximum physical contact with the baby, and being supported by the entire family during and immediately after the birth will often prevent what medical experts have labeled postpartum depression.

Myth: If You Are over Thirty-Five, Your Birth Will Be More Difficult

Today many women are delaying childbearing until their late twenties, thirties, or even forties. Career moves, postponing marriage, and a desire for self-fulfillment are some of the reasons why women are having their first babies at an older age. The National Center for Health Statistics reports that between 1975 and 1982 women who were between thirty and thirty-four years of age experienced a 23 percent increase in fertility.[43] During that same period, there was an 83 percent increase in women over the age of thirty-five having their first babies. These figures seem dramatic compared to first births for women in their twenties, which actually declined during this time.

An "older couple" feeling the intimacy of a beautiful birth experience in a birthing center.

Medicine has placed a great stigma on "older" women having babies. The current terminology is that these women are considered high risk for having gestational and birth-related complications. There are an infinite number of variables to be considered when looking at the overall health of a pregnant woman. The medical model of pregnancy wants each woman to fall within a certain set of arbitrary guidelines in order to be considered low risk: the woman should be twenty-two to twenty-four years old, she should be Rh positive with no history of a previous abortion or miscarriage, she should have had no abnormal Pap smears or childhood illnesses other than the measles, and she should have given birth within the last three years to a normal infant weighing between seven and nine pounds. Most pregnant women do not meet the standards laid out in these guidelines. Any factor that does not meet the medical model definition of a normal pregnancy can cause a woman to be labeled high risk. If she is thirty-five or older, she is considered obstetrically elderly.

Even if she is perfectly healthy and has a positive attitude about her pregnancy, a woman will be subjected to a battery of tests, precautions, and careful screening throughout pregnancy, labor, and birth. Her history and physical exam might even read, "Elderly primipara with no apparent complications or abnormalities. High risk. AFP screening with follow-up amniocentesis recommended." Today women who are too old, too young, too fat, too poor, or who have had too many prior pregnancies—or who have had none—are all considered high risk.

Women who consult with physicians before arranging for a home birth are evaluated in the same manner. They are not judged healthy and suitable for a home birth but are merely considered low risk for possible complications. Risk is a tricky subject. We all walk around at some form of risk for accident, illness, or death. Do you tell your friends that they are at low risk for an automobile accident? The mere terminology suggests a disease process, not a normal state. The medical model only associates pregnancy with the possibility of complications, either high or low.

What are the factors that make an older woman high risk? The idea that older women, especially first-time mothers, suffer more complications in pregnancy has been perpetuated for the last one hundred years. Medical texts have even stated that anyone between the ages of twenty-eight and forty is pushing the upper limit of youth. A number of seemingly conclusive studies indicated that advanced maternal age contributes to increased maternal mortality, infant mortality, perinatal mortality, pregnancy and labor complications, and a variety of birth defects, including Down's syndrome. It is possible that many studies were written in order to support the view of birth being an abnormal state, a disease state. By redefining what is normal, medicine has maintained more control. These studies have been accepted and handed down for the last two generations as being the measure of normalcy.

There are real genetic risks associated with age in both mothers and fathers. For women over thirty-five and men over fifty-five, the risk of having a baby with Down's syndrome increases every year. At twenty years of age the risk is 1 in 2,000; at thirty-five, 1 in 365; and at forty-five, 1 in 32. It seemed perfectly logical that imperfections in genetics related to age would be reflected in birth statistics. In actuality, 80 percent of Down's syndrome babies in 1986 were born to women younger than thirty-five. This could mean that many Down's babies were aborted, thereby reducing the number of genetically imperfect babies born to women over thirty-five; or it could mean that Down's syndrome is not always relegated to obstetrically elderly women.[44]

With the average life span increasing, women today are not as old at thirty-five as our grandmothers were. Older women today are generally healthier and more health conscious. What used to be considered age-related complications such as diabetes, obesity, heart problems, and high blood pressure are experienced more on an individual basis than in the general population of older females. Women who consciously choose to delay pregnancy tend to be very physically and emotionally fit for motherhood.

Positive attitudes about pregnancy, birth, and becoming a mother are increasingly important for all women but especially for older women. It is important for them to know that they have had excellent prenatal care, will be supported emotionally, and will have adequate help after the birth. These women must consider all aspects of their family lives, including their relationships, possible career obligations, and the demands of a new baby.

Myth: Baby Boys Need to Be Circumcised

For many years routine circumcision, the surgical removal of the foreskin at the end of the penis, has been a medically and socially accepted convention in the United States. Almost all newborn baby boys were circumcised before they left the hospital. Medical reasons for circumcision included the unproven belief that circumcision offered some protection against cancer or infection of the penis and cervical cancer in future female partners. Perhaps as influential was the often unspoken perception that an uncircumcised penis was somehow unhygienic. None of these "medical" reasons has ever been validated by research, and in 1975 the American Academy of Pediatrics announced that there is no absolute medical indication for routine circumcision.

Unfortunately, this statement has not precipitated a dramatic decline in the number of circumcisions being performed each year. Parents are not usually informed of the normalcy of an intact foreskin or of the risks of the operation. Some parents choose to circumcise their sons with love and honor as part of a religious ritual and have strong feelings about the issue. (Jewish parents should know that there is a growing movement to eliminate this ritual. A national organization, Jews Against Circumcision, counsels families on making this important decision.) But many parents, perhaps most, make the decision to circumcise for social rather than religious reasons. Parents who are planning to circumcise their child because the child's father or older brothers have been circumcised or because they don't want him to look different from other boys should be aware of the potential pain and trauma—both physical and emotional—the procedure entails.

During the 1980s, medical literature began slowly to refute some previously held beliefs about the abilities and sensibilities of the fetus and the newborn. For years it was believed that the perception of pain in a newborn was much less than that of an adult.[45] Babies have always responded to painful stimuli, but it was thought that their responses were mere reflexes and that they were unaware of where the pain was and had no conscious thoughts about it. It was also generally accepted that newborns did not have the capacity to remember painful experiences. Some current theories propose that the newborn is protected from pain due to an innate adaptive mechanism that gives him a particularly high pain threshold, especially for the birth process. As a consequence of these theories, babies have suffered through excruciatingly painful procedures, the most common of which is circumcision. In 1991, 1.25 million newborn males were circumcised, the majority without anesthesia.[46]

Circumcision carries inherent physical risks to the newborn. The risks associated with anesthesia are usually explained, but hemorrhage, infection, and mutilation are additional concerns that new parents should be informed about before they consent to removing their new son's sensitive foreskin. The child's future sexual response should also be considered. John Taylor, a Canadian pathologist, has studied the structure and function of the foreskin, which he describes as the sensory extension of the penis. He writes, "The prepuce is much more complex than the 'simple fold of skin' described in textbooks. Its inner mucosal surface contains a tightly pleated zone near the tip, rich in nerve endings . . . with a special sensory function."[47]

In 1987 the *New England Journal of Medicine* published an extensively researched article, "Pain and Its Effects in the Human Neonate and Fetus." The authors, both from the department of anesthesia at Harvard Medical School and Boston Children's Hospital, write from the perspective that the risks of anesthesia, both general and local, are to be considered carefully when potentially painful procedures are to be performed on neonates as well as premature infants. They believe, based on their research, that the experience of pain can be more devastating than the risks associated with anesthesia.[48] All the current research indicates that not only are babies cognizant at birth but also within the womb. Mechanisms are present for interpreting pain as early as the twentieth to thirtieth weeks of gestation.

Even with anesthesia of some kind, circumcision is painful and may produce psychological scarring on a very deep level. Noted psychiatrists now believe that a newborn's birth experience, whether it be painful or pleasant, will profoundly influence his behavior for the rest of his life. Psychiatrist Stanislav Grof states, "How one is born seems to be closely related to one's general attitude toward life, the ratio of optimism to pessimism, how one relates to other people, and one's ability to confront challenges."[49] The infant experiences the procedure as an attack and may conceptualize that his mother, the only person with whom he shares a psychological bond, has abandoned him and has willingly allowed him to be harmed. This perceived lack of protection by the mother could interrupt the formation of the baby's trust, a necessary ingredient for healthy attachment and bonding.[50]

Unfortunately, routine circumcision is also a lucrative practice for hospitals and doctors. In 1992, $250 million was spent on circumcision. In 1949, when the National Health Service in the United Kingdom decided not to pay for circumcisions, the number performed dropped immediately to less than one-half of 1 percent. The Canadian health system no longer reimburses for routine circumcision, and the number of circumcisions has steadily and dramatically dropped. Sympathetic doctors and nurses can also make a difference. In 1992 a group of twenty-two nurses at a hospital in Santa Fe issued a proclamation that they could no longer participate in newborn circumcisions. They considered themselves to be conscientious objectors. This concrete action is a step that more medical practitioners can take to protect the rights of the newborn.[51]

In the opening address at the 1989 Pre- and Perinatal Psychology Association of North America conference held at the University of Massachusetts, Dr. Lee Salk, respected pediatric psychiatrist from Columbia University, implored the audience to consider the feelings of the newly born child when caring for and handling these tiny people. He cited studies about the influence of the experience of birth and the neonatal period on a person's later behavior.

Dr. Salk also noted his own research with babies who are born prematurely and who spend time in neonatal intensive care units. His work focuses on the subsequent behavior of individuals who experience multiple invasive and painful procedures and endure consistent deprivation of human touch. What he found was an extremely high rate of behavior problems with this group as compared to a similar group of children born in the same hospital during the same time period. There was even a high rate of five- to ten-year-olds with severe psychotic behavior.[52] He concluded that we must rethink how we handle babies at birth. This new knowledge strongly suggests that humane considerations should apply as forcefully to the care of newborns and young nonverbal infants as they do to children and adults in similar painful and stressful situations.

A woman who chose to birth her baby in water and to have her husband with her.

4

A Gentle Revolution

Throughout the world, more and more people are joining the parents and practitioners who are calling for changes in maternity care. There have always been individual complaints against the increased medicalization of childbirth. Yet voices of protest were raised over fifty years ago and have continued steadily to this day. Every mother, childbirth educator, physician, or midwife who has spoken out about the normalcy of birth or written about the need for change has contributed to what has become a gentle birth revolution.

The social consciousness of women has had a profound effect on the gentle birth revolution. Women are demanding to be in control of their bodies and to fully participate in their birthing process. This change parallels women's change of status in the workplace and in the home. Economic necessity forced many mothers to enter the work force even with small children at home. In 1950 women made up only 30 percent of the work force. In 1980, 43 percent of American women worked outside the home. In 1990 almost 50 percent of women with children under the age of six worked full time. In 1992 an interesting change came about. For the first time since 1948, when the Bureau of Labor Statistics began keeping records, the percentage of women in the work force dropped because more mothers chose to stay home with their children. A record low of 18 percent of mothers with two or more children under the age of seven are now working full time.[1]

Women started choosing *when* they were going to bear children. It naturally followed that some would choose *how* they would give birth. This choice, however, remains primarily a middle-class phenomenon. Many segments of society have never had the opportunity to choose when, where, or how to have their babies. Conditions such as poverty, poor nutrition, language barriers, single and young motherhood, and lack of available services create circumstances that cause women to feel that they have no choices.

Alicia was seventeen when she became pregnant with her first baby. Neither her mother nor the baby's father could provide financial support for her, so she applied for welfare. Out of over twenty obstetricians in her home town, only one would take welfare cases. Her prenatal treatment was average. She had no complaints until she began reading about natural childbirth. Her physician flatly refused to acknowledge any of Alicia's desires, telling her she was lucky that she had a doctor who would see her.

Alicia's labor began early one morning three weeks before her due date. She immediately called her doctor to give him a progress report, then went about her usual activities. She felt very confident that everything was fine, and she knew from the reading she had done that her labor was still very mild and did not require her to be in the hospital. Late in the afternoon she received a phone call from the labor nurse at the hospital. Alicia was told in no uncertain terms that she must come to the hospital to be admitted or the sheriff would come over to pick her up and bring her in. From then on Alicia felt as if she were no more than a pregnant body. No one consulted her, informed her, or respected her feelings during the course of her labor. She wanted a completely natural birth but was given drugs to stimulate her labor and drugs to control the pain, and she was never once encouraged to be in charge. She said, "It was as if they were punishing me for getting pregnant in the first place. They acted like I wasn't even there and it was their job to get the baby out of me as quickly as possible." Alicia and her son were separated right after birth due to his low birth weight, even though he was healthy.

Alicia's lack of choice for that baby led her to seek alternative care just fifteen months later. This time she contacted midwives, came to childbirth education classes, and arranged to have a water birth. She birthed her second baby at home in warm water, empowered by being totally in charge. She said, "I can't believe the difference between the two births, not even two years apart. In the hospital I felt like it wasn't my birth or my baby. It was theirs. There is just no comparison—none!"

As more physicians and midwives embrace a perspective that views childbirth as a normal event, the gentle birth experience becomes a feasible option for all women. Birth can be experienced as an uncomplicated, natural event in which a woman can express her power, her emotions, and her sexuality and be supported by those people she loves. Her child can enter the world calmly, serenely, and joyously and can immediately become part of the family into which he has been born, being with his parents in the moments after birth and during the bonding period that follows. Childbirth can be child-centered, mother-centered, family-centered; above all, it can be gentle while still being safe.

Some of the most influential reformers of childbirth practices over the last fifty years have been physicians who have demonstrated the validity and safety of gentle birth practices. Consumers who seek changes in hospital policy have seen that the cooperation of doctors has been an essential ingredient in implementing these changes.

Birth without Fear

One of the first proponents of "natural birth" was English obstetrician Grantly Dick-Read. He was outspoken about women's ability to birth normally and without pain. In his book *Childbirth without Fear: The Principles and Practices of Natural Childbirth,* Dick-Read proposed that fear produces tension and tension produces pain. This was a radical theory in the 1930s, when anesthesia and painkillers were routinely administered for all normal births in the hospital. Read's book met strong opposition in England. He was even accused by some of his English colleagues of abusing women by refusing to medicate them. Though it was written in the 1930s, the book wasn't published in the United States until 1944.

Dick-Read's "radical" ideas asked women to view their bodies as healthy and to see pregnancy and birth as a natural process. He developed his theory of painless childbirth by watching women give birth normally, without assistance of any kind. He then analyzed the situations and noted what had helped each woman through her labor. Early in his career Dick-Read attended a home birth where the woman refused the chloroform he offered. Surprised by this, he asked the woman why she was so stoic. She turned to him, almost apologetic for her refusal of drugs, and said, "It didn't hurt, doctor. It wasn't meant to, was it?"

This now-famous quote became Dick-Read's standard and was used by the women who began the "natural childbirth movement" in the United States. Dick-Read placed great emphasis on the role of birth attendants who were supportive of women. He felt that a woman should be educated about the process of labor and participate fully in her birth, and he instructed women in a series of breathing exercises that were designed to relax them and remove stress and fear during labor.

Dick-Read emphasized that even though a woman had the ability to birth normally, her doctor ultimately knew the best way to manage her labor and birth. Dick-Read's teachings were never given the opportunity to prove themselves on a wide scale because obstetricians objected strongly to the time-consuming "natural" birth. Hospitals and birthing practices in the United States during the 1940s and 1950s made it difficult, if not impossible, for women to achieve a purely "natural" birth. When American women were discovered on labor wards with Dick-Read's book tucked into their labor beds, doctors and nurses would ridicule them for wanting to participate in the birth of their babies.

At this time, however, a few childbirth educators, like pioneer Margaret Gamper of Chicago, started classes using Dick-Read's book as a natural childbirth guide. Gamper combined Dick-Read's methods of relaxation with her own massage techniques. She began teaching Chicago-area couples in 1947 and taught childbirth education for over thirty years. She influenced many birth practitioners, including Dr. Robert Bradley of Denver, who, with his nurse Rhondda Hartman, developed the Bradley method of "Husband-Coached Childbirth."[2] Even though Gamper's teachings, based on Dick-Read's book, were successful, the rules and regulations of hospital confinement stood in the way of many women who wanted to achieve a "natural birth."

Birth without Pain

A new method of preparing for birth evolved in the 1950s. Ferdinand Lamaze and Pierre Vellay, two French obstetricians, traveled to Russia in 1951 to observe methods of childbirth that utilized concentration and mind control. The Lamaze method of conditioning techniques was originally developed from Ivan Petrovich Pavlov's behavioral research. The Soviet government had adopted techniques based on Pavlovian principles as the official method of childbirth. The Russians believed that the fear and pain that women experienced during labor and birth was a learned response. The conditioning techniques replaced the fear responses with active breathing techniques to "recondition" a woman during labor. When a contraction came, instead of tightening with fear, a woman was trained to breathe, to massage her abdomen lightly, and to focus on an external point in the room. The two French physicians took this information back to Paris where they began to train women to use these techniques in hospital births.[3]

An American woman, Marjorie Karmel, who had come to France seeking support for a natural birth experience, met Dr. Lamaze by chance. She told him that the Dick-Read method could offer childbirth without fear; Lamaze responded by assuring her that he could help her have childbirth without pain. Karmel trained with Lamaze and his nurse and gave birth to her first child in a French hospital in 1956. That same year, the Pope sanctioned the use of the Lamaze, or psychoprophylactic, techniques for childbirth. Charged by the experience, Karmel began to write about it as soon as she returned to the United States. Her article was refused for publication on the grounds that it was too controversial—perhaps because the technique came from behind the Iron Curtain. *Harper's Bazaar* finally published Karmel's article in 1957. In 1959, after giving birth a second time using the Lamaze techniques, Karmel published the stories of her birth experiences in the now-famous book *Thank You, Dr. Lamaze.*[4]

Childbirth reformer Elizabeth Bing joined with Karmel and obstetrician Benjamin Segal to begin the American Society for Psychoprophylaxis in Obstetrics in 1960. They began to introduce the idea of Lamaze training to small groups of doctors and nurses. The two women felt it would be more effective to work within the hospital system in order to introduce the method. The organization encouraged couples to work with their physicians but to never question the physicians' ultimate authority. In Bing's book *Six Practical Lessons for an Easier Childbirth*, published in 1967, she states, "If he himself [the doctor] suggests medication, accept it willingly even though you don't feel the need for it. He undoubtedly has good reasons for his decision." *Six Practical Lessons* became the bible for parents and professionals involved in studying and teaching Lamaze. The book has had twenty printings and has been published in many foreign languages.[5]

At no point in the early development of the Lamaze techniques were women encouraged to work with their bodies, feelings, or emotions. Many women who studied the techniques felt that the methods actually served to separate women from their bodies. By focusing on something outside of herself, the birthing mother simply replaced the drugs with mind-control techniques, which limit conscious participation. The birth was still conducted the way her doctor felt was appropriate. The judgment of the doctor was considered infallible, and the mother was rarely included in decisions about her own labor and birth. Most hospitals today offer courses that have the name Lamaze but in actuality prepare women more for the experience of birth in that particular hospital than does the original French method of pain control. When Marjorie Karmel wrote the first edition of her book, psychoprophylaxis was the only nondrug alternative to complete narcosis. Today these courses often teach women about additional pain-control options, including the appropriate time to request an epidural or other medication. Hospital rules about fetal monitoring and other procedures are also stressed. The content of the courses is changing, but the physician and hospital maintain control of the birth experience.

One of the keys to Lamaze preparation was the training of the support person who would "coach" the mother throughout her labor and delivery. In France this person was usually the midwife. In the United States the midwife was replaced by the husband for several reasons. The number of hospital personnel needed to instruct and support the mothers on a one-to-one basis would be too great for the hospital to justify. So the husbands, who wanted to be with their wives in most cases anyway, were converted into labor-room attendants. Unfortunately, this new role changed the husband from a loving, emotionally supportive partner to an active member of the birthing "team." The doctor now depended on the husband to keep the "little woman" under control during her labor and birth.

To become a Lamaze instructor one must have a medical background as a nurse, doctor, physiotherapist, or, most recently, "allied health professional." Experience in childbirth was not necessarily a requirement. When certified nurse-midwife (CNM) Linda Church, the mother of six children, began teaching Lamaze preparation for childbirth, she drew on her own experiences, including the frustrations that she had encountered as a patient in the hospital. Church encouraged women to take control of their births and to ask for what they wanted. Some doctors called Church to complain about the fact that their patients had to be "reinstructed" about the proper way to give birth after they had taken her class; others admired the strength and courage that these educated couples displayed.

For most couples, the Lamaze method became a compromise between parents and doctors. Husbands became coaches, timing contractions and "participating" in the birth; mothers were allowed to be awake; and doctors proceeded to monitor, give epidurals, perform episiotomies, and use forceps as necessary. The new hospital childbirth educator had done her job to "prepare" the couple for the experience, yet something was missing. What about the baby?

Birth without Violence

With the introduction of medical interventions in childbirth, the bulk of midwife knowledge, based on thousands of years of tradition, was either lost or cast aside as nothing more than old wives' tales. French physician Frederick Leboyer was the first doctor to express what many women know instinctively: A newborn is a complete being with feelings, one who possesses the ability to perceive his or her environment and to interact with it. Leboyer had attended the birth of more than nine thousand babies when he wrote *Birth without Violence*, published in 1975. He suspected that conventional hospital births were actually causing damage to newborn children. Leboyer

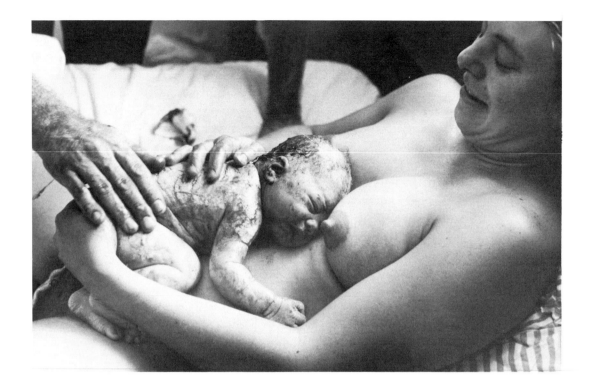

The importance of immediate skin-to-skin contact with the mother was stressed by Dr. Leboyer.

noted that in France, a nation of fifty million people, there were more than one million dysfunctional children. Leboyer wanted to know if this was related in some way to the manner in which the children were handled at birth.[6] As part of his research, Leboyer retired from his obstetrical practice and studied so-called primitive childbirth practices in a remote area of India for several years.[7]

Leboyer's premise of birth without violence was considered revolutionary at the time. He considered the birth process from the infant's point of view and suggested measures that would greatly reduce trauma for the newborn child. Leboyer instituted practices that reduced the noise and lights in the delivery room and encouraged relaxation for the woman. As soon after the birth as possible, the baby was immersed in a basin filled with warm water that closely approximated the conditions of the womb. Leboyer felt that this helped the infant recover from the stress of its birth.

Couples who read and believed in Leboyer's work often met resistance from their physicians when they requested a Leboyer-style birth. The dim lights and warm baths were not welcome additions to the routines of doctors and hospitals. Many couples began to see birth from the baby's perspective, yet Leboyer's theories virtually ignored the mother's participation in the birth of her baby. They considered the baby a victim of birth, the survivor of the "crushing" effects of the mother's uterine contractions. Women strived to have the best birth possible for the sake of the baby, but if the birth didn't go as planned or intervention became necessary, the couple was burdened with blame and guilt.

Despite this drawback, the impact of Leboyer's methods was extremely beneficial. Many midwives and couples used Leboyer's book as a reason to create alternatives for giving birth outside the hospital system. *Birth without Violence* became a best-seller in France, the United States, England, Germany, Sweden, Brazil, Italy, Holland, and other countries, indicating that the world was ready for a deeper understanding of birth.

Birth Reborn

In 1962 Dr. Michel Odent went to Pithiviers, a small town near Paris, to take charge of surgery at the public hospital. His surgical responsibilities included overseeing the hospital's small maternity clinic, which served the women of Pithiviers and nearby villages. Odent had a special advantage in being a surgeon and not an obstetrician because he was not conditioned to use the obstetric rituals of the day. Odent depended on the six midwives who worked with him and learned obstetrics from their practical experience. He also talked with women and observed them giving birth. Odent and the midwives read and discussed books such as Frederick Leboyer's *Birth without Violence* and medical anthropologist Ivan Illich's *Medical Nemesis*, which examined

Dr. Odent supports a woman in a suspended squat position while the midwife sits on the floor and waits for the baby.

what Illich described as the "disease of medical progress." Illich coined the term *iatrogenic* for "medically caused" illness, asserting that the medical establishment had become a major threat to health throughout the world.[8]

Illich's indictment of medical practices spoke strongly to the question Odent and the midwives at Pithiviers were asking themselves about childbirth: Are medical procedures and interventions necessary in a normal labor and birth? They were further inspired by their own sense of discovery while working with and observing women in labor. Odent gradually developed birthing practices based on the simplification or elimination of unnecessary medical procedures like shaving, enemas, gowning, gloving, draping, and the lithotomy position. They began to view childbirth not as a medically controlled event but as an integral part of the sexual and emotional life of a mother and her baby. Odent and the midwives saw themselves as "facilitators" whose task was to intervene as *little* as possible in this natural event, allowing the birth of a child to occur in an instinctual and gentle way. In 1976, after gentle birth practices were implemented at Pithiviers, Odent saw the perinatal mortality rate at the hospital drop to 10 deaths per 1,000 live births. The overall perinatal mortality rate in France at that time was about 20 deaths per 1,000 live births.[9]

In 1984 Odent wrote *Birth Reborn,* which recounts his experiences in the Pithiviers clinic. Doris Haire, president of the American Foundation for Maternal and Child Health, stated in the foreword, "There have been very few milestones in the worldwide movement to reform and humanize the birth experience. *Birth Reborn* is one of them. Every life has but one beginning." Just as Leboyer's *Birth without Violence* raised the public's awareness concerning gentle birth for the baby, Odent's *Birth Reborn* offered a new perspective in gentle birth for the woman.

Odent left France in 1985 and began a private practice in London, where he is presently gathering statistics and researching home birth for the World Health Organization (WHO). Odent has become a catalyst for midwives and physicians all over the world who have heard about Pithiviers and the successes there. Midwives rejoiced that finally a physician was proclaiming what they had known for years: Birth is not a medical event, and the less intervention the better. Many doctors have incorporated the philosophies prevalent at Pithiviers into their own practices. Among them, but not limited to them, are Dr. Wolf Jaskulsky in Austria, Dr. Josie Muscat in Malta, Dr. Robert Doughton in Oregon, Dr. Jan-Erik Strole in Washington State, Dr. Gustav Katz in Argentina, Dr. Bruce Sutherland in Australia, and Dr. Michael Rosenthal in California.

Birth without Rules

There has been a rediscovery by many midwives and a handful of physicians of just what the cost has been for the mothers and children who have experienced medically controlled births. Neither doctors nor women have been able to distinguish between iatrogenic complications and complications that would have developed had there not been medical interventions. Troublesome outcomes perpetuated the impression in women that their bodies were not trustworthy, so women yielded even more control to medical management. Practitioners of gentle birth advocate that the medical establishment trust women in childbirth, that they step back and respect what is natural, and that they only apply technology when it is called for.

Dr. Michael Rosenthal, a board-certified obstetrician and gynecologist, is one of those practitioners. He began his own freestanding birthing center in the quiet middle-class town of Upland, California. The Family Birthing Center, opened in January 1985, is located on a shady, tree-lined street with the San Antonio Hospital looming in the background. Rosenthal felt that his birthing center needed to be close to a major medical center because it would make women feel safer if there was a hospital in close proximity.

The approaches to birth are vastly different at the two facilities. Rosenthal provides maternity care by using only a few basic rules. The hospital next door has a procedures manual that reads like a telephone directory with standard doctors' orders for women in labor. Pregnant women come from all over the United States to use the Family Birthing Center. During the first year the birthing center was open, Rosenthal gave his clients the option of using the hospital or birthing center for their births. After that he told his clients that if they decided to use him as their obstetrician, they would have to use the birthing center.

A sunny patio with a tiled fountain greets visitors and clients as they enter the birthing center. A tour of the center conducted by Rosenthal on a busy Saturday morning reveals a warmly decorated interior, including three large birthing rooms with double beds and private toilets and showers. There are two separate bathrooms, each with large fiberglass bathtubs. The large classroom is full of very pregnant women and their spouses watching a film on birth. As we passed the classroom, Rosenthal peeked in and quipped, "I can't watch this part about C-sections; it makes me uncomfortable."

The kitchen is abundantly stocked with juices, fruit, cookies, and other snacks, and the waiting area is filled with comfortable couches and chairs. The nerve center of this facility is located behind three walls of glass, where the telephone and the busy staff can be faintly heard. Everything is immaculately clean and fresh, with colors that are harmonious, warm, and restful. Large color photographs of mothers, fathers, and newly born babies in water birth tubs decorate the walls. These photographs were taken by Rosenthal, the resident photographer.

In the reception area an older man and woman were anxiously waiting to enter one of the birthing rooms. Their daughter, who happened to be a pediatrician, had just given birth to their second grandchild in the water. Their first grandchild had been born by cesarean. The sounds of a newborn baby and the happy murmurings of his loving family could be clearly heard. On another couch in the reception area, a man and woman were holding a tiny, peaceful baby who had been born at the center just the day before.

Rosenthal worked hard in the beginning to convince women that they have the ability to birth their babies without technology and drugs. Many of the women were afraid that they would not be able to give birth without an epidural for pain. At first women were given the option of childbirth education classes at the birthing center. After a few years Rosenthal noticed that the women who actively participated in the classes, especially for their first pregnancies, had much easier births than those women who just came for their regularly scheduled prenatal visits. He now insists that all women participate in prenatal education.

Rosenthal sees the classes at the birthing center as more than teaching women how to give birth—they reinforce the normalcy of birth. The classes provide an experience of support that allows couples to feel comfortable in the birthing environment. Pregnant women often stop by the center to discuss some of their concerns about their anticipated births over a cup of tea. The importance of a casual relationship to the birthplace and the care providers cannot be underestimated. Each time a mother drops by or has a prenatal visit the birthing center becomes more familiar. When she eventu-

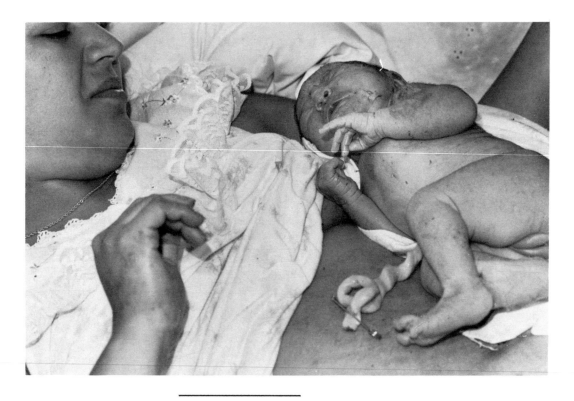

Mother and baby relax after a birthing-center birth.

ally arrives to have her baby, she does not have to cope with adjusting to a strange place.

During a prenatal class a birth will often be taking place down the hall. The mother may have even been in the class when her contractions started. A phone call from a woman in early labor is answered by Rosenthal personally. You can hear him telling her to be sure to eat, to rest if she is tired, and to call back when the contractions are longer, more intense, and closer together. He finishes by saying, "I'll probably see you tonight."

When the laboring woman arrives at the center, she and her partner and any other companions are taken to a birthing room. She is allowed to wear her own clothes and can decorate the room with personal possessions. She is also encouraged to eat lightly, and fluids are made readily available. Women may move freely about during all stages of labor and can give birth in whatever position they choose. Infants are not separated from their mothers after the birth except for valid medical reasons. Rosenthal believes that these choices allow women to focus on the *process* of giving birth. One of the only "rules" that is actively enforced at the birthing center is the requirement that the mother and baby stay for a full six hours after the birth. If complications are going to develop with the baby, they will usually occur within the first few hours.

Rosenthal feels that birthing centers such as his own will play a big part in the future of gentle birth. He acknowledges that home birth is the right place for some women. Unfortunately, doctors are restricted from attending home births by obstetrical standards for licensing and the fact that one physician would only be able to provide care for eight to ten women a month. Between fifteen and twenty-five women use the birthing center each month to have their babies.

Rosenthal is an advocate of the concept of centrally located community birthing centers where women of childbearing age can receive a wide array of services, including classes, moral support, and companionship with other pregnant women. Rosenthal's birthing center works because he takes a passive role and uses CNMs and nurses to conduct the majority of care. A woman is not left alone during her labor unless she requests privacy. The same nurse or midwife is there with the laboring mother from the moment she enters the door until she leaves with her new baby.

CNM Linda Church worked with Rosenthal from the time the center opened in February 1985 until 1991. She felt that her practice at the birthing center meant that she no longer had to fight with anyone over patients' rights. Church taught her own brand of Lamaze-prepared childbirth classes and worked in labor and delivery in several hospitals prior to her affiliation with Rosenthal. She witnessed a growing number of hospital patients who requested that their births be handled a certain way. These patients were considered pushy or downright crazy by the hospital staffs. Hospital births

Three generations of this family, including the siblings ages 4 and 10, share the excitement of birth at a California birthing center.

were sometimes reduced to a battle of wills between the couple and the doctor or nurses. Church feels that her experience as a mother has influenced her care for women as much as her midwife training. The midwife or nurse who has shared the experience of labor is usually more understanding and comforting than a young nurse who has never given birth.

"The birthing center," Rosenthal states, "is a place for the practice of midwifery." Every community should have a birthing center so that everyone can have a place to have their babies and learn about pregnancy, contraception, and parenting. Many cultures throughout history have had the tradition of central locations for giving birth. Rosenthal states emphatically, "We must move normal birth out of the hospital. Birth needs to remain a private and personal matter."[10]

Voices of Protest—Consumers Seek Change

Since the early 1950s, consumers, the recipients of maternity care, have voiced strong opinions about the necessity for a gentler, more humane system of labor and delivery. Entire organizations have evolved to deal with the results of women's birth experiences in the hospital system. In 1958 an anonymous nurse wrote a letter to the *Ladies' Home Journal* detailing the cruelty she saw in the maternity practices of the day. For well over a year the magazine was flooded with letters from mothers writing to confirm these allegations. Stories abounded of women who were left alone, tied to delivery tables, manipulated with drugs to either delay or hasten delivery (depending on the doctor's schedule), and kept from giving birth because their doctors had not yet arrived. Mothers wrote that their children had been brain-damaged as a direct result of the hospital personnel's violent treatment, even abuse, inflicted on the women during labor and delivery. During this same time, parent education groups were developing across the country in an effort to remove some of the fear surrounding the birth process and to improve birth management in local hospitals.

One such group was led by Lester Hazel and her husband Bill in the Washington, D.C., area. They went to the Maternity Center Association (MCA) in New York, which was founded in 1915, to learn about childbirth education and the Dick-Read method of childbirth. Like other parent groups, they sought improved obstetrical medical management, through the addition of services such as childbirth education, breast-feeding instruction, family participation, and rooming-in, without alienating anyone within the existing medical system.

In 1959 the MCA sponsored a gathering of all those who were interested in childbirth reform. Many of the parent childbirth education groups across the country attended. The International Childbirth Education Association (ICEA) emerged from this gathering and joined thirty parent groups together for their first national meeting in 1960.[11] The beliefs held by this organization were not radical or revolutionary, but maintained that birth belonged to the parents and not to the hospital. The members of the organization felt that each couple had the right to choose the kind of birth experience that was right for them and safe for their baby. The ICEA brought together both parents and professionals who desired change. Consultants for the group included anthropologists Margaret Mead and Ashley Montagu, who were both outspoken concerning the need for revision of maternity care in the United States. The ICEA, which has remained primarily a consumer organization, today has over 11,000 members worldwide and publishes an array of educational books, tapes, and videos. They continue to support their original beliefs that birth belongs to each individual family and that parents have the right to make informed choices.

The founding of La Leche League International (LLLI) in 1956 by a group of concerned women from the Chicago area is a strong example of a consumer-led coalition. The seven women cofounders had breast-fed their babies without the support or encouragement of their doctors or the nurses in the hospital. One of the founders, Marian Tompson, thought that it was strange that mothers who bottle-fed their babies were given much support, but women who wanted to breast-feed their babies were consistently advised to give up. The plan of the founding members was to offer encouragement and information about breast-feeding to their friends and neighbors through small support-group classes.

Doctors initially objected to these women giving out "professional medical information," but LLLI members held fast and increased their efforts in researching the effects of formula and early solids on the infant, as well as the emotional aspects of breast-feeding. League members resolved that they were, after all, the ones who were breast-feeding, not the doctors. LLLI today prints materials, sponsors seminars and support groups, trains facilitators, and encourages breast-feeding worldwide.

LLLI, though singular in its focus on breast-feeding, has provided a tangible network of support for women who seek alternative birth options. Referrals to sympathetic doctors and home-birth midwives are easily found at local LLLI meetings. Women tell of their experiences in finding supportive practitioners, as well as sharing their birth and breast-feeding stories. LLLI has been responsible for the demedicalization of breast-feeding and continues to have a strong influence on the humanization of childbirth practices.

The women's movement in the 1960s and 1970s created an atmosphere where women questioned medical practices concerning their bodies. Many feminists feel that the right to choice in childbirth is the right to ultimately control their bodies. In 1971 the Boston Women's Health Collective produced a book titled *Our Bodies, Ourselves* that stressed the importance of women reclaiming responsibility for their bodies. The authors felt it was essential for women to know how their bodies functioned, especially during pregnancy, labor, and birth. The book contained pictures of home births in the Boston area and discussed who accepted the responsibility for birth outcomes. The Boston Women's Health Collective introduced women to the idea of the transforming power of birth and to midwives who could assist them as opposed to physicians who would try to control the physiology of the birth process.

During the 1970s many counterculture groups emerged and began using *Our Bodies, Ourselves* as a guide for women's health care. These groups were most prevalent on the West Coast, but there were others sprinkled throughout the United States. One such group started The Farm in Tennessee, an intentional community of originally three hundred like-minded vegetarians and would-be farmers. In the early 1970s founders Ina May Gaskin and her husband Stephen attended the births of women in this alternative community and began teaching what Ina May called "spiritual midwifery" in her 1975 book of the same name. This couple saw themselves as traditionalists, yet at the same time they felt strongly that women had the right to choose where and how they were to give birth. In Ina May's words, "We feel that returning the major responsibility for normal childbirth to well-trained midwives rather than have it rest with a predominately male and profit-oriented medical establishment is a major advance in self-determination for women."[12]

This rise of home-birth activism in the 1970s, fueled by freedom of choice, sparked the reemergence of the midwife all across the United States. The gentle birth revolution has spread from places like The Farm to middle America. Other grass-roots organizations have formed to educate both consumers and professionals. The International Association of Parents and Professionals for Safe Alternatives in Childbirth (NAPSAC) has been working toward maternity care reform since 1975. Founded by Lee and David Stewart after the births of their five children, all born at home into the hands of their father, NAPSAC worked throughout the 1970s and 1980s to support couples and provide legal aid for midwives and doctors who found themselves battling the system. Sometimes couples would use litigation to achieve their rights to an out-of-hospital birth, relying on organizations like NAPSAC for support. NAPSAC is active to this day in the reform movement.

The dividing lines have been drawn, setting the stage for revolutionary or adversarial activity. The consumer remains the last to be consulted when decisions concerning maternity care are made. Yet birthing women do have the power—the consumer power—to change the current system. Thousands of letters in support of midwifery-based maternity services poured into the White House during the health care reform committee discussions in 1993.

Maternity care reform pioneer Dr. Michel Odent believes that we will quickly move into a "post-electronic age of childbirth" when women are again in control of birth and technology takes its rightful place as a tool for special circumstances.[13]

5
Midwifery in America—An Emerging Tradition

The term *midwife* (meaning literally "with woman") is often used to describe anyone, other than a doctor, who helps a woman through her pregnancy, labor, and birth. As we saw in chapter 3, women traditionally have attended other women in childbirth, drawing on the strength of their own experiences giving birth to support and empower them. The knowledge of birthing was passed from generation to generation. This continuity of tradition was interrupted by the development of obstetrics as a profession and the institutionalization of childbirth. The traditions of childbirth are now being restored by the women who are educating other women and helping reclaim mastery over their bodies and their ability to give birth. Traditions of prevention rather than cure, as well as respect for intimacy, privacy, family integrity, responsibility, patience, and the understanding of what it means to be a woman, are the "tools" a midwife uses during a labor and birth. It is the consumer, the birthing woman and her family, who has led this resurgence, for ultimately she is the one who gives birth; the midwife or obstetrician simply attends her. Thanks to these women the profession of midwifery, virtually eliminated by the American Medical Association (AMA) in the 1920s and 1930s, is reemerging in the United States.

A midwife making a home visit in Vermont.

The Midwifery Model of Maternity Care

The midwifery model recognizes that pregnancy and birth are natural states. It focuses on the close, natural relationship between mother and child; during pregnancy and birth, it sees the needs of mother and baby as a finely tuned integrated system. Women are encouraged to be in charge of their lives and their experiences. When a mother cooperates with her environment and a balance is established between herself and her relationships, she shares this balance with her child. All organisms on earth constantly seek a balanced state. The midwifery model of care recognizes the dynamics of the mind-body connection. Midwives often encourage women to see pregnancy as an opportunity to heal imbalances in self and relationship.

The medical model, on the other hand, views pregnancy and the birth process on a very physical level. Doctors see the potential for physical problems that could occur for the mother and baby, and they deal with them in a technological way. The midwifery model sees pregnancy as part of a life continuum incorporating all of life's experiences, including childbirth. The midwifery model also recognizes and acknowledges the influence of many factors on the outcome of pregnancy and birth.

Physicians and midwives who follow the midwifery model embrace a non-interventionist approach to childbearing that lets nature take its course during labor and birth. When they remove themselves from actively managing a birth, the practitioners experience labor and birth from a special vantage point. They can watch, listen, and observe each woman as she gives birth in a way that is powerful, life-affirming, and joyful. They become more conscious of the connections between attitude and outcome, between fear and failure, between trust and surrender. Many traditional midwives and certified nurse-midwives (CNMs) have become very adept at recognizing energy blocks that can influence the outcome of a birth. When a midwife recognizes an energy block, she can use her skills as a facilitator to eliminate the need for technical intervention by simply dealing with the emotional aspects of labor and delivery.

Traditional midwife Mary Jackson relates the story of a woman who was having her baby at home. Her labor progressed well until she reached five

centimeters' dilation. The woman continued to have contractions, but they were no longer effective in causing dilation. Jackson decided to take the woman for a walk on the beach. While they were walking, Jackson sensitively asked her if there was anything she was holding onto that would keep her from opening up. The woman finally got in touch with something that she felt might be holding her back: She had never told her husband that she had had an abortion when she was younger. She said she was afraid that he would think less of her for having had one. Jackson encouraged her to share her secret with her husband when they returned home. She left the couple alone, and the woman was able to discuss her fears with her husband. Many tears were shed by both husband and wife, and they soon called for their midwife. The woman's contractions had intensified, and within the hour their baby son was born. Without knowing what was causing the problem, Jackson had sensitively recognized the blocked energy and helped the woman get in touch with it by turning inward. The midwife had focused on the woman and her inner needs rather than providing medical intervention for a stalled labor.

COMPLICATIONS DURING A HOME BIRTH

Midwives are experienced in identifying, and are prepared to deal with, the minor complications that sometimes arise during birth. When midwives come together, whether locally in support groups and peer review meetings or nationally at midwife conventions, they share their best or their scariest birth stories. They use these sessions to educate themselves and to receive support from other practicing midwives. Actually, whenever two or more midwives meet, birth stories naturally abound. I have experienced many of these sessions and have heard hundreds of first-hand accounts of midwives dealing successfully with problem births.

A common concern of couples contemplating a home birth is how midwives handle emergencies or complications during labor and birth. Remember that midwives see healthy women and screen for problems during pregnancy. A midwife will automatically refer women with pregnancy-related problems such as high blood pressure, heart problems, high blood sugar levels, or low iron to an obstetrician. She will continually check and observe a woman's physical and emotional state during regular prenatal visits. Midwives do not hesitate to refuse to attend a home birth if they are even slightly suspicious of serious complications that may require a hospital setting.

Traditionally, midwives "try every trick in the book" when dealing with a slow or difficult labor before calling in a physician or transporting a laboring woman to the hospital. The "tricks" that midwives use include simple techniques for relaxation and breathing but may also include the use of bodywork, massage, herbs, homeopathy, and acupuncture. These techniques are utilized with the understanding that childbirth is a physical, mental, emotional, and spiritual process that needs to occur in a balanced and integrated way.

The midwife at a home birth will have all her instruments laid out, readily accessible, and the oxygen tank turned on, so that what might be an emergency becomes a matter of routine. Many couples worry that the umbilical cord may be wrapped around the baby's neck, a very common occurrence that can be easily handled by a midwife in a home birth. About 25 percent of all babies have the cord wrapped around their necks. A midwife feels the tautness of the cord and slips it over the baby's head or down over the shoulder. If it is too tight to move, the midwife clamps and cuts it, knowing that the rest of the baby must be born as quickly as possible. Such babies may also need a little help getting their breathing started.

Some babies "get stuck," a situation called shoulder dystocia. They are gently eased out with position changes of the mother, manipulations of the baby, and sometimes emergency episiotomies.

My own third birth went amazingly quickly. I spent early labor walking up and down a quiet street, occasionally hugging a tree during a strong contraction. After only two hours I climbed into our outdoor spa. There I labored for another two hours and then started to push. The midwife had climbed into the tub with me and my partner, and just after the baby's head emerged, she checked to determine whether the cord was around the baby's neck. It was not, but she did find that the cord had partially emerged with the head and was being pinched between the baby's shoulder and my pubic bone. In addition, the baby was stuck. His heartbeat decreased rapidly. The midwife acted quickly to rotate the baby's shoulders and bring him out of me, through the water, and up into my arms. Abraham was limp and blue, but he pinked up right away and nursed within the first three minutes of birth.

A midwife in southern California told of attending a twin birth at home. She finished delivering the second baby, reached up to check for the placenta, and discovered a third infant. Since she had never attended the birth of triplets, she asked the husband if he wanted them all to go to the hospital. He assured her he had confidence in her skills, and she then assisted the third baby into the world.

When a situation needs more than the midwife can offer, she has the

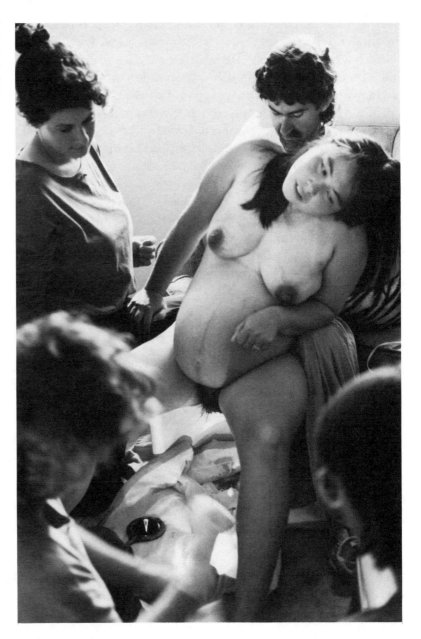

Midwives watch and wait as a woman relaxes between contractions. She chose to birth on a Dutch-style portable birth stool.

mother transported to the hospital. Midwives transport laboring women to hospitals for a variety of reasons. Most transports are for labors that progress slowly. Women with slow labors often get tired and need assistance with fluid administration and possible augmentation of labor with synthetic oxytocin. If the midwife has good rapport with the backup doctor and the hospital, the birth can often proceed as if the mother and midwife were still home. When Jill Cohen, an Oregon midwife, takes a client to the hospital, her consulting physician listens carefully, asks Jill her opinion, makes suggestions, and sometimes allows her to "catch" the baby.

Other hospitals and doctors are openly hostile to home-birth midwives and their clients. A Texas midwife called 911 and asked for immediate assistance as soon as she detected the umbilical cord coming out before the baby was born. She told the mother to get on her hands and knees; she then put her gloved hand inside the woman's vagina and held back the baby's head, thus keeping it from cutting off its own oxygen. She stayed that way during the transport to the hospital and the emergency cesarean that followed. Instead of being thanked for saving this baby's life, she was ridiculed for doing home birth and was later investigated by the state.

A prolapsed cord and a baby's lack of response to resuscitation efforts are two of the most dramatic emergency situations that can happen in a home birth. In this case, the midwife's education and experience helped her handle the problem quickly and correctly.

Midwifery Education—Education versus Experience

Empirically trained midwives the world over, especially in Third World countries, attend three-quarters of all births. These women often have no formal education and may simply be women who have given birth themselves. Their familiarity with the birth process is experiential, and their customs tell them that childbirth is normal. These midwives are usually called *lay midwives*. Lay midwives in the United States have often begun practicing after their own disappointing birth experiences in hospitals.

The lay midwives that responded to the home-birth movement of the 1970s were usually young mothers who had an awareness of the need for alternative birth choices. Many couples could not find physicians or CNMs in their area so they turned to nurses, childbirth educators, or neighbors for assistance and support. A great many couples ignored their fear of and warnings by the medical establishment and gave birth at home by themselves.

The women who stepped forth to help couples learned by doing, and they developed their own styles of care that were similar to the styles of CNMs but were not limited by legal and hospital restrictions. These providers instantly received the title of "midwife." Other couples came to these "midwives" as the word spread through the community's grapevine. The holistic health movement of the early 1980s emphasized the interrelatedness of the emotional, social, psychological, and spiritual aspects of healing and resulted in more couples seeking alternative care for pregnancy. Midwives viewed themselves as protectors of women and children and of normal birth. Many times a midwife was the birthing mother's friend and was never seen as an authority figure. Midwives did not deliver babies; they taught women how to care for themselves during pregnancy, how to acknowledge their ability to give birth, and how to care for their babies after they were born.

Lay midwives have grown up, so to speak. After attending several hundred births, some women sought even longer and more difficult apprenticeships from accredited schools or foreign programs. These early midwives were often leaders in their states, pushing for standardized education, licensing, and third-party reimbursement. Some even started midwifery schools to train and certify others. Midwives increasingly see themselves as true professionals. A lay midwife can also be referred to as an empirical, spiritual, or traditional birth attendant (TBA).

Most industrialized countries have programs that are specifically designed to teach midwifery. The United States has several of these accredited programs. The training includes studies in anatomy, physiology, biology, chemistry, psychology, and nutrition; care during pregnancy, labor, birth, and postpartum; and care of the newborn. A midwife learns how to differentiate between what is normal and what is not. She recognizes when she needs to seek assistance. These practitioners are referred to as *direct-entry midwives.*

They must pass an examination after completing the program in order to receive a license to practice. Yet the license to practice in one state does not ensure the ability to practice in another, due to the lack of common legislation governing the practice of midwifery. The United States has no federal legislation that defines the educational requirements for licensing or parameters in which a midwife will practice.

The legal status of direct-entry midwives is dependent on individual state laws. In some southern states it is only necessary for a woman who either wants to practice midwifery or who has been practicing to register at the county courthouse. California and Colorado do not have uniform laws governing the practice of midwifery. Several times in Colorado, and for twenty years in California, bills that would legalize direct-entry midwifery were voted down or killed in committee by strong lobbying from the medical associations of each state.[1]

Even in states that issue midwifery licenses, many midwives refuse to be governed by them. In Florida, licensing was mandated several years ago. Soon after dozens of midwives registered and became licensed, the state began investigating each one, revoking licenses at the slightest infraction of rules and regulations. This quickly reduced the number of midwives; others practiced illegally. On the one hand it is good for midwives to be licensed, recognized, and regulated: It assures a standard of education and provides for peer review. On the other hand licensing limits a midwife's scope of practice to whatever a state committee judges to be "normal."

The following states and territory do not provide licensing for direct-entry midwives and have laws prohibiting the practice of midwifery. It is illegal to practice midwifery in these areas, and the midwives who choose to practice do so at great personal risk.

Illinois	Maryland	Pennsylvania
Iowa	New York	West Virginia
Kansas	North Carolina	Virgin Islands
Kentucky		

The following states, federal district, and commonwealth make no determination concerning the practice of direct-entry midwifery. These areas are referred to as being "alegal." Midwives who practice in these areas are subject to random selective prosecution for practicing medicine or midwifery without a license.

Alabama	Maine	North Dakota	Vermont
Connecticut	Massachusetts	Ohio	Virginia
Delaware	Michigan	Oklahoma	Wisconsin
Georgia	Minesota	South Dakota	Wyoming
Hawaii	Missouri	Tennessee	Washington, D.C.
Idaho	Nebraska	Utah	Puerto Rico
Indiana	Nevada		

The following states have enacted legislation that regulates the practice of direct-entry midwifery. Each state has its own requirements for obtaining and maintaining a license to practice midwifery. It is up to the individual practitioner to decide whether or not to follow the state mandates in her home state to apply for licensing and to work within the guidelines of practice. Some midwives obtain licenses and others do not.

Alaska	Colorado	Montana	Oregon
Arizona	Florida	New Hampshire	Rhode Island
Arkansas	Louisiana	New Jersey	South Carolina
California	Mississippi	New Mexico	Texas

The last group of midwives, called *certified nurse-midwives* (CNMs), are those with formal medical education. In order to become a CNM in the United States, a person must attend an accredited school of nursing and receive either an associate's degree or a bachelor's degree in the applied science of nursing. The individual must pass the licensing examination in his or her state and usually must complete one year of work in a hospital labor and delivery area before being admitted to one of twenty-nine nurse-midwifery training programs in the country. CNMs are relatively recent additions to obstetric care.

All fifty states license CNMs. Almost all states regulate nurse-midwifery through the Registered Nurses Board of each state. To inquire whether a particular practitioner is licensed or registered with your state, call the state offices that govern medical practices. You may also call the American College of Nurse-Midwives (ACNM) or the Midwives Alliance of North America (MANA) for further information (see Appendix F).

The first program for the training of CNMs was the Frontier Nursing Service, founded in 1925 by Mary Breckenridge in Leslie County, Kentucky. The second school of nurse-midwifery was started in 1932 through the Maternity Center Association (MCA) in New York. Both programs were begun in an effort to provide quality care for the poor and underprivileged in America. The MCA gave entrance priority to public health nurses or practicing midwives from states with high infant mortality rates. It was expected that these CNMs would return to their states and establish public health programs for

the training and supervising of lay midwives. The ACNM, founded in 1955, was created to assure safety and quality of nurse-midwifery education. National accreditation of educational programs wasn't begun until 1970.[2]

The CNM plays a special role in health care because she can work within the established system with obstetricians or be directly hired by a hospital. CNMs are the only midwives that are allowed to deliver babies in hospitals. Working in this capacity, the CNM is no longer seen as the competitor that the traditional midwife had been. However, though it appears that she is a respected member of the health care team, she is often caught in the middle. She is sensitive and often fosters the type of family-centered care that couples had begun demanding in the 1970s, yet as she continues to seek change, the CNM is often criticized by the physicians or hospital that hires her. Doctors sometimes refuse to support the granting of hospital privileges to independent CNMs. In the United States some lay midwives have accused CNMs of catering to the physicians, of becoming handmaidens to the doctors, or worse, being mini-doctors themselves. CNMs are often targets for animosity all the way around.

Midwives Confront the System

The first awareness of the home-birth movement in the 1970s came through a highly publicized court case in Santa Cruz county in 1974. Lay midwife Raven Lang, who had taught childbirth education and provided labor support for women in the hospital during birth, began to help couples give birth at home. In 1971 Lang and seven other lay midwives opened the Birth Center in Santa Cruz in an effort to provide adequate prenatal care for women who wanted to have home births. The doctors of the county had earlier met and voted to refuse care to any woman who intended to give birth at home. The women running the Birth Center met regularly and brought knowledgeable practitioners into the area for workshops. They learned to assess fetal condition, take blood pressures, handle hemorrhages, and repair lacerations. They learned about the importance of nutrition, and they learned newborn resuscitation procedures. As the Birth Center became successful, more women in and around the Santa Cruz area began to use the services of the midwives.

In 1974 a couple used the Birth Center for prenatal care. What this couple failed to tell the midwives, who had felt uneasy about the way the couple acted, was that they were undercover agents for the state of California. When two midwives were summoned to the home of the undercover agent for a supposedly premature labor, money was forced into their hands as soon as they entered the door and they were arrested. Raven Lang, who was no longer living in the area but happened to be visiting that day, was notified about the event by one of the other midwives. Lang arrived at the Birth

Center after notifying the press. She was just in time to see the police removing everything from the house as evidence of the "midwifery ring."[3]

Three midwives were charged with treating a physical condition and practicing medicine without a license. The court case went on for several years and ended up in the Supreme Court of California. The district attorney of Santa Cruz eventually dropped the case because the Birth Center had closed and the midwives were no longer practicing. Even though the Supreme Court finally ruled against the midwives, saying that they were practicing medicine without a license, the midwives felt that they had won a small victory. The publicity helped the cause of home birth by exposing the injustice of a medical monopoly over childbirth.[4] However, the arrest and prosecution of midwives for home birth did not end in 1978 with this case.

Since 1974 there have been forty-five investigations and/or court cases involving direct-entry midwives in California alone. One California attorney, Stephen Keller, who has defended many of these midwives, has compared these investigations to a modern-day witch hunt. Many midwives have become covert in their practice or have left the state fearing prosecution. Others have become active in the California Association of Midwives (CAM), helping to push through state legislation. It took twenty years of bill introductions, revisions, defeats, and reintroductions before the very first bill recognizing midwives was passed in California in 1993. Although this first law is very conservative and restricts the scope of practice, CAM midwives hope to have it amended.

Many direct-entry midwives today are forced to practice outside legal definition. As of 1993, direct-entry midwifery was clearly *legal* in only sixteen states, clearly *illegal* in ten states, and in a legal gray area in the remaining twenty-four states, where the freedom to practice depended on the politics of state courts and regulatory boards. Arkansas is one state that in 1979 made it illegal for lay midwives to attend births, leaving many long-practicing midwives out of work and many poor rural families without access to maternity care. After ten years of court cases and vague and confusing legislation, Bill Clinton, then governor of Arkansas, finally approved a uniform midwifery law.[5]

Midwives are discriminated against in many ways, even in states where they are authorized to practice. For example, if a baby dies or is stillborn in the hospital, it is considered the will of God. If a baby dies or is stillborn at home, the midwife is charged with felony manslaughter, which is subject to the death penalty in some states and life imprisonment in others. While many of these cases have gone to trial, fortunately no midwife has been jailed for manslaughter. Nevertheless, midwives must still endure the stress of court, lawyers' fees, and loss of income, all of which can amount to hundreds of thousands of dollars.

Statistically, direct-entry midwives have an excellent record for safe and healthy home-birth practices. In New Mexico, direct-entry midwives have been legally recognized since 1980, after practicing midwifery openly since 1921. Statistics have been kept on the outcomes of home births in New Mexico. To no one's surprise, statistics for midwife-attended births are much better than those for physician-attended births in the areas of infant and maternal death, transport, episiotomy, and cesarean section.

Many opponents to midwifery argue that good statistics are due to the fact that home-birth midwives only treat normal or low-risk women. However, the statistics at the North Central Bronx Hospital in New York City put that argument to rest. At this inner-city hospital, where 60 to 80 percent of the pregnant women are considered high risk and sometimes over 30 percent are addicted, the cesarean rate is only 14 percent—the lowest in all of New York City. This is entirely due to the nurse-midwifery service, which began at the hospital as a project of the MCA.[6]

Pediatrician Marsden Wagner, former European head of the World Health Organization (WHO), Maternal & Child Health Division, has stated before legislative committees that WHO has maintained a policy for thirty years that states that "care during normal pregnancy, birth and following birth should be the duty of the midwifery profession."[7]

Midwifery in the Future

The professional CNM continues to fight to have the right to provide a midwifery model of care to a growing number of couples who seek alternatives. In 1985 the ACNM created a home-birth practice committee to assist

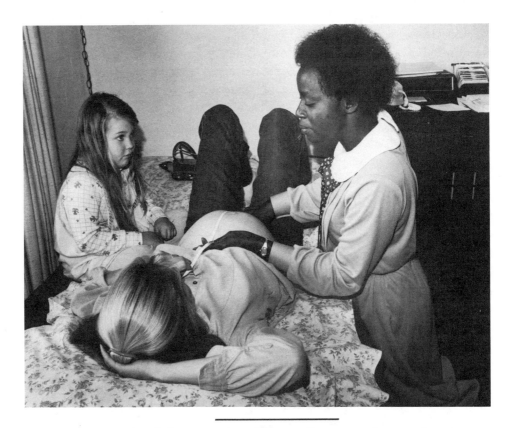

*Certified nurse midwives offer excellent prenatal care and
education in a variety of settings.*

CNMs in establishing home-birth practices. Some CNMs have worked persistently for several years to obtain hospital privileges. Today 85 percent of the four thousand CNMs in this country work in hospitals. CNMs have even done battle with the federal government and the court system to obtain their legal right to practice. The Federal Trade Commission has intervened on behalf of midwives in at least two attempts to deny them hospital privileges.[8] Many CNMs cannot practice in some states because those states require them to have a master's degree. The ACNM is working with individual state legislatures to remedy this licensing confusion. More and more midwives are being seen both by the medical profession and consumers as viable providers of safe, natural maternity care. This realization creates a separate problem—the lack of enough CNMs in the United States to provide this care.

Kitty Ernst, CNM and director of the National Association of Childbearing Centers (NACC), states that there just aren't enough midwives to fill the demand of concerned couples seeking choices in childbirth. She, along with a committee of educators across the country, has created the Community-Based Nurse-Midwifery Education Program (CNEP), which allows qualified registered nurses to study at home under the guidance of an experienced CNM mentor. The student midwife can stay in her own community, maintain her family life, and come away with a master's degree in nurse-midwifery in less than four years. Upon completion of the program, each student agrees to become a mentor so that the numbers of students will continue to increase exponentially. If the current program works in the way that Ernst and her colleagues have designed it, there will be over ten thousand midwives by the year 2001. There are currently four thousand CNMs in the United States.[9]

In 1981 Sister Angela Murdough, president of ACNM, hosted a meeting of alternative-childbirth practitioners, lay midwives, direct-entry midwives, and CNMs. The purpose of the meeting was to coalesce support for midwifery in general and to address the common causes and concerns of individual midwives. The Midwives Association of North America (MANA) was formed from this gathering. MANA later changed its name to Midwives Alliance of North America as groups with different philosophical approaches to midwifery came together. Traditionalists concerned with preserving the integrity of the family joined with feminists who were concerned with women's right to control their reproductive capacities. Both welcomed diverse cultural groups that had remained virtually hidden from public view: Amish, Mexican American, Mormon, Jewish, Muslim, and Asian women came together as midwives, but more importantly as women, in a show of solidarity. It was and is the hope of MANA that this union of midwives will not only support the work efforts of a group of dedicated women but also demonstrate that the midwifery model of maternity care is mother-centered, thus focused on human need.

CNMs and direct-entry midwives have learned to put aside differences, to respect one another's educational processes, and to work together so that more women and families can benefit from their services. Serving together on at least two national committees, CNMs and direct-entry midwives are working on creating educational standards that will help to quickly increase the number of midwives available.

Above all, midwives recognize birth as a life event where women come together, especially when that event is not invaded by the use of technology and institutional rituals. Midwives see all women in a very human way no matter what their religion, race, or nationality. Midwife and author Elizabeth Davis writes, "A strong motive for becoming a midwife is the common desire of women to come closer to one another—not just emotionally as friends but in the powerful sense of working together and establishing support systems for one another."[10]

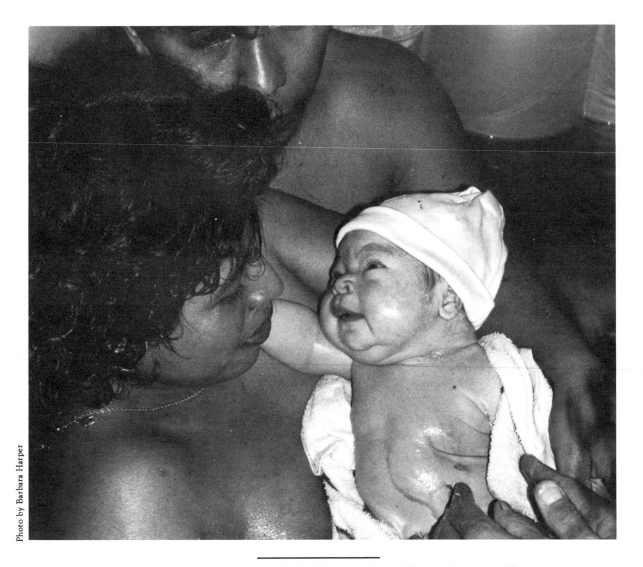

Kelly Vanessa was a very large baby. The water helped her mother to quickly change positions so the midwife could help guide the baby out.

6

Water Birth

The thought of birthing a baby into water seems startling to many people until they hear the rationale and reasons behind such an interesting approach to birth. People usually listen with curiosity, acknowledging that most women feel comfortable in water, especially when pregnant. Almost everyone draws the same conclusion: "Water birth certainly makes sense."

Most people feel relaxed and find great comfort in water. Perhaps because we begin our lives in the womb surrounded by liquid, this basic familiarity stays with us. Human beings are comprised primarily of water, and many special characteristics we have link us to aquatic mammals; perhaps we carry the memory of a time when the human species had an "aquatic interlude." A three-day-old fetus is 97 percent water; at eight months the fetus is 81 percent water. By the time a human has grown to adulthood, the adult body is still 50 to 70 percent water, depending on the amount of fatty tissue.[1]

Human beings' natural alliance with water is best witnessed by observing babies who can swim naturally and easily long before they learn to sit up or crawl. During their first year of life, babies will calmly and happily paddle under water, gazing around with eyes wide open. Babies instinctively know not to breathe while their heads are submerged under water.

Why Water Birth?

For thousands of years women have been using water to ease labor and facilitate birth. Wherever there has been even slightly warm water, there have been women bathing in it, using it ritually, and finding great comfort in it, especially in labor. Soaking in a tub of water to ease labor sounds inviting to most women. If the water is where a woman wants to be and there are no complications, then in the water is where she will feel the most comfortable. When it is time to birth the baby, there is no reason to ask the mother to get out of the water.

When a woman in labor relaxes in a warm tub, free from gravity's pull on her body, with sensory stimulation reduced, her body is less likely to secrete stress-related hormones. This allows her body to produce the pain inhibitors—endorphins—that complement labor. Noradrenaline and catecholamines, the hormones that are released during stress, actually raise the blood pressure and can inhibit or slow labor. At the 1987 Pre- and Perinatal Psychology Association of North America conference, Dr. Serge Weisel presented a study of women who labored in warm water in Belgium.[2] He stated that women with hypertension (high blood pressure) experienced a drop in blood pressure between ten and fifteen minutes after entering a warm bath. A laboring woman who is able to relax physically, is able to relax mentally as well. Many women, midwives, and doctors acknowledge the analgesic effect of water. One obstetrical nurse who had a water birth described sitting in a tub of warm water during labor as similar to "getting a shot of Demerol, but without the side effects."

Women achieve a level of comfort in water that in turn reduces their levels of fear and stress. Women's perception of pain is greatly influenced by their level of anxiety. When labor becomes physically easier, a woman's ability to concentrate calmly is improved and she is able to focus inward on the birth processes. Water helps some women reach a state of consciousness in which their fear and resistance are diminished or removed completely; their bodies then relax, and their babies are born in the easiest way possible.

Many women report being better able to concentrate once they get into the water. Doctors and midwives who attend water births find that the mere sound of water pouring into the tub helps some women release whatever inhibitions were slowing the birth, at times so quickly that the birth occurs even before the tub is filled. Oftentimes women climb into the tub to labor and the birth happens before they can get out.

Another benefit of water birth is the elasticity that water imparts to the tissues of the perineum, reducing the incidence and severity of tearing and the need for episiotomies. Dr. Michel Odent reported that in one hundred water births he had attended, no episiotomies were performed and there were only twenty-nine cases of tearing, all of which were minor surface tears.[3] A 1989 nationwide survey published in the *Journal of Nurse-Midwifery* produced statistics indicating that the use of water for labor and birth results in fewer incidents of perineal tearing with less severity.[4]

The body responses of mother and baby are intricately linked. The ease of the mother who labors and gives birth in water is transfered to the child who is born in the water. The emotions the mother feels can also be felt by the child because the hormones her body secretes in response to her emotions are absorbed by the child. In a medically controlled birth, drugs or synthetic hormones the mother receives are also received by the child. If the mother's delivery is easy and smooth, so, too, is the baby's birth. The baby spends less time in the cramped birth canal and is free from fear, frustration, or other painful emotions a long and difficult labor might arouse in the mother.

The baby emerges into the water and is "caught" either by the mother, father, or birth attendant. While in the water the child has freedom of movement in familiar fluid surroundings. A baby's limbs can also unfold with greater ease during those first moments when he leaves the mother's body and enters the water. The water offers a familiar comfort after the stress of the birth, reassuring the child and allowing his bodily systems time to organize. During the birth, babies often open their eyes, move in all directions, and use their limbs. Water mitigates the shock and sensory overload that are so often an inextricable part of birth. Lights and sounds are softer when perceived from under the water, and even the touch of his mother's skin to his own tender skin is softened by the presence of water. The same element, familiar and secure for the baby, is comforting and relaxing for the mother. Together, the mother and baby are profoundly affected by this gentlest of gentle births.

Water Birth History

In the sixth century B.C., Aristotle concluded that water was the first principle of life. He observed that the seeds of everything had a "moist nature." However, it was not until the 1700s that scientists began to understand and identify the properties of water, including its value as a form of hydrotherapy. An obscure book called *Water Cures*, printed in London in 1723, describes the benefits of water used for all kinds of conditions, including bathing during pregnancy and labor.[5] Intuitively, human beings have always been drawn to the soothing comfort of water.

Historically, there is little concrete evidence that ancient cultures practiced water birth on any scale, but it has been used by cultures all over the world. There are legends that the ancient Egyptians birthed selected babies under water. These babies became priests and priestesses. The ancient Minoans on the island of Crete are said to have used a sacred temple for water birth. Art on frescoes in the Minoan ruins depict dolphins and their special connection with humans and water. One can only speculate about the connection between these pictures and their creators. The Chumash Indians of the central California coast tell stories about their women laboring in tide pools and shallow inlets along the beach while the men of the tribe drummed and chanted. Chumash elder Grandfather Semu, now in his late eighties, recalls that when he was a boy, women would often go to the beach and labor in the shallow water. He also remembers that on many of these occasions, dolphins would appear nearby in the water, staying close to the woman until the baby was born.[6] Other Indian tribes in North, Central, and South America, as well as the Maoris of New Zealand and the Samoan people of the Pacific, may have given birth in shallow ocean or river environments. Traditions from the Hawaiian Islands maintain that certain families on the islands have been born in water for many thousands of generations.

Many midwives suspect that water birth was taking place before the advent of physicians and hospitals, even though it has not been documented. Where there was water, especially warm water, women used it to relieve labor pains. The first *recorded* modern water birth took place in France in 1803. The case, which was detailed in a French medical society journal, reports that a woman who had been laboring for forty-eight hours sought temporary relief from her nonprogressing labor in a warm bath. After just moments in the tub, the baby came out so quickly that she didn't have time to leave the water to deliver her child.[7] Subsequent reports of water birth were scattered until the 1960s, when documentation of water births began in the Soviet Union.

Around that time interesting stories emerged from the Soviet Union about the work of Igor Charcovsky, a primarily self-educated Russian scientist and healer who conducted research on animals laboring and birthing in water. He also observed human babies' behavior in water, including that of his daughter Veta, who was born prematurely in 1963. Charcovsky placed his newborn daughter in a tub of warm water for several weeks, theorizing that she would not have to combat gravity and subsequently would not waste as much energy to survive as she would struggling in the hospital incubator. Charcovsky's daughter survived, and he continued experimenting with water, newborns, and the effects of gravity on all aspects of human labor.[8]

Beyond the Leboyer Bath

During the same time period as the discoveries in Russia, Dr. Frederick Leboyer introduced the concept of the warm bath for the baby after birth. Through his search for ways to bring babies less violently into the world, Leboyer discovered the beneficial effects of warm water on newborns.

The Leboyer bath consists simply of placing the infant, directly after birth, into a basin of water heated to body temperature. The baby then can experience the comforting return to the pleasure of the fluid world it has just left behind. During Leboyer baths, babies are often wide-eyed and attentive and smile serenely as they move their arms and legs playfully in the water. They can even swim and propel themselves in the water.

Leboyer practiced in a hospital just outside Paris in the small suburb of Les Lilas. I had the opportunity to tour the hospital's maternity and labor wards in 1984. A large round tub stood in a separate room adjacent to the traditional delivery room. When asked if women ever gave birth in this tub, the midwife just threw back her head and laughed. "Of course, babies come in the water. Women just don't want to get out once they get comfortable in the water."

When I asked how the tub had become a permanent fixture in this maternity hospital, it was related that Leboyer had become friends with Dr. Michel Odent in Pithiviers in the early 1970s. Odent was the first physician to recognize the beneficial effects of warm water for labor and birth. Leboyer agreed with Odent's philosophy and incorporated the option of using birthing tubs into his hospital practice.

The midwives at the Les Lilas hospital spoke about the differences they observed in the babies born in water. "We can tell which babies have been born in water. They are like little grown-ups. You know that they understand you. It is very special to be with them."

Through his poetic writing and compelling photographs, Leboyer presented the world of the newborn infant as it had never been seen before. His contribution was a giant step toward sensitizing the world to the birth experience from the baby's perspective. Leboyer's vision, which was to eliminate the violence and trauma of birth, has more than anything else influenced the adoption of gentle birthing techniques throughout the world. Leboyer has convincingly shown the world the soothing effects of warm-water immersion for newborns.[9]

Labor Pools in France

One of the first publicly outspoken proponents of water birth was French physician Michel Odent, former head of surgery at a state hospital in Pithiviers, France. By providing women with a warm tub for labor and birth, Odent offered them more comfort and freedom than they had ever known before. "My question was how not to disturb the physiological processes of birth; and when you weigh this question, of course, it makes things different—a different kind of birthing room, water to help some women, darkness, and so on."[10]

The main focus of Odent's work has been to assist each woman to give birth in *her* own way using *her* instincts. According to Odent, understanding this principle transforms birth, making it an intensely rewarding emotional and physical experience. Warm-water baths to rest in during labor—and, for some, to give birth in—are an option for women at Pithiviers. Although he claims water births were never promoted, Odent would say smilingly to a woman in labor, "Water birth is a possibility." This stressed the idea that she should not consciously *plan* to have a water birth but should follow her instincts during labor and birth.

Many women who arrived at Pithiviers to give birth had never heard of water birth, but when they saw the large, circular blue pool full of warm water, many felt a great attraction to it. In his book *Birth Reborn*, Odent writes, "Some women who are strongly drawn to water throughout pregnancy are even more attracted to it during labor. Still others tell us that they don't like the water or can't swim. Yet as labor begins, these same women will suddenly move toward the pool, enter eagerly and not want to leave."[11] The pool, which was seven feet in diameter and two-and-a-half feet deep, was large enough to easily accommodate two people. The pool was filled with ordinary tap water at 98°F and did not contain any added salts or chemicals.

Odent found that when a woman's contractions become more painful and less efficient, resting in a warm bath often provides relief, especially for women whose dilation has not progressed beyond five centimeters. In the pool, labor almost immediately becomes easier and more efficient. In a similar situation in the hospital doctors would, without hesitation, resort to the use of interventions, including the use of drugs.

Women who choose to leave the water before delivery discover what Odent calls the "fetal ejection response." These women suddenly have an urge to leave the water. As they enter the cooler temperature of the air, the change of environment triggers an adrenaline release, and the baby comes very quickly. Odent believes that a woman who has no preconceptions about how her birth *should* be will know whether it is appropriate to remain in the water for the birth or whether she should birth the baby out of the pool.

While in Pithiviers I watched a young woman climb out of the pool and squat, supported by her husband, close to the floor where a white sheet had been spread. The midwife, Dominique Pourré, sat in front of her in complete silence. She had asked me to remain silent as well, telling me that I could better "feel" the birth with my whole self. The only sounds in that darkened room were the beautiful, primal sounds emanating from the mother as she birthed her baby. That experience of normal birth eventually influenced and changed my life.

On the occasion of his one hundredth water birth, Odent published an article summarizing his water-birth experiences for the British medical journal, the *Lancet*. In the article he states, "We have found no risk attached either to labor or to birth underwater. The use of warm water during labor requires further research, but we hope that other experience would confirm that immersion in warm water is an efficient, easy and economical way to reduce the use of drugs and the rate of intervention in parturition."[12]

Odent now lives in London and is actively involved with writing and research on what he calls "primal health." Primal health is dependent on the interconnected functioning of many organ systems in the body, which together form what he calls the primary adaptive system. Odent believes that the conditions for optimal maturation and functioning of the primary adaptive system are largely dependent on the conditions before, during, and after birth. According to Odent, medicine needs to acknowledge the profound influence of pre- and perinatal conditions on health throughout the individual's life span. He stresses that much research must be done to substantiate this hypothesis.

For Odent, water birth itself has not been a goal. Through his work at Pithiviers, Odent strove to enable all women to give birth with confidence in whatever birthing position they chose. This new freedom naturally led to the use of water as a labor and birthing option. It wasn't long before word of Odent's work spread to open-minded parents, physicians, and midwives throughout the world.

Water Birth Comes to America

In the early 1970s the practice of lay midwifery reemerged in the United States, particularly in northern California and the Boston, Massachusetts, area. This change came about in response to the increasing dissatisfaction that women experienced with the care they received in hospitals and from obstetricians. By 1981 a small group of midwives had heard about Dr. Odent's success and the pioneering research of Igor Charcovsky in the Soviet Union.

Many parents wanted to give their children a vastly different entrance into the world, one that was different from their own births, experienced in the era of "twilight sleep" and heavy sedation. Many of these concerned couples had experienced rebirthing, a technique developed in the 1970s for tapping into repressed emotions and memories, including memories of their own births. A rebirthing session involves deep, nonstop breathing, often while sitting in a tub of water, and can result in the spontaneous release of deeply buried emotions. The rebirthing community believes that the memories of your own birth affect your present life and the births of your children. "Rebirthers" began to proclaim that water birth was the only way to have a baby because it was so nontraumatic and peaceful for the baby.

During the early 1980s, when these rebirthing couples began birthing their own babies in water, most of the births were uncomplicated and fulfilling experiences. Parents sometimes left their newborn babies submerged under water for as long as twenty minutes, believing that doing so gave the babies time to completely unfold, relax, and recuperate from the stress of birth. Unfortunately, some couples attempted to birth their babies by themselves, without an experienced midwife or doctor in attendance. There were a few accidental newborn deaths, presumably from leaving the baby under the water too long. This shocked the parents and midwives who had been strong proponents of water birth, and they began to doubt its safety. The parents whose babies had died subsequently learned that the placenta can separate before the umbilical cord stops pulsating, thus leaving the baby without a source of oxygen. Today every water birth practitioner recognizes the fact that a newborn baby needs to be brought to the surface of the water immediately after birth.

As more physicians and childbirth practitioners were willing to work with women who wanted to birth in water, more information on water birth became available. In early 1989 the Waterbirth International project of the Global Maternal/Child Health Association (GMCHA) began to meet the need for accurate information on the use of water for labor and birth. Dr. Michel Odent's book, *Birth Reborn*, was published in the United States in 1984, and the following year the first U.S. birthing center to offer water birth as an option was opened by an obstetrician.

Making Waves in California

In 1985 there was one birthing center in the United States that offered women the same atmosphere that Dr. Michel Odent had created in France. The Family Birthing Center of Upland, in southern California, was opened by Dr. Michael Rosenthal. Inspired by the philosophy and work of Odent, Rosenthal transformed his practice from traditional obstetrics to a noninterventionist approach. The evolution of Rosenthal's obstetrical practice was also affected by his own observations of women giving birth naturally. Rosenthal felt that there was a big difference between parents' level of satisfaction after hospital births and the level of satisfaction of the obstetricians who attended the births. The traditional obstetrical view of a positive birth experience is a safe delivery. However, when Rosenthal talked with parents about their hospital births, they often expressed dissatisfaction. Parents wanted more options and control over giving birth.

Rosenthal's philosophical changes inspired him to open his own birthing center. He and a team of midwives provide an environment that supports women's choices in birth, enriching the birth experience for the entire family. In his former days as a traditional obstetrician, Rosenthal viewed the birth process as a medical event to be controlled on a time line. Since then he has learned to step back and empower the woman to give birth. "When women control the birth process and actively participate free of traditional interventions, they derive emotional strength and a great sense of achievement," states Rosenthal. "At the Family Birthing Center, we feel strongly that women are giving birth. They're not coming here to have their babies delivered. Part of our effort is to restore control of birth back to women. We take the term 'nonintervention' in a very literal sense. It often means that women give birth without me using my hands."

Rosenthal and Linda Church, the certified nurse-midwife (CNM) who worked at the Family Birthing Center for its first five years, have accumulated extensive experience with water birth. By the summer of 1993, almost one thousand women had birthed their babies in water at the center. There were no complications or infections in either the mothers or the babies. Because of the success rate at the Family Birthing Center, Rosenthal's and

The Family Birthing Center of Upland was the first birthing center in the United States to promote the use of water for labor and birth. Karen uses the water to relax in the later stage of labor.

CNM Linda Church listens to fetal heart tones with a doppler. Most women only need to lift their bellies out of the water to let the midwife or doctor assess fetal condition.

Karen touches her baby as it emerges and Dr. Rosenthal reaches to lift the baby out of the water.

Pure bliss as Karen holds her ten-second-old baby close to her body.

Church's work with water birth is receiving increased attention among their colleagues. In turn, women who seek this kind of birth experience have traveled great distances—from as far away as Alaska—to have their babies at the center. "Water birth is a reasonable option for reasonable people," states Rosenthal. "All their lives women have gotten into tubs when they were uncomfortable. They use a warm tub for menstrual cramps or when they've had a bad day. Women expect a warm bath to relax them, and it works." He adds, "The use of warm water for labor and birth might be viewed as radical and new in the human experience; however, from a historical perspective, the use of most obstetric interventions, such as spinal or epidural anesthesia, narcotics, and forceps, are comparatively recent. The use of water should be considered one of the most risk-free interventions. If the bath had been used earlier in this century, we might never have passed through the era of 'twilight sleep' sedation that depressed babies and removed mothers from conscious participation in birth."

An interview with Rosenthal was interrupted by a woman's birthing sounds. When Rosenthal returned, we were invited into the room where the woman was about to give birth. She was kneeling in a large salmon-colored tub filled with warm water and was attended by her husband, who was at her head. Rosenthal, at the tub's edge, was dressed in pale-blue medical scrub trousers and a maroon scrub shirt. The nurse, dressed in street clothes, was next to the father near the mother's head, wiping the mother's face with a cool cloth. The mother had been laboring for a long while and was exhausted. As the child's head crowned, Rosenthal urged the mother to look down under her belly to see the child's head. He encouraged her reach back with her hand and touch it. "Feels like hair," she said, smiling. Rosenthal reached over to a wall switch and turned out the lights in the room, leaving it dimly illuminated with the afternoon's filtered light. A few more pushes and the child had almost completely emerged under the water. The father slid across the side of the tub to get a better look and announced to the mother with a big smile, "It's a girl!" One more push and she was out.

The mother reached into the water and gently lifted her new daughter into her arms, holding her close to her breast. This woman, who just moments ago was exhausted, was now smiling and tearfully kissing her husband. Using a bulb syringe, the midwife suctioned mucus out of the baby's nasal passages and mouth. The baby, who was covered with a thick coating of vernix, rested peacefully in her mother's arms. Within a matter of seconds, the baby opened her eyes to look at her parents. The quiet was undisturbed as this new family enjoyed this precious time. In about half an hour the mother indicated that she was having some new contractions. The umbilical cord was clamped and cut, and the baby was given to the father to hold. The mother got out of the tub and spontaneously delivered the placenta. Shortly afterward mother, father, and baby retired to the large bed in their private birthing room, where they would rest and be together. There they would stay for at least six hours before returning home.

When Rosenthal discusses water birth's benefits, he is cautious about making claims because he feels more scientific documentation needs to be done. "Good parenting throughout a child's life is more important in determining his mental health than the moment of his birth," says Rosenthal. "I believe that the benefits to the fetus derive primarily from being born to a relaxed mother who is conscious and free of drugs. A significant observable fact of a water birth is that the experience is joyful and devoid of fear. The child who shares this experience with its mother reaps the benefits of her positive birth experience for a lifetime. Subsequently the child begins to fit its parents' belief that water babies are somehow special."

In reflecting on the future of water birth, Rosenthal believes it will only become more accessible to greater numbers of people when parents begin to ask for it. "Water birth is a reasonable thing to do, and there is only one way it's going to happen. It will not come from universities; it will not come from doctors; it will come from consumers, that is, mothers and fathers who demand it. As more birthing places offer water birth as an option, women will walk away from doctors who say no. The establishment will be forced to change because the consumer demands it."

Water Birth around the World

GMCHA estimates that between 1970 and 1993 more than ten thousand water births have occurred in homes, birthing centers, and hospitals worldwide, with the greatest increase occurring in the last three years. Water births have taken place in Austria, Australia, Japan, the island of Malta, England, Scotland, Wales, Ireland, Russia and several of the federations of the Newly Independant State, Germany, Belgium, Spain, France, Norway, Sweden, Switzerland, Holland, Denmark, Italy, Iceland, Israel, New Zealand, the Bahamas, Canada, the United States, Mexico, Brazil, and Argentina, among other countries. As information on the viability of water birth spreads, the number of water births increases. What is evident from talking to numerous childbirth practitioners in different countries is that water birth is an appealing choice for women who want to birth their babies naturally, without medical intervention. The birth practitioners who support water birth, whether physicians or midwives, themselves have an underlying respect and reverence for the birth process. They respect the baby as a fully conscious being who deserves exquisite treatment at the time of his or her birth. Dr. Bruce Sutherland, an obstetrician from Australia, states, "Water birth is the most spiritual kind of birth experience." Often midwives and physicians become emotional while describing particular water births they have attended. Without the many distractions of a typical hospital birth, physicians and midwives experience birth as an important passage at which they feel privileged to have been present.

AUSTRIA

Dr. Wolf Jaskulsky displayed just this attitude when talking about his work as the head of obstetrics at a small federal hospital in Austria. The father of three children who had all been born at home, he understood firsthand the importance of supporting and nurturing women during labor and birth. Jaskulsky's conventional training actually hindered him from being able to express his reverence for this process of birth. He says, "Everything I learned in medical school was rubbish. I had to go out in the country and watch midwives so I could learn what normal birth was about. I had to become a midwife." It was actually his wife who suggested that he install a tub in the hospital for warm-water labor, which he did in 1987. He stated that the other obstetricians and the older midwives were quite against his liberal practices. He quietly attended over one hundred water births in the first few years.

Word spread quickly about Jaskulsky, who is called "the midwife doctor," and women traveled from Germany and Italy to labor and give birth in water with Jaskulsky in attendance.

Jaskulsky's confidence in birth as a natural process increased. Over a period of one year, Jaskulsky had performed only one cesarean section. In contrast, during his two-week vacation, his substitute performed five cesareans. In speaking about this vast difference in practice he said, "My colleague would never admit to his anger toward women and some very deeply repressed emotions about his own mother, but it is obvious that there is a problem there. More women would benefit if physicians took the time to recognize and release through therapy this anger."[13]

Recently, however, Jaskulsky has experienced difficulty within the Austrian health care system and has had a more difficult time practicing openly. In the meantime, more midwives and doctors in Austria have been influenced by his work and at least one other clinic has begun to offer water birth.

AUSTRALIA

Water birth has gained some popularity in Australia, in part because of the pioneering work of Dr. Bruce Sutherland, medical director of the Hawthorn Birth and Development Centre. Home-birth midwives have been using water for a number of years, and several large teaching hospitals have installed new tubs in their maternity units. The creative person behind the establishment of the Hawthorn Birth and Development Centre is June Sutherland, who is a traditionally trained midwife and mother of four. Several years before the 1983 opening of the center, June had taken over as office manager for her husband Bruce's busy obstetric practice. She immediately saw the need for change in the treatment of women in labor and during birth.

June and Bruce discussed the needs of his hospital patients and the fact that many women were dissatisfied with their experiences. The women all expressed regret over giving up the control of the birth to someone else. The Sutherlands were aware that there was a need for alternatives to hospital birth, even though Bruce had practiced gentle birth in the hospital for years. He was the first doctor in Australia to use Frederick Leboyer's approach to birth. June suggested that since Bruce could not possibly attend home births

Dr. Bruce Sutherland and June Sutherland.

Photo by Barbara Harper

because of Australian governmental regulations, they should build a "home away from home" for pregnant women and their families. They encountered resistance from the traditional medical community, but June's determination never faltered. Even the health commission stood in their way by not approving the necessary building plans for the center. June went ahead and built the Hawthorn Birth and Development Centre without approved plans, paying very close attention to all the building codes. An essential part of this plan was the installation of a spa large enough to accommodate the birthing woman and all of her family if she should so desire.

Once the tub was operational, it was used for labor and birth by 80 percent of the women who came to their new freestanding birthing center. Women enjoyed the water so much that some were heard to remark, "This is better than making love." Bruce has been present at almost all of the water births at the center. Visibly moved when he speaks about water birth, he says, "It makes so much sense to me and it restores all the control to the woman. We encourage the dads to get in to 'catch' the baby if they want to. I just sit in a chair, sometimes rocking, and witness this magnificent process. It is quite a privilege to be included in such a sacred act. My fellow obstetricians accuse me of taking birth back to the dark ages. I feel sorry for them. They don't have any idea what they are missing." All the staff of the Hawthorn Birth and Development Centre live by its motto, "Love creates and heals."[14]

JAPAN
The Japanese have always incorporated the bath into their daily rituals for the relaxation and health of the family. The bath has been used as a social gathering for centuries. Prior to World War II, most births in Japan were home births attended by midwives. Formal midwifery education in Japan began in the late nineteenth century. The midwife in Japanese culture has always been respected and embraced as a member of the extended family. The medicalization of childbirth in Japan occurred during the American occupation following World War II. The scene for birth quickly shifted to the hospital and the comforts of home were left behind, including the use of warm water for labor. In recent years there has been a resurgence of home birth. Another option for Japanese women is the use of a birth home, usually the midwife's personal residence. Despite the medicalization of childbirth in Japan, midwives continue to be respected, whether attending home births or hospital births. Today there are more than twenty-three thousand medically educated midwives in Japan, whereas in the United States fewer than four thousand CNMs practice.

One Japanese midwife, Fuseiko Sei, who runs her own birth home, offers women the choice to labor and birth in water. Sei has written extensively in

Japan about her experiences, and has been one of the first Japanese midwives to present a paper on her water-birth practices.[15] Water birth is not yet prevalent in Japan, and only a few midwives openly acknowledge the use of birthing tubs. One enthusiastic water-birth midwife reports birthing her own child in water attended by her mother, who is also a midwife. Now she and her mother practice together, running their own birth house where water birth is an open alternative.

MALTA

The island of Malta seems more like the backdrop for a great spy thriller than an environment that would support a natural birthing clinic. Dr. Josie Muscat, along with several midwives, runs the St. James Natural Childbirth Clinic. Laboring women at the clinic experience such innovations as still-life videos showing scenes of waterfalls, oceans, birds, and flowers, accompanied by relaxing music. In an effort to achieve relaxation for women, Muscat has installed a large tub that was specifically designed to incorporate a birthing chair. On November 11, 1987, less than one year after opening the clinic, Muscat "caught" his first baby in the water. Since that first birth more than five hundred babies have been greeted by the warmth and security of this "expanded womb," which contains the baby's mother and father as well. Muscat firmly believes that once a mother's fear threshold is reduced, her ability to give birth naturally returns without the need for intervention. The 2 percent cesarean section rate after the first two hundred births at his center speaks for itself.[16]

UNITED KINGDOM

Carmella and Abel B'Hahn gave birth to their son, Benjaya, in 1986, just two weeks prior to the birth of my second water baby, Abraham. We met in 1987 and compared notes and babies. The two boys played alongside each other while we parents talked about our desire for the message of gentle water birth to spread all over the world. We both wanted to make the information about water labor and birth accessible to the general public. Carmella and Abel went back to England and began an information service and tub rental business. They wrote, lectured, and taught classes that many women found useful in creating a gentle birth environment, even within the hospital.

The women of England who heard about water birth and wanted to have it available to them often rented portable birth pools from people like the B'Hahns or the Active Birth Center in London. The women informed their doctors or midwives that they were going to labor in water. They asked the practitioners to help them work out the details with the hospital staff. The pioneering efforts of Janet Balaskas—founder of The Active Birth Centre and author of several books on natural childbirth—and what she has termed "the active birth movement," has empowered thousands of women to speak up and demand change in British hospitals.

Water births have been taking place in several major hospitals in London since 1987. One out-of-the-way place where water birth is happening is Maidstone Hospital in Kent, England. From the demands of one couple came the redesign of an entire delivery room, now affectionately called "the Lagoon Room" by the patients and staff. Midwife Dianne Garland has become a spokesperson for the very successful birthing unit. She says, "It took some convincing and a great deal of paperwork to push this through. Sometimes I feel like this has been my own little baby. We're now installing our third tub."[17] Over three hundred water births in five years attests to the popularity of this option.

A family-practice physician in Cornwall, Roger Lichy, so believes in water birth that he puts a portable tub on top of his van when he goes to a home birth. His statistics match those of all the other practitioners of water birth: No one has seen any infections in mother or baby, there are fewer and less severe perineal tears, there is less demand for analgesia, and the length of labor has been reduced.[18]

Midwife Margaret Brain, president of the Royal College of Midwives, says, "Any woman that wants to have a water birth should be allowed to have one—just as any woman who wants a home birth should be given the chance to do it and be attended by trained midwives with doctors acting as consultants." She continues, "We have seen that normal women do better with midwives and that home birth is safe in the hands of those who know what they are doing. We simply need more midwives practicing the way we know is best for all women, and we need a health care system that recognizes it."[19]

Epidemiologists Dr. Fiona Alderdice and Mary Renfrew state that there are now approximately twenty-nine National Health Service hospitals where water birth is a readily available option, thus making the United Kingdom the leader worldwide in this new area of gentle birth options.

RUSSIA

Water birth in Russia has been discussed and referred to by many people all over the world. Erik Sidenbladh's book *Water Babies*, which chronicles the life of water-birth pioneer Igor Charcovsky, sparked much speculation about how popular water birth was in the Soviet Union. Many mistakenly thought that it was a common practice in the maternity hospitals throughout the USSR. In actuality, the very first water birth to take place in a state hospital occurred in 1992, attended by an American midwife, Molly Lasser, who lives and works in St. Petersburg.[20] Lasser had a difficult time convincing the hospital staff that water birth was not a danger to either the mother or the baby. The only reports that the medical staff had previously heard about water birth were that it was done by fanatic "fringe" couples at home.

Those "fanatic" couples, some of whom had been trained by Igor Charcovsky, had taken their births into their own control. The hospitals and "roddoms" (from the Russian words for *birth* and *home*) that I visited on two trips to Russia, the Ukraine, and Georgia displayed the most terrifying conditions for childbirth that I had ever seen. Almost all women were drugged or unconscious; physical brutality was common; immediate separation of the mother and baby was standard and continued for two to three days; fathers were not only not allowed in the delivery room, they were not even allowed in the hospital! There is a saying in Russia that a woman who gives birth to her first baby is a hero but a woman who gives birth the second time is a fool. This judgment says more about the tortures that a woman must endure to give birth than about the merits of limiting family size. No wonder water birth and home birth had become popular options among people who were willing to take the chance to be different, risking arrest or imprisonment.

Alexi and Tatyana Sargunas were one of those couples who endured their first birth in the traditional roddom. Feeling very dissatisfied, they heard about Charcovsky and thought they would find out about his ideas. When

Photo by Alexi Sargunas

During a Black Sea birthing expedition, the Sargunas's young daughter watches as a couple prepares to give birth in the warm sea water.

Tatyana became pregnant again, they met and worked with other couples who were preparing to have home births. Charcovsky's theories involved providing women with the opportunity to get used to water during pregnancy and removing any fear of water they or their partners may have. He felt that fear influenced the outcome of a birth more than any other condition. Tatyana swam, meditated, jogged, played in the snow, and prepared herself mentally and physically to birth her second baby in a completely relaxed and peaceful manner.

All three of her daughters were born at home in a Plexiglass tank filled with water, with her husband and children either watching or assisting. During the years that they were having their own children, the Sargunases were also assisting hundreds of other couples in the Moscow area to give birth at home, either by themselves or with Tatyana acting as midwife. Tatyana considers herself a spiritual midwife who has learned through experience and necessity. The Sargunases have started an educational center in Moscow called AKBA/ AQUA—Center of Parents' Culture.

Every summer the center sponsors a water baby expedition to the Crimean coast of the Black Sea. There they teach yoga, healthy living, and swimming for adults and babies. If some of the pregnant women are lucky enough to be due during the trip, those women give birth in the warm salt water of the Black Sea. Many women in Moscow and other cities now plan their conceptions so they can participate in the expedition and deliver their babies in the sea. Approximately forty babies have been born in the sea since 1987.[21]

One couple described their birth in the sea as an incredibly unifying experience—unifying in the sense that they felt connected with all life on the planet by birthing into the abundant sea, out in the fresh salt air, with the trees above them and dolphins cavorting nearby. They felt that their baby's perceptions of the world would be very different from those babies who were born in a hospital and immediately separated from everything and everyone known and familiar. They called their birth an ecological birth and stressed that more couples should look at the impact of birth on our planet.

Although this type of birth experience sounds ideal for some women, certain factors must be considered. Currently the Black Sea is one of the most polluted bodies of water in the world. It suffers from the industrial waste of Eastern Europe and the dumping of radioactive material from nuclear power plants along its shores.

My personal suggestion to couples who seek a "dolphin experience" with their birth is to stay home, hang up a dolphin poster, and play an audiotape

Swimming lessons begin a few days after birth for the Black Sea babies.

of dolphin sounds. Keeping a birth simple and unencumbered always takes precedence over creating special effects.

Couples interested in pursuing birth in the Black Sea or participating in one of the summer expeditions can find more information in Appendix F.

OTHER COUNTRIES

As water birth becomes more common in Europe, major hospitals in Australia, Germany, Belgium, Spain, France, Norway, and Sweden have responded to consumer requests to install tubs. A hospital in Milan is having an architect who specializes in birthing environments redesign their maternity unit to incorporate the use of a tub for labor. It seems that it is only a matter of time before studies will be done in major teaching hospitals around the world on the effectiveness of water during labor and birth.

Questions Everyone Asks about Water Birth

When people first hear about water birth, there are common questions and concerns. These questions come from the doctors, midwives, and nurses—as well as pregnant women and their families—who may never have seen a water birth. Appendix D offers guidelines for those who want to pursue water birth.

HOW DOES THE BABY BREATHE UNDER WATER?

This is one of the first questions that most people ask. Understanding how a newborn takes his first breath helps to dispel any fears concerning the safety of water birth. While the child is *in utero*, it has no contact with the atmosphere and no need to breathe. The fetus's lungs do not yet work as they will once it is born and begins to breathe air. A baby in the womb "breathes" by receiving oxygenated blood from its mother via the placenta and the umbilical cord. The baby's heart pumps the oxygenated blood throughout its body. Once the blood becomes depleted of oxygen and full of waste materials, it is sent back to the mother via the umbilical cord and the placenta. The blood is purified and reoxygenated by the mother and returned to the fetus.

It is not until the newborn infant's skin makes contact with the air that the complex physiological process that results in the first breath begins. It is thought that the change in air pressure and temperature, possibly sensed by the baby's lips and nose, triggers the breathing mechanism.[22] During those first seconds after birth, when the newborn is under the water, he cannot possibly begin to breathe and continues to receive oxygen from his mother via the umbilical cord.

This is part of the gentle transition that water birth can provide. There is no undue urgency to lift the baby out of the water once the full body is birthed, but keeping the child under water for more than a few moments is not recommended. As long as the umbilical cord is intact and the placenta is functioning, the baby will remain in the same steady state it was in before and during birth. However, if the placenta were to detach from the uterine wall, it would interrupt the baby's flow of oxygenated blood. That is why it is essential for the newborn to be brought out of the water immediately after birth.

A most striking example of the gentle birth concept of allowing a baby to emerge in his own time is the baby who is born in water with the amniotic sac intact. A number of midwives have reported this occurrence. The baby floats in the water of the amniotic sac, a tiny bubble cradled and buoyant, supported by the water it has just been born into, until it moves and possibly pokes a finger through the sac. The midwife gently pulls the sac open and lifts the baby out and into his mother's arms. The child's first breath is initiated in exactly the same manner as babies born directly into warm water.

WILL THE MOTHER GET AN INFECTION FROM THE WATER?

In the 1950s women were told that it was unsafe to take a bath in the latter stages of pregnancy because the cervix was opening and the uterus could be infected by germs in the water. This edict against bathing is still printed in some childbirth books read by women today. If a woman's bag of water has ruptured before labor begins, most doctors will advise her to stay out of the bath until labor is initiated and progressing. Otherwise, bathing, especially in labor, is encouraged without worry of possible infection. The only precaution is to make sure that the water for bathing is clean. Some couples go to the extreme of using purified water for the tub in which they intend to give birth. Regular tap water is usually sufficient.

During labor everything is moving down and out. The baby is descending into the birth canal. It does not make sense that bacteria from the water would go up into the uterus. In fact, the concentration of bacteria in and around the vagina is actually diluted by the water, lessening the possibility of infection. Dr. Michael Rosenthal at the Family Birthing Center reports that

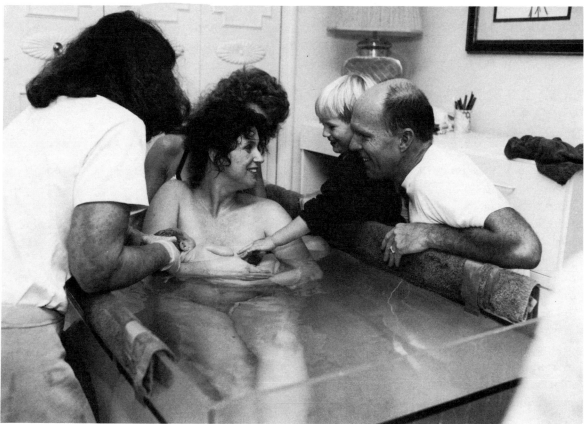

Photo by Serge McCabe

Lindy holds her new baby girl as her son and husband greet her. Lindy chose a water birth because she had pneumonia just a week prior to delivery. The water helped her conserve her energy.

there have been no maternal infections in close to one thousand cases of water births and twice that many water labors.[23] Doctors and midwives throughout the world report similar statistics.

In the early 1980s women were adding sea salt to the birthing tubs to

159

simulate the slightly saline property of amniotic fluid and to also feel safer by increasing the bacteriostatic properties of the water by making it more saline. This practice is not necessary; it neither prevents infection nor adds any benefit for the baby.

HOW ARE EMERGENCIES HANDLED IN THE WATER?

The physicians and midwives who include water birth in their practices carefully monitor the progress of the birth and the baby's status throughout labor, just as in any birth. If an emergency is encountered, the situation is assessed and the proper course of action taken. The mother may be required to get out of the tub or simply change positions. Practitioners use their own judgment and level of experience during labor and birth to guide them.

A decrease in the baby's heart rate, detected through the use of a fetoscope or ultrasound Doppler, is often seen as a cause for concern, especially in the hospital. Sometimes this situation can be easily remedied by simply asking the mother to change positions. Almost all birthing positions can be assumed in the water with minimal effort because of the water's buoyancy. A woman can squat, sit, kneel, be on her hands and knees, or sit on someone's lap. She can even lie down on her side if the tub is large enough.

Any problems associated with the actual birth can also be assessed and handled quickly when a woman is in the water. Some problems are actually resolved easier because of the water. Midwives report that a cord around the baby's neck is often easier to remove in the water because the reduced gravity results in no compression on the cord. When the baby's head emerges under the water and a cord is felt, it is simply lifted over the baby's head or a hand is slipped under the cord so that it can be passed down over the body when the baby comes out.

Another concern is that the baby may inhale meconium, the baby's first stool, during the birth. Although a rare occurrence, this is a situation that must be monitored closely. Inhaling this thick, tarry substance can be life-threatening to a baby. Midwives have stated that their ability to deal with the potential emergency that inhaling meconium presents can be dealt with as

160

easily in the water as out of it. If the meconium staining is what they classify as light or medium, they allow the birth to proceed in the water and watch as the water "washes" any meconium off the baby's face. Some midwives gently massage the baby's face during the time between the emergence of the baby's head and the birth of the body. Midwives pay particular attention to the nasal cavities, where small amounts of meconium discharge from the nostrils. Babies showing signs of meconium discharge are suctioned carefully as soon as they are brought out of the water. If the meconium staining is classified as heavy, most practitioners have the woman stand as the baby's head is crowning. As soon as the head is born, the baby should be suctioned with a DeLee mucus trap to remove the discharge.

IF I'M IN LABOR, WHEN CAN I GET INTO THE WATER?

The decision to enter the birthing tub is generally up to the mother. CNM Linda Church recommends that women try laboring in the water whenever they feel like it. However, if it is early in labor and the water relaxes a woman too much, the labor often slows down. If this is the case, the laboring woman should leave the water until her labor becomes established. Staying active during labor is the most beneficial thing a woman can do to facilitate progress. Some women alternate walking, taking showers, and bathing during labor.

Many midwives and doctors who have worked with water births see a significant correlation between entering the bath after the woman's cervix is dilated beyond five centimeters and a reduction in the remaining length of labor. It seems that if a woman waits until her labor is progressing well before getting into the water, then the contractions are more effective and complete dilation is often accomplished faster. Some women who have had water births comment that, in retrospect, they would prefer that their midwives not tell them when to get into the birthing tub. Husbands are sometimes eager for their wives to seek the comfort of the water and insist that they get in. These well-meaning people can interrupt a woman's instinctual flow so that she ends up having a water birth because someone else wanted her to, or, worse, she is forced to get out when she would rather stay in. The decision about when to get in and when to get out should be left up to the mother if everything is proceeding normally.

Water birth, although a desirable choice for many women, is simply an option, not an end to be achieved in every birth. When women have the birthing tub available, many gravitate to it without hesitation and feel safe staying in and birthing their babies.

DO YOU DELIVER THE PLACENTA IN THE WATER?

Childbirth practitioners are divided on this issue. Some allow the woman to stay in the tub for the expulsion of the placenta, and some ask the woman to stand up or leave the tub to birth the placenta. Although opinion and practice is divided on this issue, physicians and midwives who allow women to deliver the placenta in the water report that it is safe and without side effects. Using this method, the umbilical cord is not cut or clamped until the placenta is out of the woman's body. Dr. Josie Muscat, who delivers placentas in the water, states, "I believe that there is much to say in favor of this [process]. The mother is given her baby to hug while we wait for her to deliver the placenta. We do not use cord traction or abdominal pressure. We prefer a D-I-Y [do-it-yourself] method." Muscat has never seen a hemorrhage or a retained placenta.[24] Doctors and midwives have observed that there is less bleeding and that the babies almost always start nursing immediately after birth, which helps with the expulsion of the placenta. Some midwives state that the time allowed for the passage of the placenta increases slightly with birth in water. It is their general feeling that the water relaxes the uterus and that the contractions for birthing the placenta are less effective when a woman stays in the water after the baby's birth. When some women stand up to get out of the tub, however, the placenta virtually falls out.

Some women who have "planned" to have a water birth and then birth outside the tub, get back into the water to birth the placenta. Other women who have had a water birth and get out to birth the placenta often get back into a clean bath to relax and play with the baby. Once again, this seems to be a matter of choice and judgment. There are no set guidelines to follow.

CAN THE WATER BECOME CONTAMINATED?

As water becomes more accepted in hospital settings as a tool for relaxation and possible birth, the question of universal precautions arises. Universal precautions are the set guidelines that hospitals are required to follow when dealing with exposure to blood and body fluids. Almost all hospitals require doctors and midwives who attend births to gown and glove themselves as protection against contamination.

Today the doctors who deal with this potential problem routinely test their clients for blood-borne pathogens, including AIDS, HIV, and hepatitis-B. If a woman is suspected of being positive for any of these, she is usually not allowed to birth in the water. Yet in principle she can still have a water birth if protection for the caregiver is maintained. This protection includes a mask, over-the-elbow gloves, a gown, goggles, a head covering, and rubber boots. The doctor may end up looking like a space alien to the baby, but both mother and practitioner will be satisfied—as will be the hospital infection-control committee.

A woman from the Atlanta area worked diligently with her physician to help the hospital approve the use of a portable birthing tub for her labor and birth. The infection-control committee was her biggest challenge, even though she had been tested for disease and her physician considered her to be low risk. She wrote to the Occupational Safety and Health Administration (OSHA), met with the hospital staff, and asked GMCHA to write guidelines for practitioners and to supply the hospital with the names and numbers of all the doctors in the United States who were doing water births in hospitals. The hospital finally approved the use of a tub, but she delivered her baby two weeks early and had not received her rented tub yet. She feels that she has paved the way for the next woman who wants to labor and birth in water.

On occasion a birth attendant will request the woman to get out of the tub because she has released feces into the water. Most midwives and physicians who are experienced with water birth will be able to remove most floating matter with a cup, bowl, or small fish net. One home-birth midwife said that she buys several goldfish nets at a time from a pet store and gives them to couples who are planning water births. She tucks one into her birth supply bag as well for those unexpected water births. Sometimes the bowels are loose and the water becomes contaminated. If that is the case, getting out of the water is recommended.

The fact that there is a very low infant infection rate with babies born in water says that it is safe even in situations where there may be possible contaminants. As mentioned before, it is necessary to start out with clean water. An Oregon physician tells about one baby that had a staph infection after a water birth, the source of which was hard to trace. Finally a staph infection was discovered on the father's foot. The father had been in the birthing tub with his wife. Even though they are not sure that his infection was the cause of the baby's infection, it teaches practitioners an important lesson. Everyone who is going to join the mother in the tub either during the birth or directly afterward should be certain to be free of communicable disease and to shower completely before entering the tub.

WHY ISN'T WATER BIRTH AVAILABLE IN ALL HOSPITALS?

Consumer demand is gradually bringing about a change in the attitude of American hospitals. Couples who go to hospitals seeking a birth without interventions must first have a doctor who is supportive of their goals; they must then have a hospital staff that is not resistant to change.

Hospitals in England that have installed birthing tubs or allow women to bring their own rented pools are not hampered by the restrictions of the insurance companies that govern policy in American hospitals. Midwives, the predominant care providers for women in England and most of Europe, have been instrumental in changing hospital policy in England. For every two hundred midwives in England there is usually one consulting physician—just the opposite of the situation in the United States.

In 1988 Dr. Jan-Eric Strole, a Swedish-born physician now practicing in South Bend, Washington, was the first doctor in the United States to provide water for labor and birth within a hospital. His patients in Polson, Montana, relished the freedom and support they received from Strole, yet the hospital forced him to stop offering the use of water to his clients. The only explanation was that the insurance company would not cover the potential liability. Strole went to great lengths to present a case for the continuation of his water-birth practice for both the hospital and the insurance provider, but the hospital eventually made life difficult for him. He was forced to resign from the staff because the hospital would not insure the water-birth practice and Strole could not afford private liability insurance. If he were to continue, Strole would have had to pay at least $50,000 in insurance premiums for one year. While he was seeking another position out of the state, Strole continued to serve women by attending home births in the rural Montana community, offering them water for labor and birth. Strole's experience with the hospital's insurance company in Polson is an example of the extent to which birth in the United States is controlled by a few people, most assuredly men, who have no concept of what nonintervention really means.

Dr. Michael Rosenthal strongly believes that the problem is not just about putting birthing tubs into hospitals. He feels that there will be more and more hospitals that will want to remodel their maternity units to include the water-birth alternative as a "draw" for clientele. He feels that even if tubs are installed in hospitals, the rules and hospital policies that control normal birth will remain. The beautiful new Jacuzzi tubs installed in the Santa Monica Hospital maternity unit in 1991 are a case in point. Women are "not allowed" to enter the bath if their water has not broken and the baby's head has not descended into the pelvic cavity. They are also "not allowed" to enter the bath after their water *has* broken. Rosenthal does not think American hospitals will widely adopt water birth as an option: "The problem is removing obstetricians from normal birth. The problem remains of educating doctors on how to surrender into this normal process. How can a doctor, traditionally trained, even conceive of any other way to give birth if he has only seen a thousand women on their backs, hooked to fetal monitors, with legs up in stirrups?" He adds, "The concept of the birthing center works because it is a place for the practice of midwifery. More doctors need to either get out of obstetrics or become midwives."

Practices are changing as more midwives provide full maternity care within hospitals. A growing number of obstetricians also insist on incorporating water birth into hospital protocols. GMCHA has created model protocols for hospitals that wish to change and guidelines for a safe water birth for parents and practitioners (see Appendix D). GMCHA has helped several large hospitals accept water birth by working with couples who rent portable tubs, taking them right into the hospital. St. Luke's-Roosevelt Hospital in New York City is the latest to allow women this option. Dr. Lori Romanzi oversees the use of their portable tub, which never seems to get put away for long.

Michael and Mary never hesitated to make their desire for a water birth known. They first asked their doctor, then the midwives, then the hospital administration. It took perseverance, but they had a water birth in a rented tub in St. Luke's Presbyterian Hospital in Denver, Colorado. After the birth, Michael and Mary sent press releases to all the local newspapers. In less than three months, five other couples inquired whether they too could have a water birth at that hospital. This is exactly how dozens of couples in England have achieved their water births. They rented a portable tub and brought it into the hospital with them as part of their birth paraphernalia.

The most successful way of negotiating change in hospitals is consumer advocacy. One couple's request may be easily overlooked, but ten couples asking for the same service is more difficult to ignore. If you would like water birth available at your hospital, make your wishes known in the form of a letter to the hospital administration (see Appendix E for a sample letter). Send copies of your letter to everyone, including the chief of obstetrics, the head nurse on the maternity unit, your doctor, the insurance provider for the hospital, and your insurance provider if you are covered. If you don't get any response the first time, send them all a follow-up letter within two weeks. Get other couples to do the same thing. Don't be afraid to send a copy to the newspaper, either.

Water Works

We have now seen that water is useful during pregnancy, in labor, and during birth. It is also excellent for women and babies in the postpartum period for exercising and swimming. In the first few days after the birth, many women get back into the tub or birth pool with their babies. Partners and siblings delight in bathing with the baby and holding the baby in the warm water. The question of infant swimming often comes up in association with birth in water. Some couples simply want to put their babies back into the water for relaxation and fun. Others want to teach their babies to swim.

The National Swim School Association (NSSA) offers a teacher-training course for swim instructors who want to offer classes for children from one week old up to toddler age. There are qualified infant swim instructors and programs throughout the world. Babies know how to swim instinctively and usually adjust very well to pools, especially if the temperature of the water is maintained around 90°F. Swimming with babies is an especially wonderful time for fathers. Intense and focused concentration is necessary during the time in the pool; it is truly quality time for both baby and parents. If you are interested in finding out more about infant swim programs in the United States or other parts of the world, see the listings in Appendix F.

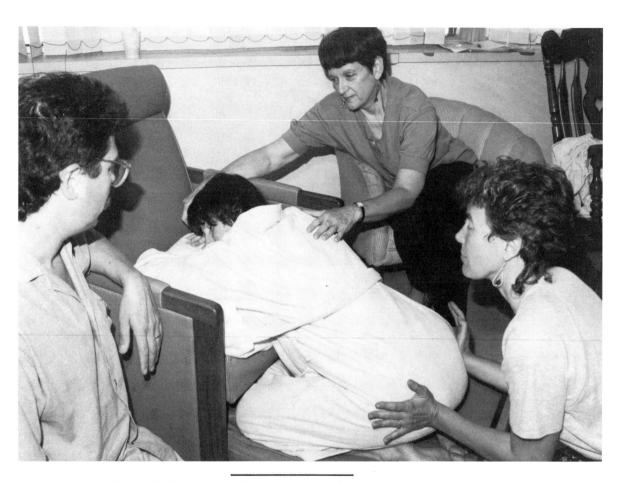

Women who listen to their bodies can direct their support persons and ask for what they need during birth, thus deriving great emotional comfort.

7

The Mind-Body Connection

The cooperation between mind and body is most evident during pregnancy and birth, and an integrated approach to health can be very effective during these times. As the option of gentle birth becomes more available, we have the opportunity to observe the birth process in its natural form. We can talk to women about why they did not need intervention and what helped them to be able to give birth gently. In this chapter we will explore the connectedness between mind and body, thoughts and actions, mother and baby.

Mind-Body Response

Labor is extremely physical, but it is also emotional and spiritual in nature. Medical science is now discovering that, in addition to its physical form, the body is made up of thoughts and emotions. Many respected physicians and scientists believe that the mind can no longer be considered separate from the body. Intelligence, once believed to be contained only in the brain and nerve cells, is now known to be an integral part of each of our cells. In his book *Quantum Healing*, endocrinologist Dr. Deepak Chopra explains that everything we experience in our lives—memories, emotions, thoughts, and stimulation—is really what forms our minds.[1]

Every emotion we experience is accompanied by a thought; every thought we think is accompanied by an emotion. All of the thoughts and emotions we think and feel emanate from our bodies on a cellular level. This is one reason that we "feel" things so intensely. Many of us have had the experience of walking into a room full of strangers and instantly liking or disliking someone. A person's appearance or manner triggers feelings and emotions in us that have been buried in our memories as well as in our bodies. A stored memory can be a resource or a hindrance during pregnancy and birth.

Amazingly enough, our bodies know how to heal themselves, filter waste products, fertilize an egg, grow a baby, and give birth. These processes that we take for granted are not things we can consciously control. They all require an uninterrupted flow of energy. The body actually experiences an energy current that flows through and around it much like the electricity that flows through the wires in the walls of your house. You don't think about electricity flowing through your house until the light doesn't turn on. Many philosophies of healing call this energy force *chi* and believe that it connects all major organs of the body along distinct pathways or meridians. Unconscious functions of the body, such as healing cancer or birthing a baby, can be strongly affected by thoughts and emotions that block the energy flow through the body.

Many childbirth educators have recognized the mind-body response. In *Childbirth without Fear*, Grantly Dick-Read noted that when a woman experiences fear (an emotion), her body tightens (a physical response), which causes pain. When she experiences the pain, her level of fear increases, causing more tension and thus more pain. A cycle of fear, tension, and pain is established and often leads to a prolonged birth process.[2] Without explaining this cycle on a cellular or chemical level, Dick-Read correctly identified the cause-and-effect relationship of emotions and the mind-body response. He emphasized the importance of being aware of the biological functions of the body as a method of dispelling learned fear and also stresses how valuable the presence of a calm and reassuring person can be throughout a woman's labor and birth.

Ferdinand Lamaze also worked within the area of mind-body response using the conditioning techniques that he perfected for labor and birth. By replacing their current thoughts with more positive ones, women were able to learn a new response to stimuli that would have otherwise produced pain.

They conditioned their bodies not to respond to the pain in the way that they had previously learned.

Listening to the Body

It is impossible to ignore the dramatic and dynamic changes that take place in the body during pregnancy. It is important for a woman to have an understanding of the physical changes that occur during her pregnancy. This focus of attention on the growing fetus and its development helps a mother shift into thinking about herself. She now has a reason for paying attention to the inner workings of her body; she may now evaluate her diet and her lifestyle in general. It is typical for women to want to know if what they are experiencing is normal. Women look to others for the answers to these questions, especially in a first pregnancy, which can be a new and possibly frightening experience.

The medical model, described in chapter 4, encourages an outward focus by insisting that pregnant women go to experts who will tell them what they are feeling. Pregnancy has to be officially diagnosed by a doctor before some women will trust what they are feeling in their bodies. The midwifery model empowers a woman to become mindful of her body, explore her inner feelings, and question herself about their meaning instead of asking an expert for an outward interpretation.

In order to be in touch with yourself it is important to be aware of the ongoing dialogue between the physical body and the mind, including emotions and thoughts. By taking time each day for an inner dialogue, you can begin a process of self-discovery. It is not necessary for this process to be mystical or complicated. It can be as simple as lying quietly and asking yourself, "What is going on in my body and how do I feel about it?" It may mean taking a walk by the ocean or in the woods. The object is to reduce the amount of outward stimulation and focus inward. Some people achieve this through prayer or meditation; others simply become "mindful." With all the distractions of our busy lives, it is sometimes difficult to set aside the time to focus inward, but when practiced daily, mindfulness becomes a valuable tool for the rest of your life, not just during pregnancy.

Pregnancy is a time of increased awareness. Most women are amazed at the process that takes place within them. For some women, being pregnant is the deepest connection that they have ever felt within themselves. Some women may be afraid to become a mother because of unpleasant experiences in their own childhood. It is important to ask yourself questions like, "How do I really feel about becoming a mother?" or "What did I like about the way in which I was mothered?" These questions will allow you to explore your feelings.

Emotions at a birth can be extremely intense. Having a baby is a major transition in a woman's life. It can be fulfilling and empowering, or it can be a struggle with unresolved emotions that can produce long-lasting effects. Many women, including grandmothers, describe their births as if they had just taken place. Their stories have the emotional intensity of the original experience. The remembrance of a woman's birth experience, if it was a negative one, needs to be cleared or processed in order to integrate it into her consciousness. If this is not done, this remembrance may influence other births and how she feels about herself and her children. When Nancy Wainer Cohen founded Cesarean/Support, Education, and Concern (C/SEC), a cesarean counseling group, she was flooded with over forty thousand letters from women who still could not deal with the emotional issues surrounding their cesarean births.[3]

The object of being aware is not so much to be in control of your body or its emotions but to recognize and work with them. This allows you to take charge of your life. A woman who keeps herself from expressing or releasing emotions is storing them on a cellular level somewhere in the body. The hormonal shifts in a woman's body during pregnancy make her emotionally vulnerable. Many people view emotions as being either positive or negative. Expressing all emotions is healthy. The key to dealing with emotions during pregnancy and birth is to first recognize them and then to release the negative ones. Most women need a support person who can encourage them to express their feelings without judgment. This person could be a friend, partner, professional counselor, doctor, or midwife.

Listening to the Baby

Babies demonstrate most dramatically the mind-body response. When a baby is born, he has been in close physical contact with his mother and has lived within her system of thoughts and emotions. If we perceive these emotions to be stimulated and released on a cellular level, as Dr. Deepak Chopra illustrates in *Quantum Healing*, then it is likely that the baby also perceives them *in utero*. Mother and baby share the same bioenergy system. Chopra describes this shared system as entrainment, a rhythmic relationship with the physical body, including all cellular activity.[4] This connection does not end at birth; in fact, it becomes stronger because the infant now has the basis for his own emotional life. While perceiving his mother's mind-body state, an infant cannot communicate with words but uses his cries and body postures as cues to indicate what is going on inside of him and what he perceives in his environment.

Birth memories reflecting these early perceptions have been activated in adult clients in response to hypnosis, psychoanalysis, LSD, psychodrama, submersion in water, and certain breathing techniques.[5] In each experience the spontaneous "remembering" of the birth experience reveals just how great its influence was on the entire psychological patterning of the individual. Psychiatrist Stanislav Grof states, "Reliving biological birth and integrating the experience into one's way of being seems to offer possibilities of psychosomatic healing, personality transformation and consciousness evolution that by far exceed therapy limited to work with biographical material from childhood and later life."[6] San Diego psychotherapist Dr. David Chamberlain came to similar conclusions in his revealing book *Babies Remember Birth*.[7]

Out of the many therapies that help people remember and resolve birth trauma, hypnosis gives us the most detailed accounts, often moment-by-moment birth reports. These amazing stories give us the advantage of a mature adult with the full use of language, but they reveal the clear thought processes and deep feelings of the infant at the time of birth. From these accounts we can now learn what birth and newborn care are like from the baby's point of view. Dr. Chamberlain did a cross-matching of mothers' accounts of birth compared to their adult children "remembering" and found an amazingly consistent correlation between perceived memories and actual events. Children even reported what their mothers were thinking during labor and birth! A short example of a taped hypnosis session will give you a much better understanding of the thoughts of a newborn.

[Dr. Chamberlain explains that Deborah, when only halfway out of her mother's body, begins a series of sharp observations.] "The doctor is looking around for something. I'm coming out, but just my eyes, I think. The doctor has black hair and a white coat and he's looking at a tray of instruments. He's turned away from me. I don't think he knows I'm coming out. Somebody better tell him I'm going to come out! I think I'm just going to do it by myself.

. . . I feel awful cold all over, especially my hands and feet. I think I'm not supposed to be this cold. My mom's trying to look around and see what's going on. They keep pushing her back down on the table. She's starting to cry because she doesn't know what's happening, and she thinks something is the matter with me. I'm all right. They're pulling on my hands and feet, kind of rubbing on them real hard. Why don't they just leave me alone? I'm all right, really I am. Just leave me alone. Everybody's all around, pulling on my fingers and rubbing them. I guess they think I'm the wrong color. That's what it is—my fingers are blue. That's why they are so cold. They put me by somebody now, on a blanket, lots of blankets.

Somebody's holding me. It's the nurse with the yellow hair. I'm all wrapped up real tight now. I can't wiggle around anymore but at least they quit mashing me. They let her [mom] hold me for a little while. My hands are still cold, wrapped up. Mom's still crying a little bit but not like she was before. Everything's okay now, so I can go to sleep. I knew I was okay. I tried to tell everybody, but they wouldn't listen. I was trying to talk but they didn't understand me. And I was trying to push them away with my hands, but there were too many of them. I was crying, trying to talk, but I guess it was just crying to them.

One of the things that really made me mad about the whole situation is this: All the time I was in there by myself, everything was just how

I wanted it. And I figured that was it. I sort of had a feeling there were other things around but not people like me. But they didn't really matter because they were outside. Then when I came out, it made me mad because I didn't have anything to say about it. When I tried to, nobody paid any attention to me. That made me mad, too, because I always thought I knew what was going on. I felt I knew a lot—I really did. I thought I was pretty intelligent. I never thought about being a person, just a mind. I thought I was an intelligent mind. And so when the situation was forced on me, I didn't like it too much. I saw all these people acting real crazy. That's when I thought I really had a more intelligent mind, because I knew what the situation was with me, and they didn't seem to. They seemed to ignore me. They were doing things to me—to the outside of me. But they acted like that's all there was. When I tried to tell them things, they just wouldn't listen, like that noise wasn't really anything. It didn't sound too impressive, but it was all I had. I just really felt like I was more intelligent than they were."[8]

Many mothers experience what they call a psychic or spiritual communication with their unborn children. When Dr. Robert Doughton of Portland, Oregon, asked his patients if they listened to their babies, he was amazed that many of the mothers were actively communicating. All humans need contact and recognition. This contact begins while we are still in the womb.

Doughton says of his work, "My original interest in having a child participate in his own birth stems from an incident that happened to me in 1976. I had delivered over fifteen thousand babies by that time, and all of a sudden, during a particularly difficult case of pre-eclampsia, I heard, for the first time, an unborn child talk to me. The baby told me to call her daddy and that everything would get better if I did that." Doughton listened to the advice of the unborn baby and complied with her wishes. Everything with the birth proceeded normally once the father appeared.

Doughton pledged to himself that he would make the attempt to invite each unborn child into the case. "My interest was to discover how to use this information clinically for the benefit of the family. It was my hope that having the unborn child participate in the birth process would prevent complications, ease labor and delivery." According to Doughton, the father and baby are just as influential as the mother. Pregnancy and birth are a family situation.

Part of the process of "listening to your baby" is listening to yourself. If the baby is particularly active or seemingly restless, ask yourself, "How am I feeling? Is there anything that is bothering me?" Remember, the baby responds to your mind-body state with a mind-body state of its own. Babies are wonderfully accurate mirrors for us, even *in utero*.

Babies do have thoughts of their own, but they are also sponges that absorb everything around them. This becomes even more evident after birth. Babies know when we are tense or upset. Their mind-body state will not allow negative emotions to be stored long, and they will cry to send the energy through. It is their natural way of moving energy to cry or fuss for us. Many mothers complain about their babies being fussy at the end of the day, commonly between 5 and 7 P.M. Nothing can calm them. Mothers who take time to sit and relax in order to release what they are storing up inside before they try to comfort their crying babies report that their babies calm down in half the time.

Visualization for a Gentle Birth

Visualization is seeing a situation or desired goal as if it has already happened. Behind every action there is first a thought. If a pregnant woman is afraid of giving birth, it may help her to visualize herself relaxing, letting go, and birthing her baby with ease. It is very important for a woman to have an image of the way in which she would like to give birth. A group of twenty women who had had cesarean sections were asked if they had visualized themselves giving birth before they went into labor. Amazingly, only one woman had seen herself actually giving birth.[9] It is good for a visualization to be built with imagery that supports a full range of feelings. In visualizing how you would like your birth to be, you make it a conscious part of your mind-body state. A creative visualization is a consciously chosen reality—one that is not subject to past thoughts and emotions.

The use of positive imagery has been proved beneficial in many areas of

health and healing. Oncologists have used visions of healthy T-cells battling cancer cells, often with the result that "terminally ill" cancer patients experience remissions. Dr. Deepak Chopra uses imagery and suggestion with patients who come to the Ayurvedic Clinic in Massachusetts. Gayle Peterson and Lewis Mehl elevated guided visualization to a science in their work in Berkeley, California. There are distinct ways to help the mother relax in order for the visualizations to be most effective. Women need to be receptive for the positive messages to be received and stored for later use.

Gayle Peterson usually uses visualization imagery with women following a massage. How does visualization work to dissolve a woman's fear and help her achieve a normal birth? Peterson explains, "Suggestion can only serve that part of the person that desires a particular outcome. When personal motivation is not present, hypnosis does not work. For example, a woman may feel that she is too 'nervous' to relax effectively for natural childbirth. She does, however, wish that she could relax. She just does not believe in her ability to do so.[10] The relaxed woman who is in an altered state is able to suspend her own ingrained belief system long enough to receive a suggestion that matches her desire for a particular outcome. During labor, women experience an altered state of consciousness. We discussed earlier that in a gentle birth the environment that a woman has created supports her in shifting between this altered state to a lighter state where she can communicate her desires. During labor the mother is suggestible to words and visualizations that her support persons might use to help her create the birth experience she desires. If she has heard these words during her pregnancy while in a state of deep relaxation, they will be even more powerful in helping her overcome her resistance. The use of imagery and visualization can support the mother by allowing her to trust in her ability to surrender to the power that moves through her. Following are a few examples of gentle visualizations for relaxation. These visualizations can be practiced throughout pregnancy and used during labor and birth.

THE WAVE
This particular visualization can be done on the floor or on a bed. It is most effective when done in a pool or hot tub. When the practitioner holds the woman as she relaxes and breathes in the water, the woman feels total support and comfort. Women who have used this process say they felt like a baby in the womb.

> See yourself lying on a warm, sandy beach with the waves softly
> moving up and back just beyond where you are lying.

I hear the waves and note their rhythmic consistency.
I listen intensely to all the sounds around me.
I breathe lightly and effortlessly.
I feel all the feelings in my body.
As I listen to the quiet between the waves, I anticipate the movement of the water.
I hear the waves coming in closer and closer until they break just beyond my feet.
As I become more aware, I feel the water touch my feet.
I do not draw away from the water.
The water is warm and soothing, comforting and relaxing.
As the next wave moves over my feet, I breathe in.
As the wave recedes, I breathe out, opening every part of my body, flowing.
I release all tension from my body as I breathe out.
The warm, nurturing, comforting waves continue to move over my body. With each wave I breathe and I become more relaxed and open.
Before long the waves have carried me into the water.
I now relax in the warm weightlessness of the ocean.
The more I relax and breathe, the more I am carried and supported by the wave.
My body opens and releases as the wave carries me.
The movement of the waves comforts me.
The waves are pleasurable.
I relax and breathe with each wave.
The wave intensifies. I breathe.
The wave is powerful. I breathe.
The wave is flowing. I breathe.
The wave eventually comes to the shore. I breathe.
The wave is calm. I breathe.
The wave is quiet. I breathe.
I now see myself lying on the warm sand.
The waves are receding.

THE ROSE

This short visualization can be used at any time during pregnancy or labor. I have brought a single rose to many mothers in labor and reminded them to watch as the rose opens, telling them that their cervix is just like the beautiful pink blossom. Every time I have brought a rose to a laboring woman, it has fully opened by the time the baby was born.

My cervix is like a rosebud.
Ready to open.
I am nurtured by those around me as the rose is nurtured by the soil.
The rosebud gradually, ever so softly, opens and blossoms.
I open and blossom.
My cervix is soft and ripe like the rosebud.
I see the outer petals of the rose falling away.
I see my cervix yielding like the outer petals of the rose.
Every contraction opens another petal of my rosebud cervix.
I welcome each contraction, which helps me open my rosebud cervix.
I welcome and receive all the nurturing around me, which helps me open.
Just like the warm sun opens the rose, the warmth I receive opens my cervix.
I yield and open.
The rose does not resist.
I open and blossom.

THE CANDLE

Women who want to use this visualization during labor often buy a special large candle just for labor, one that is likely to burn for at least twelve hours. They can use the sight of the candle to remind them to melt with the contractions.

Imagine that your pelvis is a candle with a flame in the middle.

As my contractions come, the flame burns brighter.
My body is the wax of the candle, warming and yielding to the flame.
The more I breathe, the brighter the candle burns.

The wax melts and drips with each contraction.
My body becomes looser and opens to the flame.
I see my pelvis becoming soft and warm and pliable.
I breathe. With each contraction the candle becomes softer.
I melt with the candle.
My breath helps the candle burn brighter, melting quicker.
I remain soft, warm, and yielding.

AFFIRMATIONS

Affirmations, or positive statements, are tiny positive visualizations. They counteract negative thoughts that may be hidden on a subconscious level. Your life is a manifestation of what you are thinking, so even a tiny positive thought will bring more positive actions into your life. Counseling sessions or rebirthings can end with several positive affirmations that can be written down and repeated. Binnie Anne Dansby is a psychotherapist in London who specializes in working with pregnant women. She developed a series of affirmations to be used during pregnancy and birth. You don't necessarily have to believe an affirmation to use it and have it produce results for you. If your mind only hears the affirmation while you are reading it or listening to it, it still has profound effects. Some women like to tape affirmations on their bathroom mirrors so they can see them when they get up and when they go to bed. Affirmations can be used to help you feel safe, strong, relaxed, and at ease or at peace. Some of my favorite ones are:

I am a wonderful mother.
My body is safe, even though I may feel afraid.
I am loved and appreciated.
My strength is abundant.
God takes care of me.
The more I breathe and feel, the more I relax.
With every contraction, I let go to receive my baby.
I open to receive life.
I receive all the love and support I need, I deserve it.
My baby is perfect.

There is no limit to how good I can feel.
I love and trust my body.
God's love and power flows through me.

A good way to practice affirmations is to record them on a tape, in your own voice and with your favorite music. You can even use the tape during labor. There are affirmation tapes and cards available now for those who don't want to create their own. All affirmations work with the mind-body.

The Power of Prayer

Human beings often turn to faith and prayer when a situation looks bad or is difficult. But regular devotion and prayer is a powerful tool to help women through pregnancy and birth. Just as visualization brings desired results, the outcome of prayer can be nothing less than amazing.

The physical drama of birth shows us how much we are not in control. When women surrender and literally give up trying to control the pain of labor, their bodies take over and do the work that they were meant to do. Life is very much like birth. When we surrender and commit ourselves to letting a higher power do the work, we accomplish far more. The phrase "let go and let God" has greater implications than we know.

For many women with strong religious convictions, having a baby any other way than the way God intended us to birth is letting man (yes, *man*) assume too much control. For many couples, a life without prayer would be like a life without food. It is not always easy to pray, but it can give us a time to be mindful and thankful. Prayer gives us a time to quietly assess what our needs are and to ask for help in working out the solutions.

I have seen many women suddenly turn devotional in labor. They will light candles, say prayers, and ask for protection. Some women will put on a necklace symbolizing their particular religious beliefs. They are reminded through powerful and awesome emotions and physical responses that there really is a creative and powerful force outside of themselves. I often give women a prayer to be said just before they go into labor or when they are in the early stages of labor.

As I quietly sit with you, my child, here inside of me,
I ask God to hold your hand and guide you in your journey.
You shall come to me in innocence and love.
I accept this gift and am thankful for it.
I ask that I be made strong and loving and that I be a good parent.
It's time to say good-bye to my pregnant body and open to receive the
    fullness of your love.
May your life always be filled with light.
Amen

Midwives honor women and meet them where they are in their spiritual lives. Many Christian midwives pray devotedly during a birth and have a support team of other midwives around the country praying for the mother through her pregnancy and birth. The Fellowship of Christian Midwives, with nine hundred members, has organized prayer chains. When someone calls with a particular need or request, the chain is activated. The end result is sometimes over one hundred women praying together for a particular person or situation. This network is growing and proving to be very effective.

Many cultures around the world emphasize the opportunity for a woman's spiritual awakening during the process of birth; many cultures have developed rituals to guide and protect the mother on this spiritual journey. Archetypal symbols such as Artemis, the protector of both mother and midwife, give women images of power and surrender. Artemis, the Goddess of the seasons, celebrates the rhythmic changes of the earth. As a woman's body changes during labor she mirrors this ebb and flow, this constant rhythm of creation. When a woman realizes that she cannot control the powerful rhythms of her laboring body, just as she cannot control the rain or the wind, she surrenders to the process of bringing new life into the world.

Native Americans prepare women for birth through a ceremony known as a Blessing Way. During the ceremony the pregnant woman is pampered, cared for, sung to, and made to feel totally at peace. She receives special gifts to help her through her journey. Her feet are rubbed with cornmeal, symbolizing her connection to the earth. Birth is both of the earth and of the spiritual world. Native Americans recognize that we are all spiritual beings living an earthly existence, and that childbirth opens a woman to her spiritual self like no other practice.

Many East Indian cultures purify and pray over the pregnant woman, knowing that she will be closer to the spiritual world when she is in labor. Many gurus claim that giving birth and raising a child accomplishes far more spiritually, and much faster, than sitting on a mountain top chanting for years.

The Lithuanians have an ancient tradition of consecrating a pregnant woman much in the same manner as Native Americans. A white dress is handmade and embroidered with red thread, symbolizing protection from fear and misfortune. A group of women gather with the pregnant woman very close to her time of labor and present her with gifts, sing her songs, and say special blessings. She is then washed, dressed in her new white dress, and given a necklace of amber, wood, and clay, again symbolizing her connectedness to the earth which can give her strength during labor.

No matter what a woman's relgious beliefs, there is an undeniable connectedness with all of life while a woman is giving birth. Resistance and fear, or in any way trying to control the birth process, denies her the opportunity to experience the divine nature of the creative power within.

The Sexuality of Childbirth

Surrendering to the energy that flows through her during labor and birth requires that a woman be aware of the mind-body relationship, including her feelings about her sexuality. Sexuality is our way of expressing who we are as men and women in all aspects of life. Western culture has tried to limit our sensual natures to the sexual organs and the bedroom. The guilt it associates with sex is often extended to birth as well.

A woman giving birth experiences many of the same sensations as a woman making love. In both processes, she relaxes, opens, and surrenders. Because the baby is moving through the vagina, a sexual organ, some women see birth in a sexual context. Women sometimes block the energy in their pelvis in an effort to shut off the sexual feelings or sensations they are experiencing.

185

When these women shut down, the cervix may stop opening. In many cases this energy blockage is the reason epidurals are given or cesarean sections are performed. Women who have been sexually abused as children or young adults are very susceptible to shutting down during birth. Sensitive, caring practitioners can help women work through emotions that might be devastatingly painful, thereby avoiding the additional trauma of cesarean section.

Many midwives encourage couples to express physical affection during labor. Kissing, holding, and fondling will often help a woman open up and give in to the power and intensity of her labor. I have even known midwives to recommend orgasm as a way of bringing on hard labor or helping with a stalled labor. A woman in California was giving birth at home in a portable birth tub and feeling very sexy and loving with her partner. Each time she had a contraction she would cry out, "Oh, baby, I love it. More . . . more!" Her windows were open because it was July, and soon a crowd gathered outside her home. When the baby was born amidst shouts of, "Yes!!! Yes!!! Oh, my God, yes!!!," her neighbors gave her a great round of applause. They only realized that it was a birth after they heard the cries of the baby.

If a woman feels safe, the instinctual nature of birth allows her to forget her inhibitions. Preparation, positive visualization, and mindfulness can all help a woman open and release during birth. There is a tremendous energy release when the baby comes out. Diane describes the birth of her daughter as "splitting open, having an orgasm, and seeing God all at the same time." Many women cite similar experiences and recount having powerful and life-changing orgasms. When a woman experiences joy with her body and feelings of love, acceptance, and support during her pregnancy, she often experiences the release of the baby in the same powerful way.

Redesigning Prenatal Preparation

In 1978 physician Lewis Mehl and social worker Gayle Peterson began working with pregnant women in Berkeley, California. Their research clearly demonstrated the relationship among emotional factors, body image, attitudes, and cultural patterning. Each woman who used the clinic for prenatal care was evaluated by completing a comprehensive and detailed assessment of health and probable health risks. This health-risk assessment as outlined in their book, *Pregnancy as Healing*, guides the practitioner into evaluating many different aspects of a woman's life.[11] It is important to incorporate her self-image, her past and present emotional states, and the amount of stress in her life in the evaluation. Mehl and Peterson believe that physical health reflects a combination of these factors as well as many others. Many techniques are made available to women so that they can become more aware of their thoughts and behavior patterns. Taking advantage of these techniques puts women in charge of their emotions.

Peterson used her extensive experience in working with pregnant women to create an extremely useful book, *An Easier Childbirth*. Peterson used the earlier risk assessment as a guide to help women keep an "emotional" journal during pregnancy. She says, "When women use the assessment to uncover their emotional states, their labors are easier. Women need to be listened to. If a woman is allowed to talk about her feelings, she can usually find her own answers." Peterson uses a combination of active visualization and body-centered hypnosis in working with specific issues about birth. She relates that first-time mothers who have processed emotional issues in this way often will have easier labors.[12]

It is Peterson's hope that doctors or birthing centers will provide a person in their offices who is trained to deal with emotional issues, thus giving women a new integrated approach to labor and birth. She says, "The tremendous change in identity that women go through with each pregnancy, but especially the first, is not addressed in our culture. Medical practitioners can be very sensitive, but they will unconsciously divert a woman from actually addressing her emotional concerns."

There are many techniques and practitioners that can help people access buried emotions. The hypnotherapy techniques that psychotherapist David Chamberlain uses allows individuals to access emotions by reliving the experience while in a relaxed semiconscious state. Dr. David Cheek is a retired obstetrician who uses similar techniques. He focuses on women who have already given birth to assist them in resolving trauma they may have experienced. Resolution is possible by listening to a tape of the session and following suggestions that allow the feelings to be experienced in a broader context. As discussed earlier, blocks in the energy flow of a particular situation can result in storing that emotion within the body. Dr. Deepak Chopra firmly believes that many terminal illnesses result from this blocked energy. For a woman in labor, repressed anger or fear may cause a difficult or stalled labor.

When Dr. Robert Doughton changed his style of obstetric practice in 1984 to incorporate his new view of the impact of the birth process, he readjusted the emphasis of prenatal visits from only physical assessment to include psychological assessment. It became his goal to help each family create balance within their lives. In order for them to achieve balance, Doughton felt they needed to examine their lives and deal with unresolved issues. He sought the help of midwives and psychologists in creating a birth preparation course that couples would participate in together before their births. Couples were asked to explore their individual relationships with themselves and each other, with their parents, and with their unborn baby. He even asked them to assess their religious beliefs, finding that couples who had a deep-seated belief and trust in God had better birth experiences. Doughton acknowledged that a healthy baby starts with a healthy family.

Doughton stated that his previous way of relating to his patients was to see a pregnant woman on the average of three to four hours during the entire pregnancy, possibly including the birth. One year after changing the way he practiced, Doughton noted that he saw a woman between fifty and sixty hours during her pregnancy.[13] It was a time-consuming process, but the benefits were obvious. During the five years of Doughton's new style of practice, before retiring, he helped over four hundred couples achieve gentle home births, most of which took place in water. The rate of complications and transfers was less than 5 percent.

When June and Bruce Sutherland created the Hawthorn Birth and Development Centre in Melbourne, Australia, the prenatal focus was also one of achieving balance, especially within the family. June was a trained midwife who had raised three boys and knew the importance of strengthening the family during pregnancy. She and her husband worked with other midwives and healers to design their comprehensive program for working with pregnant women and their partners.[14]

The emphasis at this freestanding birthing center has always been to experience birth as an opportunity to prepare for life as a family. The role of a parent is valued and supported. It is the opinion of the Sutherlands that birth opens a doorway that will last a lifetime. Couples go through a process of counseling similar to marriage counseling. They talk about and plan for what their life will be like with a child. Couples who already have children still go through this process. Men are supported in taking on the new role of being a father. Discussions may even include how household chores will be divided after the birth. Entire families, including grandmothers and grandfathers, are encouraged to participate in these prenatal sessions.

The center has a very popular prenatal swimming and relaxation program, developed by Cookie Harkin. Water used in this way becomes therapy for minor ailments of pregnancy, including mild hypertension and muscle strain. After they have had their babies, many couples rejoin the classes to participate in infant swimming. Similar programs are in progress in quite a few countries, including Belgium, Holland, Spain, Russia, Japan, England, and the United States.

Other options offered by the center are chiropractic adjustments during pregnancy, acupuncture, aromatherapy, and homeopathy. Assuring that the spine is in alignment enhances health by improving the innervation to all major organs. The pelvic bones can often move out of place, and a quick manipulation by a chiropractor will realign them. Women who receive regular chiropractic adjustments state that their backs don't hurt and their labors are faster and less painful.

Both the Hawthorn Birth and Development Centre and Dr. Robert Doughton have actively used rebirthing as a tool for prenatal healing. Rebirthing consists of a series of simple breathing techniques that assist a person to focus inward. Breathing in a slow, connected way helps relax the body and allows the stored memories of the mind and body to be easily and naturally revealed. Many people experience a return to a state of birth consciousness, the time when they formed their first reactions to the people around them. Rebirthing often activates those very first thoughts and emotions that we experienced as separate beings. How we interact with our environment is often based on those early thoughts and emotions. Reliving the birth experience is not the main goal of rebirthing; the theory behind the successful use of the rebirthing technique is that when we experience a painful emotion, we hold our breath, which stops the flow of energy within our bodies. The emotion is then stored somewhere in our bodies on a cellular level. When a woman has experienced similar powerful emotions during a rebirthing session before the birth of her baby, she is more likely to release and let go during her birth. It is important for her partner to have a rebirthing session before the birth as well.

Although the partner does not experience the birth on the physical level, he experiences it on his own emotional or mind-body level. The partner gains the ability to be more relaxed if he too has experienced himself as being supported and loved during a rebirthing session. Dr. Robert Doughton took the process one step further and recommended that all the people chosen to attend the birth of a child prepare themselves by being rebirthed. Doughton feels strongly that other people's emotions and thoughts can influence the outcome of a birth. He says, "I have seen it too many times. . . . It just takes one fearful person, one who has not dealt with their own feelings about love and acceptance, to stop a labor."

Rebirthing can be done with a woman in active labor. Helen Johnston, an English rebirther, was attending a birth as a support person. The mother had never had any rebirthings and had been extremely resistant to trying the technique, which she thought of as a form of religion. During the labor, the mother's pain increased and her cervix stopped dilating. The doctor suggested the use of high forceps. Helen asked the mother if she was willing to breathe with her in a connected way and to let go into the energy of the birth. The two women looked into each other's eyes and breathed together. The woman's fear melted, her body relaxed, and her baby was born naturally within an hour.

Encouraging the use of the voice is a technique first popularized by Dr. Michel Odent in Pithiviers and subsequently adapted by many midwives. Singing through pregnancy and birth is a way of opening the body and mind. The vibration that moves through the body when we sing also moves blocked energy and makes us breathe. Women who sing during pregnancy and feel the energy surge that singing can bring are often more open to vocalizing during birth. Women who are encouraged to open their throats and make

Making sounds and vocalizing in labor helps to open the cervix. When the jaw is relaxed and open, the pelvis is relaxed and open.

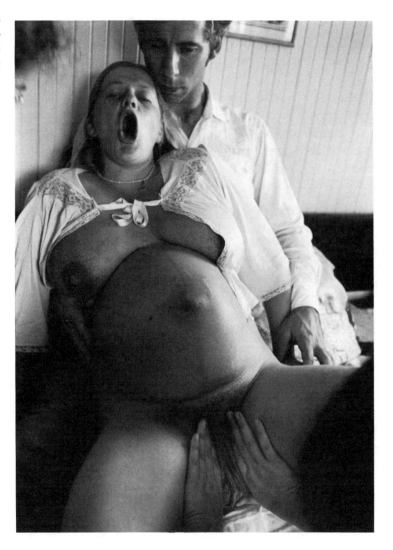

natural sounds during labor relax their jaws. As the body relaxes, the cervix opens. When Trudy, a singer, was laboring with her second baby, everyone in the room matched her original sounds. There were two men and two women attending the birth. Trudy experienced her labor as being powerful and amazing. "The sounds that everyone made went into me and helped me open even faster. It showed me that we were all working together. The energy of each contraction was matched with a very positive vibration that I could feel in every fiber of my being. It really helped me surrender to the power that God was moving through me. I could actually sense my cervix opening."

Mind, Body, Spirit in Unity

The more we can associate childbirth with life, the more we can see the influences of energy and the mind-body relationship. Childbirth is a time for exploring, examining, and realizing the creative power of life. Each and every one of us has a responsibility to live life according to our highest potential and in the will of the divine. For a baby to begin life being recognized, loved, and accepted creates a new paradigm, a new understanding of just how incredible and creative our lives can be. When life is lived in cooperation with the power of the universe, or with God—that is to say, in balance—it will be lived in cooperation with everyone and everything around us. Creating this internal balance from the very beginning is one enormously important way to create balance in the world. Gentle, conscious birth can lead the way to a better understanding of the true nature of our being. Gentle birth can bring us back to honoring how birth was meant to be.

8

Creating Gentle Birth Choices

Choices in childbirth are governed today by several major factors. To be able to choose how you give birth or what quality of care you receive, you must first have access to available and affordable options. There are far too many women who have no options. Over sixty years ago President Herbert Hoover asked the U.S. Congress to recognize children's rights by enacting legislation to create programs providing adequate prenatal and infant health care for every woman and child in the United States.[1] Though Congress acknowledged that there was a need, very few programs came into being. The health care needs of poor urban women, blacks of the rural South, and uneducated young women has remained a low priority.

The present statistics on infant mortality in the United States, especially when divided into specific regional areas, are no less than shocking. In 1990, 9.1 out of every 1,000 American babies died during their first year of life.[2] This national average reflects 8.5 infant deaths per 1,000 white babies as compared to 17.6 infant deaths per 1,000 black babies—nearly double the figure for whites.[3] A baby born in Nigeria has a better chance of survival than a baby born in the American South. The Southern Regional Project on Infant Mortality, which encompassed twenty southern states, was created in 1984 to investigate and create solutions for this incredible dilemma. A major cause of neonatal and infant mortality is low birth weight, predominantly due to inadequate prenatal care. Babies who are born to women who receive no

Midwife and clients gather outside Taos, New Mexico birth center.

prenatal care are three times more likely to be born weighing less than five pounds. Babies who weigh less than 5.5 pounds at birth have a 40 percent higher mortality rate in the first month and a 20 percent higher death rate within the first year.[4]

In many counties, a doctor or midwife is unavailable. In 1960, 25 percent of all pregnant women in the United States received no prenatal care during their first trimester; that figure has remained unchanged for the past thirty years. Five million working women in this country have no medical insurance to pay for prenatal care and childbirth.[5] Understanding the problem and having compassion for the women and babies who suffer does nothing unless a radical change in the health care delivery system is set in motion.

In May 1991 the 43d World Health Assembly gathered in Geneva to discuss the world crisis of childbirth and infant mortality. Its recommendations included the use of midwives as autonomous health care practitioners.[6] The participants felt that the education and training of midwives should be a priority for every government in the world. Creating safe and acceptable alternatives to our current system of maternity care must be approached from both the consumer's point of view and the government's point of view. The time has come, for the sake of our children and future generations, to exchange our myths for facts and turn our visions into a reality that creates safe and gentle births for all women and children.

Planning Your Birth

CHOOSING A MATERNITY CARE PROVIDER

The first and most important decision that couples need to make, ideally before they become pregnant, is who they will hire to provide prenatal care and to attend their birth. It is a decision that needs careful attention. Many factors determine the type of care a woman will choose, and choosing where you want to give birth often goes hand in hand with whom you choose as a provider. Some doctors only have privileges at specific hospitals, and you may like the doctor but not the hospital. Not all midwives have hospital privileges, just as not all midwives will attend home births. Let's first look at choosing a practitioner.

The very first factor to investigate is who the care providers are in your area. There are many places to look for all the different kinds of care offered. Physicians will be listed in the Yellow Pages or may be found by contacting the local medical society. Often certified nurse-midwives (CNMs) will also be listed as providing hospital or home-birth services. Within the last few years, direct-entry midwives have taken ads in newspapers and telephone directories. The availability of midwifery services (other than CNMs) is usually determined by the legal status of midwives in each state (see chapter 4). If a state regulates midwifery, as Oregon does, direct-entry midwives practice and advertise openly. But in California, where selective prosecution for practicing medicine without a license has still threatened midwives, they tend to keep a low profile.

How does one find a good midwife? Individual state midwifery organizations keep records of midwives who are members. The Midwives Alliance of North America (MANA) also keeps statistics on all members, and the Global Maternal/Child Health Association (GMCHA) provides a computer referral network of all home-birth midwives, birthing centers, and hospitals who are registered as supporting gentle birth. Check local alternative and parenting newspapers, resource centers, and bulletin boards in children's stores and health-food stores.

Talk with friends and family members and other women with whom you share common values concerning birth. Ask them about their birth experiences. If you know women who have had one cesarean and then a good vaginal birth, find out who their care provider was. As soon as you have a few referrals, make interview appointments. Remember that you are the prospective client conducting the interview and doing the hiring. You will find convenient lists of questions to ask potential care providers, both midwives and doctors, listed in Appendixes A and B. Finding a caregiver who will truly support you in having the best birth experience possible will, in most cases, automatically determine where you will give birth.

If you are unable to find a referral in your local area, look a little farther afield. Think about driving to the next city or even across state lines. Most first labors progress slowly enough to allow time for travel, although riding in a car while in labor is not one of the most thrilling experiences of a woman's life. Many couples do choose travel in order to find the care they want. Dr. Michael Rosenthal of the Family Birthing Center in Upland, California, never thinks it unusual when birthing couples travel a long distance to use his facility or his services. Ruth and Tim didn't contemplate very long in deciding to travel from Alaska to California for the birth of their third baby. Ruth flew down three weeks before her due date, and Tim followed when labor began. Ruth, who had had two previous cesareans, was thrilled when she was referred to Rosenthal through the International Cesarean Awareness Network (ICAN). Rosenthal assured her there was no reason that she couldn't deliver normally. His confidence in her ability helped her birth her baby in warm water after eighteen hours of labor.

Other couples have traveled halfway around the world seeking extraordinary birth experiences, especially those wanting water births. I most often recommend that keeping the birth simple and close to home usually works the best. But if you have no other choices, traveling can be worth the added hassle.

WHAT DOES IT COST TO HAVE A BABY TODAY?

The cost of maternity care and insurance coverage is the next major determining factor in seeking the care you want. Doctors' and midwives' fees vary among individual practitioners and in different geographic areas. Most providers charge pregnant women a set fee that includes prenatal visits, labor and delivery management, and postpartum follow-up. Not included in this fee are required blood tests, diagnostic testing such as ultrasound or amniocentesis, all hospital or birthing center costs, anesthesia and anesthesiologist fees, newborn care, and pediatrician charges.

In determining where you want to give birth and with whom, cost is all too often the most influential factor. The cost of a normal vaginal birth in a hospital is between $3,000 and $5,000. The average physician fee is $1,800.[7] The cost of neonatal intensive care for one low-birth-weight infant is $14,698.[8] Full maternity care in birthing centers is approximately half of combined physician and hospital charges. Midwife fees vary drastically because of differences in education, qualifications, and geographic location. Suburban midwives charge more than rural midwives. The average cost of a midwife-

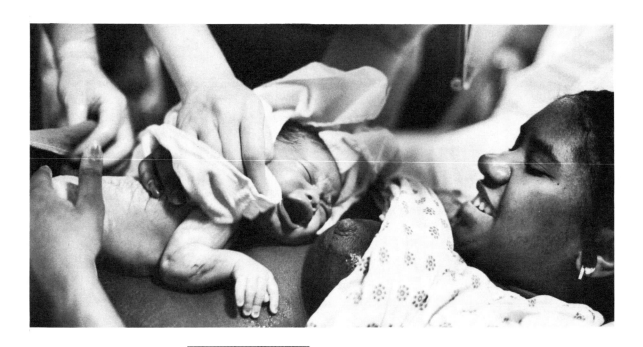

*A sixteen-year-old mother, treated with respect in a birthing center,
greets her newborn with joy and wonder.*

attended birth in the United States is $1,200 and includes far more quality
hours of prenatal care, labor and birth support, and postpartum visits.

Before making any decisions about maternity care, take out your insurance policy and read it. Write a letter to the company if you are in doubt as
to whether the type of birth experience you want is covered completely,
partially, or not at all. Group insurance plans, such as Health Net or others,
may restrict choices. With this type of coverage, you are usually restricted to
choosing from a pool of physicians who provide services for that insurance
company.

A young couple in Santa Barbara was determined to have their first baby
at home even though their insurance company would not pay for the services
of a CNM. They wrote letters to the insurance company and found out that

the midwife expenses would be covered if a doctor in their medical group would refer them to a qualified CNM for care. Of course, none of the doctors was willing to do that. But after their daughter was born at home, they went back to one of the doctors in the medical group and asked him to retroactively refer them to the CNM who had attended their birth. The doctor agreed and the insurance company reimbursed all midwife fees.

As mentioned, over five million employed women have no health care coverage for pregnancy and birth. When a woman is forced to seek public assistance through Medicaid or another state health insurance plan, her choices are automatically limited. Health care costs may be covered, but she becomes part of a heavily burdened system that usually does not allow for individuality. Her voice *can* be heard if she herself knows what she wants.

Julie, who had no insurance coverage when she became pregnant, applied for Medical (California Medicaid). There was only one doctor, in the town of over ninety thousand people, who would provide care for Medical patients. Even though Julie was forced to go to this particular physician, she supplemented her regular prenatal visits with a birth class at a local resource center. There she was encouraged to ask for what she wanted. The course included writing a birth plan, which plainly stated that she would like freedom of movement and nothing to initiate or augment labor unless it was medically advisable.

When she awoke one morning having mild contractions about a week before her due date, Julie called her doctor and he told her to meet him at the hospital within the next hour. She was placed on a fetal monitor as soon as she checked in; a vaginal examination by hospital staff revealed that she was only two centimeters dilated. When the doctor arrived, he also examined her, taking an unusual amount of time. When Julie asked him what he was doing, he didn't answer her but the nurse told her that he was preparing to break her bag of water. She was shocked and asked him if he had forgotten the birth plan they had discussed. He told her that *he* was the one in charge and that he viewed it as necessary to speed up the labor. When she refused, he became defensive, trying to make her feel guilty for her choice. "You might be in labor for a long time. Do you want to be responsible for what may happen to your baby?" She assured him that she was quite willing to take on all the responsibility for her decision. She checked out of the hospital against his advice. Her mild labor stopped, probably from the emotional stress of the confrontation.

Julie gave birth easily a week later to a healthy boy. She knew what she wanted and she had acted on it. Not having the financial power to purchase the health care that you ideally want does not preclude the option of taking control of your birth as Julie did.

After reviewing financial concerns, some couples decide to forego insurance coverage and opt for a home- or birthing-center birth that may not be reimbursable. Jim reluctantly went along with Maggie's desire to have a home water birth, even though his insurance policy could afford them the "best" doctor and hospital. Their location restricted them to the choice of a reputable but nonreimbursable direct-entry midwife. Jim talked about the experience after his son's birth: "At this point I don't care what it would have cost me. To know that Maggie was in control and that she wouldn't have to have another cesarean was worth every penny. I've decided to start a fund for our next baby's birth. It's the best investment you can make for your child's future—a gentle birth."

WRITING A BIRTH PLAN

A written birth plan is a tool that can be used for negotiation in any birth setting. It helps define what you want and how you may possibly give birth. The idea of writing a birth plan evolved during the past decade. A birth plan needs to be well thought out and clearly written, depicting your desires for your birth and for postnatal care. The details may vary according to where you choose to give birth, but there are many similar elements. A careful consideration of all your needs is important. Many childbirth instructors will assist women in creating a plan. Some hospital personnel look disdainfully at birth plans and become defensive if a woman presents what they perceive as a demand list. Others welcome the plan and understand that it represents a woman's desire for having the birth she wants.

When Corrie was planning to have a vaginal birth after a cesarean (VBAC) at her local hospital, she went directly to the chief of obstetrics well before her due date and learned about hospital policy for VBAC births. She determined that their policy was too strict for her. She wrote a plan that met her needs and presented it to the hospital board. A copy went to her physician, the president of the hospital, and the insurance provider. She worked to negotiate a situation that would give her freedom to labor without intervention and still meet the hospital requirements for safety. She did not want continuous fetal monitoring or an intravenous (IV) line, but agreed to be on the monitor twenty minutes out of every hour and to use a heparin lock (an IV needle placed in a vein to keep it open) in her hand. Because of all the hospital restrictions, Corrie eventually chose to give birth at home with the help of a lay midwife. She knew, however, that she had helped change the policy for the next woman who wanted to have a VBAC in that hospital.

One objection to birth plans is that they may create false expectations and result in disappointment if the plan is not followed. Flexibility is necessary in birth, but a birth plan keeps everyone aware of the mother's desires and allows the woman to be more in charge of her care. It is at times difficult for some care providers to simply turn over the decision-making process to someone else, but a well-thought-out plan shows that the woman is not only willing but able to accept that responsibility.

Preparing a birth plan is an educational process that can help you focus on what you want your birth to be like. It is not just looking over a xeroxed sheet from the hospital and crossing off what you want or don't want. Creating a comprehensive birth plan takes cooperation between you and your care provider. It is also a beneficial process for a woman who is planning a home birth. It can be fun deciding simple things like the kind of food to have available or the kind of music to play during labor. For a sample birth plan for a hospital birth, see Appendix C.

WHERE TO BIRTH YOUR BABY

Determining a caregiver and deciding how you'll pay for maternity care sometimes automatically determine where you will give birth. Yet often the decision process is reversed. You may already know that you want to have the baby at home or in a hospital. You must then find the practitioner who will work with you. Today more women are successfully negotiating for what they want. The number of midwife-attended out-of-hospital births increased from 9,727 in 1975 to over 20,000 in 1990.[9] Let's take a look at some of the considerations in creating choices in all birth settings and environments.

Home Birth

The demand for home birth is increasing, but the lack of qualified midwives is evident. Just compare four thousand American CNMs, the majority of whom work in hospitals, with England's thirty-four thousand midwives. In a landmark 1992 report, the House of Commons Health Committee stated that "the needs of mothers and babies (should be) placed at the centre, from which it follows that the maternity services must be fashioned around them and not the other way round."[10] Now any woman in England can request a home birth; it is up to the local health service to work out the details.

Women who want to be in charge of every element in their environment usually elect to have their babies at home. Many couples find that their desire for privacy and intimacy takes precedence over any financial or legal obstacles they may encounter. Many must finance the birth out of their own pockets because of lack of insurance coverage or refusal of third-party reimbursement for midwives. Couples who choose a home birth accept more responsibility than those who choose to birth at a hospital or birthing center.

Many prospective parents who are considering a home birth wonder if it is legal. Home birth is absolutely legal. As witnessed in England, it has now become a legislative mandate. Here in the United States, the legal gray area still depends on the status of midwives in each state. The midwife who provides prenatal care and attends the home birth assumes the legal responsibility for the life of the mother and baby. If there is no midwife involved, the parents then become legally responsible if anything happens to the baby during the birth. There are child abuse and neglect laws in force now in every state. If a child dies during an unattended home birth any third party can conceivably charge the parents with child abuse and manslaughter. These instances are very rare and are seldom carried through the court system.

Parents who decide they want a home birth are often faced with the lack of doctor support or backup. Some couples who are committed to home birth hire a midwife but also see an obstetrician throughout their pregnancy, just so they have help available in case of an emergency. When midwives work

Obstetrician Carol Knight gathers with some of her clients and their babies at her center in Palo Alto, California. Dr. Knight attended all these women in their homes.

independently, without doctor backup, they must rely on the doctors in the local emergency room to take over if there is a complication that requires transport to a hospital. In states where midwifery is not licensed or regulated, midwives often cannot even accompany their clients into the hospital for fear of prosecution. A midwife who is lucky enough to develop a working relationship with a doctor and hospital is considered a respected member of the health care team. Her presence and expertise are not only acknowledged but called upon.

Couples often wonder about the materials and supplies necessary in a home birth. Not much is really needed. Home birth kits are readily available from birthing supply companies (see Appendix F). The kits contain sterile gloves, gauze pads, straws, a cotton hat for the baby, drop cloths, waterproof covers for the bed, a thermometer, and a pan for sitz baths after birth. Midwives bring everything else needed, including the technology of birth, to the home. Fetal heart tones are monitored with fetoscopes or ultrasonic stethoscopes. Oxygen tanks stand ready in case either mother or baby needs oxygen. Midwives carry drugs that can be administered to slow or stop a hemorrhage. Most midwives also bring with them special herbal preparations, homeopathic remedies, massage techniques, and even acupuncture needles. IV lines can be started at home; tears or episiotomies can be stitched. (See Appendix B for areas of possible concern that you will want to discuss with your practitioner.)

Choosing to have a home birth demands commitment, cooperation, and trust. For many couples, however, it is the most satisfactory choice. Trudy and Ned recall feelings of absolute awe overwhelming them after the birth of their second son at home. Their first son was born in the hospital and it was a good experience, but Trudy said of her second birth, "I just didn't realize there could be so much difference between home and hospital. Here [at home] everyone was focused on me and my needs; there [the hospital] everyone just wanted the baby to come out. I almost felt like I wasn't a part of it. Having everyone here and feeling the baby come out and having his dad be the first one in this world to touch him.... That's the way God intended birth to be."

There are literally thousands of stories just like Ned and Trudy's. Many couples who have one or two births in the hospital and then try a home birth come away with a confidence that is unparalleled.

Birthing Center Birth

There is a vast difference between birthing centers that are attached to hospitals and birthing centers that are freestanding and owned and operated independently by CNMs or physicians. Besides the absence of expensive medical equipment, there is an obvious difference in attitude about birth. We have discussed the Family Birthing Center of Upland, California, and the Hawthorn Birth and Development Centre of Melbourne, Australia, in previous chapters, so you have a good idea of their philosophies and of the family-centered care they offer. Freestanding birthing centers focus on serving the needs of the women and families who use them.

The majority of birthing centers serve primarily the educated middle class, who either have the money to pay out of pocket for their births or have an insurance provider who will cover it. Access to birthing centers for poor or working women has been limited, which is why the Birth Place in San Diego opened in 1990. The Birth Place has been incorporated to ensure that at least 40 percent of their clients are women on welfare.

Because women who have access to care from a birthing center are more involved in their care, birthing centers can offer a viable alternative to the dilemma of high infant mortality. They have more prenatal visits, fewer instances of prematurity, and babies with higher birth weights. The National Association of Childbearing Centers (NACC) has been working since 1983 to help establish a network of community-based birthing centers throughout the United States. There are approximately 130 accredited birthing centers across the country and about the same number in the process of accreditation.

One of the first jobs that CNM Kitty Ernst tackled as head of NACC was the licensing and regulation of freestanding birthing centers. A task force was set up to create the guidelines that individual states would eventually adopt as their licensing procedures. The political process began, and legislation regulating birthing centers was established in twenty-seven states. This initial push for licensing legitimized birthing centers and allowed insurance companies to reimburse fees. The next major push was for a national standard of accreditation for birthing centers.

Ernst states, "NACC refers over a thousand parents a year to birthing centers in their areas. Birth centers offer quality nurse-midwifery care for half the cost. When mothers realize just what they could be getting for half the price of a two-day stay in a hospital, they will begin to demand these

*As well as providing prenatal and birth care, birthing centers become
a place for new mothers to receive support and encouragement as parents.*

services. As taxpayers we should be looking at this because of all the dollars
that go into medically subsidized maternity care."[11]

The Natural Childbirth Institute in Culver City, California, focuses on
women's needs by giving them complete freedom of choice. Director Nancy
McNeese, CNM, and her staff help over one hundred families a year in the
central Los Angeles area achieve gentle noninterventionist births. One-third
of these births are in warm water. McNeese feels that her center provides a
valuable community service—one that she admits is time-intensive. "We put

women in charge of their birth experience," she states, "and keep the costs reasonable."

There is great client satisfaction at birthing centers. The homelike atmosphere and relaxed attitudes help make women feel safe. Women bring their personal items, their chosen music, and most important, any and all of their family members.

When Mary Breckenridge founded the Kentucky Frontier Nursing Service in 1925, she understood that health care starts in the home with the women who take the responsibility for raising children. Breckenridge had a deep love and concern for children; she also knew that if you take care of a mother, she is better able to care for her baby. Freestanding birthing centers, offering care based on the midwifery model, are designed to take care of mothers for almost a year or beyond. The total focus of care is on the development of health through creating a balance in women's lives. Women are nurtured, and their self-confidence in their inherent abilities to give birth and nurture their children is increased. Kitty Ernst describes birthing centers as "family places where there is no generation gap and where children and grandparents alike are invited to share in one of life's most special events. They are places where health care for all can begin now and grow."

Hospital Birth

Negotiating for what you want in a hospital birth can be a challenging but rewarding experience. In the last decade many couples throughout the United States have succeeded in having satisfying birth experiences within an institutional setting. Not every hospital is resistant to change. Hospitals in Europe, especially in the United Kingdom, are adjusting to requests for water birth by installing tubs. More and more American hospitals are remodeling their birthing units. They are providing rooms in which the mother may labor, give birth, and stay with her baby after birth.

Some of these birthing units, however, have become masterful reproductions of homelike environments that merely conceal the standard hospital technology. Everything needed for a medically controlled birth either pops out of the wall or conveniently rolls into the room. The consumer must be aware of whether a hospital just advertises the availability of gentle birth or truly provides it. Make sure you talk with both the hospital and your doctor so that you feel confident you will be allowed to create the experience you want within the hospital. Some doctors will sit with women in labor and let the process unfold in an undisturbed way. There are also many hospitals who employ CNMs in their clinics.

Don't be dependent on your doctor to tell you everything about the hospital. Call the administration yourself and ask about their policies and whether they offer tours of the maternity area. Even if you have a great relationship with your doctor and you write a detailed birth plan, you may be faced with the limits of hospital policy the minute you are admitted. You might set aside some time to visit the maternity unit and talk to some of the nurses who work there. If they are too busy to answer your questions, ask for their phone numbers and set a time to call them at home. Talk to other women who have given birth at that hospital. Write down your questions so you know what to ask. By asking questions, sometimes simple ones, you make hospital staffs more aware of the growing concerns for gentle birth choices. You will find a very complete list of questions for doctors and midwives, any of which may be addressed to hospitals, in Appendices A and B.

When Peggy toured the maternity unit three weeks before her second baby was due, she suddenly changed her mind about giving birth in that hospital. Fortunately she was able to hire a CNM at that late date, and she had a beautiful and quick home birth. She said, "It's not that I didn't have a good experience with my first baby in the hospital, but I just knew it wasn't for me after I saw it again." Find out what you really want before you are in labor, and don't make the mistake of assuming anything.

An ideal situation for women giving birth in a hospital was created several years ago at Beth Israel Hospital in Newark, New Jersey. The hospital rented an entire floor to an independent birthing center. The Birth Center at the Beth functions as a freestanding birthing center even though it is on the seventh floor of a large city hospital. The center maintains its own staff, procedures, and protocols, yet it has a referral arrangement with the obstetric and pediatric staff. When a woman needs more intervention than the birthing center is equipped to handle, she is simply transferred down a few floors to the hospital's maternity unit. So far the reaction of the community, the hospital, and the staff of the birthing center has been great. The center has even offered women the opportunity to labor and give birth in water. CNM Donna Roosa, the center director, says, "We quite literally have the best of both worlds here. There is no reason why any other hospital in the United States could not adapt what we have created here to their particular needs. We hope it is just a matter of time until they do."

WHO ELSE SHOULD BE AT YOUR BIRTH?

Sheila Kitzinger calls the people you choose to support you at your birth your "birth companions." It is a very important decision to consider. Many women say that one of the reasons they chose a home birth was that they were able to have friends and family around them. More hospitals are allowing mothers to have more than one person with them for birth. The baby's father is usually the one person most women want to be with them. They draw on the strength and love of their partner and seek his support through this most powerful and emotional transition. Most couples find that sharing the birth experience strengthens their relationship and bonds them as a family. Some women want only their partner and their doctor or midwife in order to maintain intimacy, but most women like to have at least one other woman as part of her support team.

Mothers, sisters, or close female friends are most often chosen by pregnant women as that added support person. Women need to feel mothered during the birth process. The emotional demands of labor can often be met by another woman who has given birth herself. Midwives sometimes fill this role for women, especially if they have formed a close bond with the mother during her pregnancy. Sometimes a nurse in the hospital can serve this function very well. There have been studies that show that when one person focused on the mother, labor time was cut in half and the number of complications was reduced.[12] Studies also show that mothers had a stronger response to their newborns, cuddling and bonding with them in the first hour after birth.

There is a growing number of women, especially those who have given birth already, who help women during and after their births. These women, who are not trained as midwives, are called childbirth advocates, labor assistants, or doulas. Their role is to support the mother emotionally, give simple comfort measures during labor, and protect her rights if she is giving birth in the hospital. Labor assistants are also a great support for fathers. They may quietly encourage fathers to be present with their wives and give them back rubs and food when they need it. Women who help out after the birth are often called doulas, from the Greek for "helper."

Programs designed by organizations such as Informed Homebirth/Informed Birth and Parenting or the National Association of Childbirth Assistants teach the art of labor assisting. Some trained midwives also serve in this capacity for women giving birth in hospitals. Having a trained labor support person can be an essential component in achieving a gentle birth experience.

Robin and Ted had decided to have their first baby in the hospital and to hire a labor assistant to be with them for their birth. The assistant came to their home when Robin was in early labor and monitored her there for several hours. The three of them worked and bonded well together. When the assistant suggested that they go to the hospital, they made a smooth transition. Her support continued in the hospital and their baby was born after thirty minutes, much to the surprise of the hospital staff and doctor.

When considering hiring a childbirth assistant or labor support person, you need to interview a candidate just as you would a midwife or doctor. What is her education and birth experience? What does she charge? Is she available and on call any hour of the day or night? Does someone take over for her if she cannot come for some reason? Are you able to discuss your specific needs with her, and is she flexible? If you are interested in becoming a childbirth assistant, contact one of the birthing organizations listed in Appendix F for more information.

In consciously choosing whom you want around you at your birth, it is beneficial to have someone with whom you share a deep love. Think about those people who are willing to give to you physically and emotionally without putting demands on you. The last thing you need during your labor is to take care of someone else's needs. This is why some women don't want to be responsible for their small children during labor and birth. Women know that the children may demand their attention and may not understand why mommy is making funny noises and can't talk or play with them. Most children do very well at birth when they are adequately supported, especially when birth is viewed as normal and natural. Children who grow up actually experiencing birth have a much broader view of life than those who only see pictures or movies about birth.

A woman must choose the number of people who will be present at a birth with caution. Often if there are too many people, it will slow down or stop labor. Women who invite their entire family to their births often report afterward that they felt like they were performing. Diane and Allen had decided early in their pregnancy that they wanted their home birth to be very intimate, with only the midwife and Diane's mother present. When Diane's stepfather came during the night with her mother, Allen very quickly asked him to find a hotel room in town until the baby was born. It may have been difficult, but Allen truly supported Diane in respecting her plans of whom she wanted with her. It is very important to be able to clearly communicate your needs to the people you invite to attend your birth.

A labor assistant or doula can be extremely helpful after the birth as well. She may continue to come to the home to help for up to two weeks. A doula traditionally takes care of the mother and provides whatever service she may need, like watching the new baby while the mother bathes, eats, or takes a nap or taking care of the other children so the mother can focus her attention on the baby. So much attention is focused on the birth that sometimes it is hard to conceive that there is actually going to be a baby to take care of and parent for the next twenty to twenty-five years. A labor assistant or doula adds a very meaningful component to creating gentle birth choices for women.

Consumers Create Choices

Be demanding options and taking steps to create them, the consumer has made progress in taking back control of the birth process. Changes have taken place in hospitals where administrators have been willing to listen and in legislatures where lawmakers have been influenced by politically active individuals and groups. Consumer Advocates for the Legalization of Midwifery (CALM) organized a statewide campaign in California in 1991 to spread public awareness about midwifery.[13] Groups like CALM are powerful

Consumer advocacy is one way to create gentle birth choices.

tools for negotiating change and are helping to define what "good medical practice" is. Change will come when the gathered data demonstrates that gentle birth choices, like home birth and water birth, are not only desired by the parents but safe and reasonable for the baby.

In March 1993 the Ontario, Canada, government called for funding proposals for three new out-of-hospital birthing centers. Over seventy inquiry packages were sent out and ten were returned by the cut-off deadline in June.

The Ontario government expects to have these three new centers open by September 1994. Elana Johnson, an Ontario midwife responsible for submitting one of the proposals, recalls that the birthing center process began with consumers. "There were actually four birth-center committees in different cities that came together as a coalition. Each committee had parents and midwives working together. In September 1992, almost five years after we first started meeting loosely as a group, we presented a brief to the health minister about the potential cost-effectiveness of midwifery-run birthing centers and their relevance in our health care system." Johnson continues, "It is quite obvious that there is a consumer demand for midwifery-run centers and also a community need. Midwives, as it was legislated in 1991, were mandated to work for pregnant women in all settings: hospital, birthing centers, and homes."[14]

When Sister Angela Murdaugh, CNM, began the Holy Family Services birth and health center in West Laco, Texas, she was tired of what she calls the "hassle index" that comes with government-funded programs. CNMs in this area of the Texas–Mexican border who serve the low-income migrant population have persevered in a long struggle for recognition as Medicaid providers. Physician backup and liability insurance have also created stumbling blocks. The perseverance has paid off, though, with 40 percent of the births in this area of Texas taking place out of the hospital—20 percent in birthing centers and 20 percent as home births. The area's neonatal mortality rate is much lower than the national average, even for this severely impoverished area.[15] Holy Family Services, which receives no federal funding and is dependent on Catholic Charities and public support, is a true example of combined community effort.

Kitty Ernst, CNM, believes consumers represent a great untapped power that can change the way birth is conducted in this country. The Childbearing Center, the country's very first freestanding birthing center, was founded in New York City in 1975 by the Maternity Center Association (MCA), a voluntary health agency. MCA director Ruth Watson Lubic, CNM, states, "Its board consists of consumers working with professional advisory groups. Since its founding in 1918, MCA has been responsible for initiating prenatal care, prenatal parent education, prepared childbirth classes, nurse-midwifery edu-

Teenage girls who are cared for by midwives have better birth experiences and are much better prepared to mother their children. This sixteen-year-old gave birth with dignity and joy and approaches motherhood in the same way.

cation, and freestanding birthing centers in the United States. It has helped other consumer groups and families make their voices heard."[16] Consumers *can* come together to establish birthing centers and change maternity-care practices. Most centers start that way.

Health Care for All Women and Children by the Year 2000

We have looked at why the medicalization of childbirth took place, the effects that this has had on women and families, and why it is necessary to give birth to a cooperative and systematic restructuring of maternity care. Women need to know that they can create the alternatives they want by demanding necessary change. Dr. Michael Rosenthal says, "I tell women they can have their babies the way they want here. They can have it the way they want anywhere, they just have to be willing to ask."

Creating gentle birth choices has become very necessary. We must change the way birth is managed and the way babies are brought into their new lives. These changes will not happen overnight and they certainly will not be easy. Dr. Marsden Wagner, pediatrician and former responsible officer for Maternal/Child Health in the World Health Organization (WHO), aptly addresses the issue of change. He predicts there will be opposition to creating change within the maternity care system for birthing women. He says, "Change won't come easy. We have an incredibly obstinate obstetrical profession. It's all about territory. It's about power. It's about control. And at the end of the day, it's about money."[17]

We have an opportunity, if not an obligation, to take our new understanding and create a maternal-child health care system that works: a system that acknowledges that birth is a normal physiological process and not a medical event; a system that embraces midwifery as the best possible care for healthy birthing women; and a system that allows women to choose how, where, and with whom they give birth. When we develop and utilize a health care system based on these precepts, we will begin to see healing take place in all levels of our society. Our families will be stronger, babies will be healthier, women will glow with self-confidence and power. Birth changes women's lives forever. As we approach a new millennium, let us make sure that women's lives are changed in positive, healthy, and empowering ways and that all parents have plenty of gentle birth choices.

Appendix A

Questions to Ask
a Doctor

What is your general philosophy concerning pregnancy and birth?

When you interview obstetricians, it is important to assess right away how liberal or traditional they are in their own practice. Are they open to new ideas or do they practice by the book?

How long have you been practicing?

Some women may want a doctor who has attended a few thousand births, others may want to work with someone who is just starting out in practice and has fresh energy and openness about all birth situations.

Are you board-certified? If not, why?

Each specialty of medicine has its own examining board that certifies doctors by written and oral examination. Being board-certified states that this doctor holds to a very high set of standards within the obstetric profession; however, this is no assurance of a particular physician's ability. Some physicians voluntarily choose not to be certified; others have been denied certification.

Do you have any children and how were they born?

Having a female obstetrician will not automatically guarantee a lower intervention rate, but sometimes you will find a compassionate doctor who actually gave birth at home or in a birthing center or who has caught his own children. They are more likely to understand your requests for freedom of choice.

Do you use midwives in your practice?

Not all obstetricians will advertise the existence of midwives on their staffs. If they do work with a midwife, request her services.

What are your guidelines for "normal" and "high-risk" pregnancies?

Screening requirements vary from doctor to doctor. Some view all women over thirty-five as high risk; others do not see age as a significant factor. Standard obstetrics today views a woman who has had three children as high risk as well as the woman who is having her first baby. The set of guidelines that each doctor uses provides him or her with a picture of possible complications. By concentrating on the person and not the picture, better maternity care can be provided.

What is your regular fee? What does this fee include?

Normal prenatal care usually includes all tests performed within the doctor's office (blood tests for hemoglobin, urinalysis, and blood glucose levels) and delivery at the hospital. What fees do not cover are extra lab tests or the initial diagnostic work-up. These fees are paid directly to the laboratory.

What routine tests do you require?

Under what circumstances would you require the following tests?

Ultrasound during pregnancy

Alpha-fetoprotein (AFP)

Chorionic villi sampling (CVS)

Amniocentesis

Glucose tolerance test (GTT)

How often do you do cesarean sections and for what reasons?

Definitely assess this doctor's cesarean-section rate and ask for the reasons for them.

If my baby is breech, can I give birth vaginally?

In 1990 most medical schools were not even teaching the procedures for vaginal breech birth.[1] A breech baby, no matter what position, was classified as an automatic reason for a cesarean section. There are some doctors who will allow women to attempt a vaginal breech.

Do you encourage women who have had one cesarean section to give birth vaginally?

Do you have specific recommendations concerning weight gain, diet, and exercise?

Doctors are less likely today to insist on a restricted weight gain and more likely to recommend a healthy diet and exercise plan. Keeping active throughout pregnancy will enhance your ability to labor and give birth and decrease your chances of gestational diabetes.

Do you require or suggest that I take a childbirth class?

All first-time couples benefit greatly from taking an informative and practical birth preparation class, and doctors are recognizing the value of preparation.

How often will I see you?

Visits are scheduled once a month until the seventh month, every two weeks until thirty-six weeks, and once a week after that. Extra appointments can be scheduled at any time between regular visits.

Do you return calls personally or ask your nurses to call?

If the nurses on staff in the doctor's office can handle normal questions, it can be pleasant to develop a relationship with them. But it is good to know how calls and questions are handled before they arise.

If there is more than one doctor in the practice, what is your rotation policy? How often are you on call? Will I be seen by each doctor in the practice? Who will actually be at my birth? Do I have a choice? Will the other doctors respect the agreements you make with me?

It is very important to meet either the other partners in your doctor's practice or whoever covers his practice when he is out of town or unavailable. If your doctor has a busy practice, it is not reasonable to assume that he or she can attend every birth. Therefore, interview the other doctors and make sure they share your philosophies and goals and that they understand how you want your birth to be. Don't wait until you are in labor to be disappointed.

Where do you have hospital privileges? Can I choose which hospital if you have privileges at more than one?

Take a tour of each hospital and choose the one you want to birth in. Your doctor may not want to travel across town or out of his area. Hospitals often grant privileges to other doctors in special circumstances.

Does the hospital allow the patient to follow her written birth plan?

This is a question for the hospital, but it may also be asked of the physician.

Could you tell me how a routine vaginal birth is handled at that hospital?

When do I need to check into the hospital?

The longer you stay at home in early labor, the less possibility there will be for interventions.

Can I labor and give birth in the same room?

The concept of labor, delivery, recovery, and postpartum (LDRP)in the same room has been promoted for the last ten years. If your prospective hospital is one that still transfers women into the delivery room, request that they make an exception in your case. Also be aware of the "cosmetic cover-up" discussed in chapter 7. Not all LDRP rooms are alike, and not all allow women to do what they want.

Do I have to have an IV?

Do I have to have an electronic fetal monitor on during labor?

How often does someone do a vaginal exam to assess progress?

Can I refuse vaginal exams?

How soon after my labor begins will you (or the doctor on call) come to see me?

Will you stay with me during labor?

Can my partner stay with me the entire time?

Can the rest of my family members, including my children or my mother and father, be present during labor and birth?

Does the hospital have showers or baths in each room?

Can I eat and drink during my labor?

Do you encourage women to walk, squat, or be on their hands and knees during labor?

Understanding the philosophy behind why you need to remain active during labor encourages women to move. Lying still on a bed during labor is probably the hardest thing for women to cope with.

Can I birth the baby in the position of my choice?

Hospital beds often break apart at the foot to "allow" a woman to semi-squat. What some women have found easier is to simply put the mattress on the floor or be supported by their partners while they squat on the floor. Assess early on if those alternatives are acceptable to your doctor and the hospital.

Can I use a warm bath for pain relief during my labor, even if my water has broken?

One woman at Santa Monica Hospital was promised that she would be able to use the brand-new tubs that had been installed for labor. What her doctor did not tell her was his list of restrictions: A woman could not use the tub if her water had not broken and the baby's head had not engaged into the pelvis (for fear of a cord prolapse), and she could not enter the water after her water had broken (for fear of infection). She never once used the tubs and ended up with an epidural and a low-forceps delivery.

Can I stay in the water to deliver my baby?

Find out right away what position your doctor takes on water birth. It might be your opportunity to educate him.

What kind of pain medication do you generally use?

Do you have any experience with acupuncture for pain relief?

Some hospitals now have acupuncturists on call for pain relief and special problems during labor. Breech babies have been turned through acupuncture; nausea has been controlled; and labor has been kept active with needles instead of drugs. It is worth investigating this alternative.

If I want an epidural, what are your guidelines?

There is a relatively new form of epidural that administers such a low dose that women can actually move their extremities and "feel" more. Some doctors offer this "walking epidural" with certain restrictions. Question your doctor carefully about the kinds of medication used and the procedures with which they are administered.

Do you do episiotomies? Why? What percentage?

Does your doctor think that episiotomies are necessary? Is he or she willing to allow you to try other techniques? If a doctor cuts more than 10 percent of birthing clients, look for a new doctor.

Do you ever use hot packs on the perineum or use perineal massage?

Do you routinely order enemas or pubic shaves?

Do you ever use a vacuum extractor? What percentage?

Vacuum extractors were developed to take the place of low forceps. A large suction cup (usually made of hard plastic and sometimes silicone) is placed on the baby's scalp. The cup is attached to a tube that is attached to a vacuum. When a suction on the baby's head has been achieved, constant suction will quite literally pull the baby out within ten to twenty minutes.[2] There are some risks with extraction, such as perineal lacerations, hematomas on the baby's scalp, and pain for both the mother and baby. It requires a fully dilated cervix, a baby with at least some part of the scalp visible in the birth canal, and the cooperation of the mother. Vacuum extraction is preferred over the use of forceps.

Do you ever use forceps? What percentage?

What is your policy concerning stripping or rupturing membranes?

Rupturing membranes is often the first intervention that doctors do to "get a labor going." Ask your doctor if a labor can progress normally and slowly without rupturing the membranes? Will you be informed of his or her desire to break your water? Do you have the right to refuse this intervention?

What is your policy concerning interventions after my water breaks by itself?

Some physicians view ruptured membranes as a potentially dangerous situation for both mother and baby. Others watch carefully, encouraging women to walk and remain active, especially if labor has not yet started. Assess your doctor's guidelines for ruptured membranes. How long will he or she allow you to go without starting labor? What lab tests are required? Some doctors take white blood counts every twenty-four hours and body temperatures every four hours and leave a woman alone. Others want her hospitalized immediately and induce labor with Pitocin. Studies have shown that women who walk and remain active have fewer cesarean sections and always deliver before those who receive Pitocin.[3]

How long will you allow me to labor before starting interventions?

Does your doctor go by the book in judging length of labor? What are his or her considerations: maternal exhaustion, nutritional needs, movement?

What is your policy for using Pitocin in labor? What percentage?

How does your doctor judge a slow or ineffectual labor? Do you really have a "lazy" uterus or do you need to get up and move around?

How long will you wait to cut the cord and deliver the placenta?

Can my partner cut the cord?

Is cord cutting viewed as a medical procedure or simply part of the process of birth that the couple has shared? Are fathers included in this process?

What do you put in the infant's eyes after birth?

State laws mandate that an antibacterial agent be put into the baby's eyes to reduce the incidence of blindness from venereal disease that has been passed from the mother to the baby. The use of silver nitrate has been abandoned by most hospitals. More common antibiotic agents are now used. Find out from your doctor what he or she recommends, and ask if you can choose not to use anything at all if you have been screened for all venereal diseases.

Do you routinely give vitamin K shots to newborns?

Vitamin K is routinely given to prevent hemorrhagic disease in newborns. The incidence of intracranial hemorrhage is extremely low. The administration of vitamin K has also been given to counteract the possibilities of bleeding after circumcision. There has been an unusually high incidence of childhood cancer linked to vitamin K shots. Oral vitamin K has not shown any relationship to cancer in children.[4] Ask your doctor if oral vitamin K may be substituted and if he has access to the latest research.

Can I breast-feed immediately after birth?

Can the baby stay with me in my room (rooming-in)?

How do you feel about circumcision?

If your doctor has no opinion about circumcision, please use the opportunity to educate him or her.

How soon after the birth can we leave the hospital?

Most doctors recommend a short stay in the hospital. Some are even willing to discharge after twenty-four hours. Find out if your doctor is open to discharge after six to twelve hours, especially if you have given birth vaginally and you have adequate help at home.

Appendix B

Questions to Ask a Midwife

What is your education and training as a midwife?

You must discern if you are hiring a certified nurse-midwife (CNM), a lay midwife, or a direct-entry midwife with formal training from a midwifery program in the United States or abroad. The three groups represent vast differences in educational experience but not necessarily in the way they practice.

How many years have you been practicing?

Do you want to trust a midwife who is just starting out in independent practice or do you continue your search for a more experienced midwife? Find this out right away.

What is your general philosophy about pregnancy and birth?

Midwives in general hold the philosophy that normal birth is not a medical event and needs to be respected for the creative process that it is. I would be surprised if you found a midwife who viewed birth as a potential emergency to be prepared for.

Are you a mother yourself? How old are your children now?

If you are choosing a midwife with young children, how will she be able to attend your birth if there are family needs? Are you open to her bringing her young and perhaps nursing child with her to your birth?

How were your babies born?

Many women become midwives after a not-so-wonderful birth experience. Find out about your midwife's births. Some argue that midwives who have never given birth cannot be as good as those who have had children. I don't agree with this assumption; I know some wonderful, talented, caring midwives who have not had the opportunity to give birth.

Do you work alone or with a partner or assistant? If you work with someone, what is his or her experience?

It is important to meet all the people who will have any responsibility concerning your prenatal care, labor, or birth. Some midwives take on apprentices or students. Find this out in the beginning.

How many births have you attended as the primary caregiver?

How long has your midwife been in independent practice? Has she always worked with an experienced partner? Ask for references from former partners and clients.

Do you attend births in a birthing center or hospital?

Perhaps this midwife has hospital privileges or attends births at home and in a birthing center.

How many births are you attending now?

For a home-birth practice, the most births that one midwife with one assistant can possibly attend is six to eight per month. If she tries to attend more, there could be two women in labor at the same time, leaving one with no coverage. Midwives in birthing centers can handle many more births per month because there they can attend more than one laboring woman at a time.

Who takes over for you if you go on vacation or get sick?

A very important consideration is who will take over the midwife's practice if she is unable to continue or needs to leave for a certain period of time. Make these plans with your midwife early on in your pregnancy. Know that you will be covered if anything happens to your midwife.

Do you have guidelines or restrictions about who can give birth at home?

A midwife should have the same screening criteria as a doctor screening for risk factors. Most women cannot stay at home if they have had a low hemoglobin level within one week prior to their due date, hypertension, an active herpes lesion, multiple births, breech presentation, or any vaginal bleeding prior to labor. All of these cases would be referred to a physician.

Do you require that I see a physician during my pregnancy even if everything is all right?

A visit to a backup physician is usually in order just so you can meet and he or she can establish a chart on you. If your midwife does not have an active relationship with a backup physician, it may be your responsibility to obtain a doctor and see him or her.

What are your fees and what do they include?

Just as with a doctor, most midwives' fees cover all prenatal care, birth, newborn assessment, home care, and follow-up for six weeks. Any lab tests, diagnostic tests, or extra doctors' visits are not included. Also not included are the costs of a hospital transfer, including ambulance, hospital, and doctors' fees.

Can you submit your charges to my insurance company?

I don't know of a single lay midwife in this country who can bill an independent insurance company for reimbursement, but several states do allow reimbursement for state-licensed midwives who care for low-income women. Many CNMs can bill insurance companies and state Medicaid. Some midwives have an arrangement with a physician to add their charges to the doctor's bill, which is turned in to the insurance provider for payment. Find out if your midwife has made any of these arrangements.

What payment arrangements do you make?

Most midwives will take payments throughout pregnancy. Many even have payment forms and billing systems on home computers. Payment of services is usually required before delivery, because after birth it can be difficult to collect the bill. Be considerate about the midwife's bill and make easy and early arrangements for payment. Historically midwives have given their services away. Perhaps that is why so many birthing centers run by midwives go out of business.

How often will I see you?

Visits are scheduled once a month until the seventh month, every two weeks until thirty-six weeks, and once a week after that. Extra appointments can be scheduled at any time between regular visits.

What are your guidelines concerning weight gain, nutrition, and exercise?

Weight gain and diet will be monitored throughout the pregnancy. Most midwives are educated about modern nutrition and work with women to get the most out of their diets. Many midwives have special education in the use of herbs and homeopathy for pregnancy.

Do you require that I take a childbirth education class? Do you teach a childbirth preparation class?

Midwives usually teach their own preparation classes. Some midwives feel that they give so much individualized attention that couples do not need extra classes to prepare for birth.

If I am planning a home birth, do you come to my home anytime before I go into labor?

Midwives generally make at least one home visit before they come to the house for labor. They assure that the home is adequate and clean, and they help plan any necessary details with the couples, such as where the water birth tub should go.

When should I call you after my labor begins?

Each midwife sets her own protocols about when and the reasons why to call after labor begins. Generally midwives want to know as soon as contractions begin so they can plan their day (or night). They usually don't arrive until the contractions are "long and strong" and close together.

How do you handle emergencies?

Ask very carefully just what kind of emergencies she is prepared to deal with and has dealt with in different situations.

How many women whom you have attended have had to go to the hospital?

Assess your midwife's transport rate. Inquire if there is any one problem for which she transfers the most.

In what situations would I have to go to the hospital?

Be very specific and find out exactly why you might be transported. Situations that require backup might include prolonged labor, premature labor, prolapsed umbilical cord, bleeding in labor, severe drop or increase in fetal heart tone, maternal hypertension, meconium in the amniotic fluid, or problems with the baby right after birth.

Would you stay with me in the hospital?

Most midwives can accompany their clients into the hospital and stay with them, but in some places where lay midwifery is illegal, the midwife cannot come into the hospital and admit that she has been attending a home birth. Find out if your midwife has a good working relationship with a local hospital. Sometimes hospitals will not admit a woman in labor, so carefully plan your backup arrangements with your midwife.

What is your experience with water for labor and birth?

Midwives traditionally have used water for pain relief during labor. Many are now advocating its use by all of their clients.

Can I give birth in water?

Ask if your midwife has a tub that she uses for water birth or if she knows where you can rent or purchase one. Find out if she really is supportive of water birth. I have talked with many women who have said that their midwives professed to support water birth but then asked the mother to get out of the tub at the last minute.

What is your experience with breech births? How many have you attended?

What is your experience with twins? How many have you attended?

Do you suture perineal tears?

Unless your midwife sutures well, you will have to travel to a hospital if you need stitches. This might influence your choice of practitioners.

What is your experience with a vaginal birth after a cesarean [VBAC]?

Will you attend a VBAC at home? in the hospital?

Many midwives cannot legally attend a first-time VBAC at home because of licensing restrictions. Some are willing to look the other way in order to give the woman a chance. This is a very serious consideration that requires much discussion with your midwife.

Have you ever had to resuscitate a baby?

Assess the resuscitation skills of the midwife. Midwifery organizations and nursing schools teach courses in neonatal resuscitations, and your midwife should have a current certificate. Ask to see it.

What kind of equipment do you bring to a birth?

Find out what kind of drugs, oxygen, resuscitation equipment, intravenous (IV) equipment, and other emergency equipment your midwife keeps in her bags.

Do you examine the baby after birth?

Do you put drops in the baby's eyes? Do you give the baby a vitamin K shot?

Many midwives do not use either eye drops or vitamin K shots for the baby after a home birth. Find this out ahead of time and decide if you want to take these precautions.

Do you have a pediatrician you work with or recommend?

Will you allow my partner to be as active at the birth as desired (catching the baby, cutting the cord)? Can I have my other children with me during my labor and birth?

Is your midwife willing to "allow" the family to conduct the birth under her supervision? Is she willing to give you complete control? Will she instruct your partner on how to catch the baby?

How often do you come to see me after I give birth?

Home-birth midwives generally come back for follow-up visits after twenty-four hours, two days, five days, and ten days.

Do you provide or know of anyone who will help new mothers after birth?

Some home-birth services provide a doula or can recommend one for help after the baby's birth. There is generally an extra charge that is well worth every penny.

Will you help me with breast-feeding?

Midwives are on call twenty-four hours a day, seven days a week, for all problems after birth, especially breast-feeding. Many even have special classes or private sessions to evaluate breast-feeding readiness and answer any questions.

How do you feel about circumcision?

I don't know of very many midwives who will present both viewpoints about circumcision unless their clients are Jewish. If there is a religious consideration, the thoughtful midwife will support her clients' decision.

Sample Birth Plan for a Hospital Birth

I understand that all of my requests presume that I have a normal pregnancy and birth. If there is a situation that constitutes a medical emergency for either myself or my baby, I agree to accept medical judgments only with informed consent. I would prefer to have the following set of requests honored.

It is my wish to have clear and adequate explanations of all procedures, of my progress as assessed by medical staff, and of any possible complications as soon as they occur.

I wish to have the following:

- No separation from my birth partner during hospital stay
- More than one support person if desired
- No enema or pubic shave
- Freedom to wear my own clothes during labor and birth
- Freedom to use food and drink during labor as I choose
- No use of electronic fetal monitor, either external or internal, in the absence of fetal distress; use of a fetoscope instead
- No drugs during labor or delivery
- No routine IV unless in an emergency
- Freedom to walk and move during labor

- No artificial rupture of membranes
- No Pitocin
- Freedom to use warm water immersion for labor and/or birth (even if my membranes are ruptured)
- Freedom to give birth in any position I choose
- Lights dimmed, room quiet
- No episiotomy; use of perineal massage instead
- Delay in cutting cord until it has stopped pulsating, unless it is wrapped around baby's neck; my partner and I should be allowed to cut cord if we desire
- In case of cesarean, my partner will be allowed to accompany me to the operating room and recovery room. My partner will be allowed to hold the baby immediately after delivery and accompany him or her to the nursery
- Immediate skin-to-skin contact and nursing immediately after birth
- Use of Neosporin for baby's eyes to be delayed for one hour after the birth to allow optimal sight for bonding
- No vitamin K shot; use oral vitamin K instead
- Baby is not to be removed from mother's sight; newborn exam is to be done in mother's presence
- Breast-feeding only; no introduction of anything artificial for the baby
- No bath; vernix should be rubbed into the baby's skin
- No Pitocin used for placental expulsion, only nipple stimulation or nursing
- Allow at least thirty to forty-five minutes for delivery of placenta

- No cord traction or manual removal of placenta unless there is evidence of an emergency
- Massage of uterus every fifteen minutes for an hour after expulsion of the placenta
- Discharge as soon after birth as possible, unless there are complications, in which case the baby will room-in with me

Appendix D

Procedures and Protocols for Hydrotherapy for Labor and Birth

What follows is a compilation of protocols from several birthing centers and the recommendations that are given by the Global Maternal/Child Health Association (GMCHA). We wish to acknowledge Maidstone Hospital, Kent, England; A Shared Beginning: The Westchester Birth Center of Yonkers, New York; the Family Birthing Center of Upland, California; Monadnock Community Hospital of Peterborough, New Hampshire; and Sparks Family Hospital of Sparks, Nevada, for contributing their protocols.

These protocols are intended for use by midwives or physicians considering incorporating water birth into their practice. They can also be used by couples negotiating with hospitals for the right to use water for labor and birth. Couples may copy them and give them to the head of labor and delivery as well as to their doctor or midwife.

I. OBJECTIVES
  A. To provide the laboring mother with a flexible, low-risk alternative to delivering in a bed
  B. To enhance the normal physiologic process of birth
  C. To assist in restoring control of the birth process to the mother

D. To enhance the mother's relaxation and minimize the need for medical intervention, recognizing two major concepts:
   1. Her relative weightlessness in water provides comfort and relief
   2. With relaxation, less adrenalin is produced while endorphin and oxytocin production are increased
E. Provide a gentler transition to the world for the newborn

II. ELIGIBILITY

A. A woman is eligible to use the tub for hydrotherapy during labor if the following conditions are met
   1. She wishes to use it
   2. She takes a shower with germicidal soap before entering the tub
   3. She has no recent history of vaginal, urinary tract, or skin infections
   4. Maternal and fetal vital signs are within normal limits
   5. Maternal and fetal vital signs continue to be monitored
   6. The tub is cleaned prior to use according to standard procedures
   7. Woman agrees to follow instruction from midwife, doctor, or nurse, including getting out of the tub if told to do so

III. CONTRAINDICATIONS FOR USE OF WATER FOR LABOR OR BIRTH

A. A woman may not use hydrotherapy if any of the following conditions are noted
   1. Anticipated birth complications
   2. Meconium staining in amniotic fluid
   3. Any obstetrical risk that would be cause for transfer to a high-risk unit
   4. Use of narcotic medication less than two hours prior to using tub

5. Fetal distress

6. The use or administration of Pitocin or magnesium sulfate

7. Extended period of time between rupture of membranes and onset of labor (selectively)

IV. WATER TEMPERATURE

A. Temperature may vary within a range of 90–101°F

B. The woman should be able to control temperature, not to exceed 101°F

V. OBSERVATIONS DURING LABOR AND BIRTH

A. The following observations need to be noted during labor and birth in water

   1. Status of membranes

   2. Cervical dilatation and effacement

   3. Position of fetus

   4. Progress of labor, including contraction pattern

   5. Maternal vital signs

     a) If mother experiences dizziness, assist her in getting out of the tub immediately

     b) Keep in mind that a sudden change in environment and temperature close to time of birth may initiate the fetal ejection response

   6. Hydration of the mother (women in warm water tend to dehydrate)

   7. Fetal well-being

VI. OBSERVATIONS DURING DELIVERY

A. The mother may adopt any desired position that is safe and comfortable for her

B. Delivery of the head is facilitated by gentle pushing by the mother

C. Manipulation of the head is usually not necessary in order to birth the shoulders because of the buoyancy of the water

D. If heavy meconium is noted at delivery, the mother is asked to stand so that the mouth, oropharynx, and hypopharynx of the baby can be suctioned

E. If no meconium is noted or if the meconium staining is light or medium, the delivery may proceed in the water

F. Once the infant is birthed, the baby's head should be brought above the water rapidly (within twenty seconds). The infant may then rest on the mother's chest while the oropharnyx and narres are suctioned, if necessary.

G. The mother and baby may stay in the tub until the umbilical cord has stopped pulsating

H. The mother is encouraged to breast-feed immediately to assist in the contracting of the uterus and expulsion of the placenta

VII. DELIVERY OF THE PLACENTA

A. Keep as a goal delivery of the placenta and perineal/vaginal inspection within forty minutes

B. Delivery of placenta in water
1. Umbilical cord is not clamped or cut
2. A lightweight container should be on hand to facilitate floating the placenta until the cord is cut close to the baby
3. Parents are given the opportunity to cut cord with instruction
4. Estimated blood loss is assessed according to darkening of the water

C. Delivery of placenta out of water
1. Umbilical cord is clamped and cut
2. Baby is handed to a significant other (father, parent, friend, or nurse)
3. Mother is assisted out of the tub either into the bed, to a squatting position on the floor, or against the side of the tub
4. Make sure mother is dried and wrapped in warm blanket

VIII. EVALUATION OF NEWBORN

A. While mother is still in tub with newborn on chest
1. Apgar assessment is made according to standard guidelines
2. If fetal tachycardia is present, water should be cooled or mother and baby assisted out of the tub
3. Suctioning or DeLee trap may be used as indicated
4. Keep baby's body in warm water or cover with towels

B. After cord is cut and baby is removed from water
1. Standard baby warmer should be in tub room
2. After physical assessments are made by pediatrician or midwife, baby is wrapped warmly and given to mother or significant other

IX. CLEANING OF THE TUB

A. Instructions for cleaning apply to any portable tub, Jacuzzi, or bath
1. Scrub tub with bacterial agent and/or 50 percent solution of bleach and water; run the water through the jets and drains
2. Benzalkonium spray (diluted to 4 percent) used after the scrub
3. Take bacterial cultures monthly
4. Any debris that accumulates while mother is in the water must be strained out as quickly as possible

Sample Letter to Hospital

Mary Q. Public
Any Street
Anywhere, Any State 11101

January 17, 1994

Community Hospital
Any Street
Anywhere, Any State 11101
Attn: [name of Administrator]

Dear [Administrator's name]:

It has come to my attention that your hospital restricts the use of hydrotherapy for labor and birth. My doctor has consented to my desire to use water to ease labor pains but informs me that it is hospital policy to keep women in bed on fetal monitors during labor.

Many articles in respected medical journals stress the efficacy of the use of water for non-narcotic pain relief. It is considered by many doctors as the single most effective pain-management tool. I would be happy to bring this research, along with some books on the subject, to your office.

I want to be able either to use one of the hospital tubs to labor in or to bring my own portable inflatable tub into your hospital. I am due at the end of March and am willing to work with you and your staff to achieve this goal.

I want to remind you of the economics of this request. More and more women are going to be requesting access to water during labor and for birth. Your hospital is within twenty minutes from my home, and I do not want to have to take my insurance money to another hospital or birth facility. However, I do know what I want during my labor and birth and will make whatever arrangements necessary to ensure that my birth experience is a satisfactory one.

Please consider this reasonable request and respond as soon as possible.

Sincerely,

Mary Q. Public

Be sure to send copies to the chief of obstetrics at the hospital, the head nurse, the perinatologist, your insurance company, your doctor, and the local newspaper.

Appendix F

Resources

Academy of Certified Birth Educators (ACBE)

2001 E. Prairie Circle, Suite I
Olathe, KS 66062
913-782-5116
ACBE offers courses on childbirth education.

Active Birth Centre

55 Dartmouth Park Road
London NW5 1SL
England
011-44-71-267-3006
Active Birth Centre, founded by author Jane Balaskas, offers various prenatal classes, tub rentals, and consultations for women who are seeking alternatives to obstetric birth.

AKBA/AQUA

Center of Parents' Culture
51-2-163 Kashirskoye Shosse
Moscow 115612
Russian Federation
011-7-095-344-94-85
Alexi and Tatyana Sargunas are midwives and water birth parents. They lead seminars and workshops in Moscow and at the Black Sea on water birth, infant development, and baby swimming.

American Academy of Husband-Coached Childbirth (AAHCC)

P.O. Box 5224
Sherman Oaks, CA 91413-5224
800-423-2397
This organization, which began the Bradley method of childbirth preparation, sponsors workshops, publishes a newsletter and pamphlets, and certifies childbirth educators in this method.

American College of Nurse-Midwives (ACNM)

818 Connecticut Avenue N.W.
Washington, DC 20006
202-728-9860
ACNM was founded in 1955 to establish and maintain standards for the practice of nurse-midwifery. Information about midwifery and referrals to nurse-midwives can be received from the national headquarters. For referrals in your area, call toll-free twenty-four hours a day: 888-MIDWIFE.

American Society of Psychoprophylaxis in Obstetrics (ASPO Lamaze)

1840 Wilson Boulevard, Suite 204
Arlington, VA 22201
800-368-4404

ASPO-Lamaze introduced the Lamaze method to the United States and continues to offer classes and certification for childbirth educators.

Australian Swim School

1202 Banbury Cross
Santa Ana, CA 92705
714-731-6666

Infant swim programs for moms and babies as well as certification for instructors.

Birthworks

42 Tallwood Drive
Medford, NJ 08255
609-953-9380

National childbirth education and certification.

Cascade Healthcare & Birth and Life Bookstore

141 Commercial Street N.E.
Salem, OR 97301
800-443-9942

Home birth supplies and educational books and materials available through mail order for couples. The most complete line of supplies for midwifery professionals. Now incorporates the Birth and Life Bookstore, which has the largest available selection of books and videos about pregnancy, birth, parenting, and midwifery.

Cesarean/Support, Education, and Concern (C/SEC)

22 Forest Road
Framingham, MA 01701
518-877-8266

C/SEC offers information and support for cesarean prevention and vaginal birth after cesarean, as well as nationwide training workshops for childbirth educators. Representatives are available for telephone consultations in your area.

Childbirth Education Associations of Australia (NSW) Ltd.

P.O. Box 413
Hurtsville, NSW 2220
(02) 580-0399

Co-Creations

290 North Main Street, Suite 8
Ashland, OR 97520
541-488-3446

Doula services, childbirth education classes, early parenting classes.

Consumer Advocates for the Legalization of Midwifery (CALM)

P.O. Box 7902
Citrus Heights, CA 95621-7902
916-791-7831

CALM continues to introduce legislation in California to legalize midwifery in this state.

The Farm

156 Drakes Lane
Summertown, TN 38483

The Farm publishes a quarterly newsletter, *The Birth Gazette,* and produces videos on many aspects of childbirth.

Fellowship of Christian Midwives

P.O. Box 642
Parker, CO 80134
313-841-2128

Provides Christian midwives with support, classes, materials, and conferences. Will provide referrals for couples seeking midwives or doctors with a committed Christian approach to birth. Full midwifery training course for those called to be Christian midwives.

Global Maternal/Child Health Association (GMCHA) and Waterbirth International

P.O. Box 366
West Linn, OR 97068
800-641-BABY or 503-682-3600

GMCHA, a membership organization, was founded in 1989 by Barbara Harper in order to preserve, protect, and enhance the well-being of women and children throughout pregnancy, birth, infancy, and early childhood. This organization provides the most complete resources for water birth: it rents and sells portable tubs for water labor and birth and sells books and videos about natural childbirth. It also offers computer referrals to midwives, doctors, and birthing centers in the U.S. and other parts of the world; a water-birth certification course for birth professionals; and water-birth workshops for parents.

Home Birth Access

P.O. Box 66
Broadway
Sydney NSW 2007
Australia

Informed Homebirth/ Informed Birth and Parenting

P.O. Box 3675
Ann Arbor, MI 48106
313-662-6857

Childbirth education seminars are offered nationwide; newsletter and books on home birth and early childhood education are available; childbirth assistant trainings are held nationwide.

International Association of Parents and Professionals for Safe Alternatives in Childbirth (NAPSAC)

Route 1, Box 646
Marble Hill, MO 63764
573-238-2010

NAPSAC publishes books and pamphlets supporting the alternative birth movement and offers an international directory of alternative birth services.

International Childbirth
Education Association
(ICEA)
P.O. Box 20048
Minneapolis, MN 55420-0048
612-854-8660
ICEA certifies childbirth educators and publishes a journal and a catalog of books, pamphlets, and videos on childbirth and family-centered maternity care.

International Confederation
of Midwives
57 Lower Belgrave Street
London, England SW1W 0LR
International conferences every three years. Publishes a quarterly newsletter.

International Lactation
Consultant Association
(ILCA)
210 Brown Avenue
Evanston, IL 60202-3601
847-492-1648
ILCA provides support and up-to-date material about breast-feeding.

International Twins
Association (ITA)
P.O. Box 77386, Station C
Atlanta, GA 30357
ITA members support each other with information, both locally and nationally, through newsletters and conferences.

La Leche League
International (LLLI)
1400 N. Meacham Road
P.O. Box 4079
Schaumburg, IL 60168-4079
847-519-7730
Hotline: 800-LA LECHE
Call the hotline between 9 A.M. and 3 P.M. (CST) for breast-feeding help or a referral to a local LLLI support group. LLLI also publishes many informative books on breast-feeding.

Maternity Center Association
(MCA)
48 East 92nd Street
New York, NY 10128
212-369-7300
Responsible for opening the first birthing center in the United States, MCA conducts classes and conferences and publishes many booklets on childbirth.

Midwifery Contact Centre
1A Shoalwater Road
Shoalwater, WA 6169
Australia

Midwifery education
For a complete list of all midwifery education programs, both direct-entry midwifery and nurse-midwifery, call the office of Global Maternal/Child Health Association (GMCHA) at 503-682-3600.

Midwifery Today Magazine

P.O. Box 2672
Eugene, OR 97402
800-743-0974

This magazine is geared toward birth professionals but has excellent articles about home birth, natural childbirth, and midwifery that parents will also find useful.

Midwives Information and Resource Service (MIDIRS)

Institute of Child Health
Royal Hospital for Sick Children
St. Michael's Hill
Bristol BS2 8BJ
England
011-44-272-251-791

MIDIRS publishes the most comprehensive digest of reprinted articles and abstracts about childbirth, midwifery, and related issues.

Mothering Magazine

P.O. Box 1690
Santa Fe, NM 87504
505-984-8116

This quarterly magazine offers a variety of advice for parents about pregnancy, childbirth, infancy, parenting, and education. Reprints are available on circumcision, vaccination, and midwifery.

National Association of Childbirth Assistants

265 Meridian Avenue, Suite 7
San Jose, CA 95123
408-225-9167

Offers conferences, classes, and training for this new area of birth professionals.

National Organization of Circumcision Information Resource Centers (NOCIRC)

P.O. Box 2512
San Anselmo, CA 94960
415-488-9883

NOCIRC provides information about the devastating effects of circumcision through newsletter, conferences, books, and telephone consultations.

National Swim School Association (NSSA)

1158 35th Avenue North
St. Petersburg, FL 33704
813-896-7946 (phone and fax)

NSSA holds conferences, publishes a newsletter, and gives referrals to infant swim instructors across the United States.

National Women's Health Network

514 10th Street, N.W., Suite 400
Washington, DC 20004
202-347-1140

The network monitors federal policies that affect women's health, especially in the area of reproductive rights and environmental and occupational health. A newsletter and other publications are available.

New Zealand Midwives'
Association
24 Ashton Road
Mount Eden
Auckland
New Zealand

Point of View Productions
2477 Folsom Street
San Francisco, CA 94110
415-821-0435
Point of View Productions was responsible, under the direction of filmmaker Karil Daniels, for releasing the first and still the most comprehensive film on water birth. *Water Baby: The Experience of Water Birth* won nine awards and is a landmark presentation. 57 minutes. Available in VHS and PAL.

Pre- and Perinatal Psychology Association of North America (PPPANA)
1600 Prince Street, 509
Alexandria, VA 22314-2838
703-548-2802
PPPANA provides a professional journal on the latest research about prenatal psychology. Conferences are held every other year. A newsletter is available.

Primal Health Research Institute
59 Roderick Road
London NW3 2NP
011-44-71-485-0095

Maternity Care Health Index

Excerpted with permission
from *Mothering*, vol. 68.

Health care costs for the United States in 1992: $838.5 billion

Percentage of U.S. Gross National Product spent on health care in 1965: 6%

Percentage spent in 1992: 12%

Percentage by which U.S. health care expenditures exceed those of Canada: 40%, Germany: 90%, Japan: 100%, the leading industrialized nations (averaged): 100%

Population of the United States: 256,749,000

Percentage who are uninsured or underinsured: 37%

The 12 countries with higher life expectancies than the U.S.: Japan, Iceland, Andorra, Italy, Sweden, Australia, Finland, France, New Zealand, Denmark, England, and Wales

The 22 countries with lower infant mortality rates than the U.S.: Japan, Sweden, Finland, Switzerland, Canada, Singapore, Hong Kong, Netherlands, France, Ireland, Germany, Denmark, Norway, Scotland, Australia, Northern Ireland, Spain, England and Wales, Belgium, Austria, Italy

Percentage of countries with lower infant mortality rates than the U.S. that provide universal prenatal care: 100%

Percentage in the U.S. who have no private health insurance: 25%

Percentage of women in the U.S. who receive little or no prenatal care: 25%

Chances that a woman with little or no prenatal care will give birth to a low-birthweight (less than 5.5 pounds) or premature (less than 37 weeks of gestation) baby: 1 in 2

The factor most closely associated with infant death: low birthweight

Percentage of infant deaths linked to low birthweight: 60%

Chances that a low birthweight infant will die during the first month of life: 1 in 40

Average cost of long-term health care (through age 35) for a low-birthweight baby: $50,558

Average cost of long-term health care (through age 35) for a baby of average weight: $20,033

Cost of newborn intensive care for 1 infant: $20,000–$100,000

Cost of prenatal care for 30 women: $20,000–$100,000

Health care cost savings obtainable by providing universal prenatal care to all women in the U.S.: $7–$10 billion a year

Percentage of births attended principally by midwives (certified nurse-midwives and direct-entry midwives) in the U.S.: 4%

Percentage of births attended principally by midwives in European nations: 75%

Percentage of countries with lower infant mortality rates than the U.S. in which midwives are the principal birth attendants: 100%

Average cost of a midwife-attended birth in the U.S.: $1,200

Average cost of a physician-attended vaginal birth in the U.S.: $4,200

Health care cost savings obtainable by utilizing midwifery care for 75% of pregnancies in the U.S.: $8.5 billion a year

Cost per year of utilizing routine electronic fetal monitoring during childbirth: $750 million

Number of well-constructed scientific studies in which electronic fetal monitoring has been proven more effective than the use of a simple stethoscope (fetoscope): 0

Health care cost savings obtainable by eliminating the routine use of electronic fetal monitoring: $675 million a year

Endnotes

Chapter 1

1. National Center for Health Statistics, *Monthly Vital Statistics Report*, Jan. 1993.
2. World Health Organization, *Report: Recommendations for Birth*, May 1990.
3. National Center for Health Statistics, *Monthly Vital Statistics Report*, Jan. 1993.
4. Bruce Flamm, *Birth after Cesarean: The Medical Facts* (New York: Prentice Hall, 1990), 19.
5. The Public Citizen Health Research Group, *Health Letter* 5:3 (1989): 2.
6. World Health Organization, *Report on Maternal-Child Health Statistics,* May 1990.
7. Beth Shearer, "Crisis in Obstetrics," *C/SEC Newsletter* 13:3 (1988).
8. Global Maternal/Child Health Association (GMCHA) practitioner survey on gentle birth practices, 1992.
9. Janet Balaskas, *Encyclopedia of Pregnancy and Birth* (New York: McDonald, 1987), 33.
10. Michel Odent, *Birth Reborn* (New York: Pantheon, 1984), 15.
11. Roberto Caldeyro-Barci, et al., "Effect of Position Changes on the Intensity and Frequency of Uterine Contractions during Labor," *American Journal of Obstetrics and Gynecology* 80 (1960): 284–90.
12. Judith Goldsmith, *Childbirth Wisdom* (Brookline, Mass.: East-West Health Books, 1990), 32.
13. Nancy Berezin, *Gentle Birth Book* (New York: Simon & Schuster, 1980), 35.
14. Ibid., 39.
15. Dr. Donald Sutherland, interview with author, July 1990.
16. Berezin, *Gentle Birth Book*, 63.
17. International Confederation of Midwives/ World Health Organization, *Project on Safe Motherhood*, May 1990.
18. Doris Haire, *The Cultural Warping of Childbirth* (Minneapolis: International Childbirth Education Association Publications, 1973), 14.
19. *Mothering*, Summer 1988.
20. Sheila Kitzinger, *The Complete Book of Pregnancy and Childbirth*, 11th ed. (New York: Knopf, 1986), 278.
21. Sheila Kitzinger, *Breastfeeding* (New York: Random House, 1991).

Chapter 2

1. Judith Leavitt, *Brought to Bed: Childbearing in America 1750-1950* (New York: Oxford University Press, 1986), 23.
2. Ibid., 269.
3. National Center for Health Statistics, *Monthly Vital Statistics Report*, Feb. 1993.
4. Howard Haggard, *Devils, Drugs, and Doctors* (New York: Blue Ribbon Books, 1929), 48.
5. Barbara Katz-Rothman, *Giving Birth: Al-*

ternatives in Childbirth. (Harmondsworth, U.K.: Penguin, 1982), 24.

6. Paul Starr, *The Social Transformation of American Medicine* (New York: Basic Books, 1982), 49–50.

7. Barbara Ehrenreich and Dierdre English, *Witches, Midwives, and Nurses* (New York: Feminist Press, 1973), 20.

8. Eugene O'Neill, *Mourning Becomes Electra*. In the play O'Neill makes references to his mother's drug habits.

9. Leavitt, *Brought to Bed*, 117.

10. Deborah Sullivan and Rose Weitz, *Labor Pains: Modern Midwives and Home Birth* (New Haven, Conn.: Yale University Press, 1988), 23.

11. Margot Edwards and Mary Waldorf, *Reclaiming Birth: History and Heroines of American Childbirth Reform* (Freedom, Calif.: Crossing Press, 1984), 153.

12. Ibid., 155.

13. Judith Litoff, ed., *The American Midwife Debate* (Westport, Conn.: Greenwood Press, 1986), 11.

14. Leavitt, *Brought to Bed*, 289.

15. Judith Rooks, "Nurse-Midwifery: The Window Is Wide Open," *American Journal of Nursing* 90:12 (1990): 12.

16. *Webster's Third New International Dictionary* (Springfield, Mass.: Merriam, 1976).

17. Joseph B. DeLee, "The Prophylactic Forceps Operation," *American Journal of Obstetrics and Gynecology* 1:1 (1920): 34–44.

18. Leavitt, *Brought to Bed*, 12.

19. Leavitt, *Brought to Bed*, 174.

20. Penny Armstrong and Sheryl Feldman, *A Wise Birth* (New York: William Morrow, 1990), 95.

21. Leavitt, *Brought to Bed*, 134.

22. Dorothy Wertz and Richard Wertz, *Lying-In: A History of Childbirth in America* (New Haven, Conn.: Yale University Press, 1989), 165.

23. Leavitt, *Brought to Bed*, 269.

24. Christine Kelley-Buchanan, *Peace of Mind during Pregnancy* (New York: Dell, 1988), 23.

25. Yvonne Brackbill, June Rice, and J. D. Diony Young, *Birth Trap* (New York: Warner Books, 1984), 171.

26. Kelley-Buchanan, *Peace of Mind during Pregnancy*, 173.

27. Leavitt, *Brought to Bed*, 269.

Chapter 3

1. National Center for Health Statistics, *Monthly Vital Statistics Report*, Jan. 1993.

2. Brigitte Jordan and Robbie Davis-Floyd, *Birth in Four Cultures* (Prospect Heights, Ill.: Waveland Press, 1993), 63.

3. Michel Odent, *Planned Home Birth in Industrialized Countries* (Copenhagen: World Health Organization, 1991), 2.

4. Stanley Sagov, et al., *Home Birth: A Practitioner's Guide to Birth outside the Hospital* (Rockville, Md.: Aspen Systems, 1984), 30–32.

5. Sullivan and Weitz, *Labor Pains*, 115.

6. Judith Rooks, et al., "Outcomes of Care in Birth Centers: The National Birth Center Study," *New England Journal of Medicine* 321 (1989), 1806.

7. Ibid.

8. Harlow Johnson, *California Alternative Birthing Methods Study*, Summary Report, Oct. 1986, and interview with Nancy McNeese, CNM, member of evaluation team, California legislature.

9. Kitty Ernst, CNM, ed., *National Association of Childbearing Centers Newsletter*, October 1990, 3.

10. American College of Nurse-Midwives data, May 1991.

11. Japanese Midwives Association data (34,000 trained midwives), October, 1990.

12. Barry Levy, Fredrick Wilkinson, and William Marine, "Reducing Neonatal Mortality Rate with Nurse-Midwives," *American*

Journal of Obstetrics and Gynecology 109:1 (1971): 50–58.

13. Edwards and Waldorf, *Reclaiming Birth*, 178.

14. World Health Organization, "Action for Safe Motherhood" (Geneva: World Health Organization, Maternal and Child Health and Family Planning Division of Family Health, 1991).

15. Paul Hon, "Clinical Fetal Monitoring versus Effect on Perinatal Outcome," *American Journal of Obstetrics and Gynecology* 118 (1974): 529–33.

16. Karin Nelson and Jonas Ellenberg, "Antecedents of Cerebral Palsy," *American Journal of Diseases of Children* 1 (1985): 39.

17. Dr. Michael Rosenthal, personal communication with author, 1991.

18. National Institutes of Health, "Health Letter," Sept. 1980.

19. Ruth Shearer, ed., *C/SEC Newsletter* 13:3 (1988): 2.

20. Ibid.

21. "Is the EFM Accurate?" *Journal of Nurse-Midwifery* (1990): 32.

22. K. Leveno, et al., "A Prospective Comparison of Selective and Universal Electronic Fetal Monitoring in 34,995 Pregnancies," *New England Journal of Medicine* 315:10 (1986): 315.

23. Roger Freeman, "Intrapartum Fetal Monitoring: A Disappointing Story," *New England Journal of Medicine* 322:9 (1990): 624–25.

24. Flamm, *Birth after Cesarean*, 3.

25. Sidney Wolfe, "One Hundred and Six Hospitals with the Highest Cesarean Rates," *Public Citizen Health Research Group Health Letter* 5:3 (1989): 1.

26. Mortimer Rosen and Lillian Thomas, *The Cesarean Myth: Choosing the Best Way to Have Your Baby* (Harmondsworth, U.K.: Penguin Books, 1989), 23.

27. Ibid., 24.

28. Dr. Michael Rosenthal, personal communication with author, 1990.

29. American College of Obstetrics and Gynecology, Committee on Obstetrics: Maternal and Fetal Medicine, *Guidelines for Vaginal Delivery after Cesarean Birth*, Committee Opinion no. 64, Oct. 1988.

30. Flamm, *Birth After Cesarean*, 65.

31. Michael Rosenthal, *Gentle Birth Choices* (videocassette), West Lynn, Or.: GMCHA/Win/Win Productions, 1993.

32. Kelley-Buchanan, *Peace of Mind during Pregnancy*, 29.

33. Jude Roedding, "Birth Trauma and Suicide: A Study of the Relationship between Near-Death Experience at Birth and Later Suicidal Behavior," *Pre- and Perinatal Psychology Journal* 6:2 (Winter 1991): 48.

34. Kitzinger, *The Complete Book of Pregnancy and Childbirth*, 241.

35. Doris Haire, *The Cultural Warping of Childbirth* (Minneapolis: International Childbirth Education Association Publications, 1972), 6.

36. Sheila Kitzinger, "Episiotomy," *Mothering* 55 (Spring): 64.

37. Eakin Chalmers, et al., *Effective Guide to Care in Pregnancy* (New York: Oxford University Press, 1986): 355.

38. Niles Newton, "Experimental Inhibition of Labor through Environmental Disturbance," *Obstetrics and Gynecology* 27 (1966): 371–77.

39. Marshall Klaus, et al., "Effect of Social Support During Parturition on Maternal and Infant Morbidity," *British Medical Journal* 293:6547 (1986): 585–87.

40. Sosa, et al., "Effect of a Supportive Companion on Perinatal Problems, Length of Labor and Mother-Infant Interaction," *New England Journal of Medicine* 303:11 (1980): 597–600.

41. Marsden Wagner, "Hospital Birth Deemed Too Risky," *Chicago Sun Times*, April 2, 1989. As reported in *Mothering* 55 (Fall 1989): 75.

42. Helen Varney, *Nurse-Midwifery* (Boston: Blackwell Scientific Publications, 1980), 385.
43. Phyllis Mansfield, "Maternal Age: What Is Really High Risk?" *Mothering* 41 (Fall 1986): 64–69.
44. Ibid.
45. Jill Larson, "The Politics of Newborn Pain," *Mothering* (Fall 1990): 45.
46. Marilyn Milos, ed., *NOCIRC Newsletter,* Spring 1992, 2.
47. John Taylor, "The Prepuce Defined." Syllabus of Abstracts, The Second International Symposium on Circumcision, San Francisco, April 30, 1991: 19.
48. K. J. S. Amand and P. R. Hickey, "Pain and Its Effects in the Human Neonate and Fetus," New England Journal of Medicine 317:21 (1987): 1321–29.
49. Stanislav Grof and Joan Halifax, *The Human Encounter with Death* (New York: E. P. Dutton, 1977), 116.
50. Rima Laibow, "Circumcision and Its Relationship to Attachment Impairment." Syllabus of Abstracts, The Second International Symposium on Circumcision, San Francisco, April 30, 1991: 14.
51. Marilyn Milos, NOCIRC president, interview with author, Jan. 1993.
52. Lee Salk, keynote speech, Pre- and Perinatal Psychology Association of North America conference, Amherst, Mass., 1989.

Chapter 4

1. Ellen Kleiner, ed., "Good News," *Mothering* 64: (Fall 1992): 26.
2. Edwards and Waldorf, *Reclaiming Birth,* 32.
3. Ibid.
4. Marjorie Karmel, *Thank You, Dr. Lamaze* (Garden City, N.Y.: Doubleday, 1965), 35.
5. Elizabeth Bing, *Six Practical Lessons for an Easier Childbirth* (New York: Bantam Books, 1977), 139.
6. Frederick Leboyer, *Birth without Violence* (New York: Knopf, 1975), 15.
7. Women and Children's Hospital midwife staff, Paris, interview with author, June 1984.
8. Ivan Illich, *Medical Nemesis: The Expropriation of Health* (New York: Random House, 1976), 32.
9. Odent, *Birth Reborn,* 36.
10. Dr. Michael Rosenthal, interview with author, July 1990.
11. Edwards and Waldorf, *Reclaiming Birth,* 62–63.
12. Ina May Gaskin, *Spiritual Midwifery* (Summertown, Tenn.: The Book Publishing Co., 1977).
13. Dr. Michel Odent, interview with author, April 1992.

Chapter 5

1. Jessica Mitford, *The American Way of Birth* (New York: Penguin Books, 1992), 225.
2. Helen Varney, *Nurse-Midwifery,* 156.
3. Edwards and Waldorf, *Reclaiming Birth,* 164.
4. Suzanne Arms, *Immaculate Deception* (Boston: Houghton-Mifflin, 1975).
5. Ellie Becker, Meria Long, Vicki Stamler, and Pacia Sallomi, *Midwifery and the Law* (Santa Fe: Mothering, 1990), 14.
6. Ibid., 8.
7. Dr. Marsden Wagner, interview with author, Dec. 1991.
8. Edwards and Waldorf, *Reclaiming Birth,* 179–80.
9. Kitty Ernst, interview with author, May 1991.
10. Elizabeth Davis, *Heart and Hands: A Guide to Midwifery,* 2nd ed. (Berkeley, Calif.: Celestial Arts), 2.

Chapter 6

1. Lyall Watson and Jerry Derbyshire, *The Water Planet: A Celebration of the Wonder of Water* (New York: Crown, 1988), 111.

2. Serge Weisel, "Benefits of Warm Water Immersion during First Stage Labor," paper presented at the Pre- and Perinatal Psychology Association of North America conference, San Francisco, 1987.

3. Michel Odent, "Birth under Water," *Lancet* 2:147 (1983): 67.

4. Waterbirth International, "Survey of Waterbirth Practice," *Journal of Nurse-Midwifery* 34:4 (1989): 86. The results of the surveys are still being compiled by the author. The first twenty surveys produced the statistics as mentioned.

5. I found this book at Samuel Weiser's Bookstore in the rare book collection, where it was priced at $800. I left it on the bookshelf but only after poring over it for several hours.

6. Grandfather Semu, personal communication, Nov. 1987.

7. Karil Daniels, *Water Baby: The Story of Waterbirth* (videocassette), San Francisco: Point of View Productions, 1985.

8. Erik Sidenbladh, *Water Babies* (New York: St. Martin's Press, 1983).

9. Frederick Leboyer, *Birth without Violence*, 72–90.

10. Dr. Michel Odent, interviews with author, July 1987, Aug. 1989, May 1990.

11. Odent, *Birth Reborn*, 46.

12. Odent, "Birth under Water," 148.

13. Dr. Wolf Jaskulsky, interview with author, Aug. 1989.

14. Dr. Bruce Sutherland, interview with author, May 1990.

15. Fuseiko Sei, "A Study of Waterbirths after Informed Consent of Client," paper presented at the International Confederation of Midwives conference, Kobe, Japan, Oct. 1990.

16. Josie Muscat, personal correspondence, Sept. 1990.

17. Diane Garland, member of the Board of Directors of Global Maternal/Child Health Association, interviews and correspondence with author, 1990–1993.

18. Roger Lichy, Water Birth Practitioner Survey, personal correspondence, Aug. 1990.

19. Margaret Brain, Conference of the American College of Nurse-Midwives, Minneapolis, May 1991, interview with author.

20. Molly Lasser, personal correspondence, Dec. 1992.

21. Alex and Tatyana Sargunas, interview with author, Sept. 1992.

22. Odent, "Birth under Water," 147.

23. Michael Rosenthal, "Warm-Water Immersion for Labor and Birth," *Female Patient*, Aug. 1992.

24. Josie Muscat, response to Global Maternal/Child Health Association survey and personal communication.

Chapter 7

1. Deepak Chopra, *Quantum Healing: Exploring the Frontiers of Mind/Body Medicine* (New York: Bantam, 1989).

2. Grantly Dick-Read, *Childbirth without Fear: The Principles and Practices of Natural Childbirth* (New York: Harper & Row, 1944), 16.

3. Nancy Wainer Cohen and Lois Estner, *Silent Knife: Cesarean Prevention and Vaginal Birth after Cesarean* (South Hadley, Mass.: Bergin and Garvey, 1983), 6.

4. Deepak Chopra, telephone interview with author, Dec. 1991.

5. Chamberlain, "The Expanding Boundaries of Memory," 175.

6. Jane English, *Different Doorway: Adventures of a Cesarean Born* (Point Reyes Station: Ca.: Earth Heart, 1985), 22.

7. David Chamberlain, *Babies Remember Birth* (New York: Ballantine, 1990), 152.

8. Ibid., 152–57.

9. Gayle Peterson, *An Easier Childbirth* (Los Angeles: Jeremy Tarcher, 1991), 17.

10. Ibid.

11. Lewis Mehl and Gayle Peterson, *Pregnancy as Healing* (Berkeley, Calif.: Mind Body Press, 1984), 58.

12. Gayle Peterson, personal communication, May 1992.

13. Dr. Robert Doughton, interview with author, June 1989.

14. June Sutherland, interview with author, July 1990.

Chapter 8

1. Dr. William Tuxton, American College of Nurse-Midwives conference, Atlanta, May 1990.

2. National Center for Health Statistics, *Monthly Vital Statistics Report*, April 1990.

3. Singh, et al., *Prenatal Care in the United States: A State and County Inventory*, The Alan Guttmacher Institute 1 (1989): 15.

4. National Center for Health Statistics, "Advance Report of Final Natality Statistics," *Monthly Vital Statistics Report* 39 (1989): 12.

5. General Accounting Office, "Prenatal Care: Medicaid Recipients and Uninsured Women Obtain Insufficient Care," Sept. 1987, 14.

6. *International Confederation of Midwives Newsletter* 5:2 (Summer 1992).

7. National Center for Health Statistics, *Monthly Vital Statistics Report*, April 1990.

8. General Accounting Office, "Prenatal Care," 12.

9. National Center for Health Statistics, *Monthly Vital Statistics Report*, Feb. 1993.

10. United Kingdom, House of Commons, *Second Report of the Health Committee on Maternity Services* 1 (1992).

11. Kitty Ernst, personal communication, May 1991.

12. Sosa, et al., "Effect of a Supportive Companion on Perinatal Problems, Length of Labor, and Mother-Infant Interaction," 597–600.

13. *California Association of Midwives Newsletter*, Summer 1991.

14. Elana Johnson, interview with author, June 1993.

15. Sister Angela Murdaugh, CNM, interview with author, Sept. 1991.

16. Ruth Watson Lubic, "Evaluation of an Out-of-Hospital Maternity Center for Low-Risk Patients." From *Health Policy and Nursing Practice*, L. Aiken, ed. (Boston: McGraw-Hill, 1980), 3.

17. Dr. Marsden Wagner, interview with author, Dec. 1991.

Appendix A

1. Telephone survey of eleven United States medical schools, March 1990.

2. S. Cavanagh and E. Williams, "The Acceptance of the Ventouse," *MIDIRS Midwifery Digest* 2:4 (1992): 431–34.

3. Erik Hemrinki, et al., "Ambulation Versus Oxytocin in Protracted Labor: A Pilot Study," *European Journal of Obstetrics, Gynecology, and Reproductive Biology* 20 (1985): 199–208.

4. D. Hull, "Vitamin K and Childhood Cancer," British Medical Journal 305:6849 (Aug. 1992): 326–27.

Bibliography

Abrams, Richard. *Will It Hurt the Baby?* Reading, Mass.: Addison-Wesley, 1990.

ACOG Committee Opinion. Guidelines for Vaginal Delivery after a Previous Cesarean Section. Number 64, Oct. 1988.

Aderhold, K., and L. Perry. "Jet Hydrotherapy for Labor and Postpartum Pain Relief." *American Journal of Maternal/Child Nursing* 16:2 (1991): 97–99.

Arms, Suzanne. *Immaculate Deception.* Boston: Houghton-Mifflin, 1975.

Armstrong, Penny, and Sheryl Feldman. *A Wise Birth.* New York: William Morrow, 1990.

Armstrong, Sue. "Conference Renames Circumcision." *Safe Motherhood Newsletter* 5 (March–June 1991): 2.

Ashford, Janet. *Whole Birth Catalog: A Sourcebook for Choices in Childbirth.* Freedom, Calif.: Crossing Press, 1986.

——. "Sitting, Standing, Squatting in Childbirth." *Mothering* 41 (Fall 1986): 58–63.

——. "The History of Midwifery in the United States." *Mothering* 54 (Winter 1990): 64–69.

Balaskas, Janet. *Encyclopedia of Pregnancy and Birth.* New York: McDonald and Co., 1987.

——. *Natural Pregnancy.* Brooklyn, N.Y.: Interlink Books, 1990.

——. *Active Birth: The New Approach to Giving Birth.* Cambridge, Mass.: Harvard Common Press, 1992.

Baldwin, Rahima. *Special Delivery.* Berkeley, Calif.: Celestial Arts, 1979.

——. "Becoming a Midwife in the Nineties." *Mothering* 65 (Winter 1992): 76–80.

Baldwin, Rahima, et al. *Pregnant Feelings: Developing Trust in Birth.* Berkeley, Calif.: Celestial Arts, 1986.

Bar-Yum Bromberg, Naomi. "The Trouble with Ultrasound." *Mothering* 57 (Fall 90): 73–77.

Bean, Constance. *Methods of Childbirth.* New York: William Morrow, 1990.

Becker, Ellie, Meria Long, Vicki Stamler, and Pacia Sallomi. *Midwifery and the Law.* Santa Fe: Mothering, 1990.

Berezin, Nancy. *Gentle Birth Book.* New York: Simon & Schuster, 1980.

Bing, Elizabeth. *Six Practical Lessons for an Easier Childbirth.* New York: Bantam Books, 1967.

Boehm, John. "Resuscitation of the Newborn and Prevention of Asphyxia." *Gynecology and Obstetrics* 3: 1–11.

Boutelier, C., L. Bougues, and J. Timbal. "Experimental Study of Convective Heat Transfer Coefficient for the Human Body in Water." *Journal of Applied Physiology* 42: 1 (1977): 93–100.

Brackbill, Yvonne, June Rice, and J. D. Diony Young. *Birth Trap*. New York: Warner Books, 1984.

Bradley, Robert. *Husband-Coached Childbirth*. New York: Harper & Row, 1981.

Breckenridge, M. *Wide Neighborhoods: A Story of the Frontier Nursing Service*. Lexington: University Press of Kentucky, 1981.

Brown, C. "Therapeutic Effects of Bathing during Labor." *Journal of Nurse-Midwifery* 27:1 (1982): 13–16.

Burman, Salee, and Victor Burman. *The Birth Center*. New York: Prentice Hall, 1986.

Bursztajn, Harold, Richard Feinbloom, Robert Hamm, and Archie Brodskey. *Medical Choices, Medical Chances*. New York: Routledge Publishing, 1981.

Caldeyro-Barci, Roberto, et al. "Effect of Position Changes on the Intensity and Frequency of Uterine Contractions during Labor." *American Journal of Obstetrics and Gynecology* 80 (1960): 284.

Chalmers, Eakin, et al. *Effective Guide to Care in Pregnancy*. New York: Oxford University Press, 1986.

Chamberlain, David. *Babies Remember Birth: And Other Extraordinary Scientific Discoveries about the Mind and Personality of Your Newborn*. New York: Ballantine Books, 1990.

——. "The Expanding Boundaries of Memory." *Pre- and Perinatal Psychology Journal* 4:3 (Spring 1990): 171–89.

——. "Is There Intelligence before Birth?" *Pre- and Perinatal Psychology Journal* 6:3 (1992): 217–37.

Chard, Tim, and M. Richards, eds. *Benefits and Hazards of the New Obstetrics*. Philadelphia: Lippincott, 1977.

Charlish, Anna, and Linda Hughey Holt. *Birth Tech: Tests and Technology in Pregnancy and Birth*. New York: Facts on File, 1991.

Chopra, Deepak. *Quantum Healing: Exploring the Frontiers of Mind/Body Medicine*. New York: Bantam, 1989.

Church, D. *Communicating with the Spirit of Your Unborn Child*. San Leandro, Calif.: Aslan Publishing, 1988.

Church, Linda. "Water Birth: One Birthing Center's Observations." *Journal of Nurse-Midwifery* 34:4 (1989): 165–70.

Clark, Matt, D. Seward, and E. Bailey. "Giving Birth Underwater." *Newsweek*, January 16, 1984, 70.

Clausen, Joy Princeton. *Maternity Nursing Today*. New York: McGraw-Hill, 1979.

Cohen, Nancy Wainer, and Lois J. Estner. *Silent Knife: Cesarean Prevention and Vaginal Birth after Cesarean*. South Hadley, Mass.: Bergin and Garvey, 1983.

Cohn, Anna, and Lucinda Leach. *Generations*. New York: Pantheon, 1987.

Coleman, L., and A. Coleman. *Pregnancy: The Psychological Experience*. New York: Noonday Press, 1971.

Cook, William. *Natural Childbirth: Fact and Fallacy*. Chicago: Nelson Hall, 1982.

Coulter, Harris L. *Divided Legacy: The Origins of Modern Western Medicine*. Berkeley, Calif.: North Atlantic Books, 1988.

Cowley, Geoffrey. "Children in Peril." *Newsweek*, special summer issue, 1991, 18–21.

Crelin, Edmond S. *Functional Anatomy of the Newborn*. New Haven, Conn.: Yale University Press, 1973.

Davis, Elizabeth. *Heart and Hands: A Guide to Midwifery*, 2nd ed. Berkeley, Calif.: Celestial Arts, 1987.

Davis-Floyd, Robbie. *Birth as an American Rite of Passage*. Berkeley, Calif.: University of California Press, 1992.

DeLee, Joseph B. "The Prophylactic Forceps Operation." *American Journal of Obstetrics and Gynecology* 1:1 (1920): 34–35.

Dick-Read, Grantly. *Childbirth without Fear: The Original Approach to Natural Childbirth*, 5th ed. New York: HarperCollins, 1987.

Dreifus, Claudia. *Seizing Our Bodies: The Politics of Women's Health*. New York: Random House, 1977.

Eagan, Andrea. "200 Years of Childbirth." *Parents Magazine*, December 1985, 174–76.

Edwards, Margot, and Mary Waldorf. *Reclaiming Birth: History and Heroines of Amercian Childbirth Reform*. Freedom, Calif.: Crossing Press, 1984.

"EFM, Intermittent Asculation Found Comparable," *American College of Obstetrics and Gynecology Newsletter* 32 (1988): 11.

Ehrenreich, Barbara, and Dierdre English. *Witches, Midwives, and Nurses*. New York: Feminist Press, 1973.

———. *For Her Own Good*. New York: Doubleday/Dell Publishing, 1978.

English, Jane. *Different Doorway: Adventures of a Cesarean Born*. Point Reyes Station, Cailf.: Earth Heart, 1985.

Epstein, M. "Water Immersion and the Kidney: Implications for Volume Regulation." *Undersea Biomedical Research* 11:2 (1984): 113–21.

Fanaroff, Avroy, and Richard Martin. *Neonatal-Perinatal Medicine: Diseases of the Fetus and Infant*. St. Louis: C. V. Mosby, 1983.

Fetherolf, Josala. "Esther B. Zorn: CPM Movement." *Mothering* 52 (Fall 1989): 56–63.

Fisher, John, and Giuseppe Sant'Ambrogio. "Airway and Lung Receptors and Their Reflex Effects in the Newborn." *Pediatric Pulmonology* 1:2 (1985): 112–26.

Flamm, Bruce L. *Birth after Cesarean: The Medical Facts*. New York: Prentice Hall, 1990.

Freeman, Roger. "Intrapartum Fetal Monitoring: A Disappointing Story." *New England Journal of Medicine* 322:9 (1990): 624–25.

Gaskin, Ina May. *Spiritual Midwifery*. Summertown, Tenn.: The Book Publishing Co., 1977.

General Accounting Office. "Prenatal Care: Medicaid Recipients and Uninsured Women Obtain Insufficient Care." Sept. 1987, 14.

Gilbert, Elizabeth, and Judith Harmon. *High-Risk Pregnancy and Delivery*. St. Louis: C. V. Mosby, 1986.

Goldsmith, Judith. *Childbirth Wisdom*. Brookline, Mass.: East-West Health Books, 1990.

Goodlin, R., K. Engdahl-Hoffmann, N. Williams, and P. Buchan. "Shoulder-out Immersion in Pregnant Women." *Journal of Perinatal Medicine* 12 (1984).

Greenleaf, J. "Physiological Responses to Prolonged Bed Rest and Fluid Immersion in Humans." *Journal of Applied Physiology* 57:4 (1984): 619–33.

Greenspan, Stanley, and Nancy Thorndike Greenspan. *First Feelings*. New York: The Book Press, 1985.

Grof, Stanislav, and Joan Halifax. *The Human Encounter with Death*. New York: E. P. Dutton, 1977.

Haggard, Howard. *Devils, Drugs and Doctors*. New York: Blue Ribbon Books, 1929.

Haire, Doris. *The Cultural Warping of Childbirth*. Minneapolis: International Childbirth Education Association, 1973.

Harned, H., and J. Ferreio. "Initiation of Breathing by Cold Stimulation: Effects of Change in Ambient Temperature on Respiratory Activity of the Full-term Fetal Lamb." *Journal of Pediatrics* 83:4 (1973): 666–69.

Hatch, Frank, and Lenny Maietta. "The Role of Kinesthesia in Pre- and Perinatal Bonding." *Pre- and Perinatal Psychology Journal* 5:1 (Spring 1991): 253–70.

Hemrinki, Erik, et al. "Ambulation Versus Oxytocin in Protracted Labor: A Pilot Study." *European Journal of Obstetrics, Gynecology, and Reproductive Biology* 20 (1985): 199–208.

Hillan, Edith. "Electronic Fetal Monitoring: More Problems than Benefits." *MIDIRS Midwifery Digest* 1:3 (1991): 249–51.

Hon, Paul. "Clinical Fetal Monitoring versus Effect on Perinatal Outcome." *American Journal of Obstetrics and Gynecology* 118 (1974): 529–33.

Hull, D. "Vitamin K and Childhood Cancer." *British Medical Journal* 305: 6849 (August 1992): 326–27.

Illich, Ivan. *Medical Nemesis: The Expropriation of Health*. New York: Random House, 1976.

Johnson, Harlow. *California Alternative Birthing Methods Study*. Summary Report, Oct. 1986.

Jones, Carl. *Alternative Birth: The Complete Guide*. Los Angeles: Jeremy Tarcher, 1992.

Jones, Joy. "Gestational Diabetes: Myth or Metabolism?" *Mothering* 50 (Winter 1989): 58–67.

Jordan, Brigitte, and Robbie Davis-Floyd. *Birth in Four Cultures*. Prospect Heights, Ill.: Waveland Press, 1993.

Karmel, Marjorie. *Thank you, Dr. Lamaze*. Garden City, N.Y.: Doubleday, 1965.

Kasindorf, Jeanie. "Mommy Oldest: Having Babies at 45 and Beyond." *New York Magazine*, July 1989, 25–29.

Katz, V., R. Ryder, R. Cefalo, S. Carmichael, and R. Goolsby. "A Comparison of Bed Rest and Immersion for Treating Edema in Pregnancy." *Obstetrics and Gynecology* 75:2 (1990): 147–51.

Katz-Rothman, Barbara. *Giving Birth: Alternatives in Childbirth*. Harmonds-worth, U.K.: Penguin, 1982.

——. *The Tentative Pregnancy: Prenatal Diagnosis and Future of Motherhood*. New York: Viking-Penguin Books, 1987.

——. *Recreating Motherhood: Ideology and Technology in a Patriarchal Society.* New York: Norton, 1989.

Kelley-Buchanan, Christine. *Peace of Mind during Pregnancy.* New York: Dell, 1988.

Kellogg, Carol. "Postnatal Effects of Prenatal Exposure to Psychoactive Drugs." *Pre- and Perinatal Psychology Journal* 5:3 (Spring 1991): 233–49.

Kitzinger, Sheila. *Birth over Thirty.* Harmondsworth, U.K.: Penguin, 1985.

——. *Breastfeeding.* New York: Random House, 1991.

——. *The Midwife Challenge.* Pandora Press, 1988.

——. *Pregnancy Day by Day.* New York: Knopf, 1990.

——. "Episiotomy." *Mothering* 55 (Spring 1990): 62–67.

——. *The Complete Book of Pregnancy and Childbirth,* 11th ed. New York: Knopf, 1986.

Klaus, M., P. Klaus, and J. Kennell. *Mothering the Mother: How a Doula Can Help You Have a Shorter, Easier Birth.* Reading, Mass.: Addison-Wesley, 1993.

Korte, Diana. "Infant Mortality: Lessons from Japan." *Mothering* 62 (Winter 1992): 82–87.

Korte, Diana, and Roberta Scaer. *A Good Birth, A Safe Birth.* New York: Bantam, 1984.

Kryukova, Nina. "Child of the Sea." *Soviet Life* 3 (1987): 22–25.

La Leche League International. *The Womanly Art of Breastfeeding.* Chicago, 1958.

Larson, Jill. "The Politics of Newborn Pain." *Mothering* 57 (Fall 1990): 41–47.

Leavitt, Judith. *Brought to Bed: Childbearing in America 1750–1950.* New York: Oxford University Press, 1986.

Leboyer, Fredrick. *Birth without Violence.* New York: Knopf, 1975.

——. *The Art of Breathing.* Dorset, U.K.: Element Books, 1983.

Lederman, R. P., E. Lederman, B. Work, Jr., and D. McCann. "The Relationship of Maternal Anxiety, Plasma Catecholamines and Plasma Cortisol to Progress in Labor." *American Journal of Obstetrics and Gynecology* 153 (1985): 870–77.

Leiberman, E., and K. Ryan. "Birth Day Choices." *New England Journal of Medicine* 321 (1989): 26.

Leidloff, Jean. *The Continuum Concept.* Reading, Mass.: Addison-Wesley, 1985.

Lenstrup, C., et al. "Warm Tub Bath during Delivery." *Acta Obstetric Gynecology Scandinavia* 66 (1987): 709–12.

Leveno, K., et al. "A Prospective Comparison of Selective and Universal Electronic Fetal Monitoring in 34,995 Pregnancies." *New England Journal of Medicine* 315:10 (1986): 615–19.

Leventhal, E., H. Leventhal, S. Shacham, and D. Easterling. "Active Coping Reduces Reports of Pain from Childbirth." *Journal of Consulting and Clinical Psychology* 57:3 (1989): 365–71.

Levy, Barry, Fredrick Wilkinson, and William Marine. "Reducing Neonatal Mortality Rate with Nurse-Midwives." *American Journal of Obstetrics and Gynecology* 109 (1971): 50–58.

Litoff, Judith, ed. *The American Midwife Debate.* Westport, Conn.: Greenwood Press, 1986.

Lubic Watson, Ruth. "Evaluation of an Out-of-Hospital Maternity Center for Low-Risk Patients." *Health Policy and Nursing Practice* (1980): 3–27.

MacGregor, Eve. "Dilemmas in Genetic Screening." *Nursing* 4:41 (1991): 13–15.

Mansfield, Phyllis. "Maternal Age: What Is Really High Risk?" *Mothering* 41 (Fall 1989): 64–69.

McKay, Susan, and Charles Mahan. "Laboring Patients Need More Freedom to Move." *Contemporary OB/GYN* (July 1984): 92–119.

McKay, Susan, and J. Roberts. "Obstetrics by Ear—Maternal Caregiver Perceptions of the Meaning of Maternal Sounds during Second-Stage Labor." *Journal of Nurse-Midwifery* 35:5 (1990): 266–73.

Mehl, Lewis, and Gayle Peterson. *Pregnancy as Healing.* Berkeley, Calif.: Mind Body Press, 1984.

Mendelsohn, Robert. *Confessions of a Medical Heretic.* Chicago: Contemporary Books, 1979.

———. *Male Practice: How Doctors Manipulate Women.* Chicago: Contemporary Books, 1981.

Minchin, Maureen. *Breastfeeding Matters: What We Need to Know about Infant Feeding.* Armadale, Australia: Alma Publications, 1989.

Mitford, Jessica. *The American Way of Birth.* New York: Penguin Books, 1992.

Montagu, Ashley. *Touching: The Human Significance of Skin.* New York: Harper & Row, 1972.

Myers, Stephen, and N. Gleicher. "A Successful Program to Lower Cesarean Section Rates." *New England Journal of Medicine* 319 (1988) : 1511–16.

National Center for Health Statistics. "Advance Report of Final Natality Statistics," *Monthly Vital Statistics Reports* 1989, 1990, 1993.

National Women's Health Network. *How the FDA Determines the "Safety" of Drugs: Just How Safe Is Safe?* Washington, D.C.: National Women's Health Network, 1990.

Nelson, Karin, and Jonas Ellenberg. "Antecedents of Cerebral Palsy." *American Journal of Diseases of Children* 1 (1985): 39.

Newton, Niles. "Experimental Inhibition of Labor through Environmental Disturbance." *Obstetrics and Gynecology* 27 (1966): 371–77.

———. "Effect of Fear and Disturbances on Labor." In Stewart and Stewart, eds., *21st Century Obstetrics Now!* Marble Hill, Mo.: NAPSAC Publications, 1977.

Oakley, Ann. *The Captured Womb: A History of the Medical Care of Pregnant Women.* New York: Basil Blackwell, 1984.

Odent, Michel. *Birth Reborn.* New York: Pantheon, 1984.

———. "Birth under Water." *Lancet* 2:147 (1983): 67.

———. *Entering the World: The Demedicalization of Childbirth.* New York: Marion Boyers, 1984.

———. *Primal Health.* London: Century Hutchinson, Ltd., 1986.

———. *Planned Home Birth in Industrialized Countries.* World Health Organization Report, 1991.

———. *The Nature of Birth and Breastfeeding.* South Hadley, Mass.: Bergin and Garvey, 1992.

Parfitt-Rowe, Rebecca. *The Birth Primer.* Philadelphia: Running Press, 1977.

Pelka, Fred. "Electronic Fetal Monitoring." *Mothering* 65 (Winter 1992): 70–75.

Pert, Candice. "Neuropeptides: The Emotions and Bodymind." *Advances* 3:3 (Summer 1986): 13–18.

Peterson, Gayle. *Birthing Normally: A Personal Growth Approach to Childbirth.* Berkeley, Calif.: Shadow and Light, 1981.

———. *An Easier Childbirth.* Los Angeles: Jeremy Tarcher, 1991.

————. "Body-Centered Hypnosis for Pregnancy and Childbirth." *Mothering* 63 (Spring 1992): 80–85.

Prentice, A., and T. Lind. "Fetal Heart Rate Monitoring during Labor: Too Frequent Intervention, Too Little Benefit?" *Lancet* (12 December 1987): 1375–77.

"Preventing Unnecessary Cesareans." *Mothering* 52 (Fall 1989): 64.

Renfrew, Mary, Chloe Fisher, and Suzanne Arms. *Bestfeeding: Getting Breastfeeding Right for You.* Berkeley, Calif.: Celestial Arts, 1990.

Rice, Ruth D. "Maternal-Infant Bonding: The Profound Long-term Benefits of Immediate, Continuous Skin and Eye Contact at Birth." In Stewart and Stewart, eds., *21st Century Obstetrics Now!* Marble Hill, Mo.: NAPSAC Publications, 1977.

Roedding, Jude. "Birth Trauma and Suicide: A Study of the Relationship between Near-Death Experience at Birth and Later Suicidal Behavior." *Pre- and Perinatal Psychology Journal* 6:2 (Winter 1991): 145–67.

Rooks, Judith P. "Nurse-Midwifery: The Window Is Wide Open." *American Journal of Nursing* (December 1990): 31–36.

Rooks, Judith, et al. "Outcomes of Care in Birth Centers: The National Birth Center Study." *New England Journal of Medicine* 321 (1989): 1804–11.

Rosen, Mortimer, and Lillian Thomas. *The Cesarean Myth: Choosing the Best Way to Have Your Baby.* Harmondsworth, U.K.: Penguin Books, 1989.

Rosenthal, Michael. "Warm-Water Immersion for Labor and Birth." *Female Patient* 16 (August 1992): 35–47.

Sagov, Stanley, et al. *Home Birth: A Practitioner's Guide to Birth outside the Hospital.* Rockville, Md.: Aspen Systems, 1984.

Samuels, Mike, and Nancy Samuels. *The Well Pregnancy Book.* New York: Simon & Schuster, 1986.

Sanders, Lauren. "A Birthing Center Grows in the Bronx." *Mothering* 64 (Summer 1992): 86–91.

Scholten, Catherine. *Childbearing in American Society 1650-1850.* New York: New York University Press, 1985.

Sidenbladh, Erik. *Water Babies.* New York: St. Martin's Press, 1983.

Simkin, Penny. "Stress, Pain and Catecholamines in Labor. Part 1: A Review; Part 2: Stress Associated with Childbirth Events: A Pilot Survey of New Mothers." *Birth* 13:4 (1986): 227–40.

————. "Siblings at Birth." *Mothering* 45 (Fall 1987): 60–65.

Singh, et al. *Prenatal Care in the United States: A State and County Inventory.* The Alan Guttmacher Institute 1 (1989): 11–23.

Sosa, et al. "Effect of a Supportive Companion on Perinatal Problems, Length of Labor, and Mother-Infant Interaction." *New England Journal of Medicine* 303:11 (1980): 597–600.

Starr, Paul. *The Social Transformation of American Medicine.* New York: Basic Books, 1982.

Sullivan, Deborah, and Rose Weitz. *Labor Pains: Modern Midwives and Homebirth.* New Haven, Conn.: Yale University Press, 1988.

Tatje-Broussard, Nancy. "Second Stage Labor: You Don't Have to Push." *Mothering* 57 (Fall 1990): 70–81.

Taylor, M'haletta. *Under Water Birth: A Personal Account—An Interview with Carmella and Abel B'Hahn*. West Midlands, England (self-published), 1987.

Ulrich-Thatcher, Laurel. *A Midwife's Tale*. New York: Random House, 1990.

United Kingdom. *Second Report of the House of Commons Health Committee on Maternity Services*. 1992.

Varney, Helen. *Nurse-Midwifery*. Boston: Blackwell Scientific Publications, 1980.

Verny, Thomas. "The Scientific Basis of Pre- and Perinatal Psychology, Part I." *Pre- and Perinatal Psychology Journal* 3:3 (Spring 1989): 157–70.

Verny, Thomas, and Pamela Weintraub. *Nurturing the Unborn Child*. New York: Dell, 1991.

Vyass, H., et al. "Determinants of the First Inspiratory Volume and Functional Residual Capacity at Birth." *Pediatric Pulmonology* 2:4 (1986): 189–93.

Wagner, Marsden. "Hospital Birth Deemed 'Too Risky.'" *Chicago Sun-Times*, April 2, 1989, as reported in *Mothering* 53 (Fall 1989): 75.

——. "Midwifery Practice: An Urgent Need." *Mothering* 54 (Winter 1990): 69.

——. "Appropriate Technology for Birth." *New Zealand College of Midwives* 3 (1991): 10–11, 14–15.

Waldenstrom, Nilsson. "Warm Tub Bath after Spontaneous Rupture of the Membranes." *Birth* 19:2 (1992): 57–63.

Ward, Charlotte, and Fred Ward. *The Home Birth Book*. New York: Dolphin Books, 1977.

Watson, Lyall, and Jerry Derbyshire. *The Water Planet: A Celebration of the Wonder of Water*. New York: Crown, 1988.

Wertz, Dorothy, and Richard Wertz. *Lying-In: A History of Childbirth in America*. New Haven, Conn.: Yale University Press, 1989.

Wolfe, Sidney. "Unnecessary Cesarean Sections: How to Cure a National Epidemic." *Public Citizen Health Research Group Health Letter* 5:3 (1989): 2.

Wymelenberg, Suzanne. *Science and Babies: Private Decisions, Public Dilemmas*. Washington, D.C.: National Academy Press, 1990.

Zander, Luke, and Luke Chamberlain. *Pregnancy Care for the 1980s*. New York: Macmillan, 1984.

Index

infant mortality, 9, 33, 34; at birthing centers, 55; and bottle feeding, 25–26; by country, **53,** 193; and home birth, 51–54; with midwives, 57, 58, 128; in United States, 9, 193. *See also* baby; fetus; health

infection, 33–34, 41, 70–71, 81, 84, 88, 89, 158–160, 163–164

insurance, 197–200

International Cesarean Awareness Network (ICAN), 63, 197

International Confederation of Midwives (ICM), 58–59

IV lines, 10, 67, 78, 201. *See also* drugs

Japan: infant mortality in, 53; midwifery in, 57, 189; water birth in, 150–151

Kitzinger, Sheila, 30, 209

kneeling, for birth position, 18. *See also* birth positions

labor: affection in, 185–186; drugs for, 16, 43, 66–67, 96; and food, 76–79; myths about, 40; natural, 12, 14–15, 117–118; positions for, 18–19, 60, 62, 75–76, 102; visualizations for, 176–181; and water birth, 161–162. *See also* birth; pregnancy

La Leche League International (LLLI), 110–111

Lamaze method, 97–99, 107, 170. *See also* breath

Leboyer method, 20–21, 99–101, 137–138

light levels, at birth, 15, 20–21, 101, 135

lithotomy position, 18, 40, 54

loss. *See* emotions

love, 12, 13, 19, 48, 58, 80–81, **185.** *See also* sexuality; support

Malta, 12, 151

maternal sensitive period, 82. *See also* bonding

maternity care, 94, 126, 129; costs of, 197–198; and doctors, 57–59; lack of, 195; midwifery model for, 57–59, 115–120; redesigning, 186–192. *See also* labor; pregnancy

Maternity Center Association (MCA), 109–110

meconium, 27, 80, 160–161

medical intervention, 7–10, 12, 31–48, 81, 117; and fetal monitors, 61–62; at gentle birth, 14, 54, 165; at hospitals, 15–17, 18, 28; results of, 47–48, 104

medicalization of birth, 9, 31–48, 49, 115, 165

Medical Nemesis, 101–102

midwives: American, 113–132; at birthing center, 54–56; costs of, 197–198; direct-entry, 121–126; and doctors, 1, 34–36, 38–41, 198–199; education for, 39, 57, 120–126; European, 9, 52–53; future for, 128–132; at gentle birth, 3, 16–17, 85, 103, 108, 115–120; historical, 31–33, 113; and hospitals, 129–130, 195–196; lay midwives, 120–121; legal status of, 121–128; legitimization of, 55–59, 211–212; locating, 2–3, 94, 196–197; for maternity care, 115–120; and obstetrics, 57–58; spiritual, 111. *See also* certified nurse-midwife

mind-body response, 169–192

miscarriage, 45, 87

mothering: and breastfeeding, 27; empowerment for, 11, 13–14, 85, 209

movement, freedom of, 17–18, 71, 107

Netherlands, 9, 189; infant mortality in, 52–53; midwifery in, 57, **122**

neural tube defects, 44–45